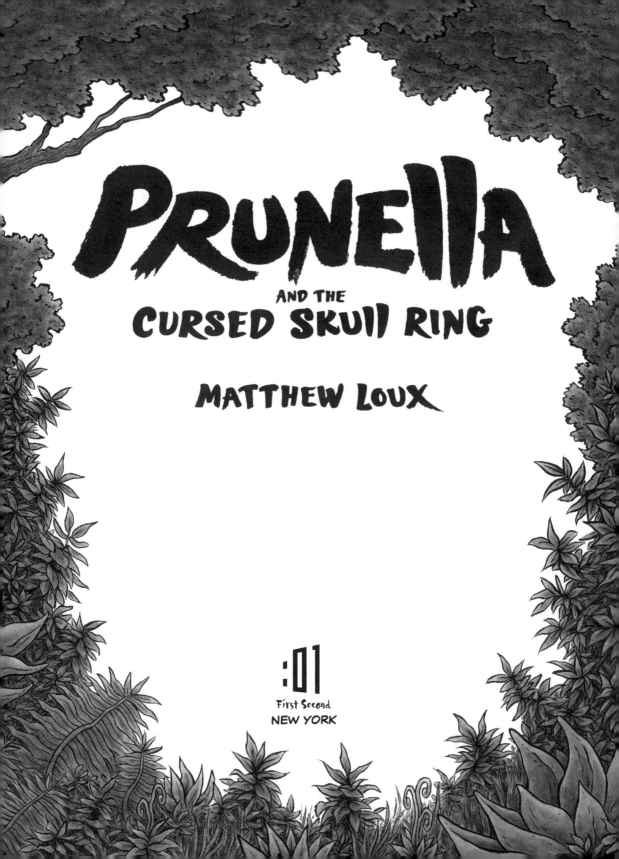

PRUNELLA

AND THE
CURSED SKULL RING

MATTHEW LOUX

:01
First Second
NEW YORK

THIS BOOK IS DEDICATED TO ABBY.

:01

First Second

PUBLISHED BY FIRST SECOND
FIRST SECOND IS AN IMPRINT OF ROARING BROOK PRESS, A DIVISION OF HOLTZBRINCK
PUBLISHING HOLDINGS LIMITED PARTNERSHIP
120 BROADWAY, NEW YORK, NY 10271
FIRSTSECONDBOOKS.COM
MACKIDS.COM

LIBRARY OF CONGRESS CONTROL NUMBER: 2022904243

OUR BOOKS MAY BE PURCHASED IN BULK FOR PROMOTIONAL, EDUCATIONAL, OR BUSINESS
USE. PLEASE CONTACT YOUR LOCAL BOOKSELLER OR THE MACMILLAN CORPORATE
AND PREMIUM SALES DEPARTMENT AT (800) 221-7945 EXT. 5442 OR BY EMAIL AT
MACMILLANSPECIALMARKETS@MACMILLAN.COM.

FIRST
EDITION

FIRST EDITION, 2022
EDITED BY MARK SIEGEL AND MICHAEL MOCCIO
COVER DESIGN BY KIRK BENSHOFF
INTERIOR BOOK DESIGN BY SUNNY LEE, YAN L. MOY, AND MADELINE MORALES
PRODUCTION EDITING BY KAT KOPIT

PENCILED WITH STAEDTLER HB MARS CARBON. INKED WITH WINSOR & NEWTON BLACK INDIAN
INK USING SERIES 7 KOLINSKY SABLE BRUSHES, SIZE 0. PAINTED BY HAND USING VARIOUS
WATERCOLOR PAINTS, SYNTHETIC BRUSHES, AND PAPER TYPES. LETTERED WITH CHATTERBOX
FONT BY COMICRAFT.

PRINTED IN CHINA BY TOPPAN LEEFUNG PRINTING LTD., DONGGUAN CITY, GUANGDONG PROVINCE

ISBN 978-1-250-16261-8
10 9 8 7 6 5 4 3 2 1

DON'T MISS YOUR NEXT FAVORITE BOOK FROM FIRST SECOND! FOR THE LATEST UPDATES
GO TO FIRSTSECONDNEWSLETTER.COM AND SIGN UP FOR OUR ENEWSLETTER.

BY ART
WE LIVE

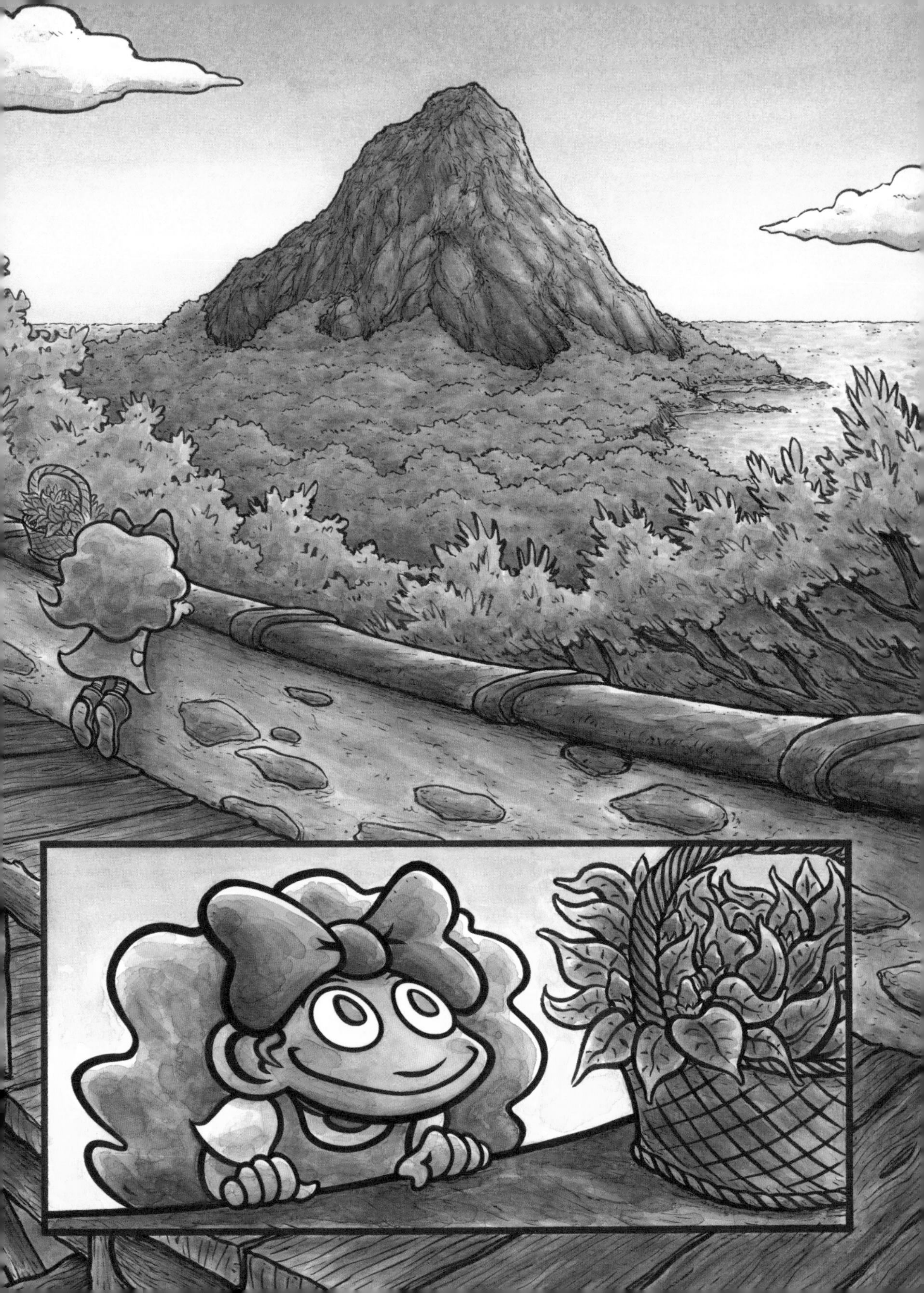

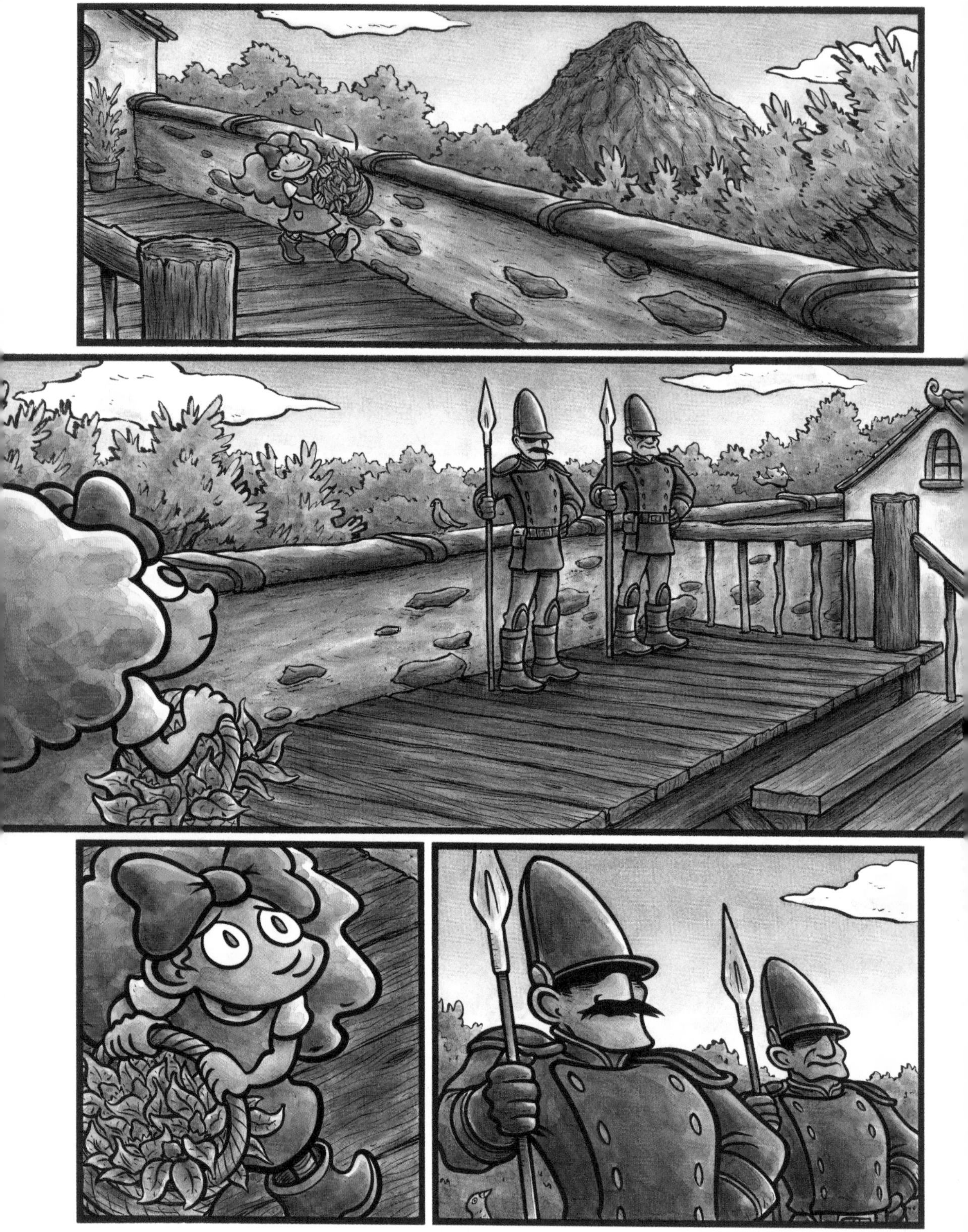

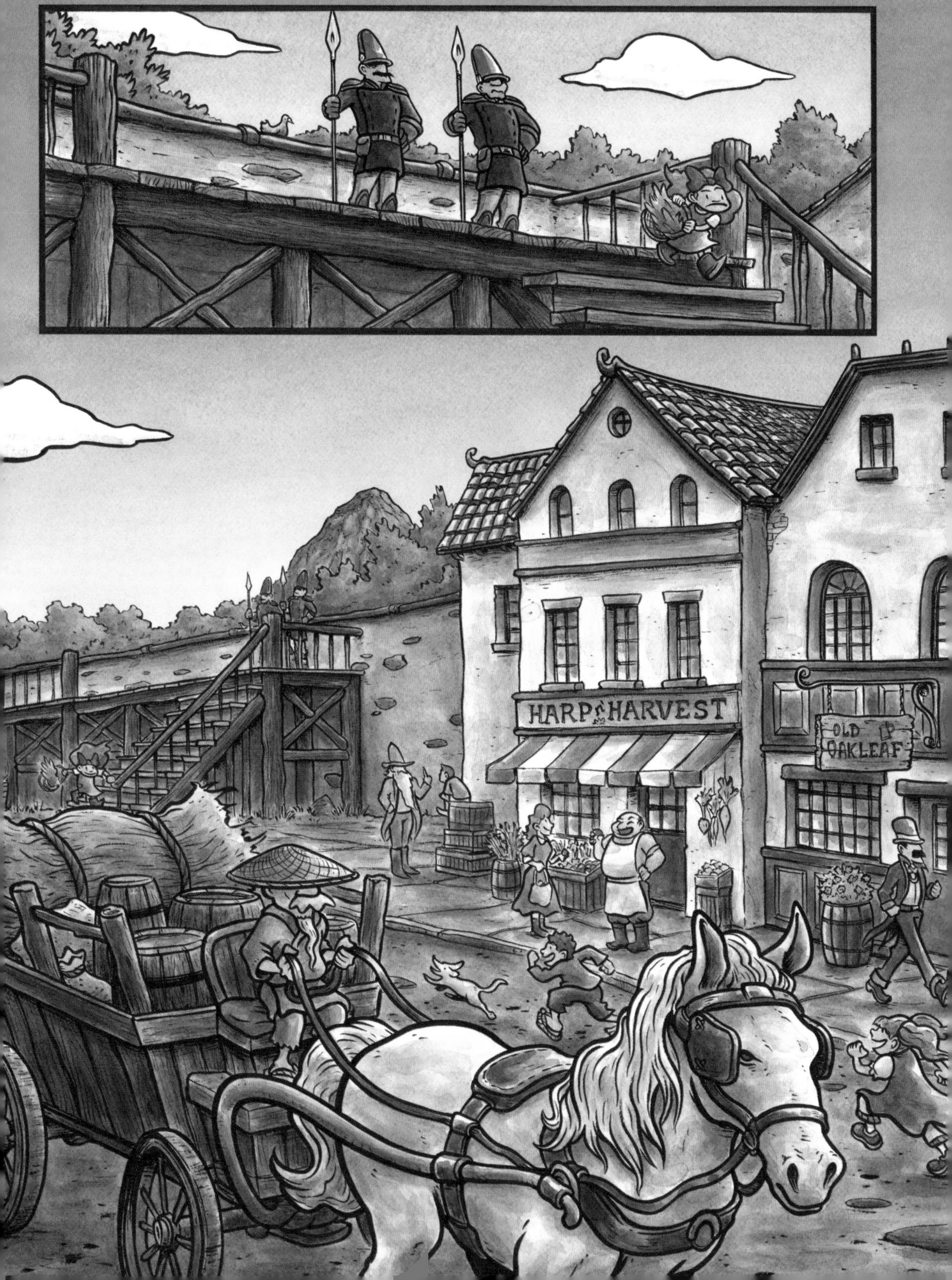
HARP & HARVEST
OLD OAKLEAF

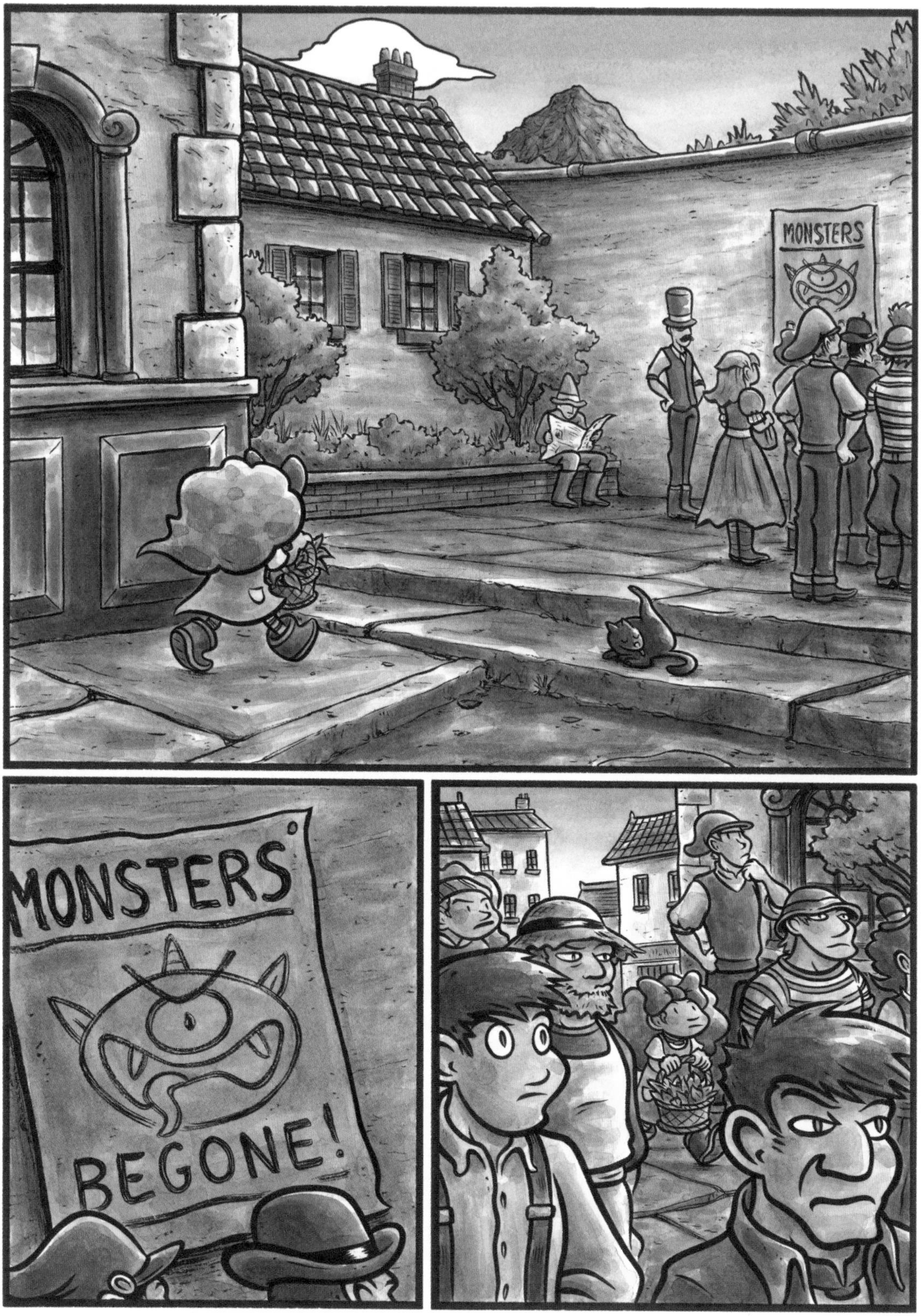
MONSTERS
MONSTERS
BEGONE!

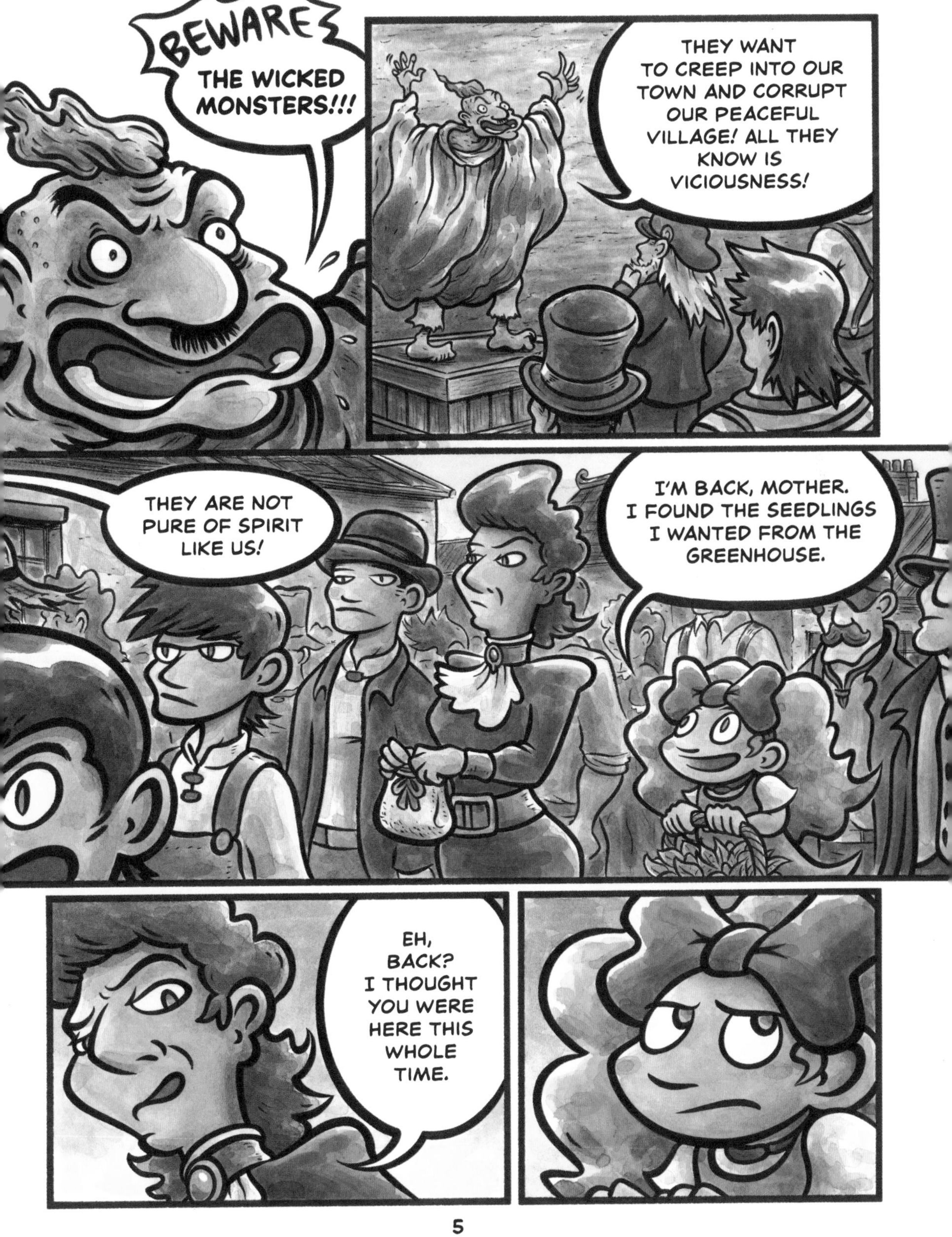
BEWARE THE WICKED MONSTERS!!!
THEY WANT TO CREEP INTO OUR TOWN AND CORRUPT OUR PEACEFUL VILLAGE! ALL THEY KNOW IS VICIOUSNESS!
THEY ARE NOT PURE OF SPIRIT LIKE US!
I'M BACK, MOTHER. I FOUND THE SEEDLINGS I WANTED FROM THE GREENHOUSE.
EH, BACK? I THOUGHT YOU WERE HERE THIS WHOLE TIME.

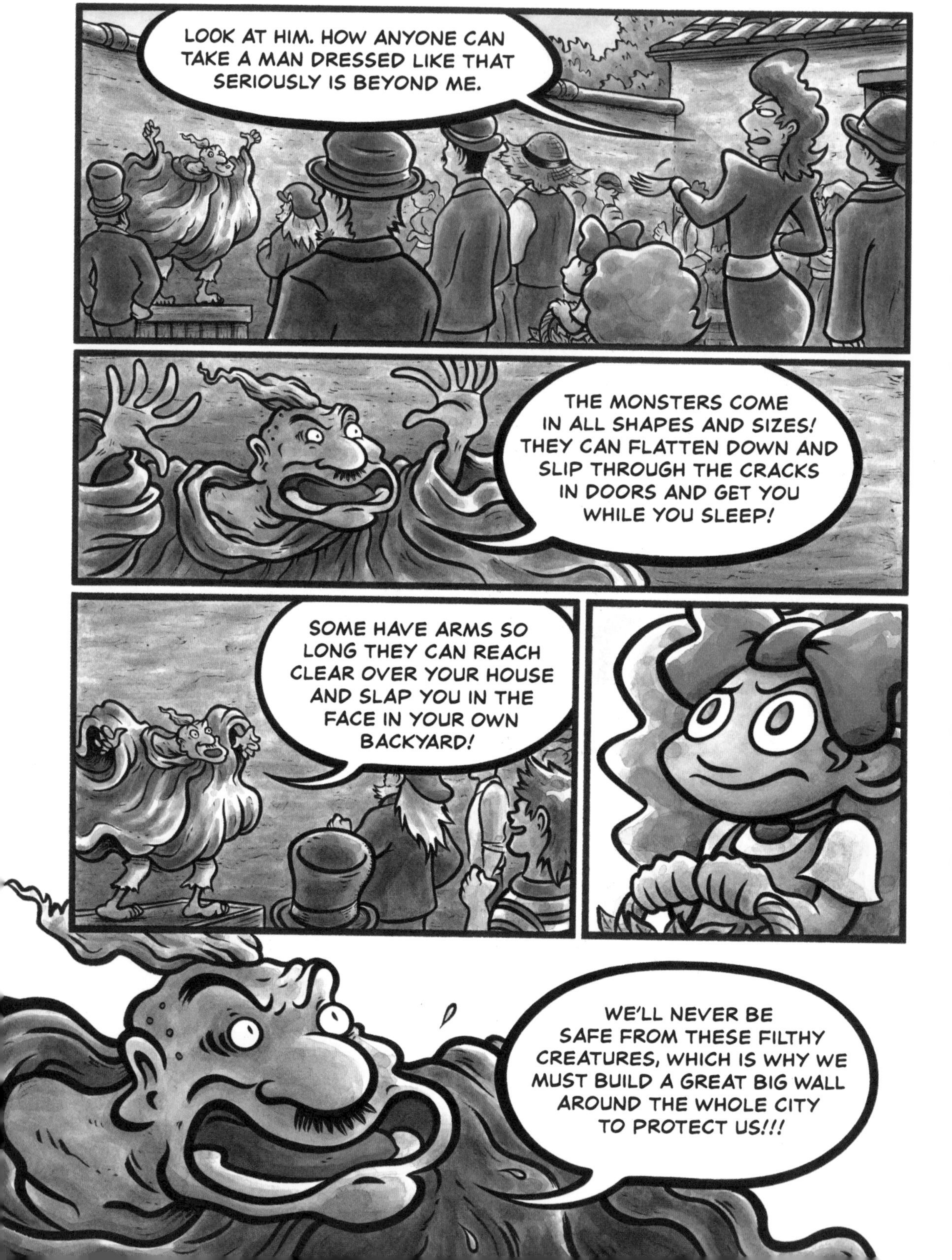
LOOK AT HIM. HOW ANYONE CAN TAKE A MAN DRESSED LIKE THAT SERIOUSLY IS BEYOND ME.
THE MONSTERS COME IN ALL SHAPES AND SIZES! THEY CAN FLATTEN DOWN AND SLIP THROUGH THE CRACKS IN DOORS AND GET YOU WHILE YOU SLEEP!
SOME HAVE ARMS SO LONG THEY CAN REACH CLEAR OVER YOUR HOUSE AND SLAP YOU IN THE FACE IN YOUR OWN BACKYARD!
WE'LL NEVER BE SAFE FROM THESE FILTHY CREATURES, WHICH IS WHY WE MUST BUILD A GREAT BIG WALL AROUND THE WHOLE CITY TO PROTECT US!!!

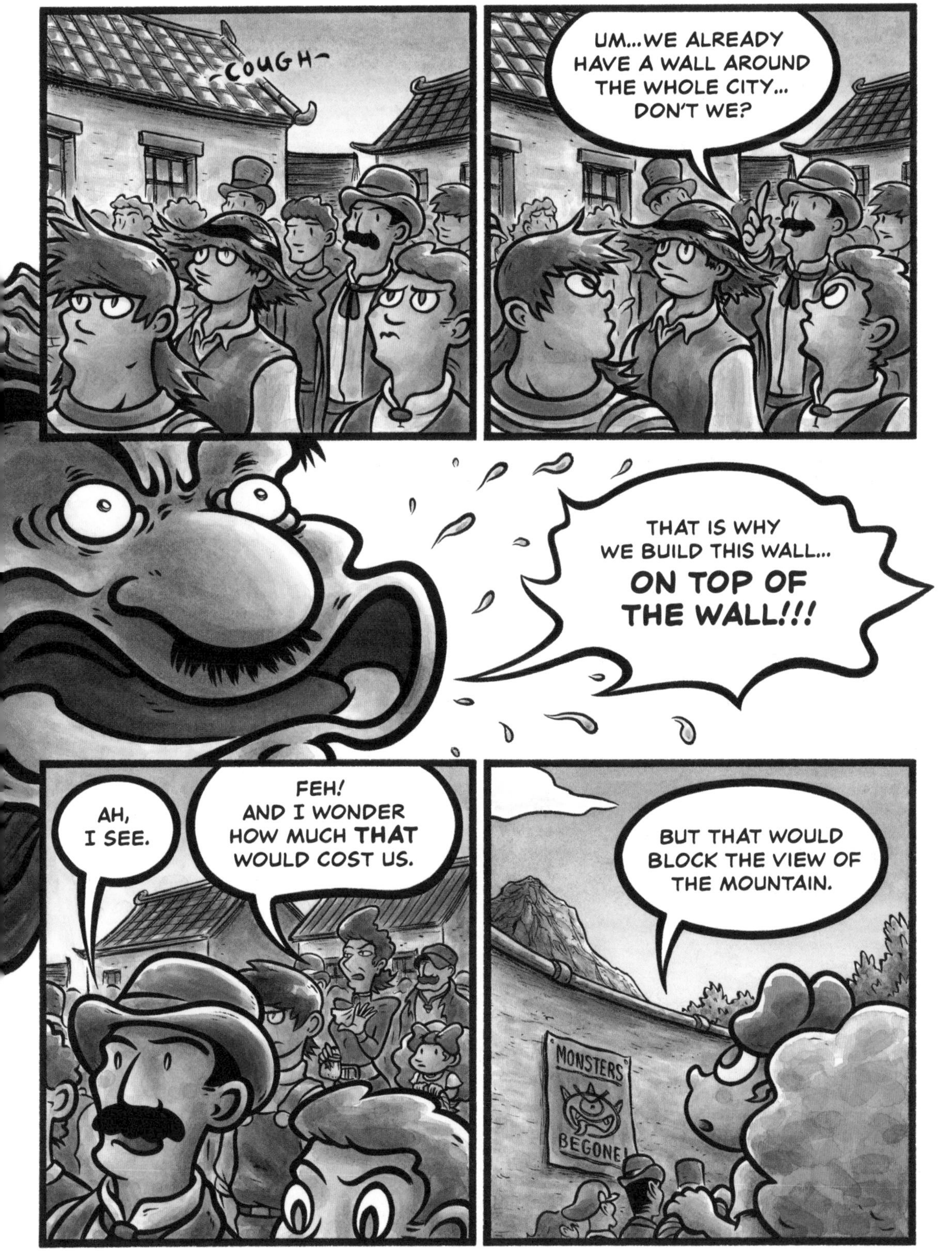
-COUGH-
UM...WE ALREADY HAVE A WALL AROUND THE WHOLE CITY... DON'T WE?
THAT IS WHY WE BUILD THIS WALL... **ON TOP OF THE WALL!!!**
AH, I SEE.
FEH! AND I WONDER HOW MUCH **THAT** WOULD COST US.
BUT THAT WOULD BLOCK THE VIEW OF THE MOUNTAIN.
MONSTERS BEGONE!

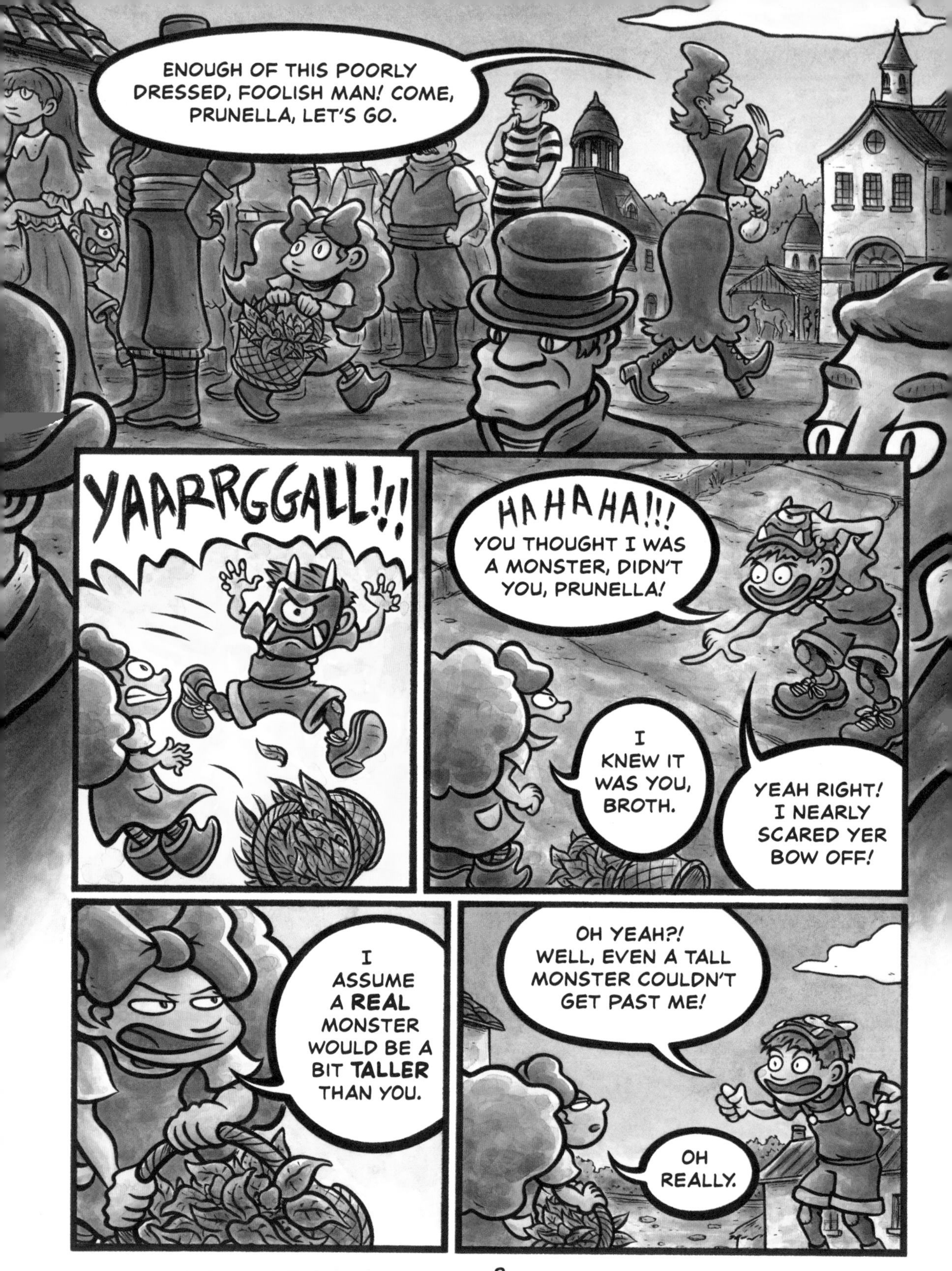

ENOUGH OF THIS POORLY DRESSED, FOOLISH MAN! COME, PRUNELLA, LET'S GO.
YAARRGGALL!!!
HAHAHA!!! YOU THOUGHT I WAS A MONSTER, DIDN'T YOU, PRUNELLA!
I KNEW IT WAS YOU, BROTH.
YEAH RIGHT! I NEARLY SCARED YER BOW OFF!
I ASSUME A REAL MONSTER WOULD BE A BIT TALLER THAN YOU.
OH YEAH?! WELL, EVEN A TALL MONSTER COULDN'T GET PAST ME!
OH REALLY.

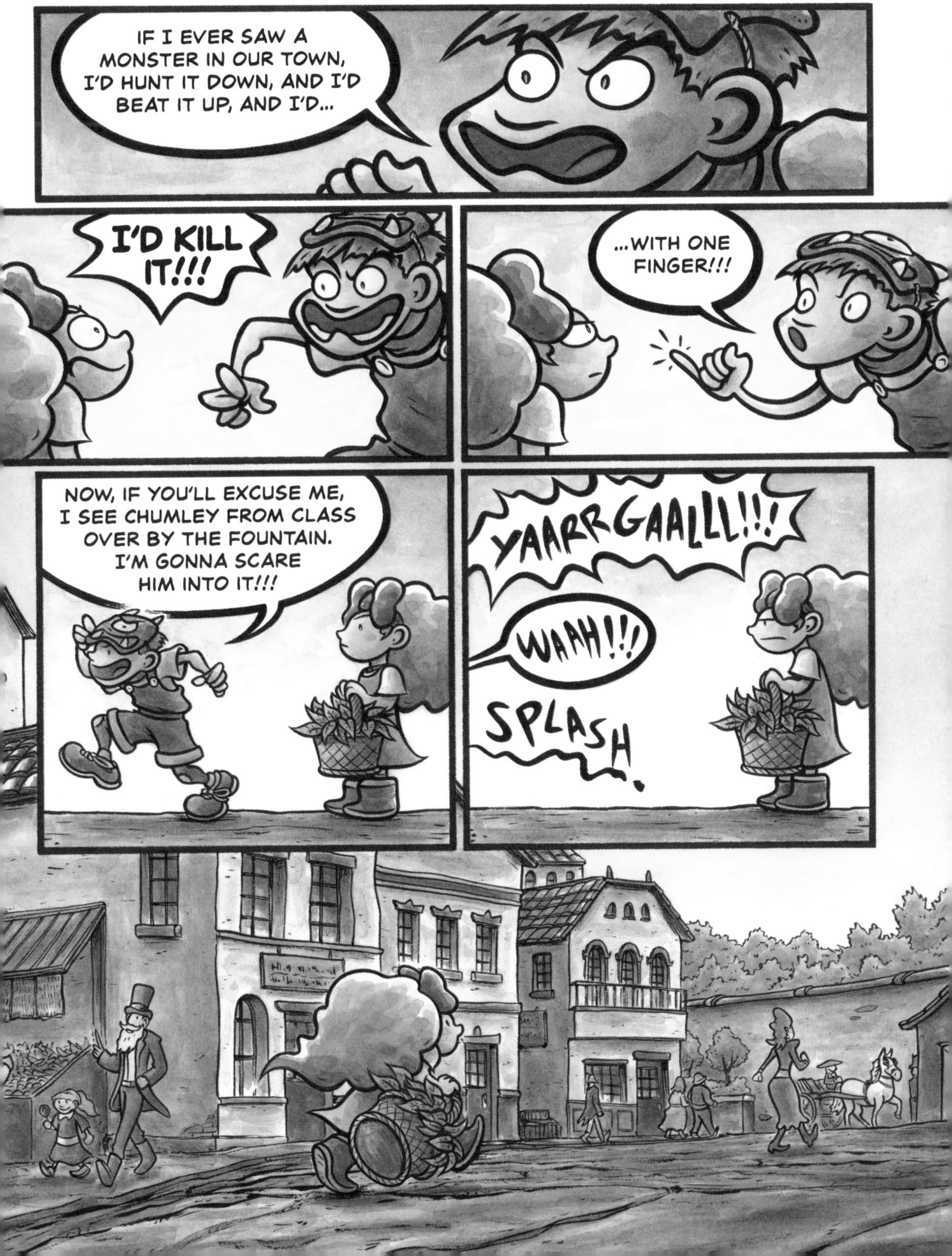
IF I EVER SAW A MONSTER IN OUR TOWN, I'D HUNT IT DOWN, AND I'D BEAT IT UP, AND I'D...
I'D KILL IT!!!
...WITH ONE FINGER!!!
NOW, IF YOU'LL EXCUSE ME, I SEE CHUMLEY FROM CLASS OVER BY THE FOUNTAIN. I'M GONNA SCARE HIM INTO IT!!!
YAARRGAALLL!!!
WAAH!!!
SPLASH

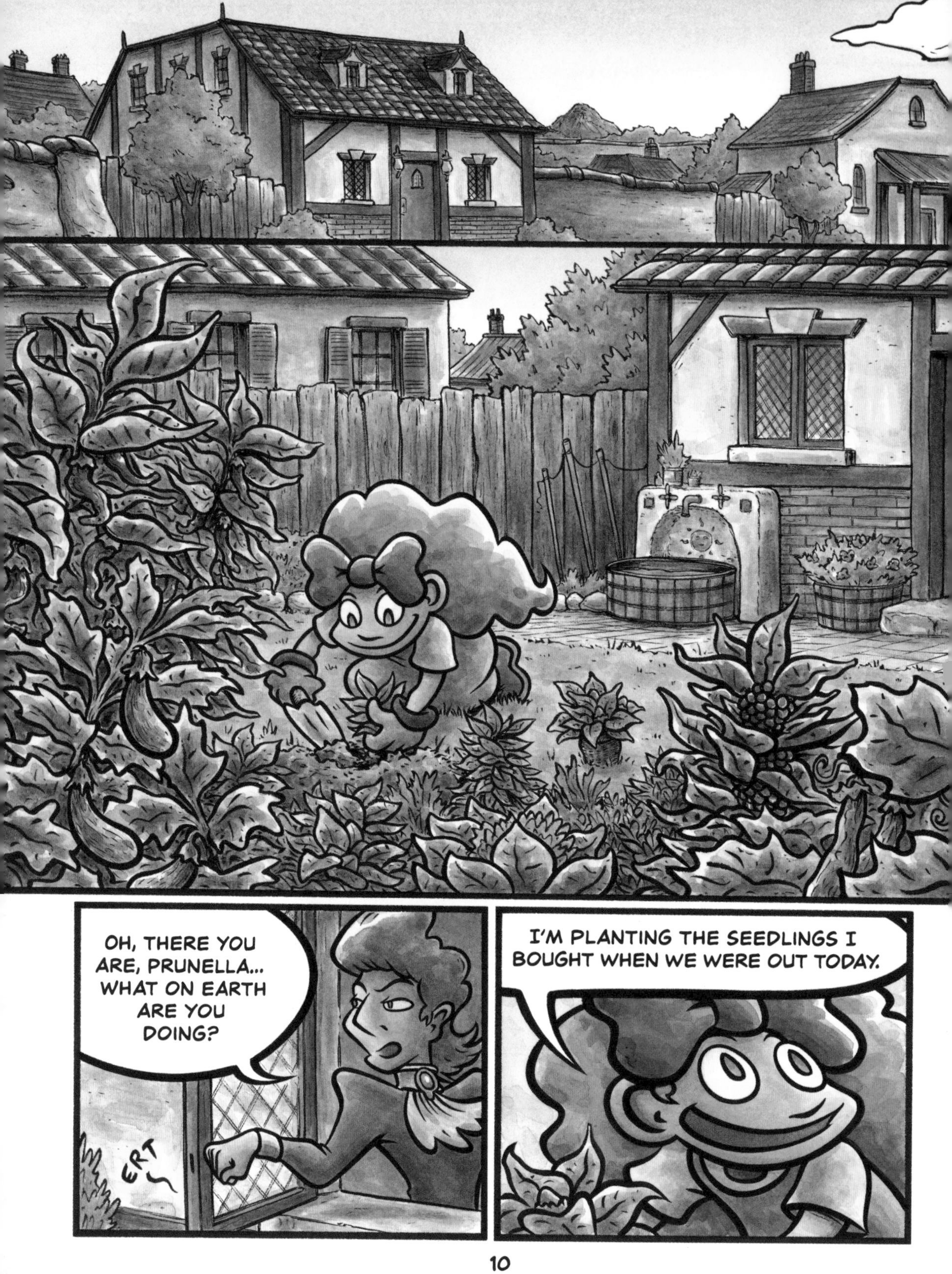
OH, THERE YOU ARE, PRUNELLA... WHAT ON EARTH ARE YOU DOING?
ERT
I'M PLANTING THE SEEDLINGS I BOUGHT WHEN WE WERE OUT TODAY.

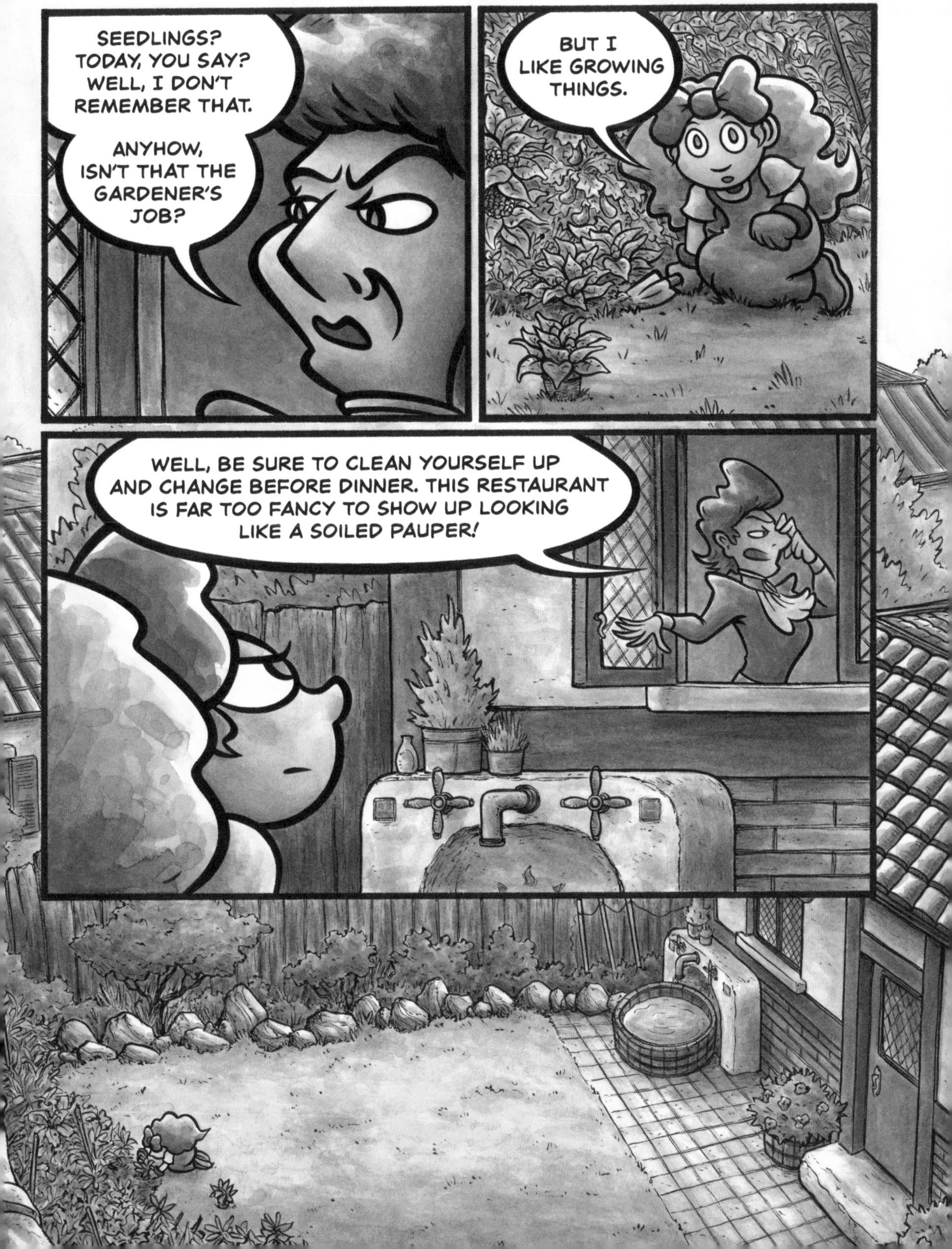
SEEDLINGS? TODAY, YOU SAY? WELL, I DON'T REMEMBER THAT.
ANYHOW, ISN'T THAT THE GARDENER'S JOB?
BUT I LIKE GROWING THINGS.
WELL, BE SURE TO CLEAN YOURSELF UP AND CHANGE BEFORE DINNER. THIS RESTAURANT IS FAR TOO FANCY TO SHOW UP LOOKING LIKE A SOILED PAUPER!

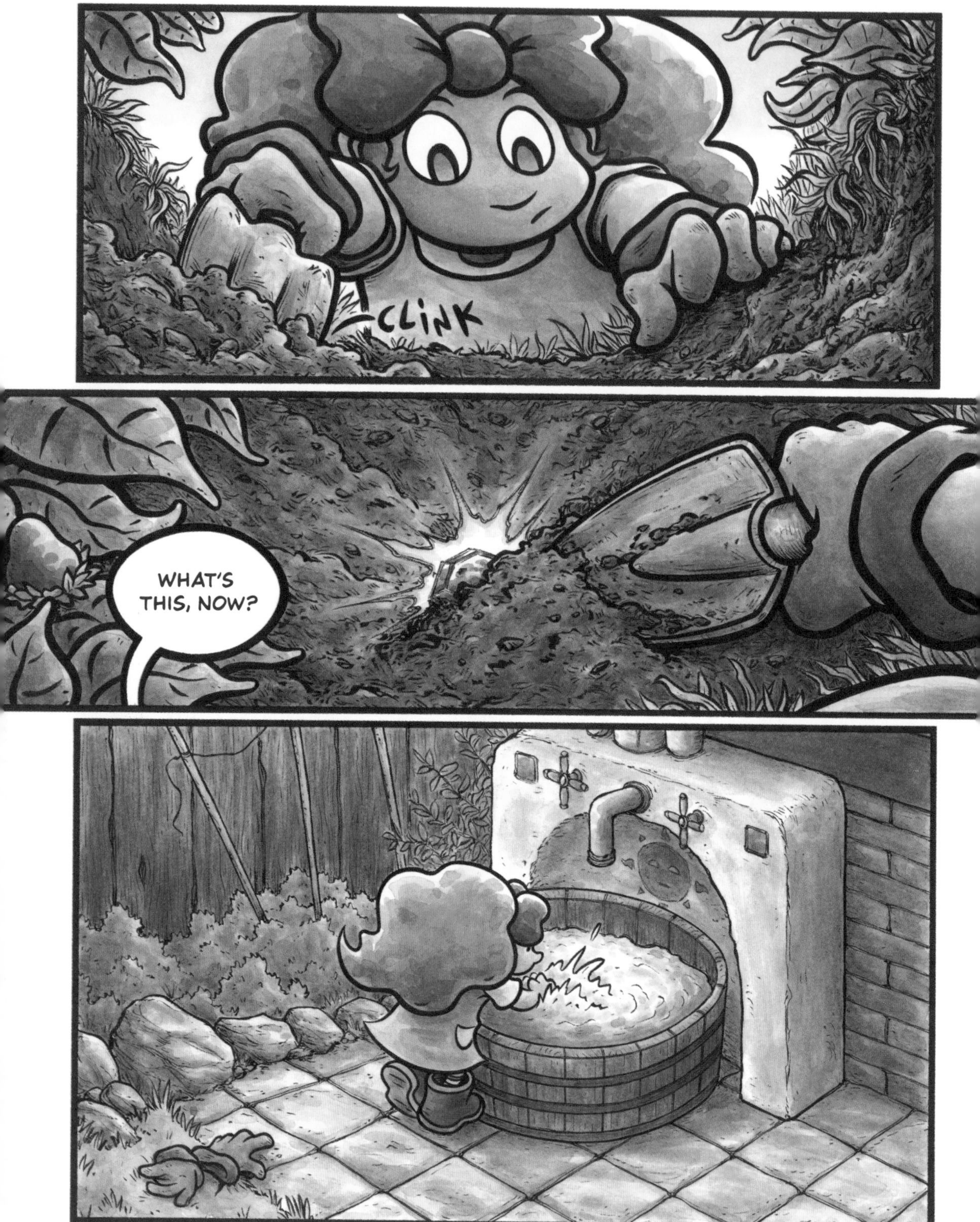
CLINK
WHAT'S THIS, NOW?

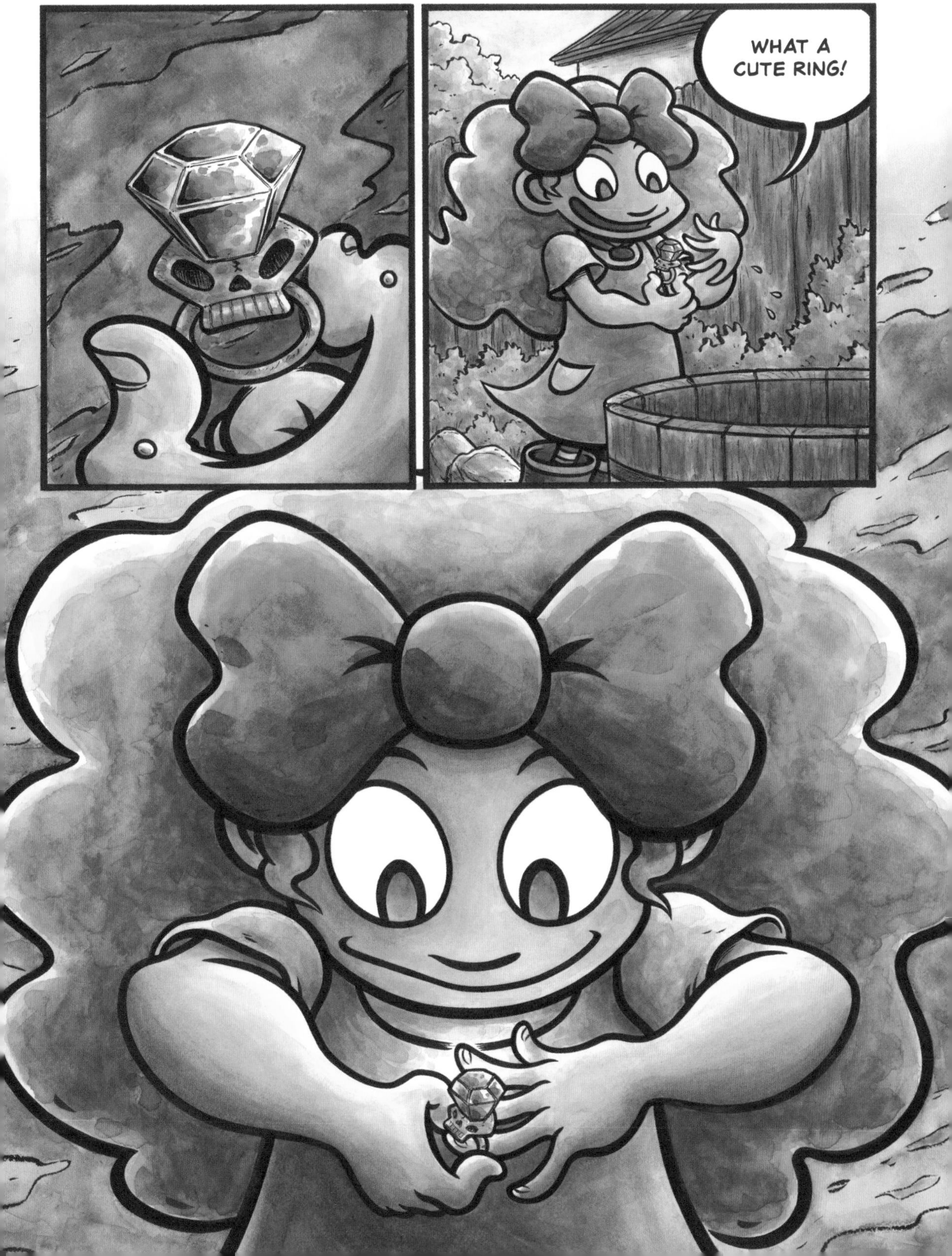
WHAT A
CUTE RING!

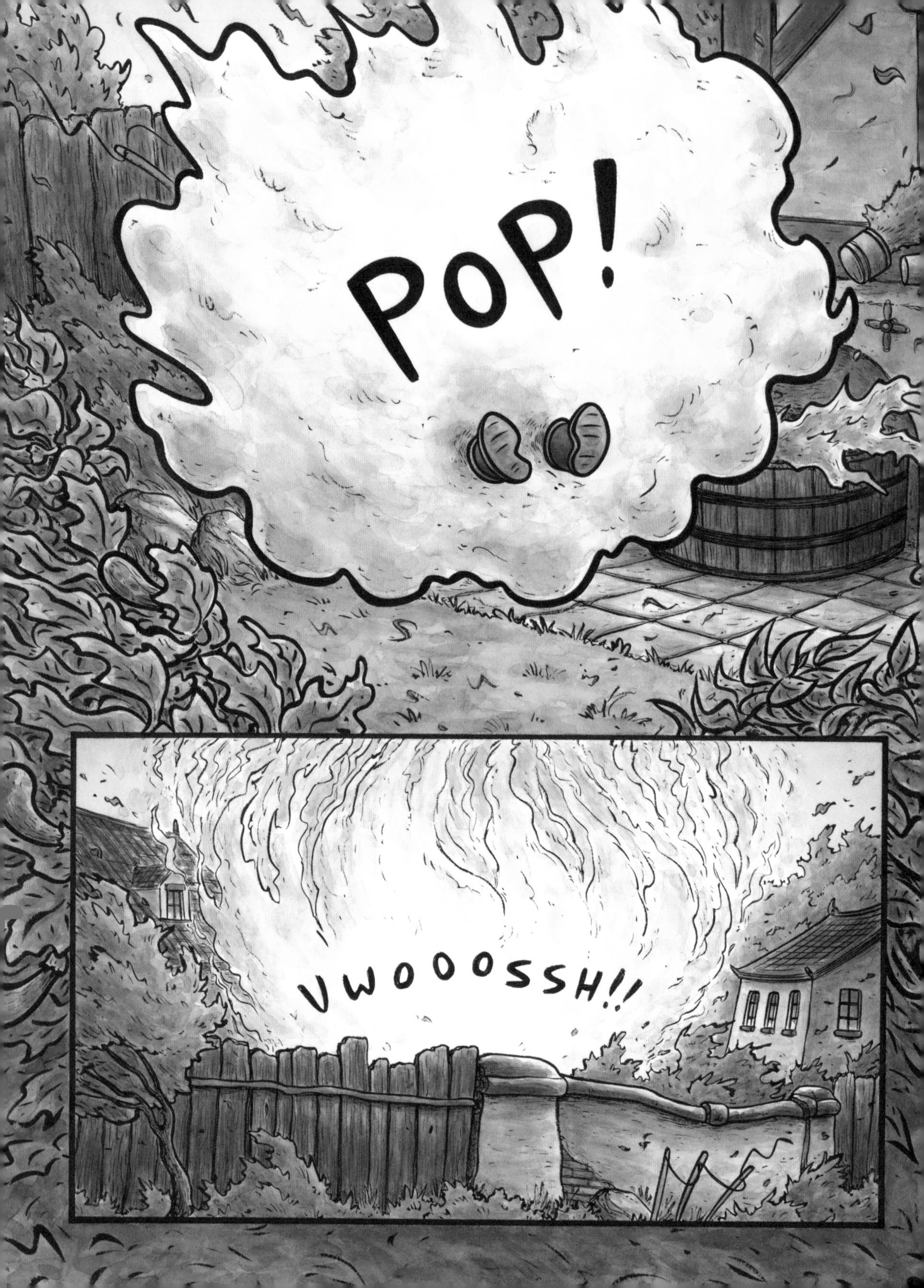
POP!
VWOOOSSH!!

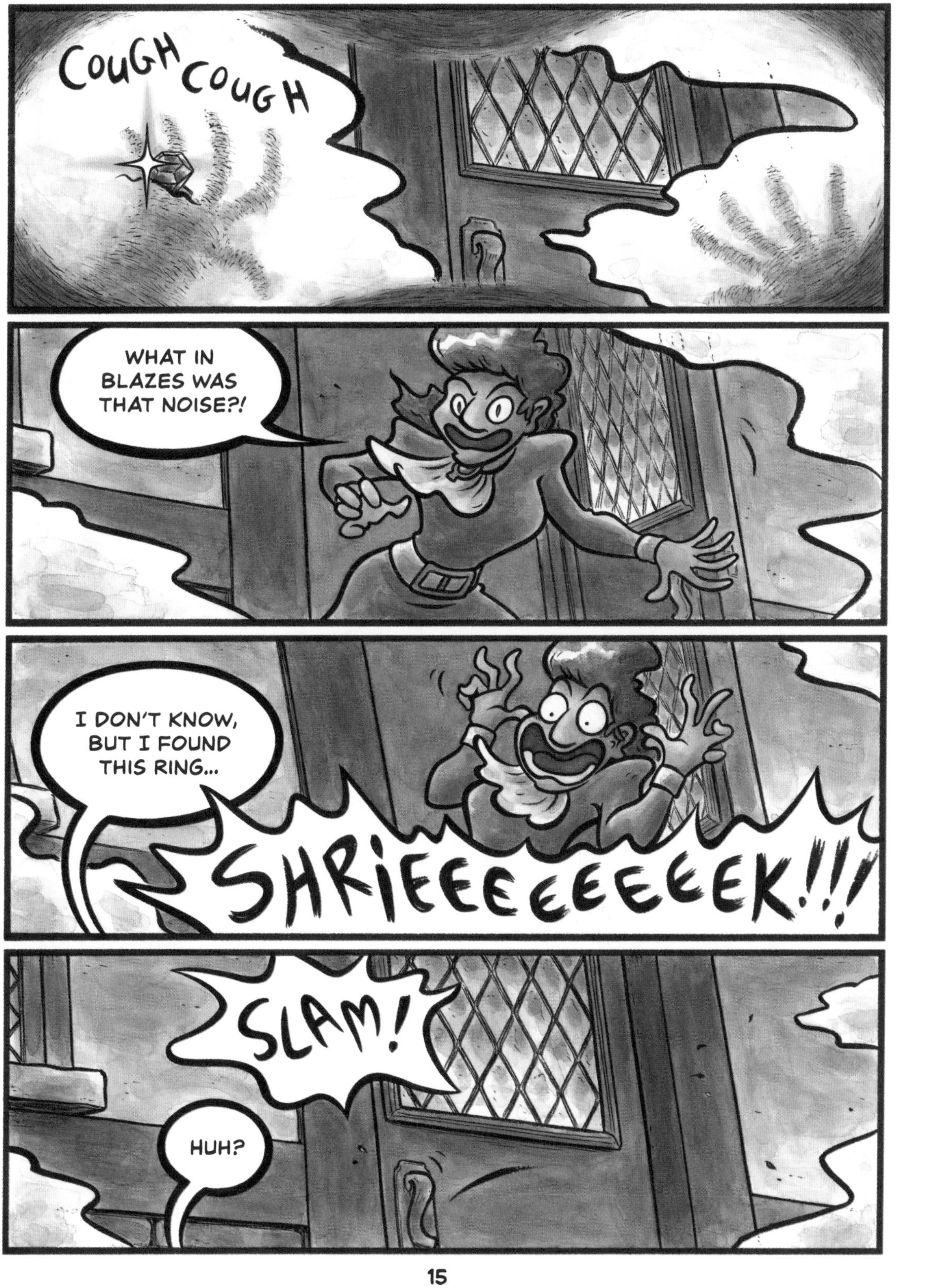
COUGH COUGH
WHAT IN BLAZES WAS THAT NOISE?!
I DON'T KNOW, BUT I FOUND THIS RING...
SHRIEEEEEEEEEK!!!
SLAM!
HUH?

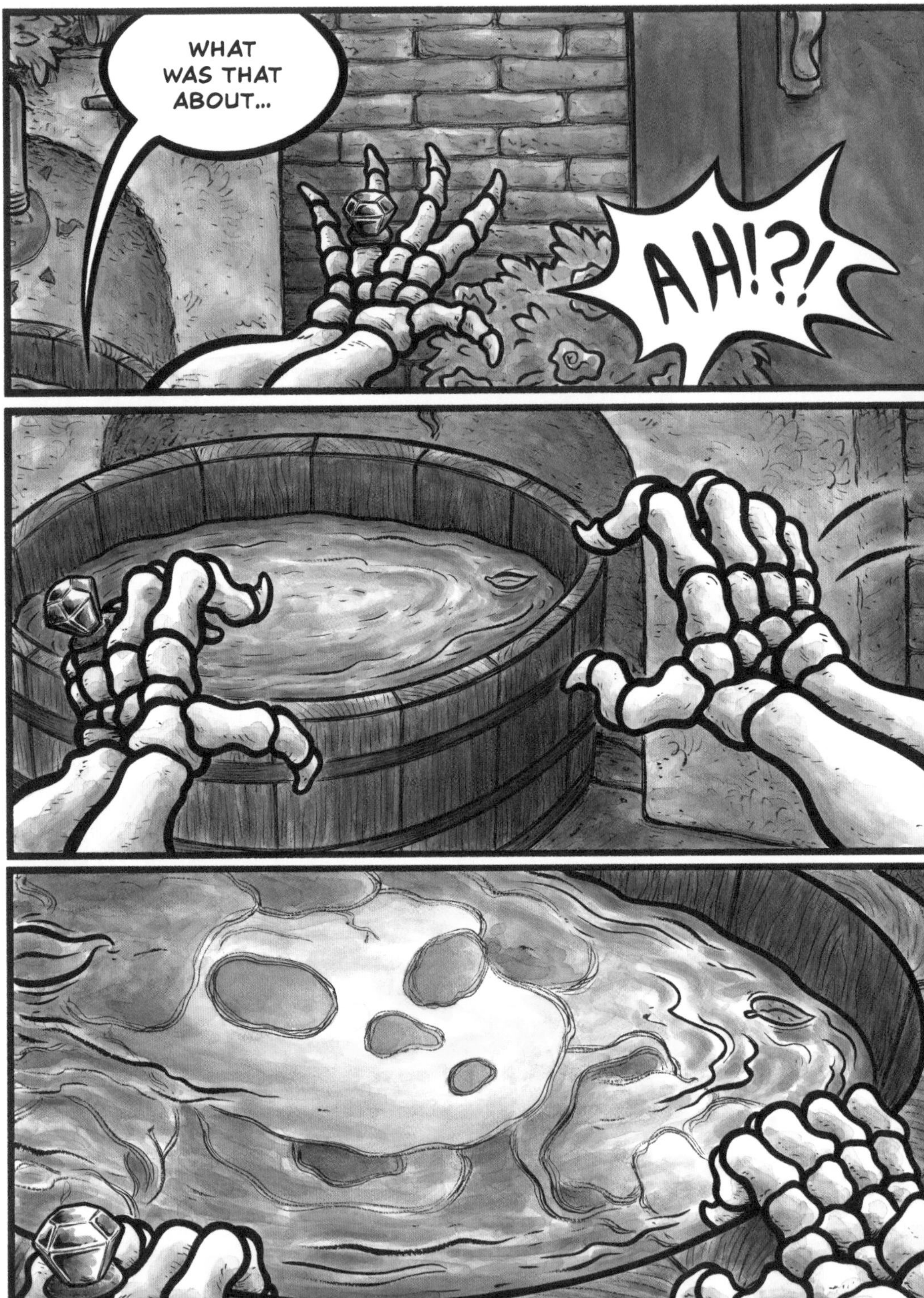
WHAT WAS THAT ABOUT...
AH!?!

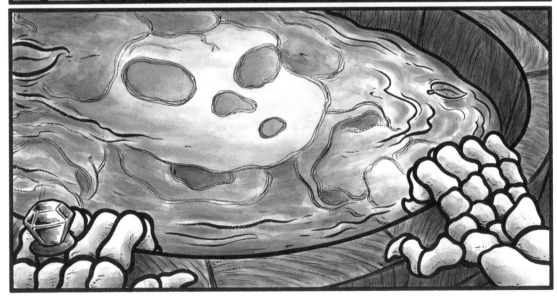

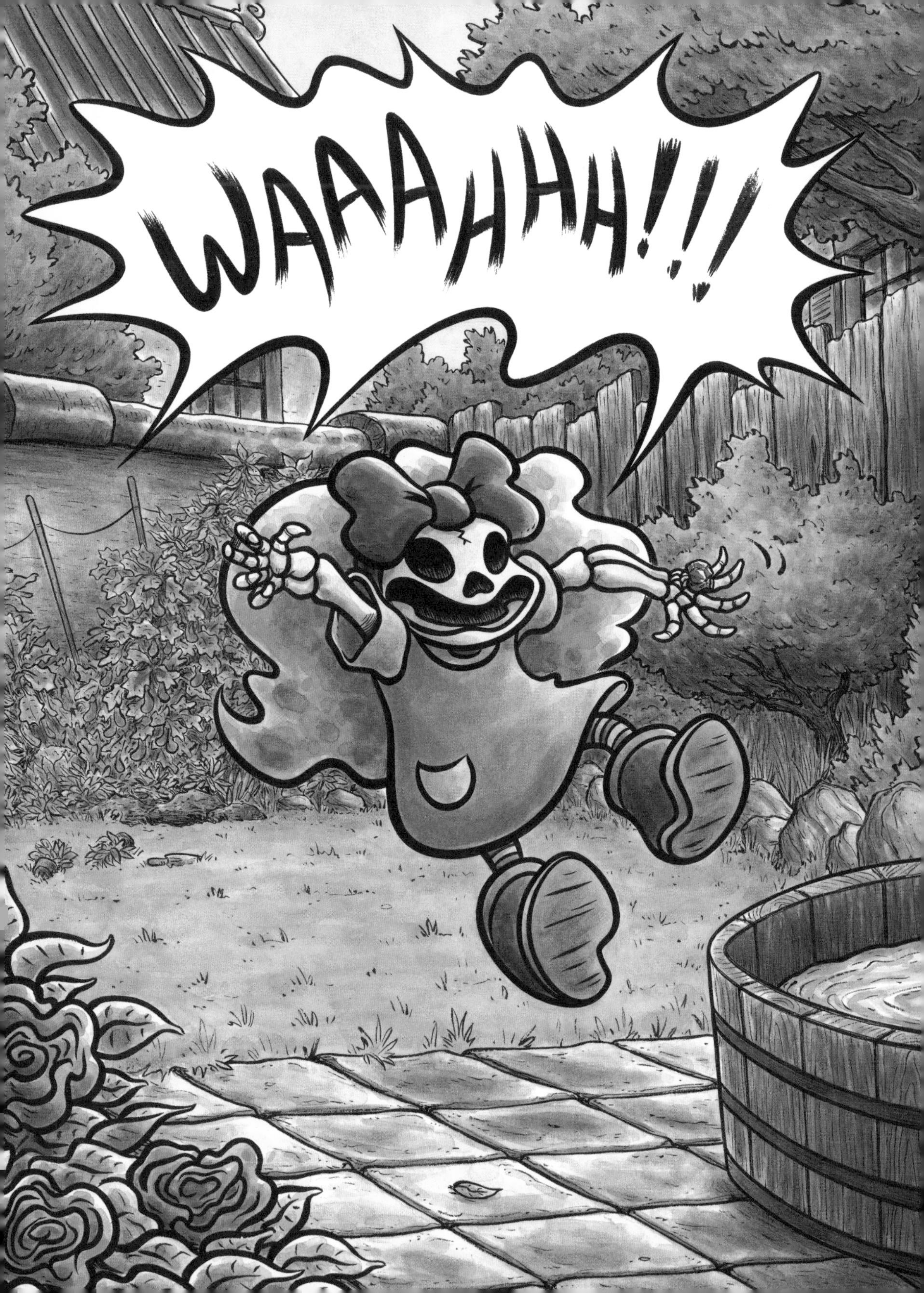
WAAAHHH!!!

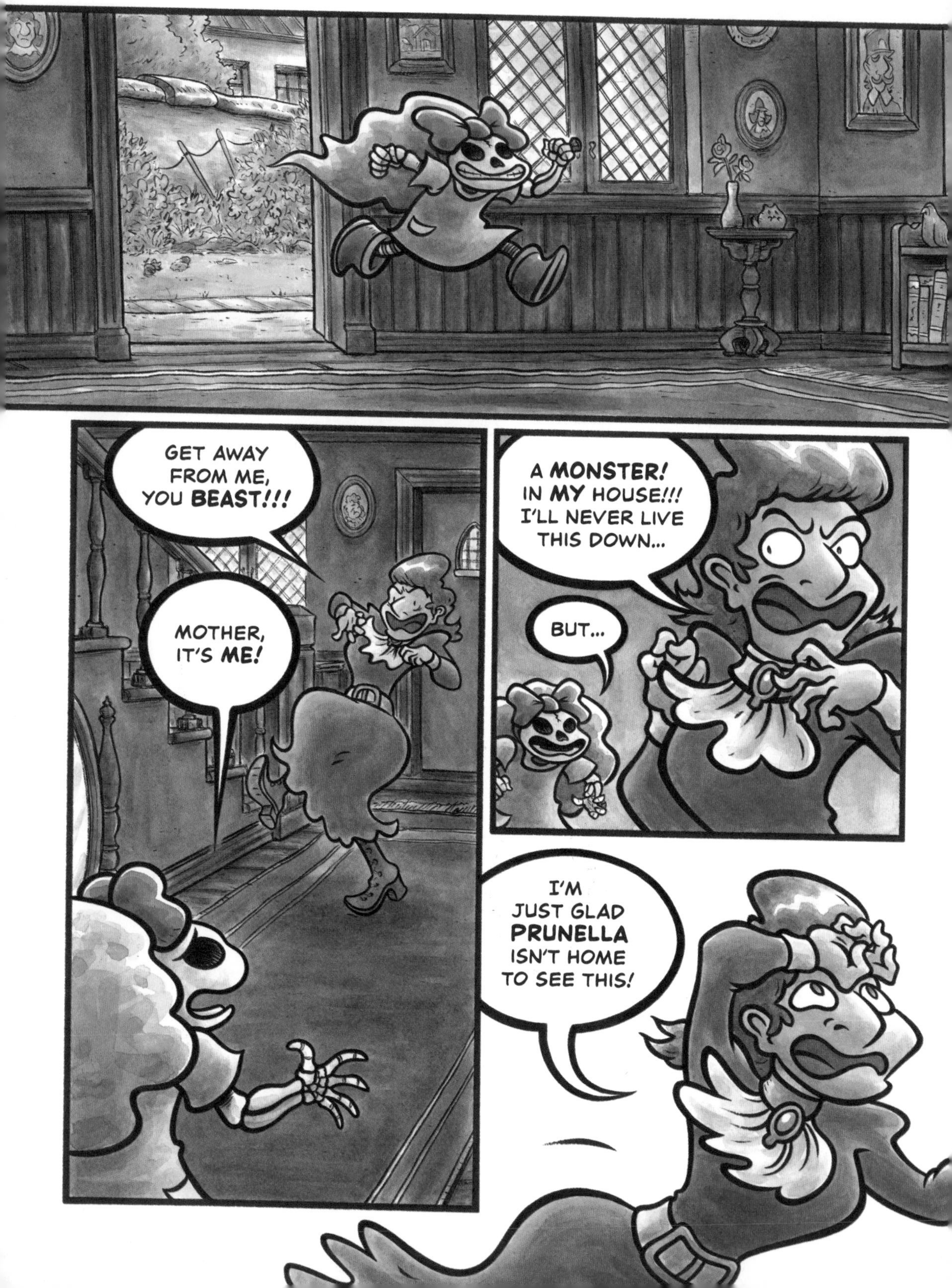
GET AWAY FROM ME, YOU **BEAST!!!**
MOTHER, IT'S **ME!**
A **MONSTER!** IN **MY** HOUSE!!! I'LL NEVER LIVE THIS DOWN...
BUT...
I'M JUST GLAD **PRUNELLA** ISN'T HOME TO SEE THIS!

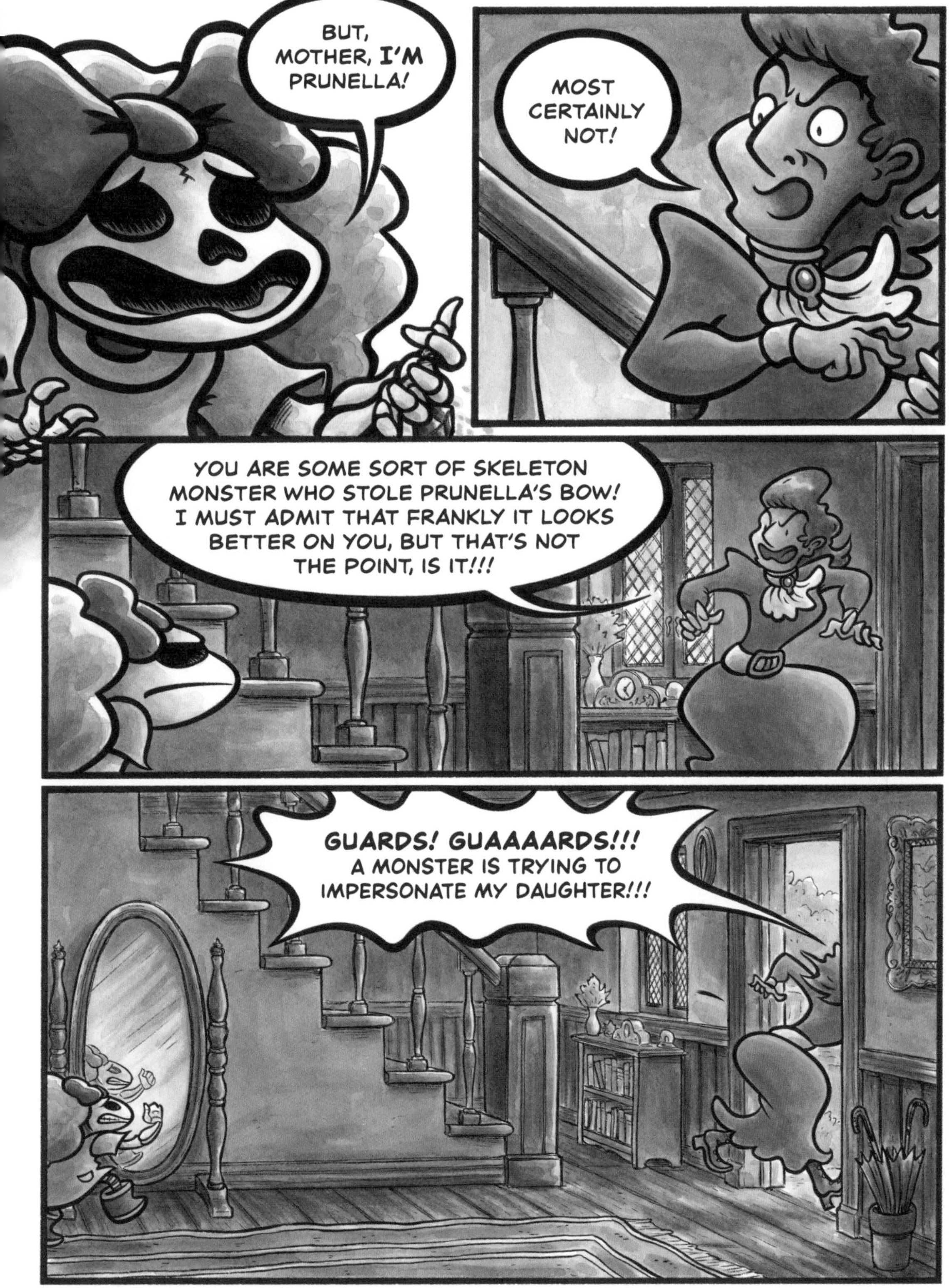
BUT, MOTHER, I'M PRUNELLA!
MOST CERTAINLY NOT!
YOU ARE SOME SORT OF SKELETON MONSTER WHO STOLE PRUNELLA'S BOW! I MUST ADMIT THAT FRANKLY IT LOOKS BETTER ON YOU, BUT THAT'S NOT THE POINT, IS IT!!!
GUARDS! GUAAAARDS!!! A MONSTER IS TRYING TO IMPERSONATE MY DAUGHTER!!!

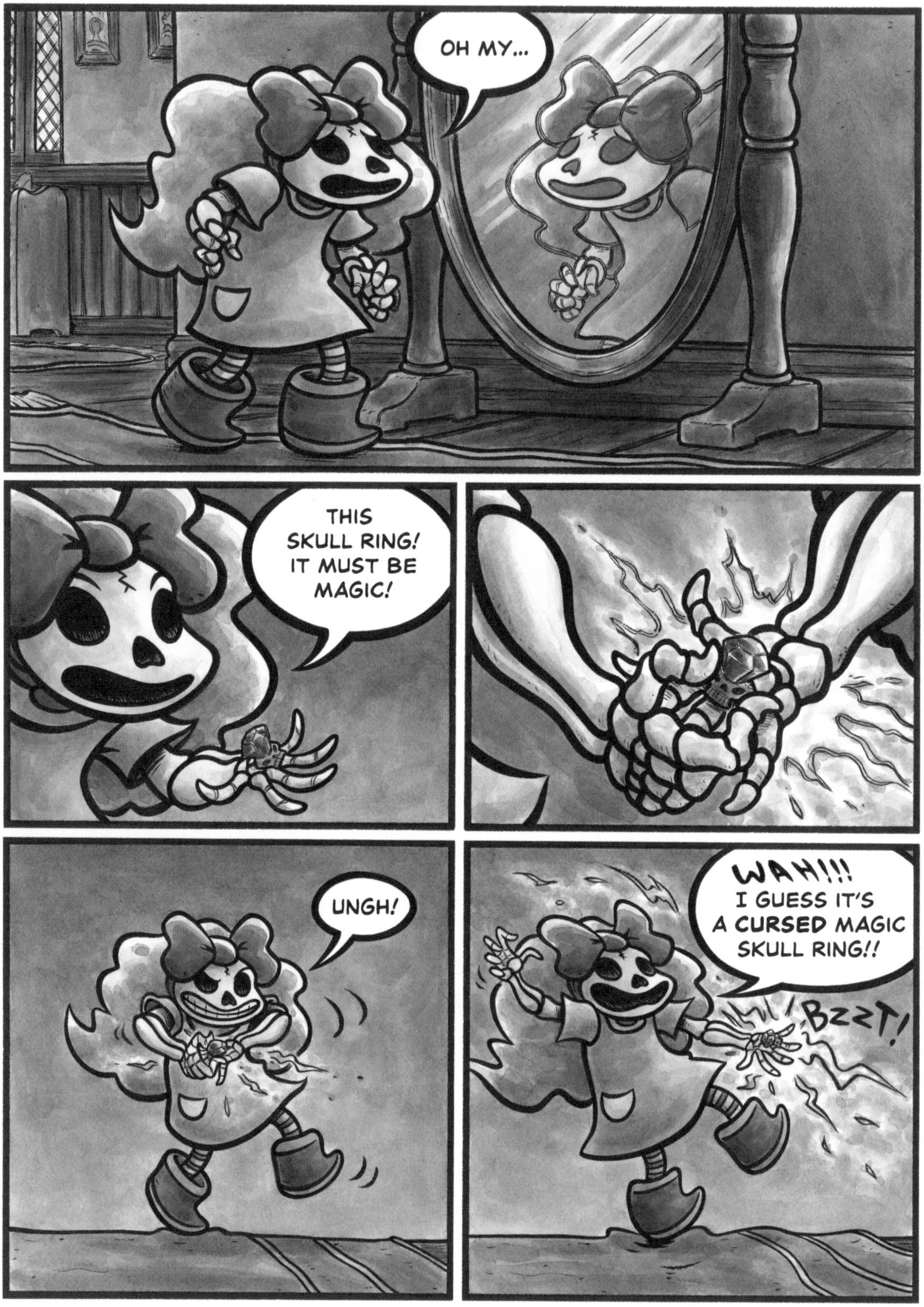
OH MY...
THIS SKULL RING! IT MUST BE MAGIC!
UNGH!
WAH!!!
I GUESS IT'S A CURSED MAGIC SKULL RING!!
BZZT!

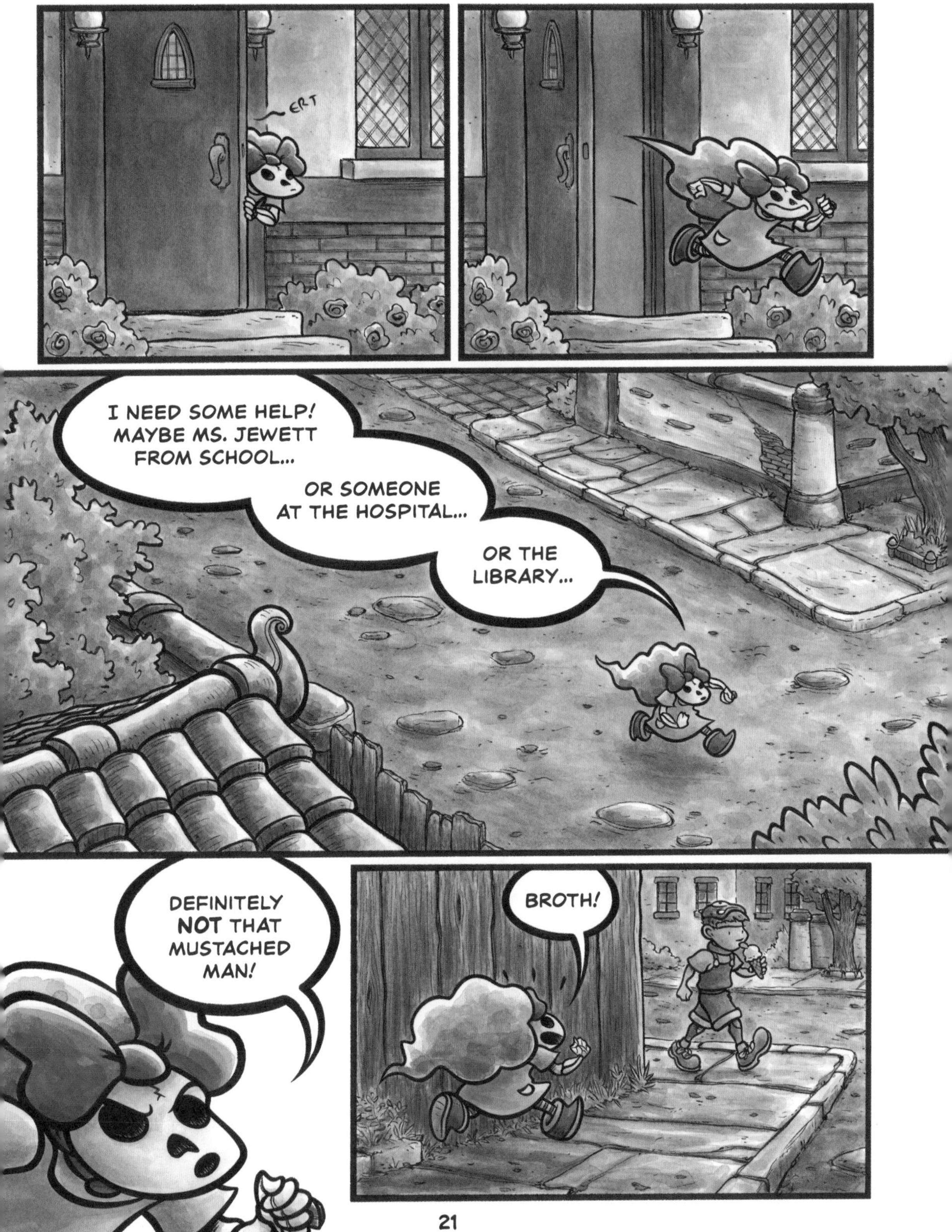
ERT
I NEED SOME HELP! MAYBE MS. JEWETT FROM SCHOOL...
OR SOMEONE AT THE HOSPITAL...
OR THE LIBRARY...
DEFINITELY NOT THAT MUSTACHED MAN!
BROTH!

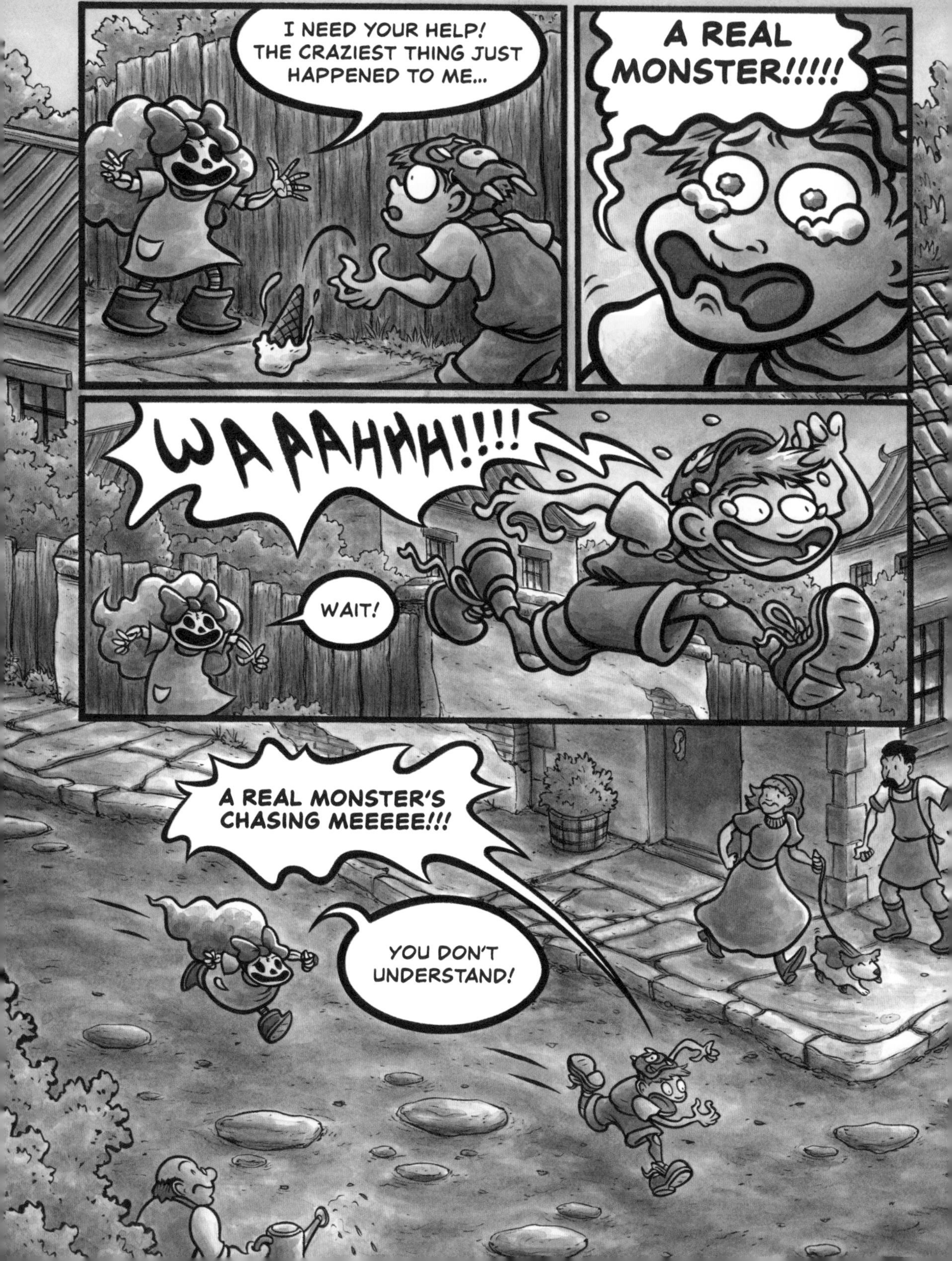
I NEED YOUR HELP! THE CRAZIEST THING JUST HAPPENED TO ME...
A REAL MONSTER!!!!!
WAAAHHH!!!!
WAIT!
A REAL MONSTER'S CHASING MEEEEE!!!
YOU DON'T UNDERSTAND!

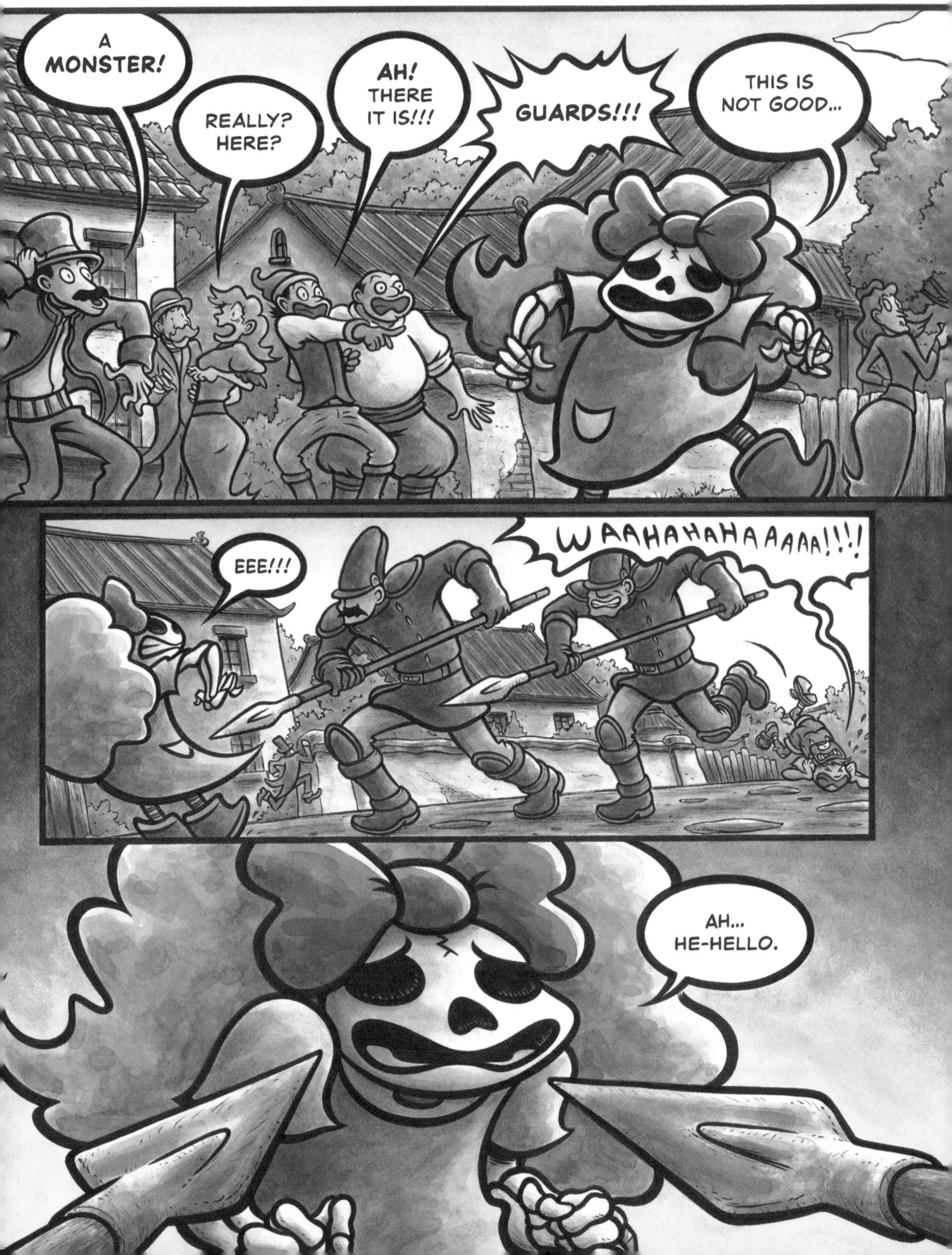
A MONSTER!
REALLY? HERE?
AH! THERE IT IS!!!
GUARDS!!!
THIS IS NOT GOOD...
EEE!!!
WAAHAHAHAAAAA!!!!
AH... HE-HELLO.

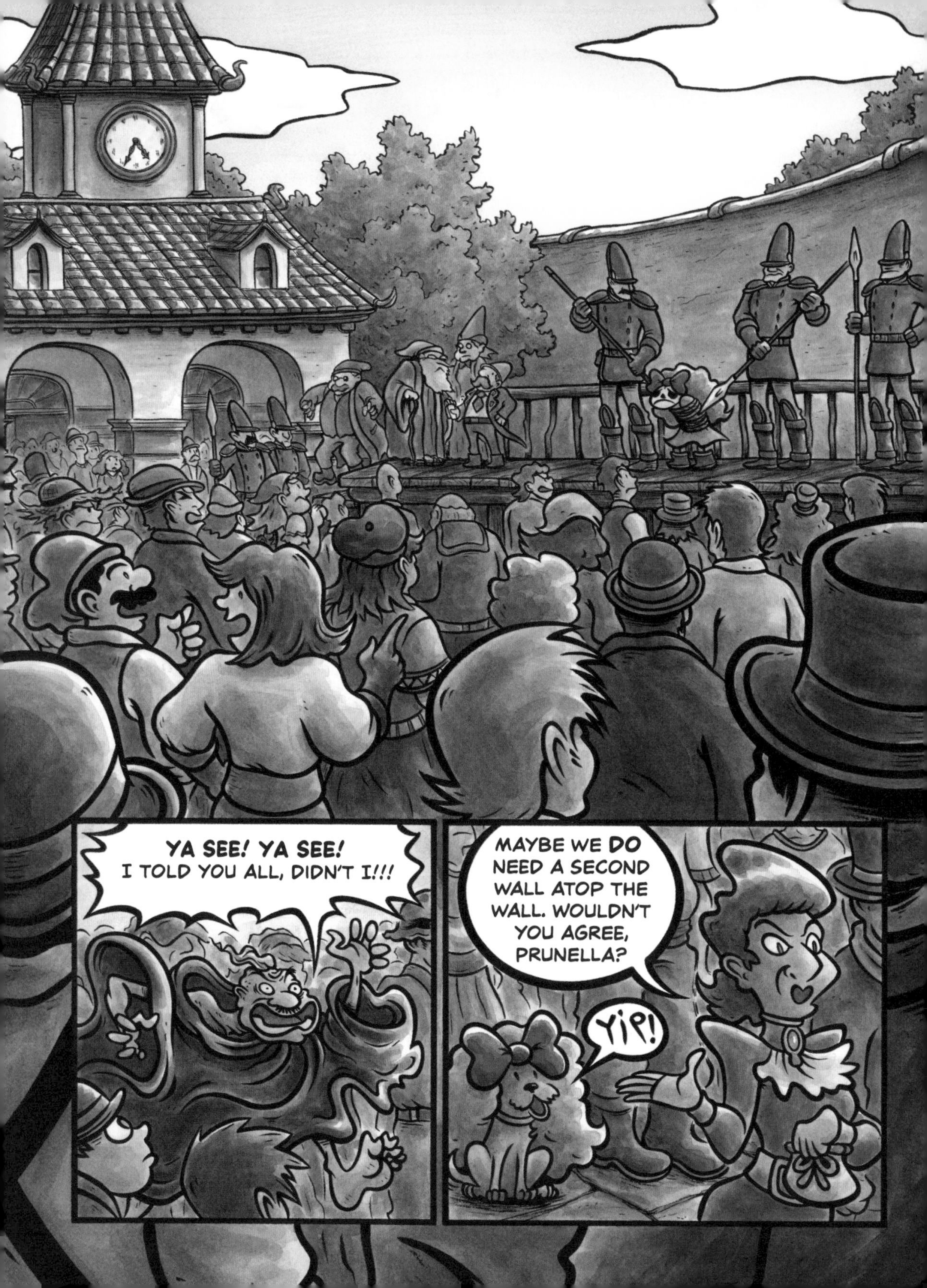
YA SEE! YA SEE!
I TOLD YOU ALL, DIDN'T I!!!
MAYBE WE DO NEED A SECOND WALL ATOP THE WALL. WOULDN'T YOU AGREE, PRUNELLA?
YIP!

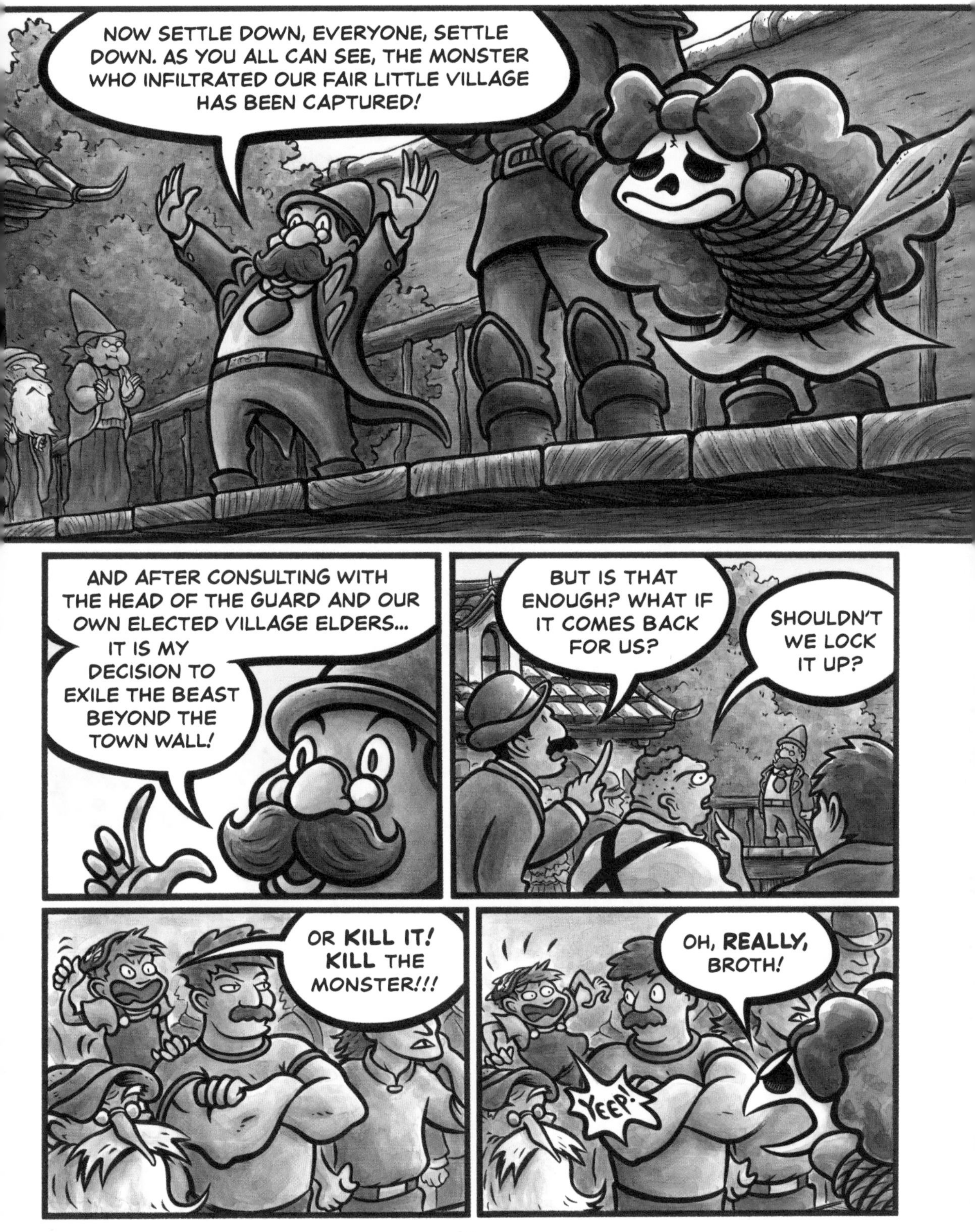
NOW SETTLE DOWN, EVERYONE, SETTLE DOWN. AS YOU ALL CAN SEE, THE MONSTER WHO INFILTRATED OUR FAIR LITTLE VILLAGE HAS BEEN CAPTURED!
AND AFTER CONSULTING WITH THE HEAD OF THE GUARD AND OUR OWN ELECTED VILLAGE ELDERS...
IT IS MY DECISION TO EXILE THE BEAST BEYOND THE TOWN WALL!
BUT IS THAT ENOUGH? WHAT IF IT COMES BACK FOR US?
SHOULDN'T WE LOCK IT UP?
OR **KILL IT! KILL** THE MONSTER!!!
OH, **REALLY,** BROTH!
YEEP!

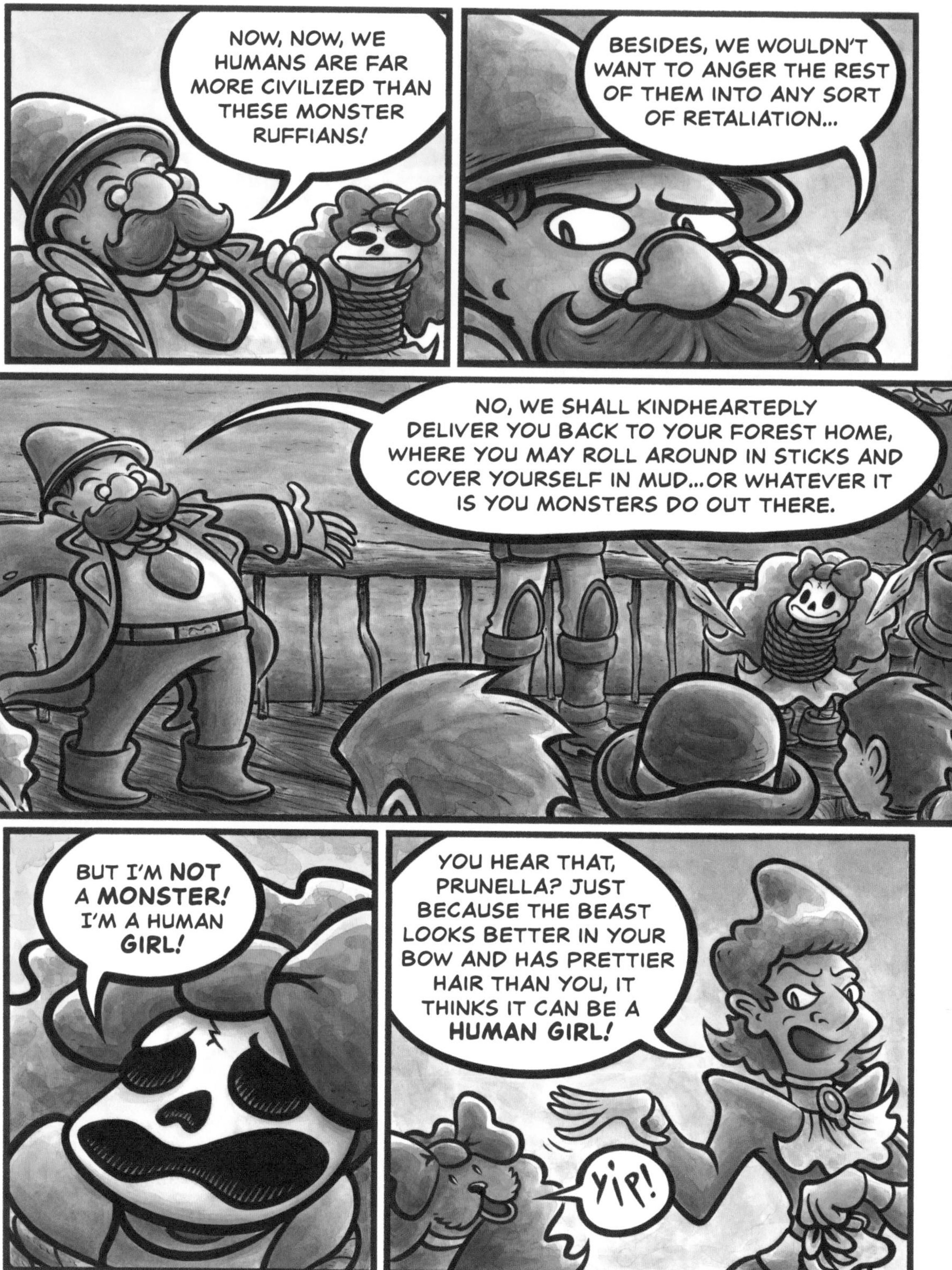
NOW, NOW, WE HUMANS ARE FAR MORE CIVILIZED THAN THESE MONSTER RUFFIANS!
BESIDES, WE WOULDN'T WANT TO ANGER THE REST OF THEM INTO ANY SORT OF RETALIATION...
NO, WE SHALL KINDHEARTEDLY DELIVER YOU BACK TO YOUR FOREST HOME, WHERE YOU MAY ROLL AROUND IN STICKS AND COVER YOURSELF IN MUD...OR WHATEVER IT IS YOU MONSTERS DO OUT THERE.
BUT I'M **NOT** A **MONSTER**! I'M A HUMAN **GIRL**!
YOU HEAR THAT, PRUNELLA? JUST BECAUSE THE BEAST LOOKS BETTER IN YOUR BOW AND HAS PRETTIER HAIR THAN YOU, IT THINKS IT CAN BE A **HUMAN GIRL**!
YIP!

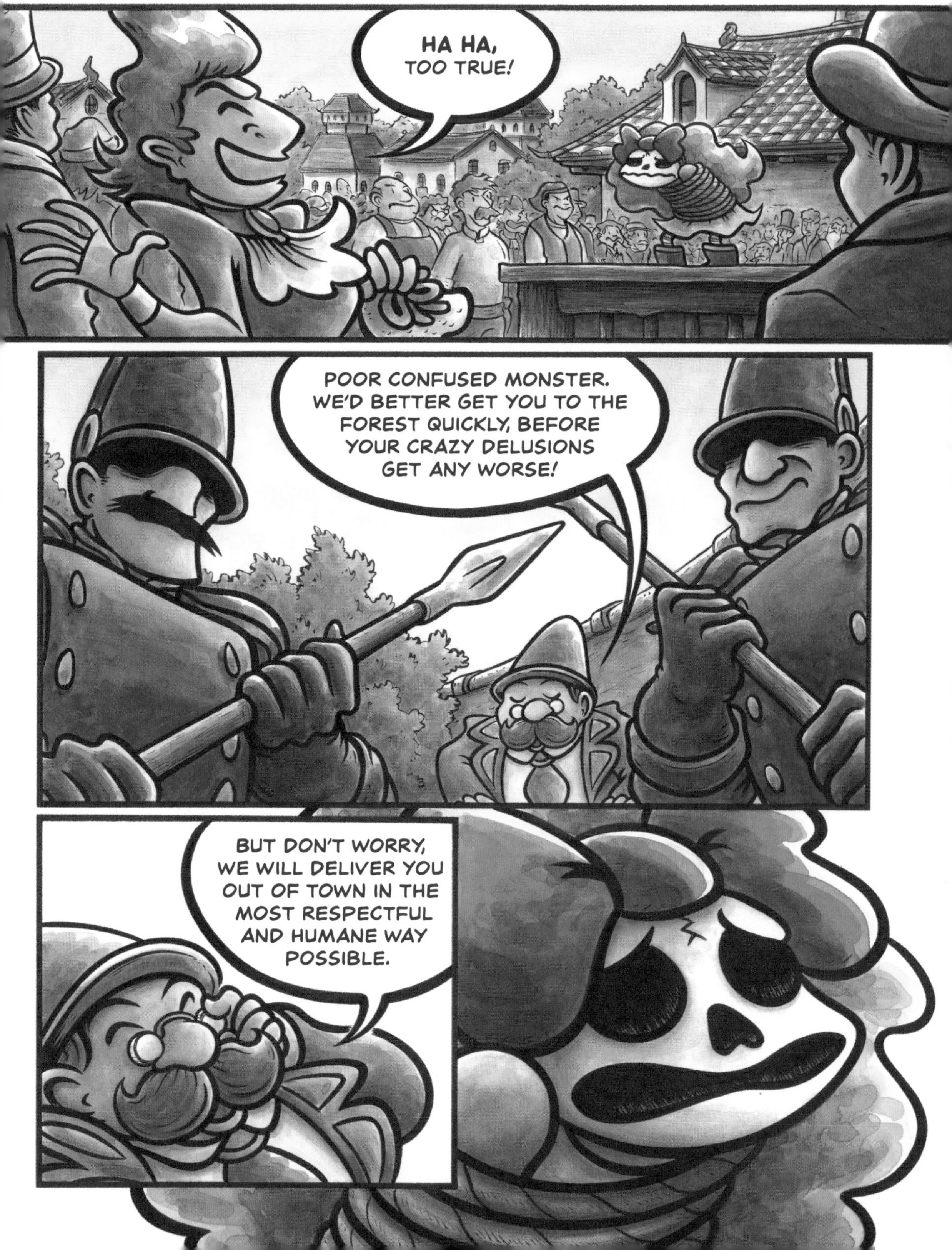
HA HA,
TOO TRUE!
POOR CONFUSED MONSTER. WE'D BETTER GET YOU TO THE FOREST QUICKLY, BEFORE YOUR CRAZY DELUSIONS GET ANY WORSE!
BUT DON'T WORRY, WE WILL DELIVER YOU OUT OF TOWN IN THE MOST RESPECTFUL AND HUMANE WAY POSSIBLE.

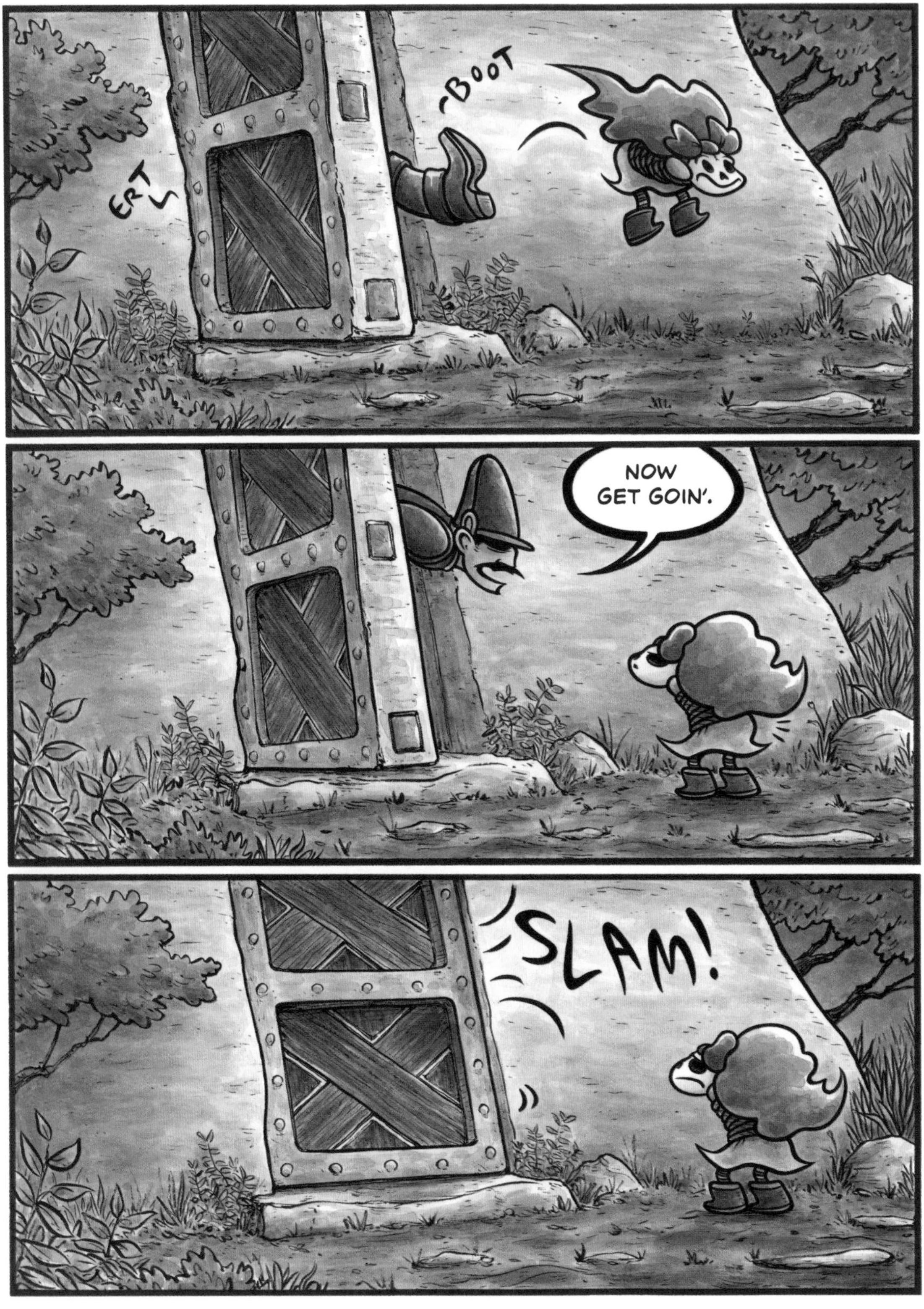
ERT
BOOT
NOW GET GOIN'.
SLAM!

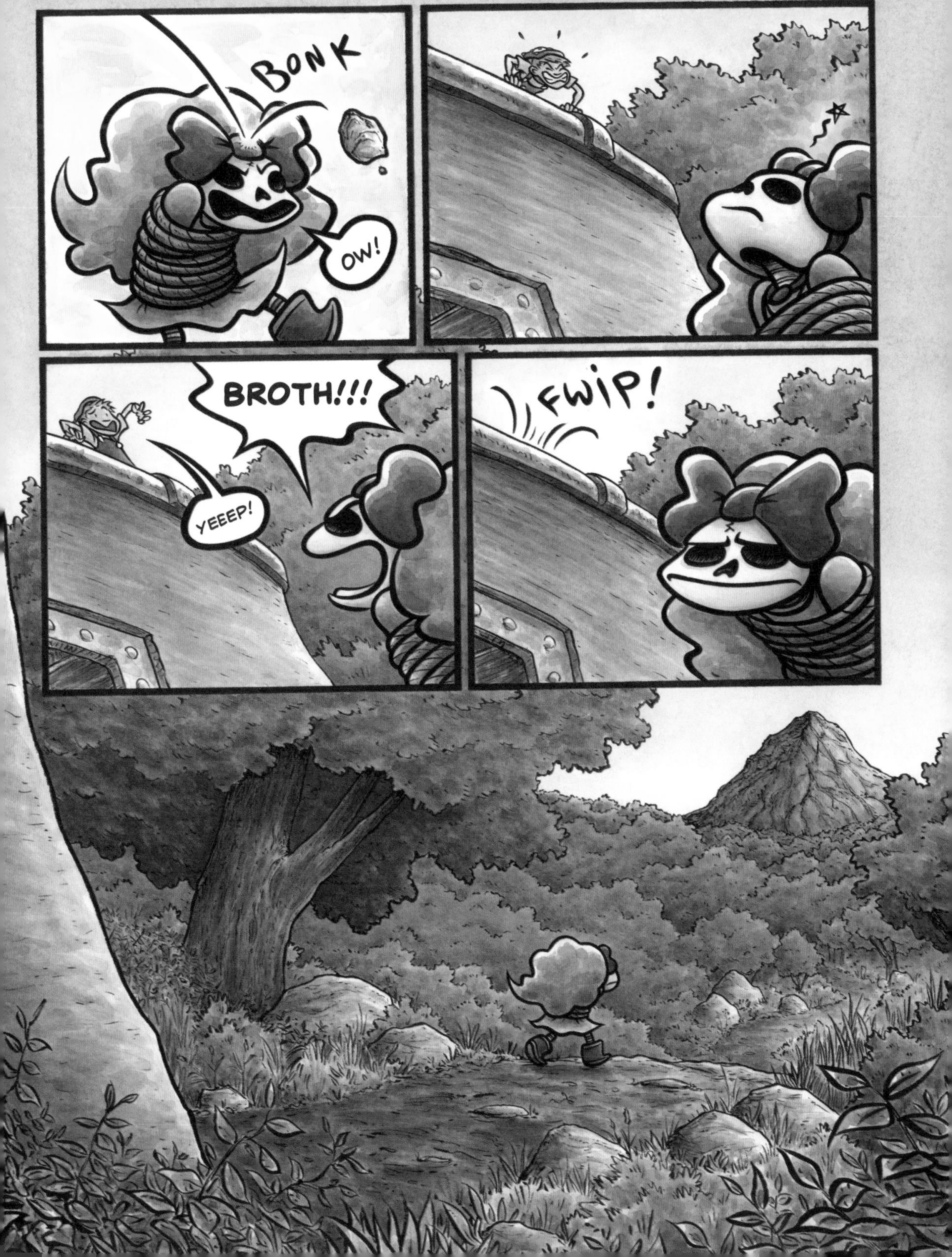
BONK
OW!
BROTH!!!
YEEEP!
FWIP!

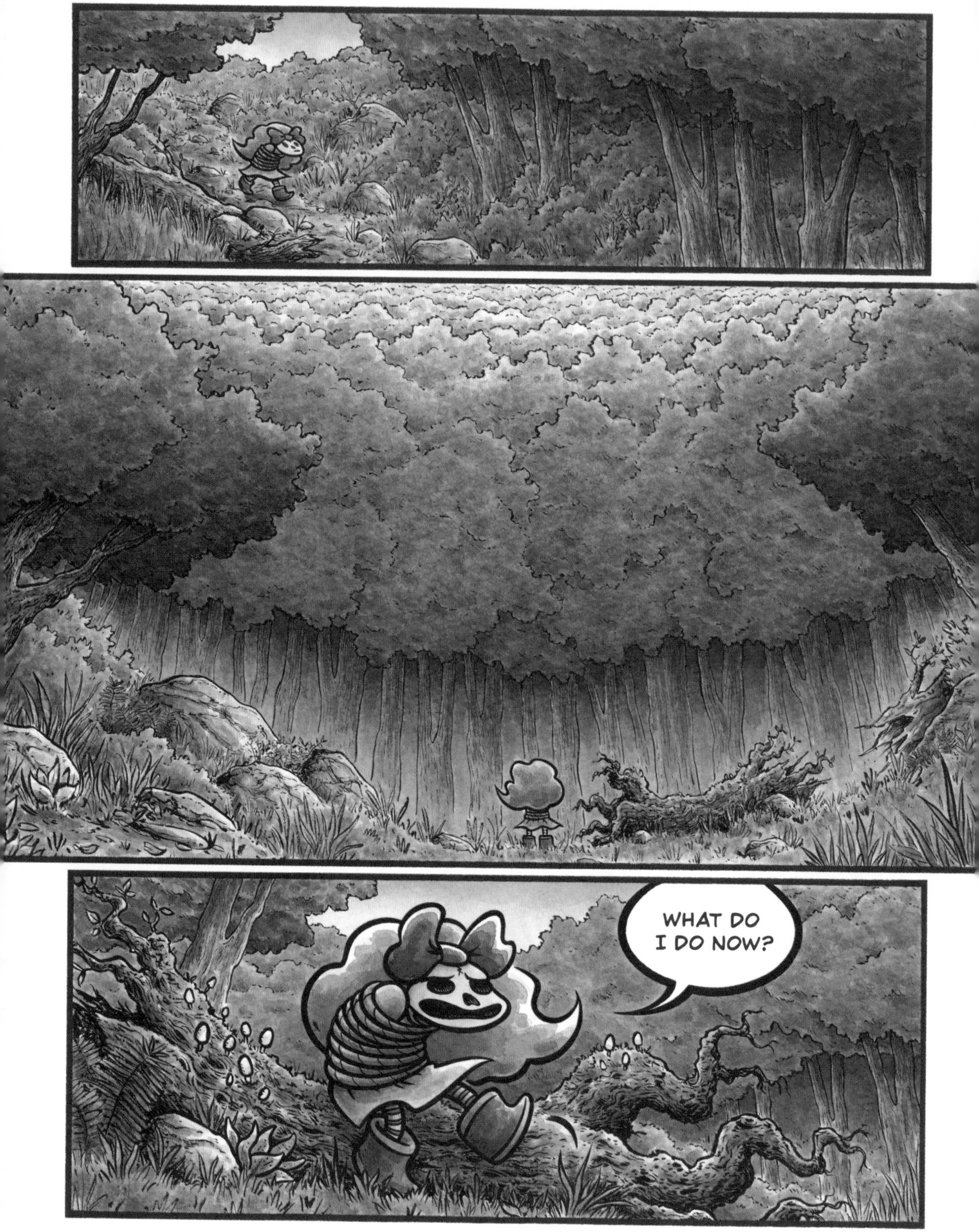
WHAT DO I DO NOW?

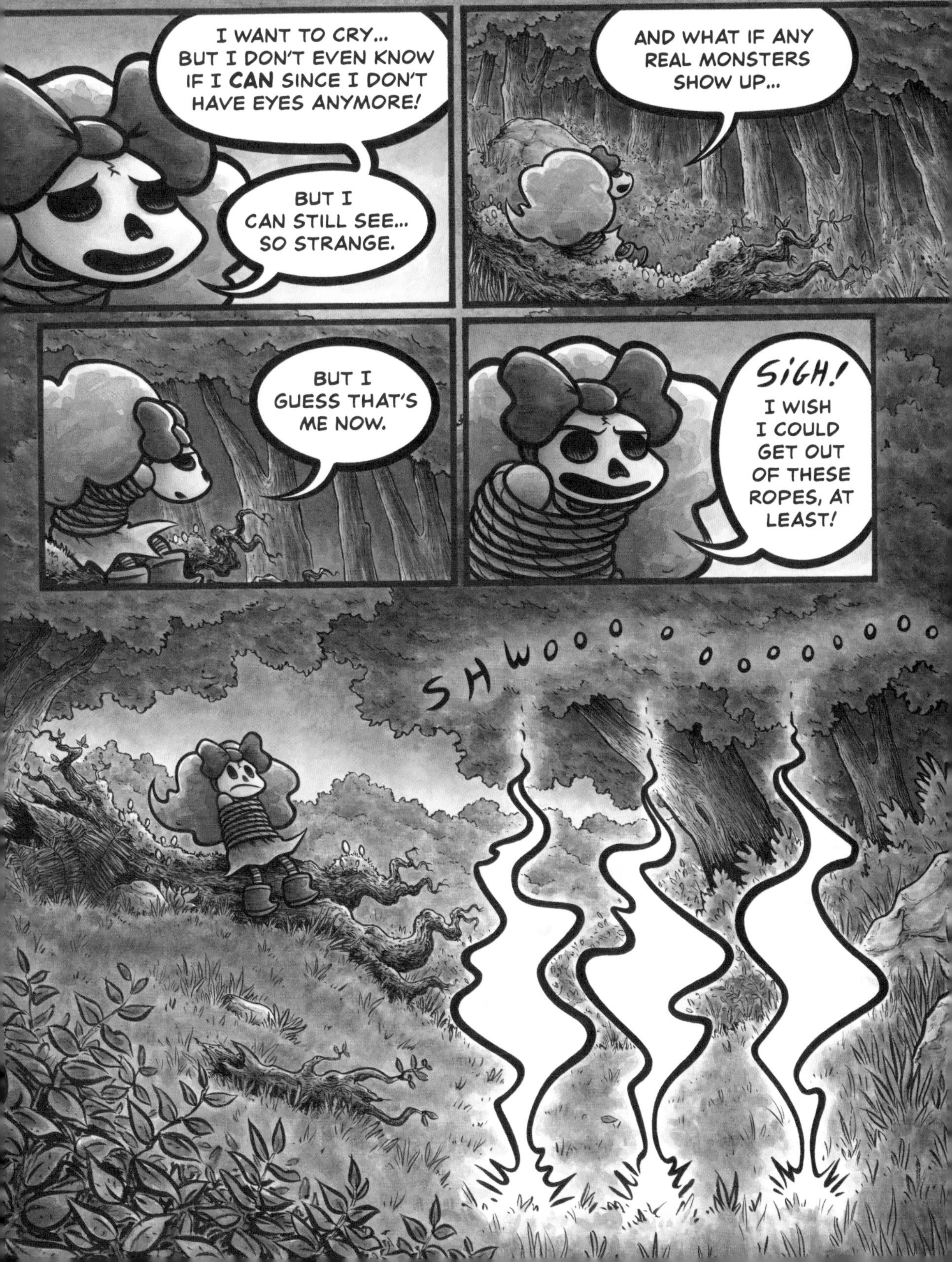
I WANT TO CRY... BUT I DON'T EVEN KNOW IF I **CAN** SINCE I DON'T HAVE EYES ANYMORE!
BUT I CAN STILL SEE... SO STRANGE.
AND WHAT IF ANY REAL MONSTERS SHOW UP...
BUT I GUESS THAT'S ME NOW.
SIGH! I WISH I COULD GET OUT OF THESE ROPES, AT LEAST!
SHWOOOOOOOOOOOOOOO

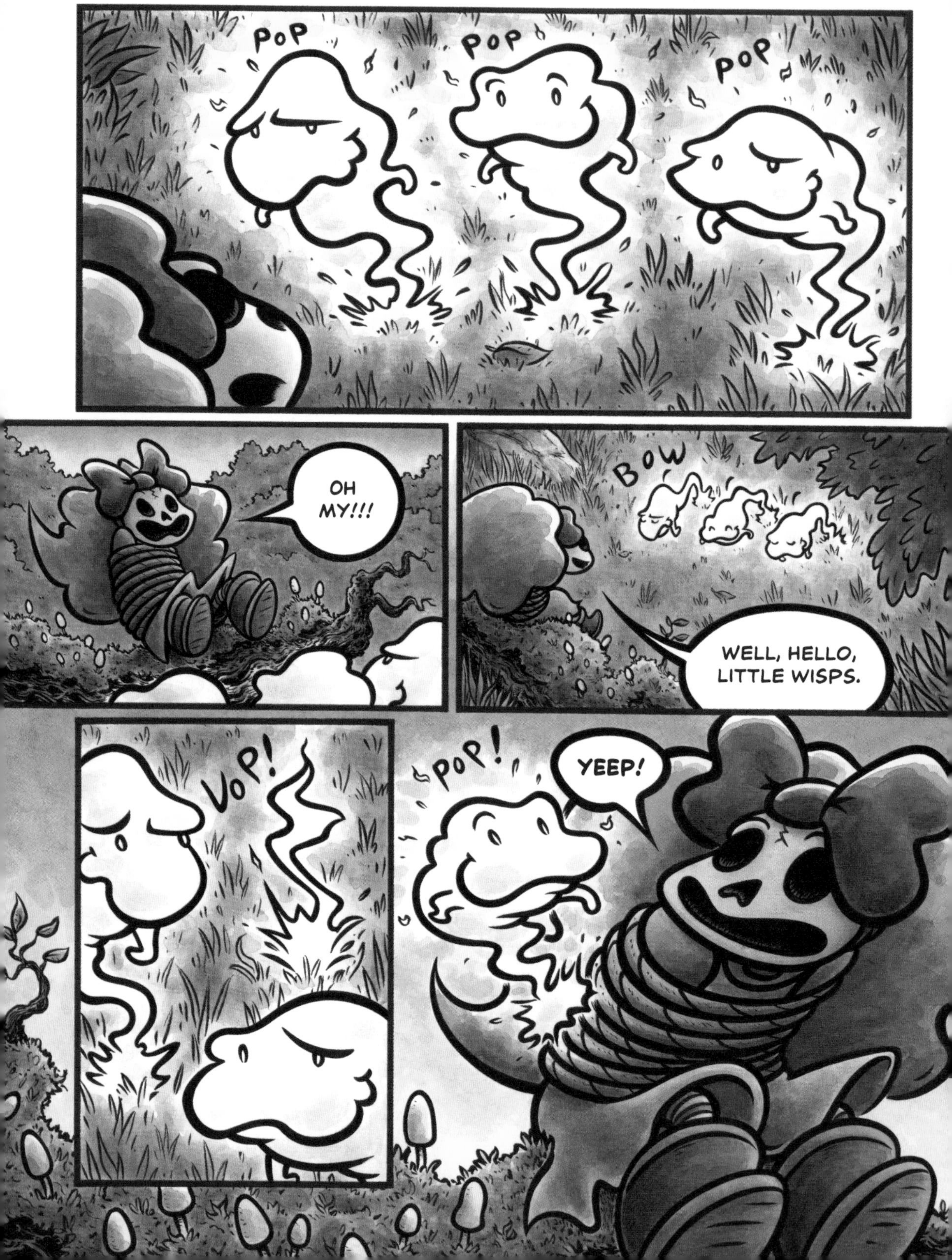
POP
POP
POP
OH MY!!!
BOW
WELL, HELLO, LITTLE WISPS.
VOP!
POP!
YEEP!

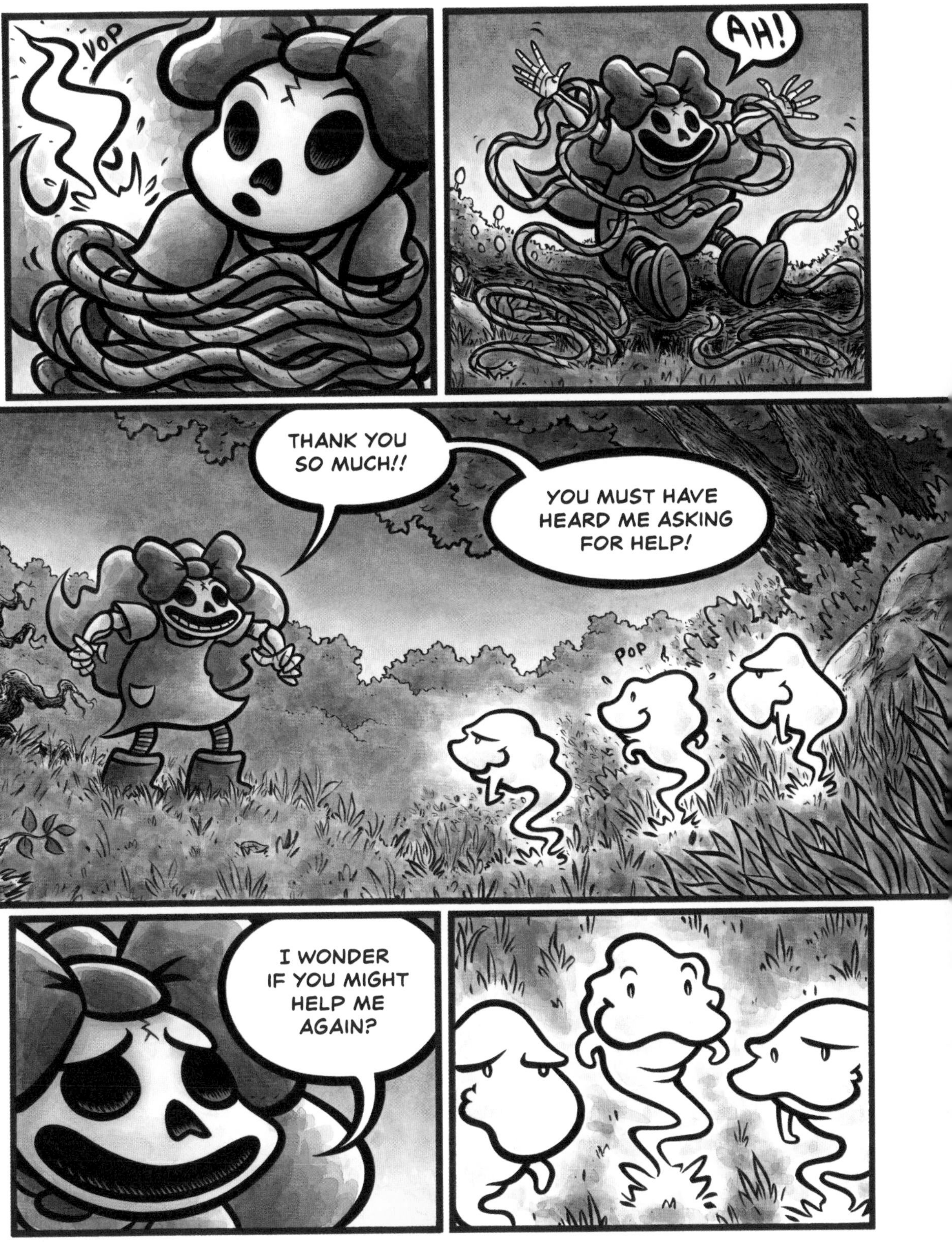
VOP
AH!
THANK YOU SO MUCH!!
YOU MUST HAVE HEARD ME ASKING FOR HELP!
POP
I WONDER IF YOU MIGHT HELP ME AGAIN?

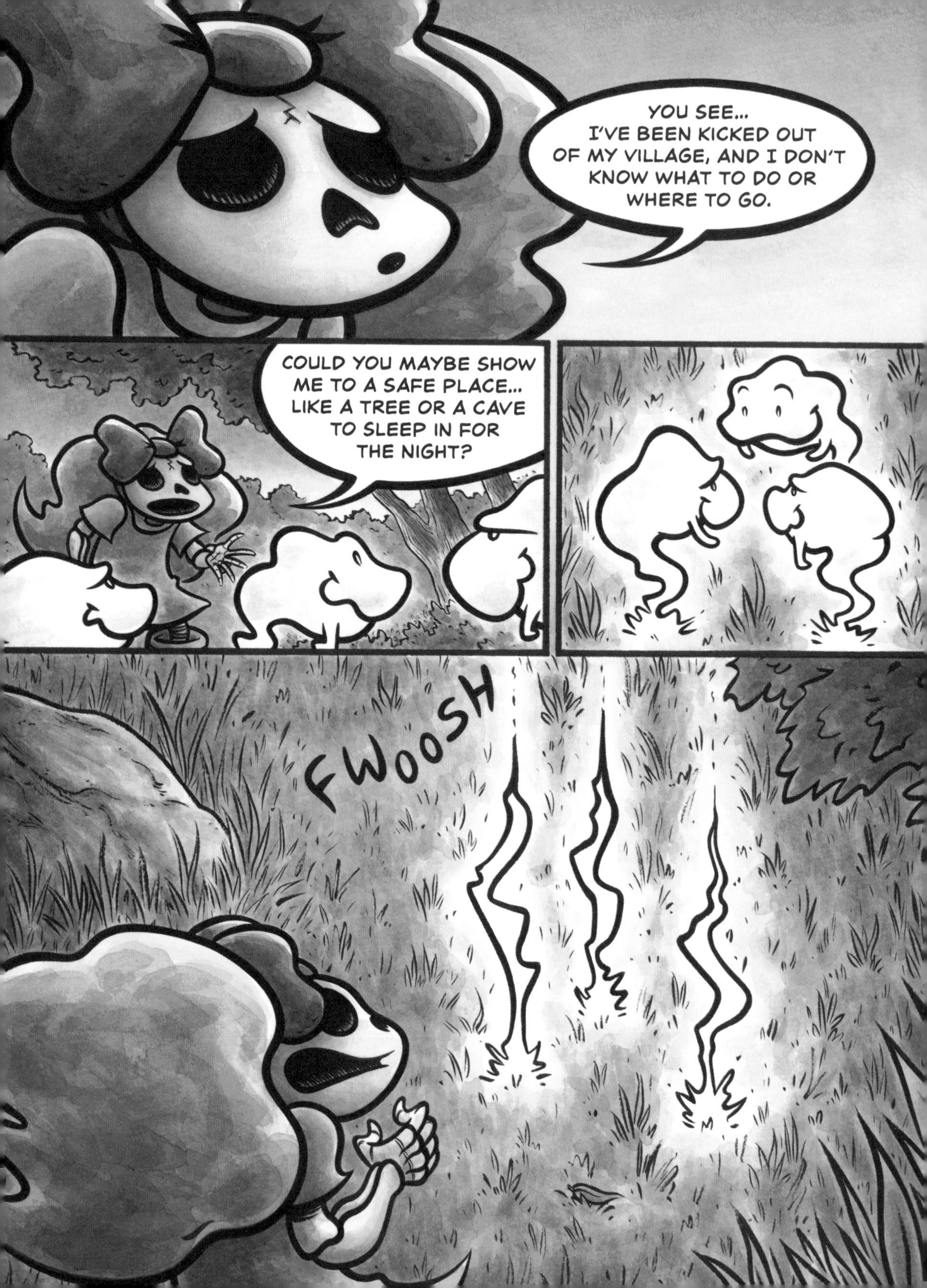
YOU SEE... I'VE BEEN KICKED OUT OF MY VILLAGE, AND I DON'T KNOW WHAT TO DO OR WHERE TO GO.
COULD YOU MAYBE SHOW ME TO A SAFE PLACE... LIKE A TREE OR A CAVE TO SLEEP IN FOR THE NIGHT?
FWOOSH

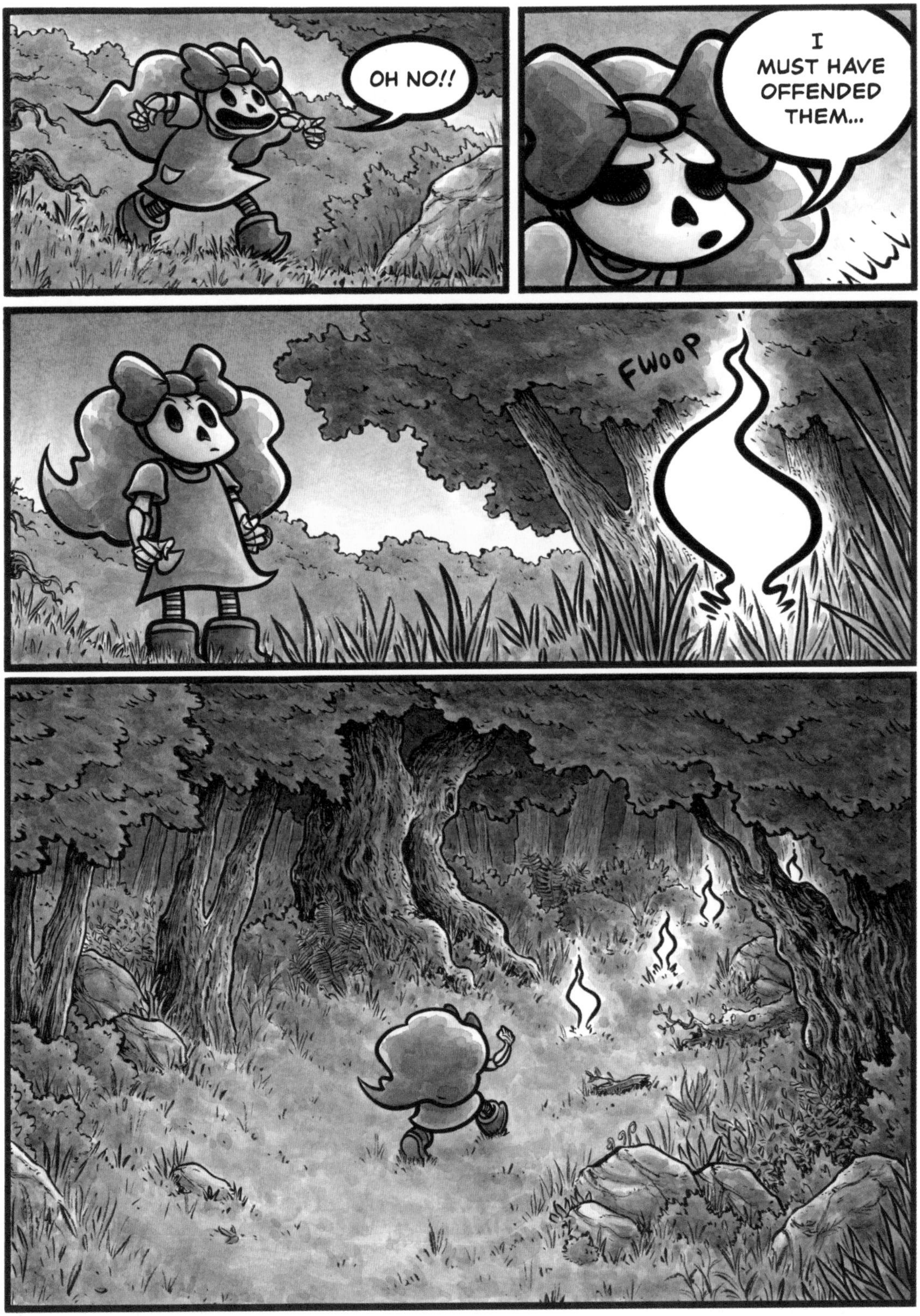
OH NO!!
I MUST HAVE OFFENDED THEM...
FWOOP

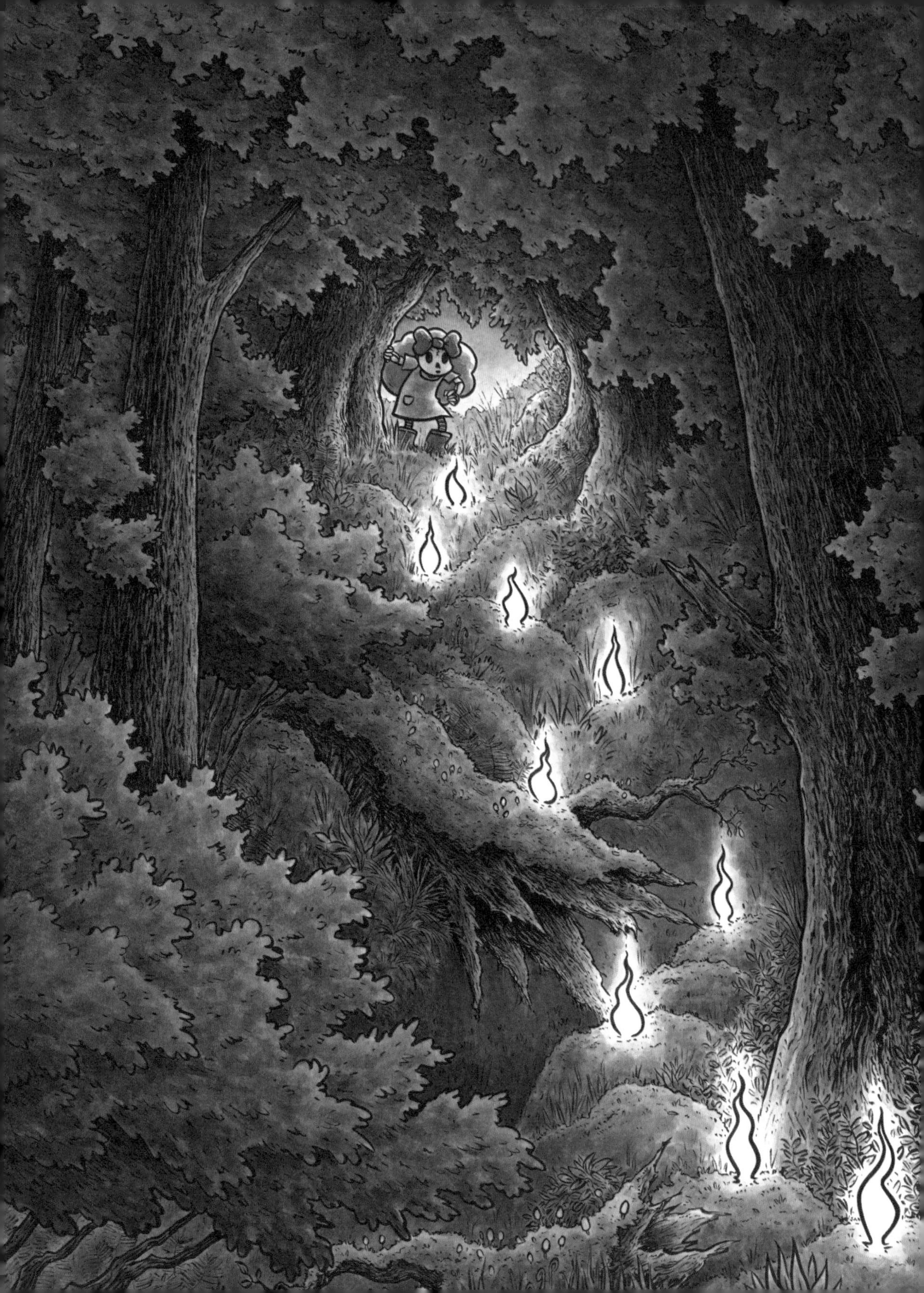

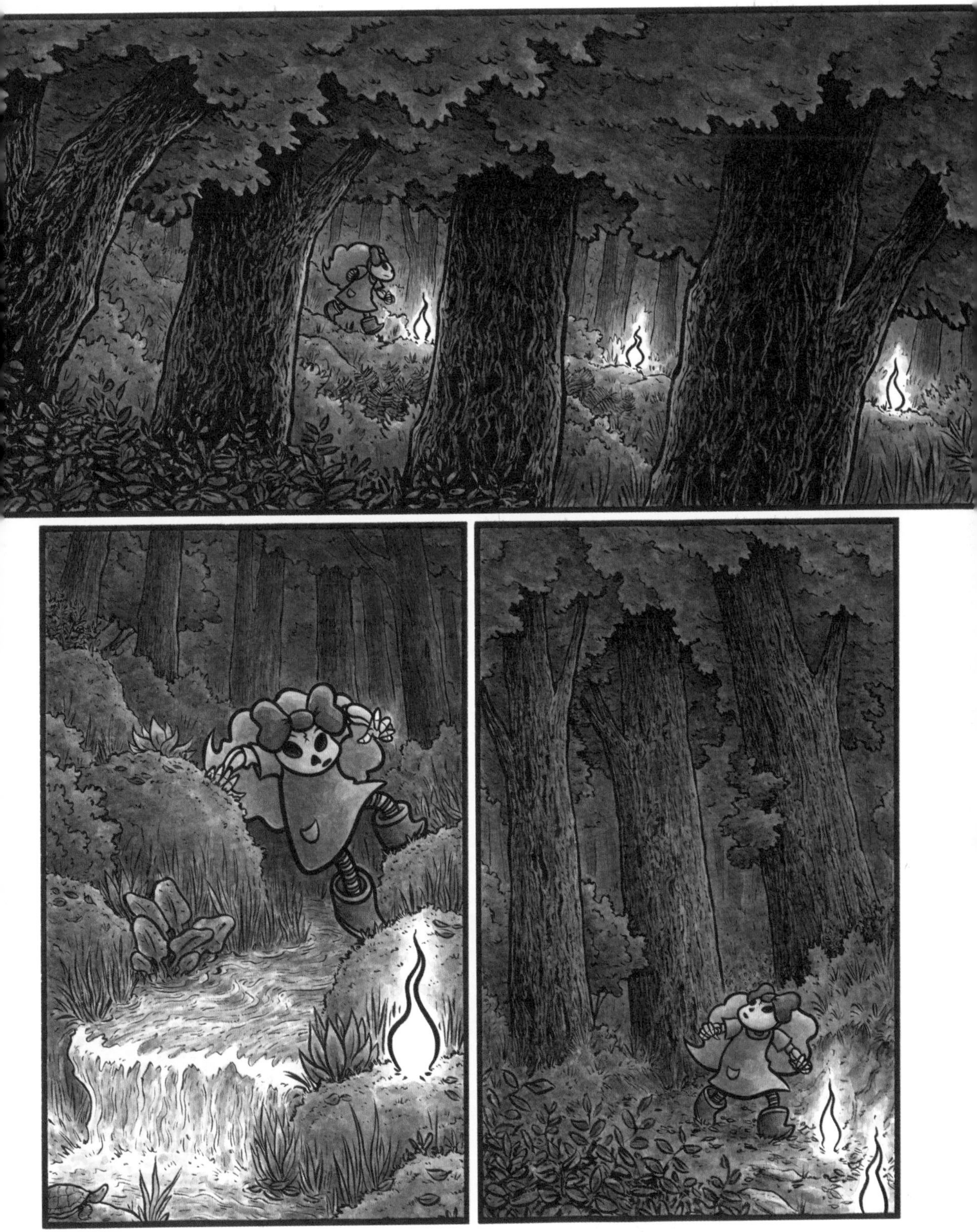

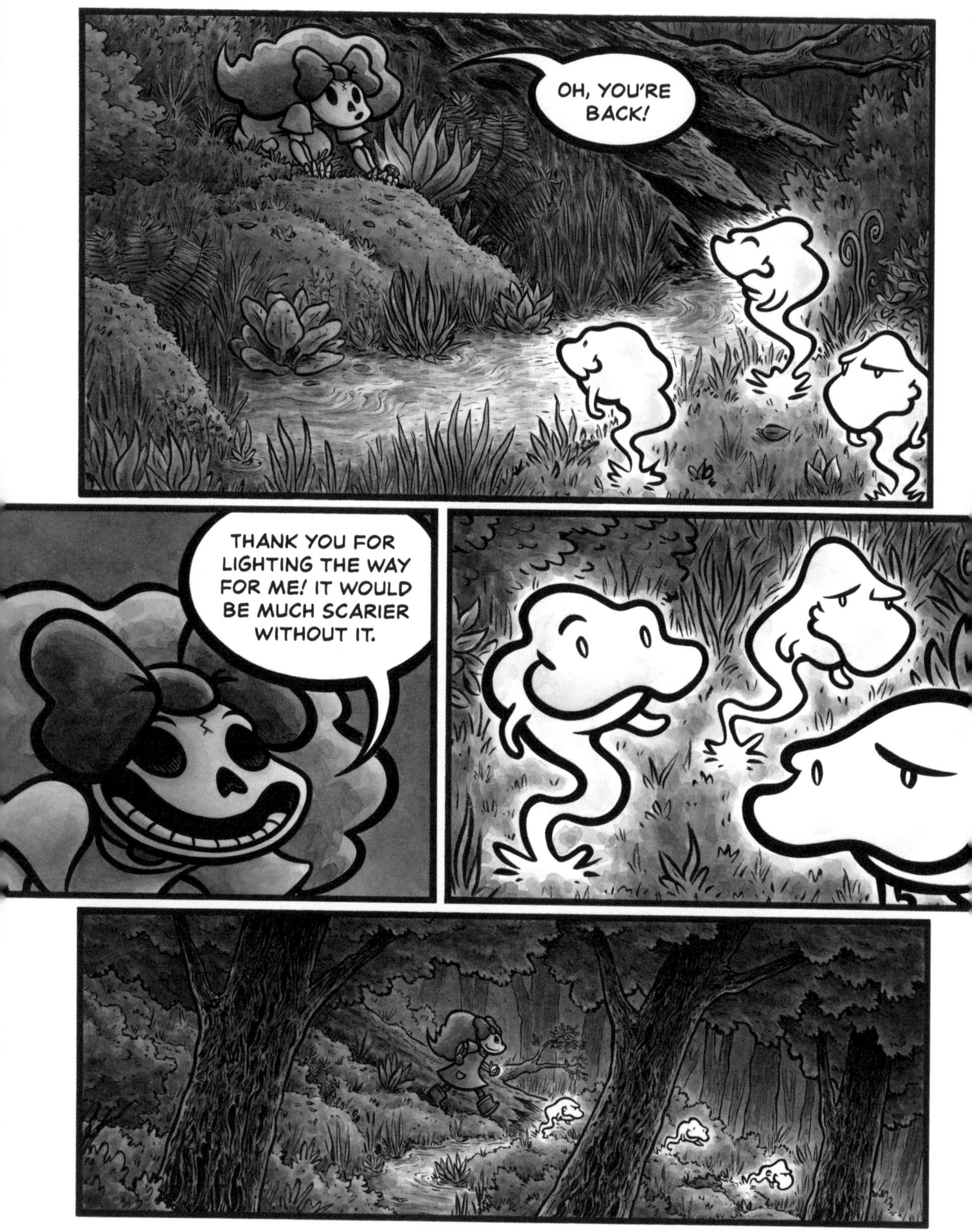
OH, YOU'RE BACK!
THANK YOU FOR LIGHTING THE WAY FOR ME! IT WOULD BE MUCH SCARIER WITHOUT IT.

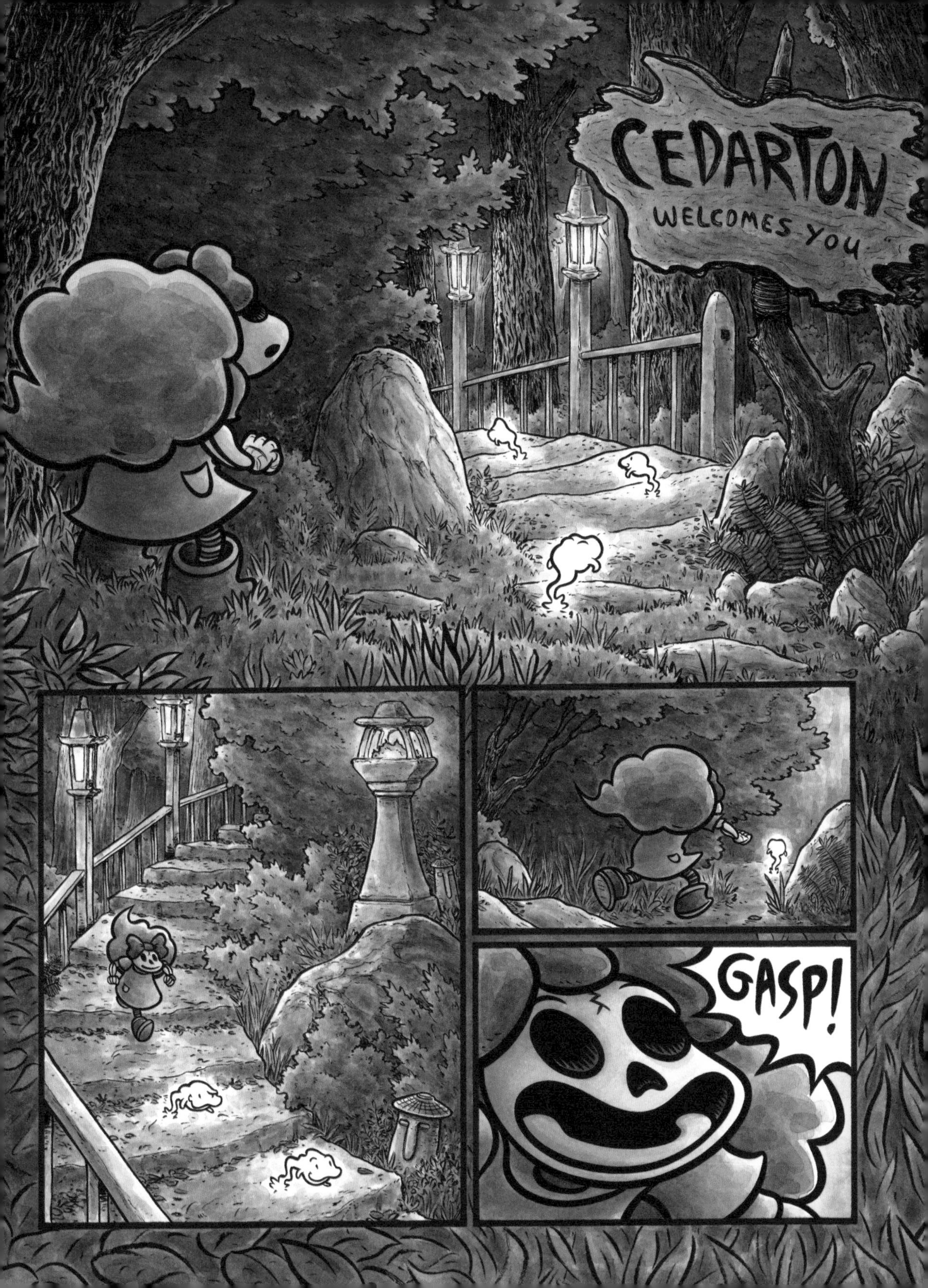
CEDARTON
WELCOMES YOU
GASP!

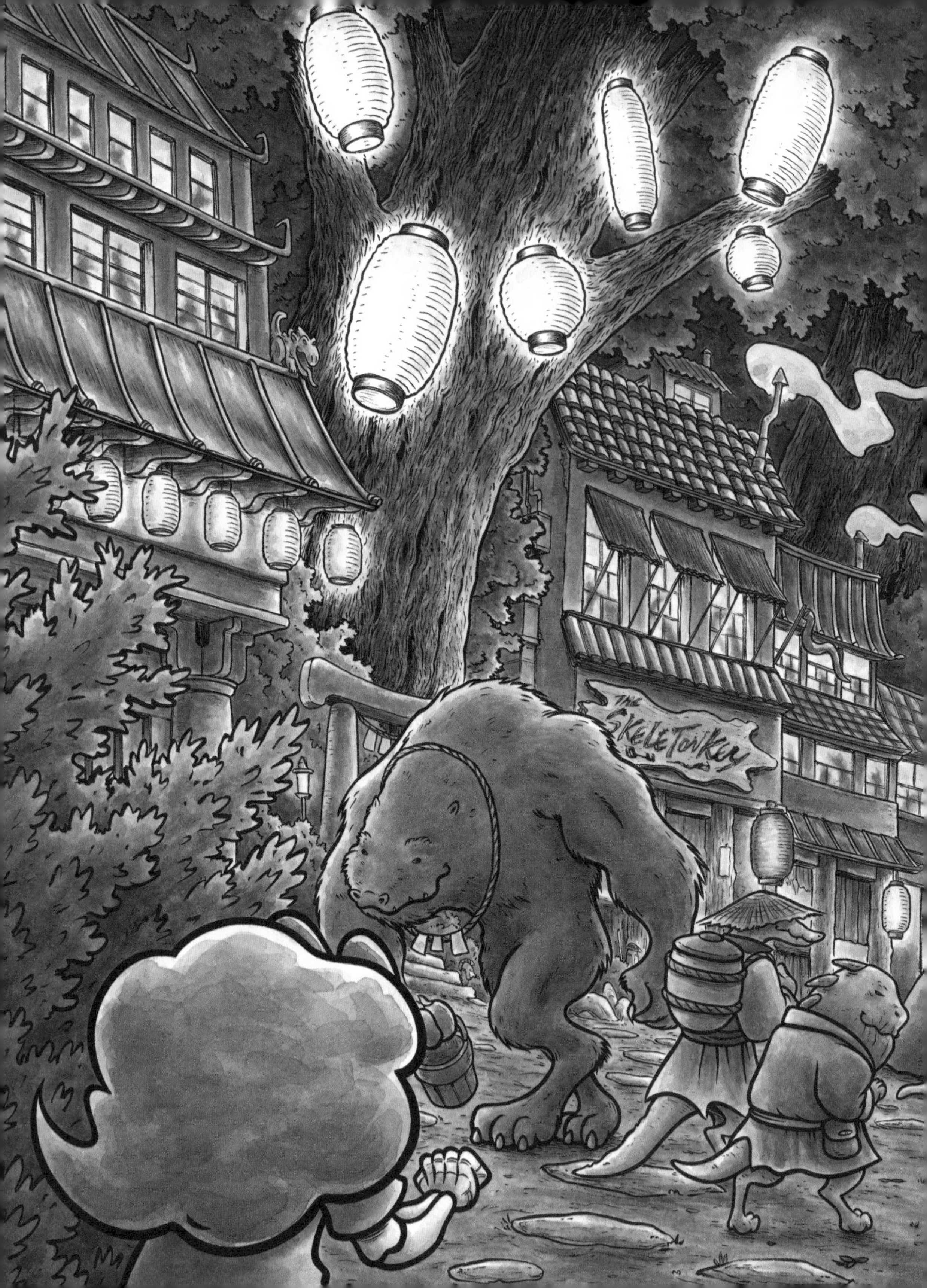
THE
SKELETONKEY

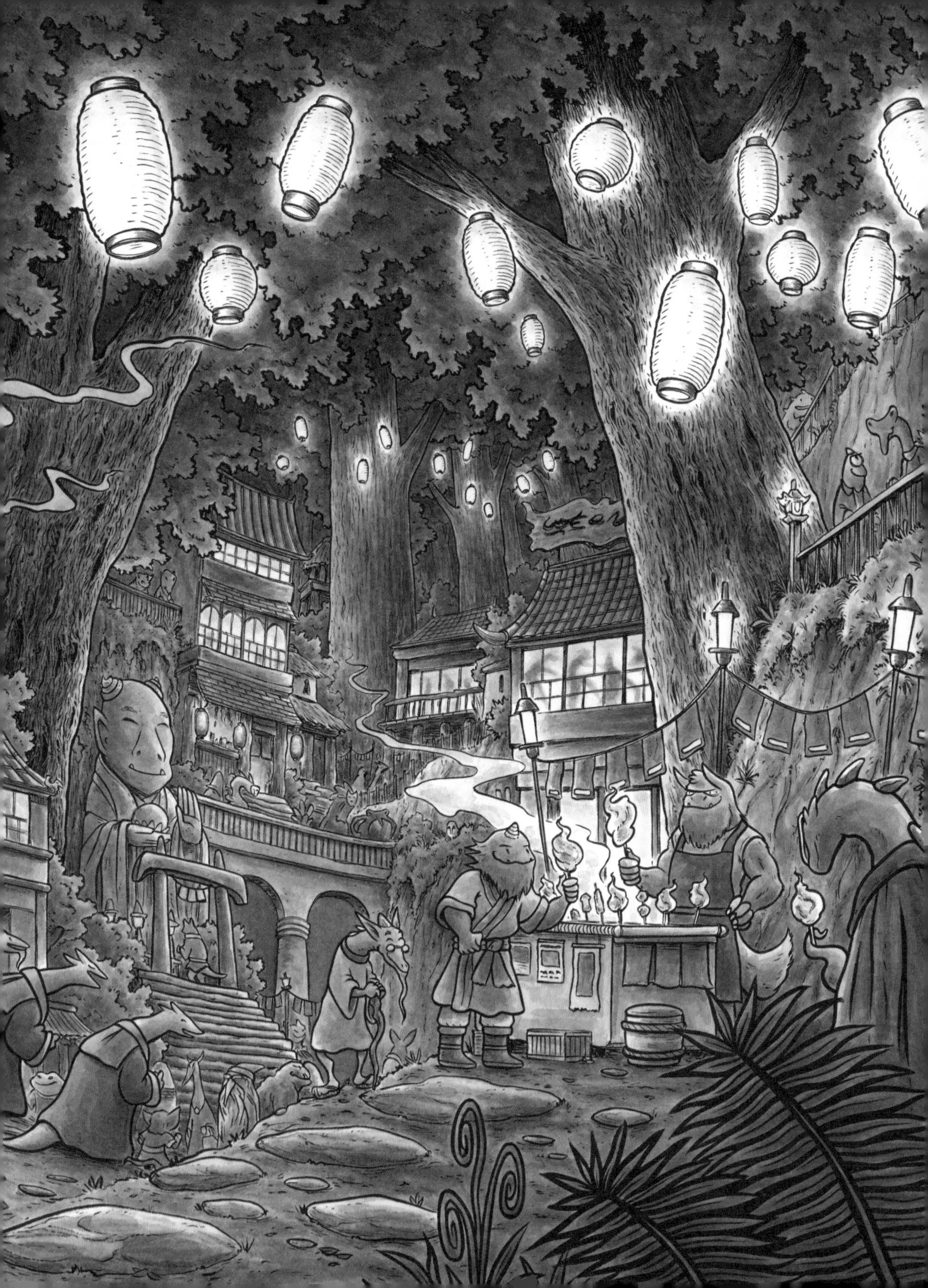

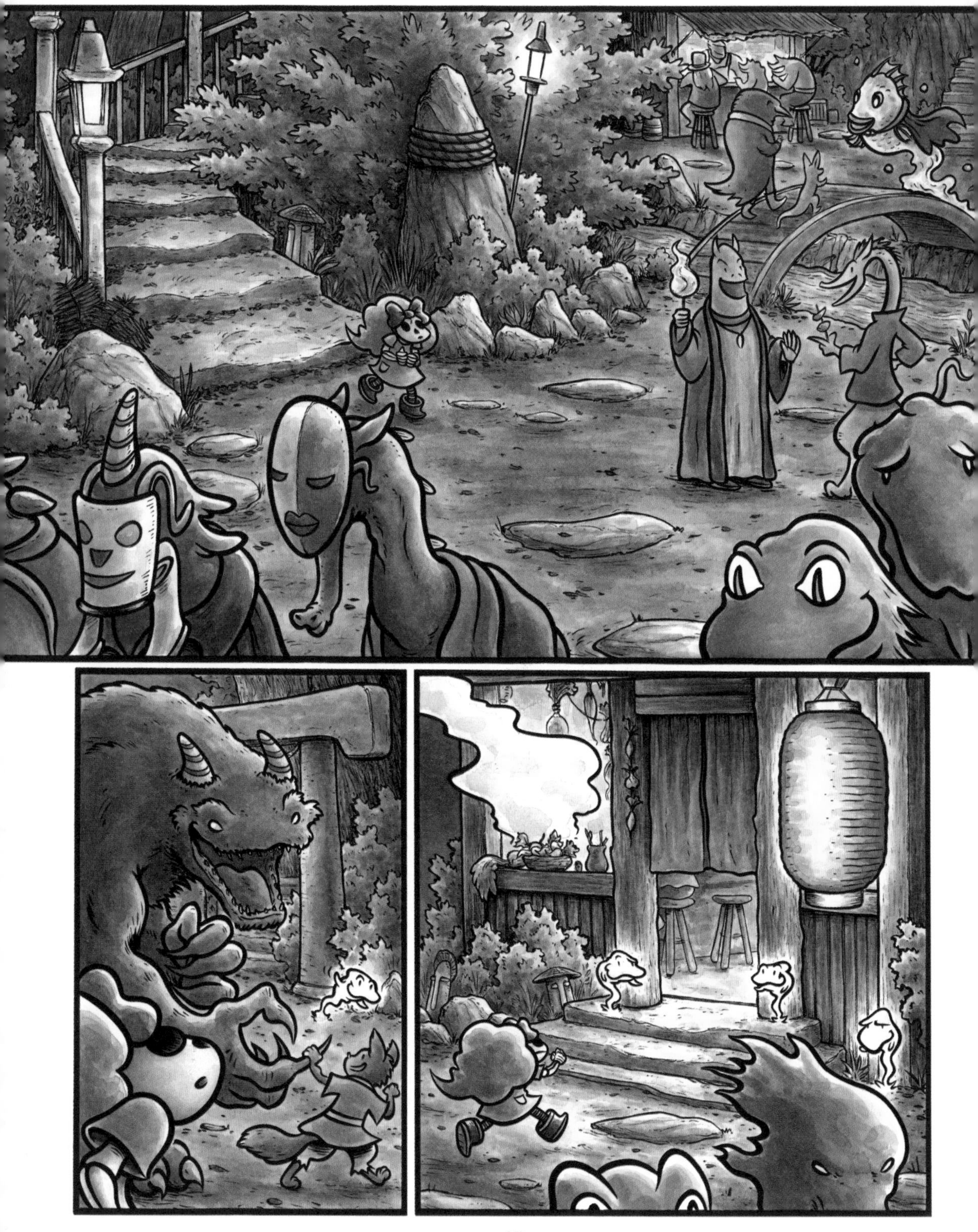

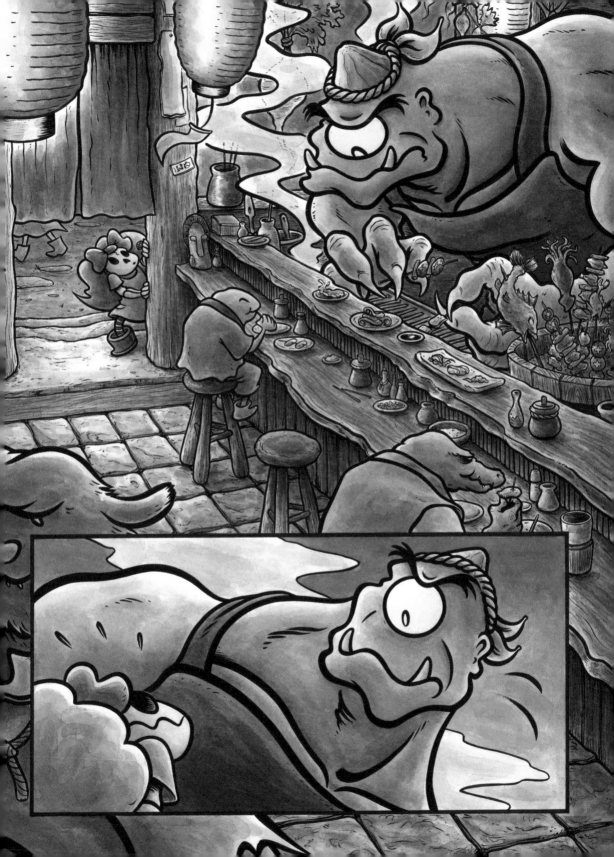

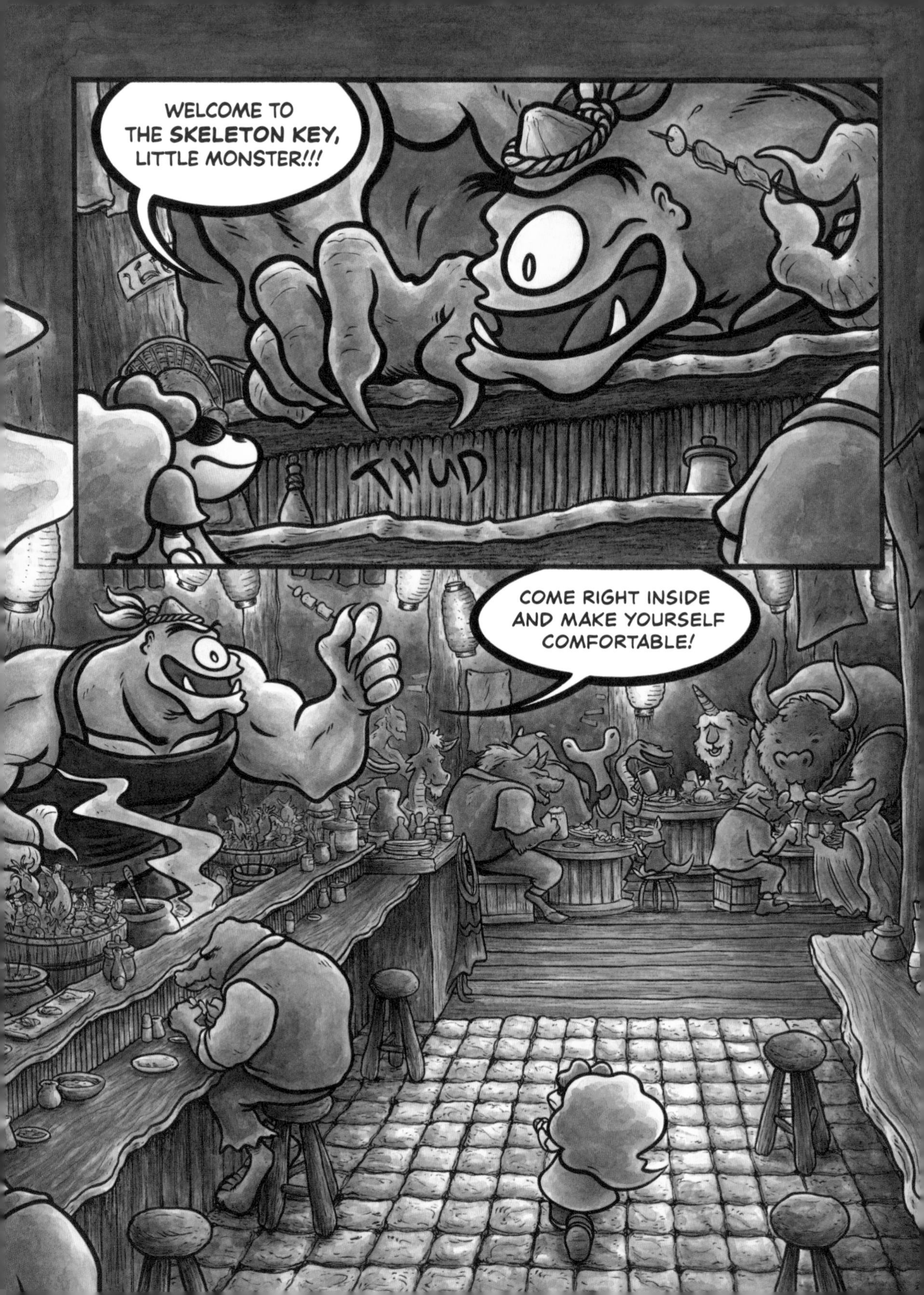
WELCOME TO THE SKELETON KEY, LITTLE MONSTER!!!
THUD
COME RIGHT INSIDE AND MAKE YOURSELF COMFORTABLE!

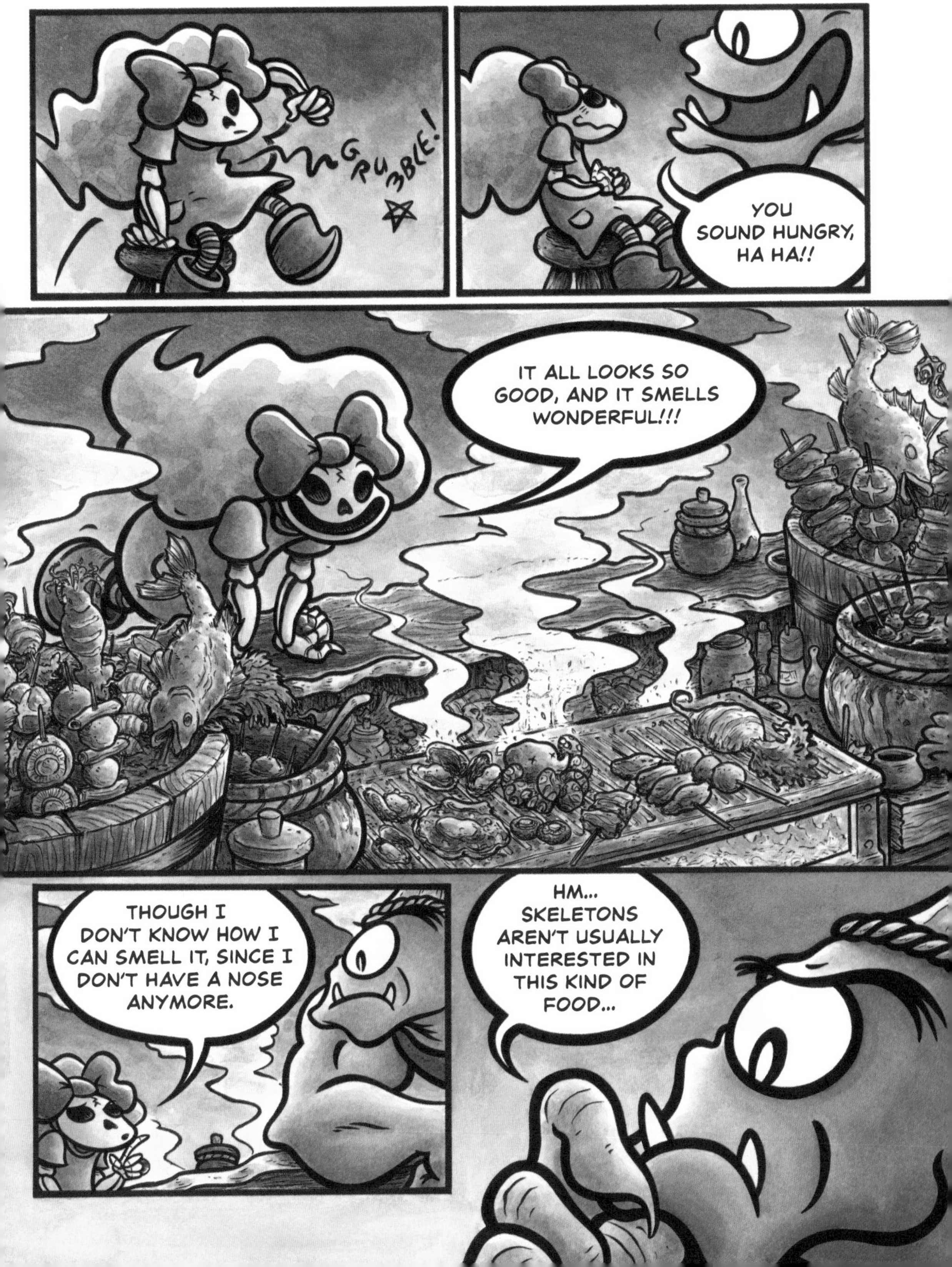
GRUMBLE!
YOU SOUND HUNGRY, HA HA!!
IT ALL LOOKS SO GOOD, AND IT SMELLS WONDERFUL!!!
THOUGH I DON'T KNOW HOW I CAN SMELL IT, SINCE I DON'T HAVE A NOSE ANYMORE.
HM... SKELETONS AREN'T USUALLY INTERESTED IN THIS KIND OF FOOD...

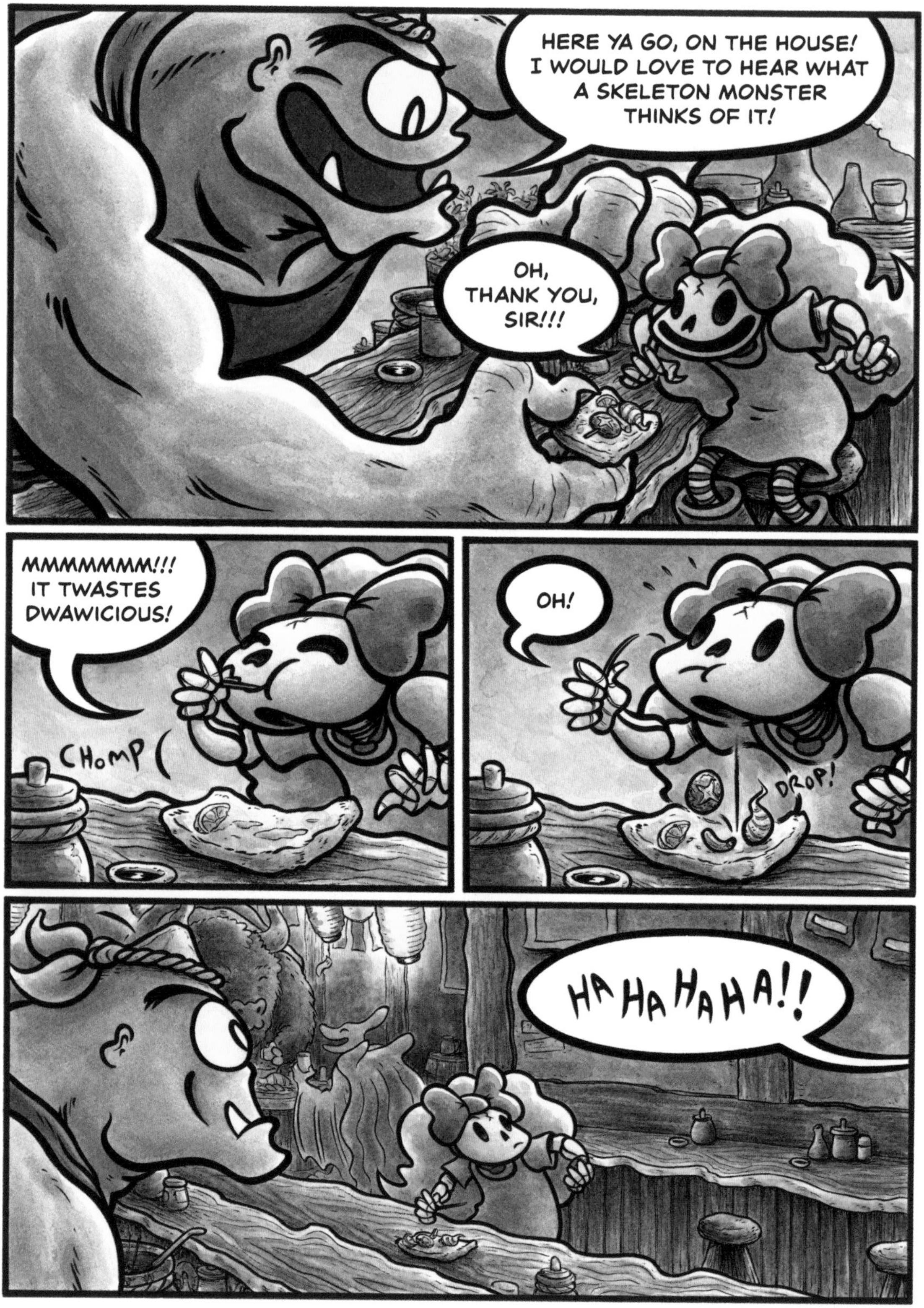

HERE YA GO, ON THE HOUSE! I WOULD LOVE TO HEAR WHAT A SKELETON MONSTER THINKS OF IT!
OH, THANK YOU, SIR!!!
MMMMMMM!!! IT TWASTES DWAWICIOUS!
CHOMP
OH!
DROP!
HAHAHAHA!!

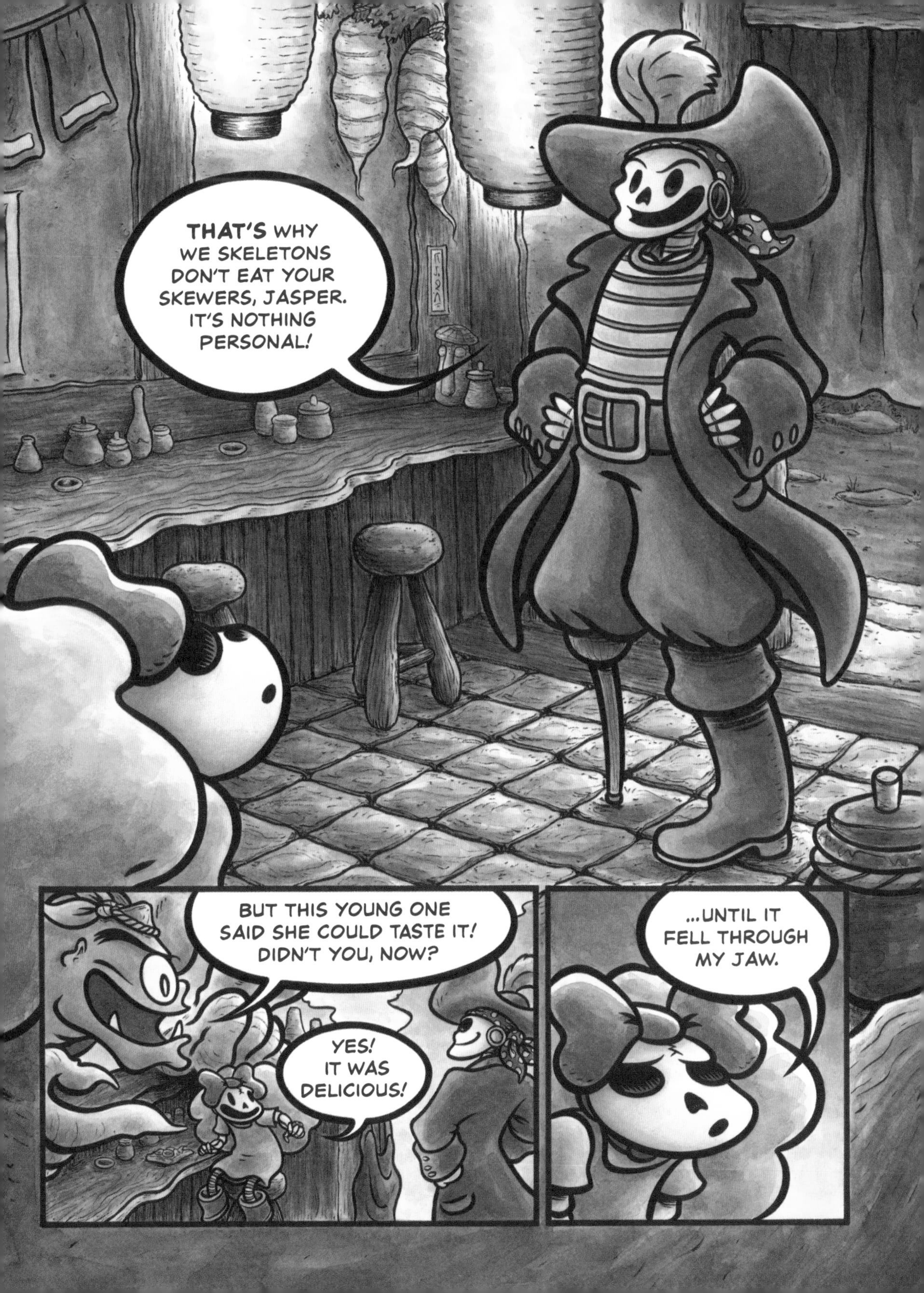
THAT'S WHY WE SKELETONS DON'T EAT YOUR SKEWERS, JASPER. IT'S NOTHING PERSONAL!
BUT THIS YOUNG ONE SAID SHE COULD TASTE IT! DIDN'T YOU, NOW?
YES! IT WAS DELICIOUS!
...UNTIL IT FELL THROUGH MY JAW.

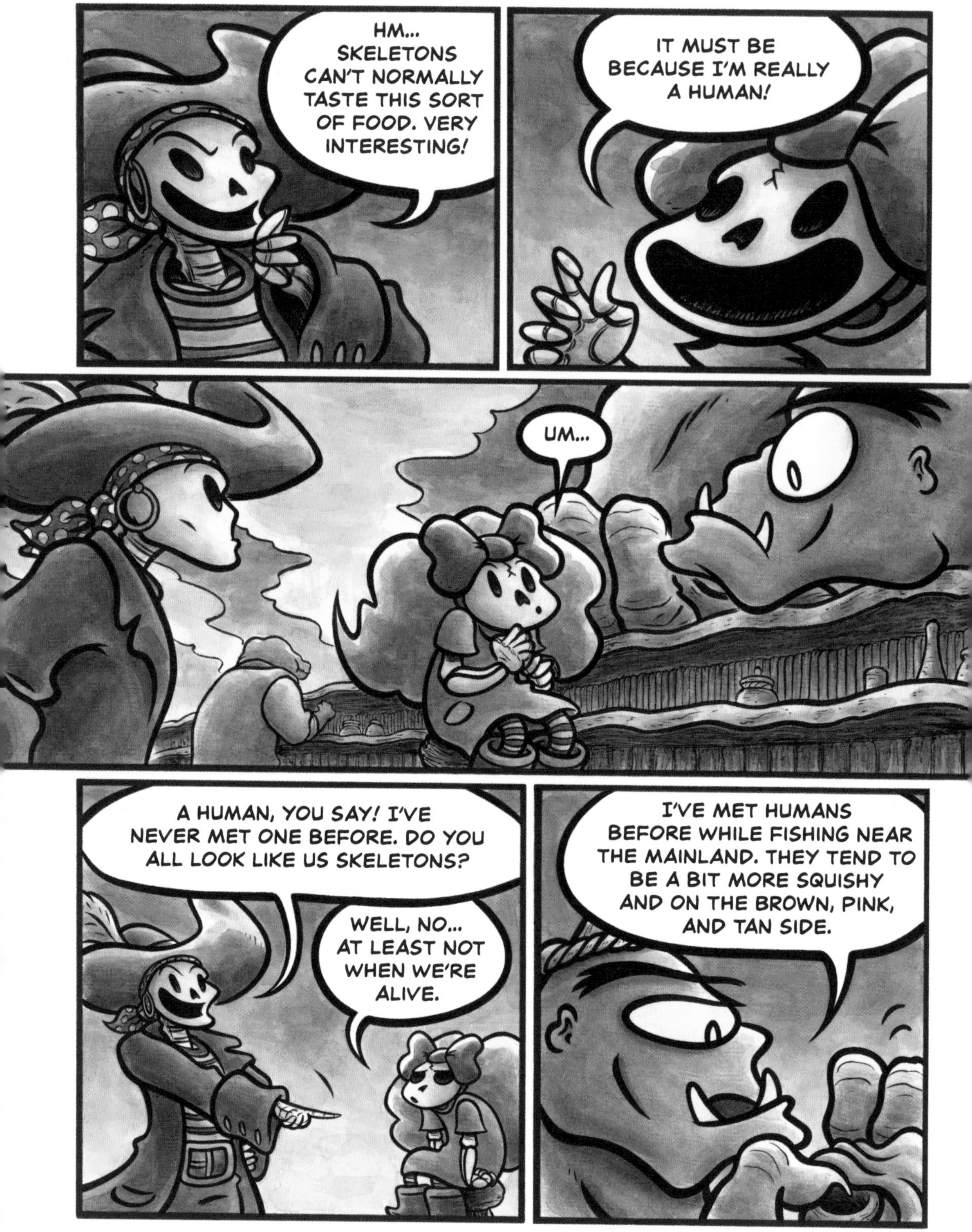
HM... SKELETONS CAN'T NORMALLY TASTE THIS SORT OF FOOD. VERY INTERESTING!
IT MUST BE BECAUSE I'M REALLY A HUMAN!
UM...
A HUMAN, YOU SAY! I'VE NEVER MET ONE BEFORE. DO YOU ALL LOOK LIKE US SKELETONS?
WELL, NO... AT LEAST NOT WHEN WE'RE ALIVE.
I'VE MET HUMANS BEFORE WHILE FISHING NEAR THE MAINLAND. THEY TEND TO BE A BIT MORE SQUISHY AND ON THE BROWN, PINK, AND TAN SIDE.

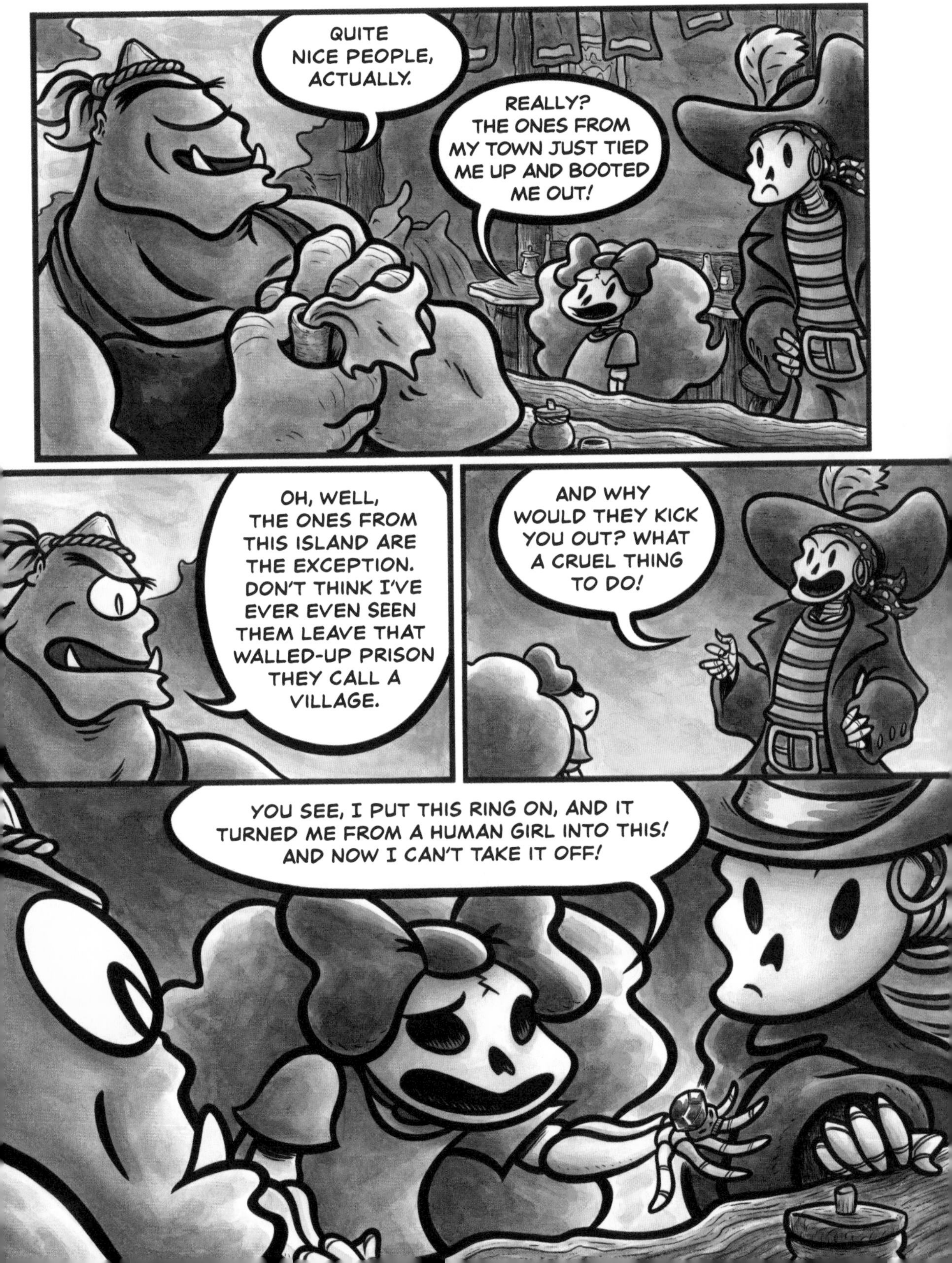
QUITE NICE PEOPLE, ACTUALLY.
REALLY? THE ONES FROM MY TOWN JUST TIED ME UP AND BOOTED ME OUT!
OH, WELL, THE ONES FROM THIS ISLAND ARE THE EXCEPTION. DON'T THINK I'VE EVER EVEN SEEN THEM LEAVE THAT WALLED-UP PRISON THEY CALL A VILLAGE.
AND WHY WOULD THEY KICK YOU OUT? WHAT A CRUEL THING TO DO!
YOU SEE, I PUT THIS RING ON, AND IT TURNED ME FROM A HUMAN GIRL INTO THIS! AND NOW I CAN'T TAKE IT OFF!

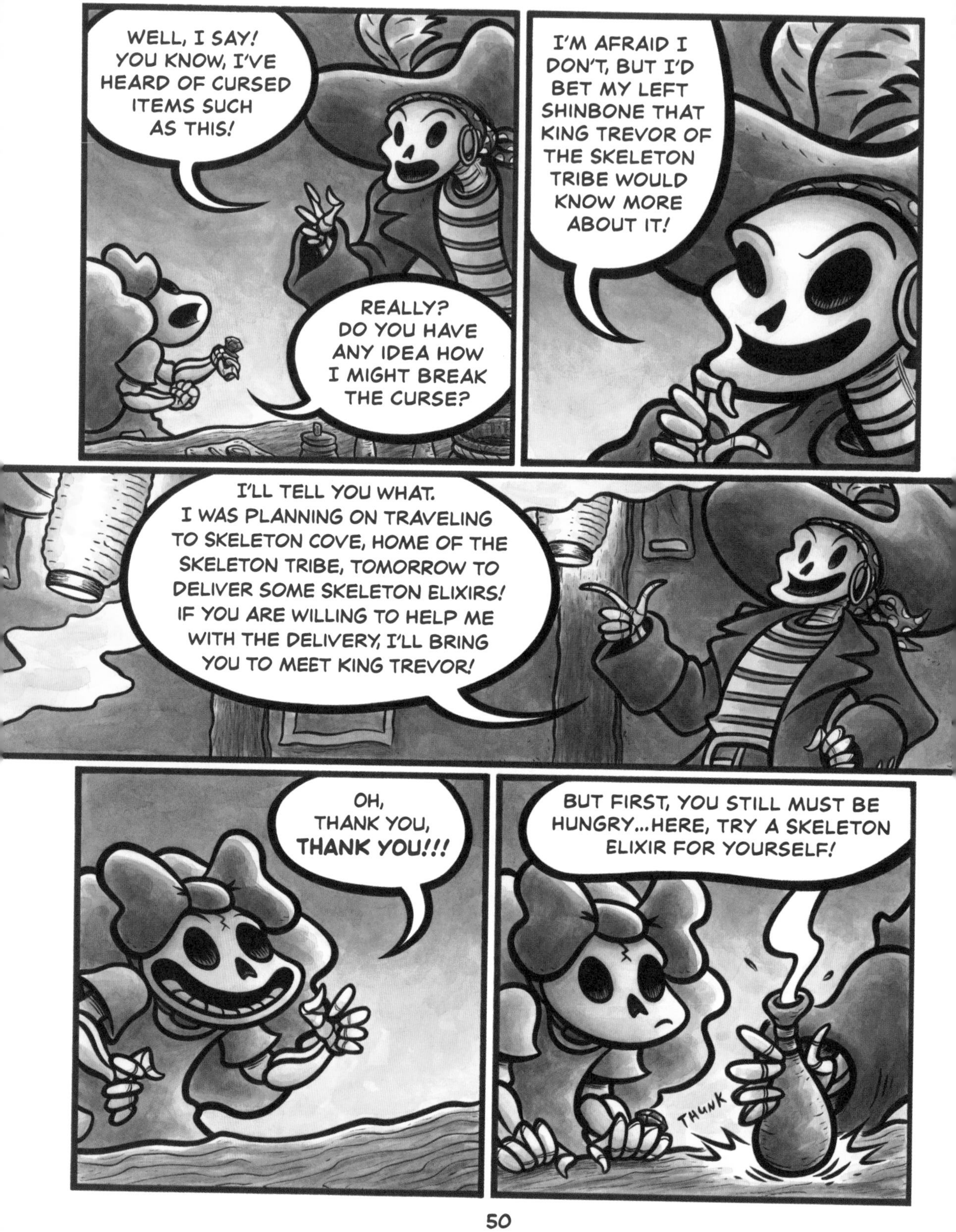
WELL, I SAY! YOU KNOW, I'VE HEARD OF CURSED ITEMS SUCH AS THIS!
REALLY? DO YOU HAVE ANY IDEA HOW I MIGHT BREAK THE CURSE?
I'M AFRAID I DON'T, BUT I'D BET MY LEFT SHINBONE THAT KING TREVOR OF THE SKELETON TRIBE WOULD KNOW MORE ABOUT IT!
I'LL TELL YOU WHAT. I WAS PLANNING ON TRAVELING TO SKELETON COVE, HOME OF THE SKELETON TRIBE, TOMORROW TO DELIVER SOME SKELETON ELIXIRS! IF YOU ARE WILLING TO HELP ME WITH THE DELIVERY, I'LL BRING YOU TO MEET KING TREVOR!
OH, THANK YOU, **THANK YOU!!!**
BUT FIRST, YOU STILL MUST BE HUNGRY...HERE, TRY A SKELETON ELIXIR FOR YOURSELF!
THUNK

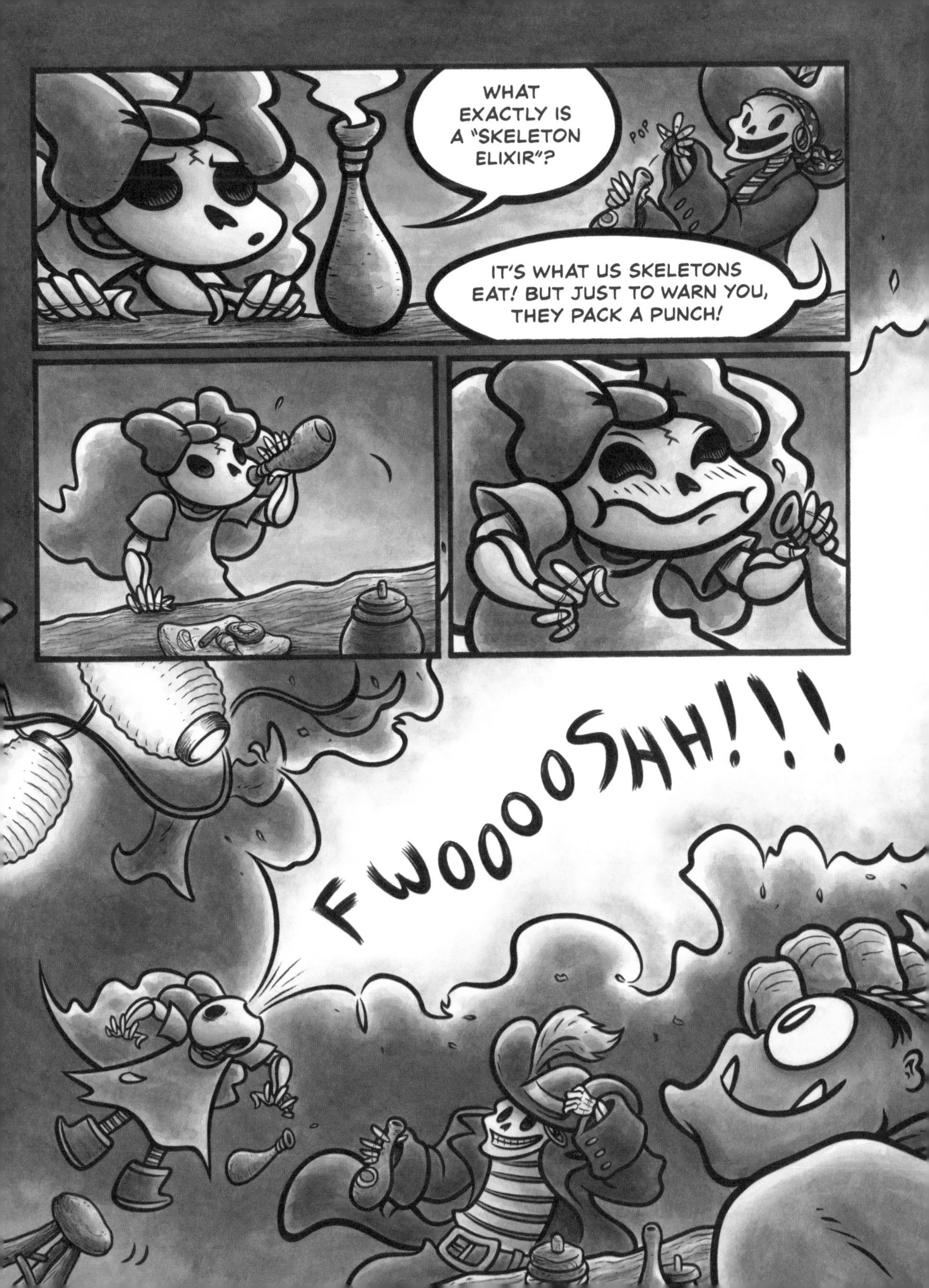
WHAT EXACTLY IS A "SKELETON ELIXIR"?
POP
IT'S WHAT US SKELETONS EAT! BUT JUST TO WARN YOU, THEY PACK A PUNCH!
FWOOOOSHH!!!

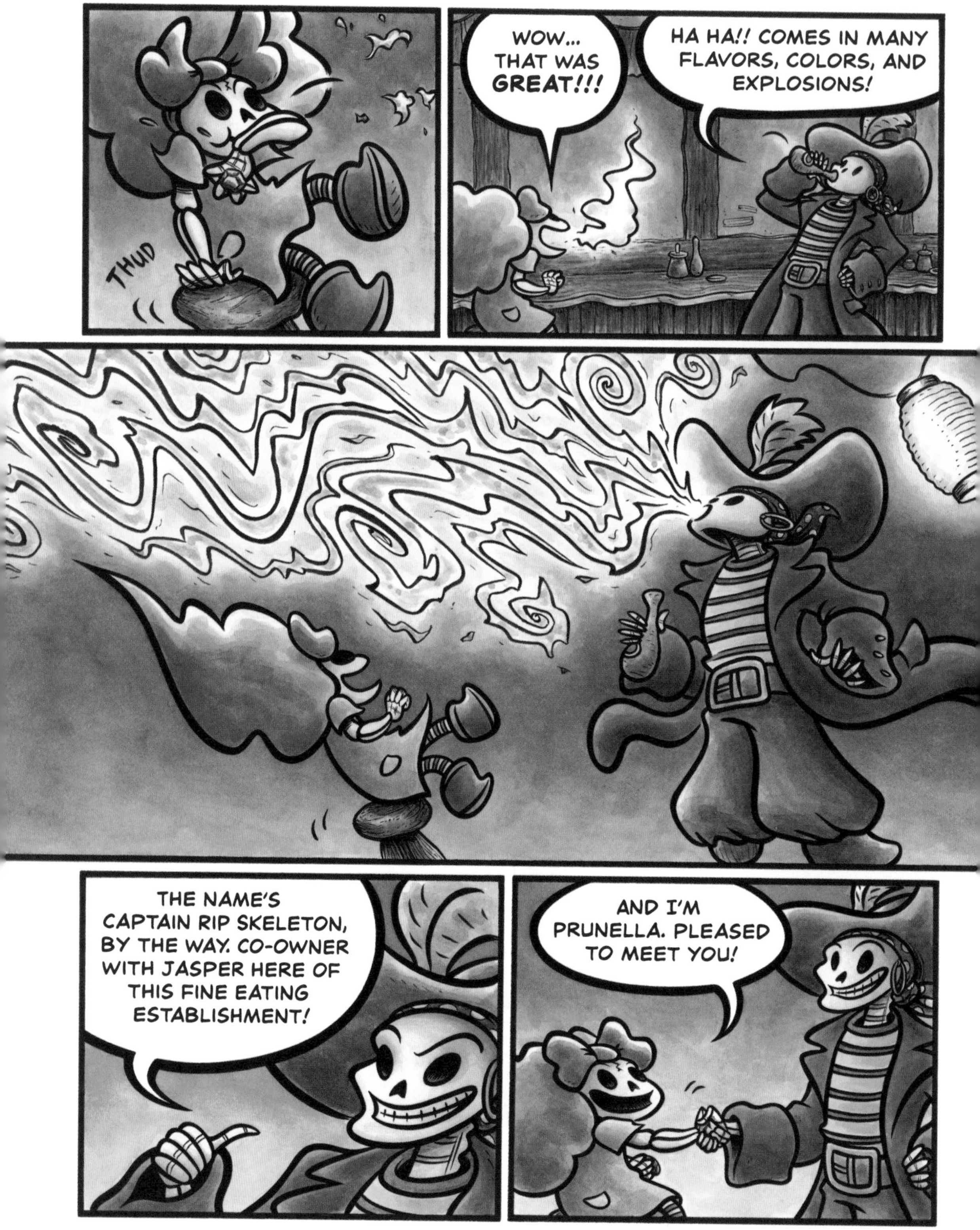
THUD
WOW... THAT WAS GREAT!!!
HA HA!! COMES IN MANY FLAVORS, COLORS, AND EXPLOSIONS!
THE NAME'S CAPTAIN RIP SKELETON, BY THE WAY. CO-OWNER WITH JASPER HERE OF THIS FINE EATING ESTABLISHMENT!
AND I'M PRUNELLA. PLEASED TO MEET YOU!

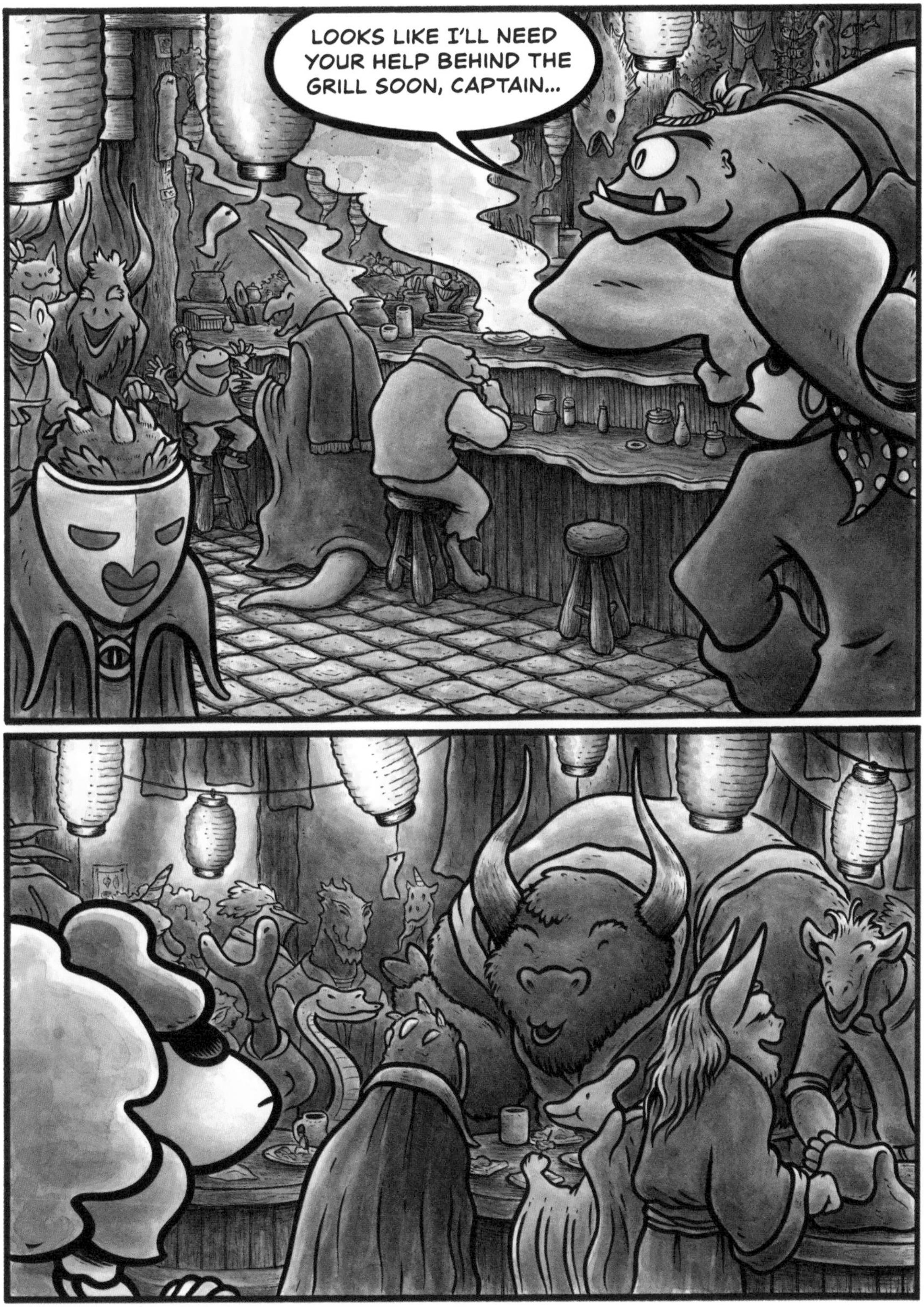
LOOKS LIKE I'LL NEED YOUR HELP BEHIND THE GRILL SOON, CAPTAIN...

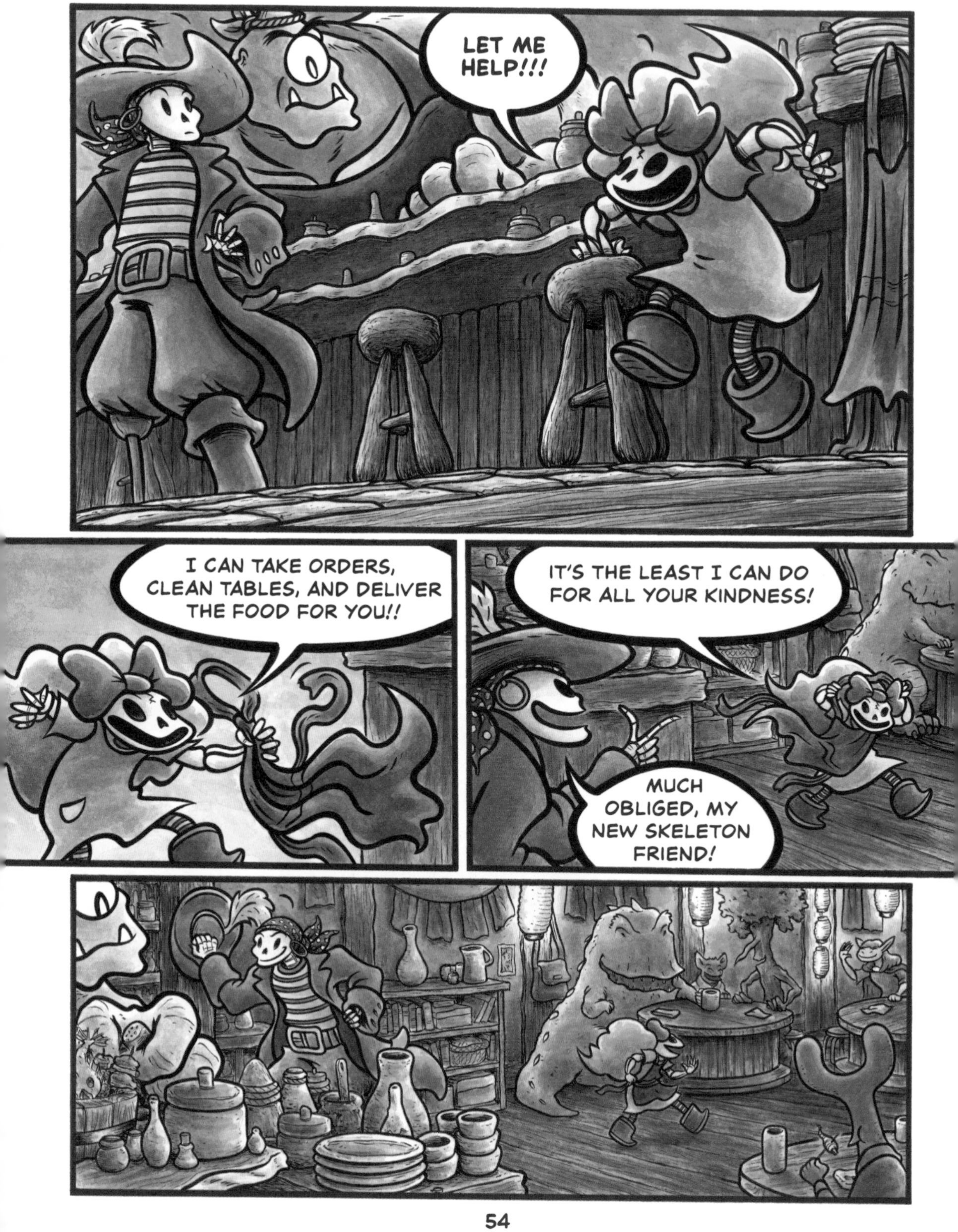
LET ME HELP!!!
I CAN TAKE ORDERS, CLEAN TABLES, AND DELIVER THE FOOD FOR YOU!!
IT'S THE LEAST I CAN DO FOR ALL YOUR KINDNESS!
MUCH OBLIGED, MY NEW SKELETON FRIEND!

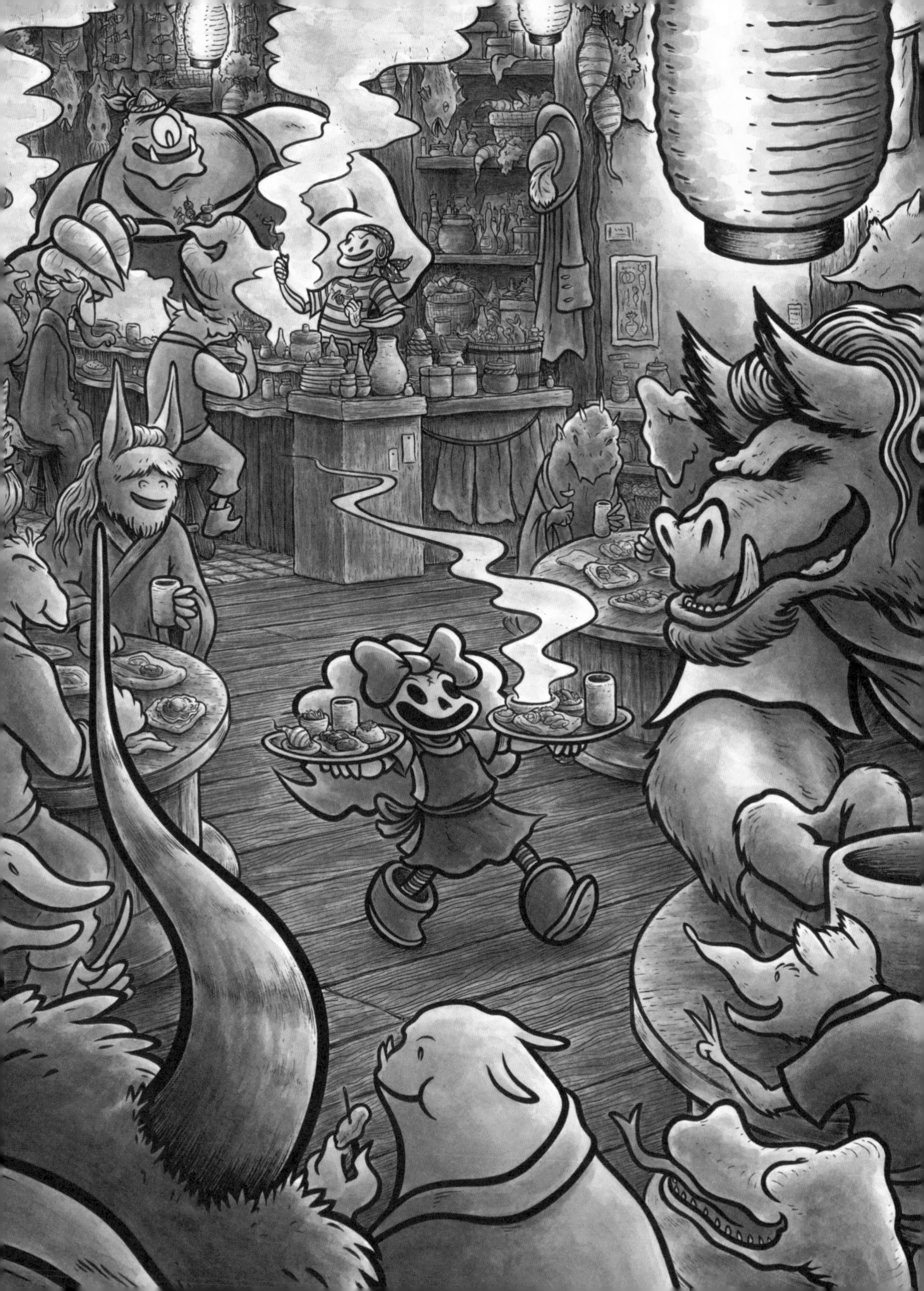

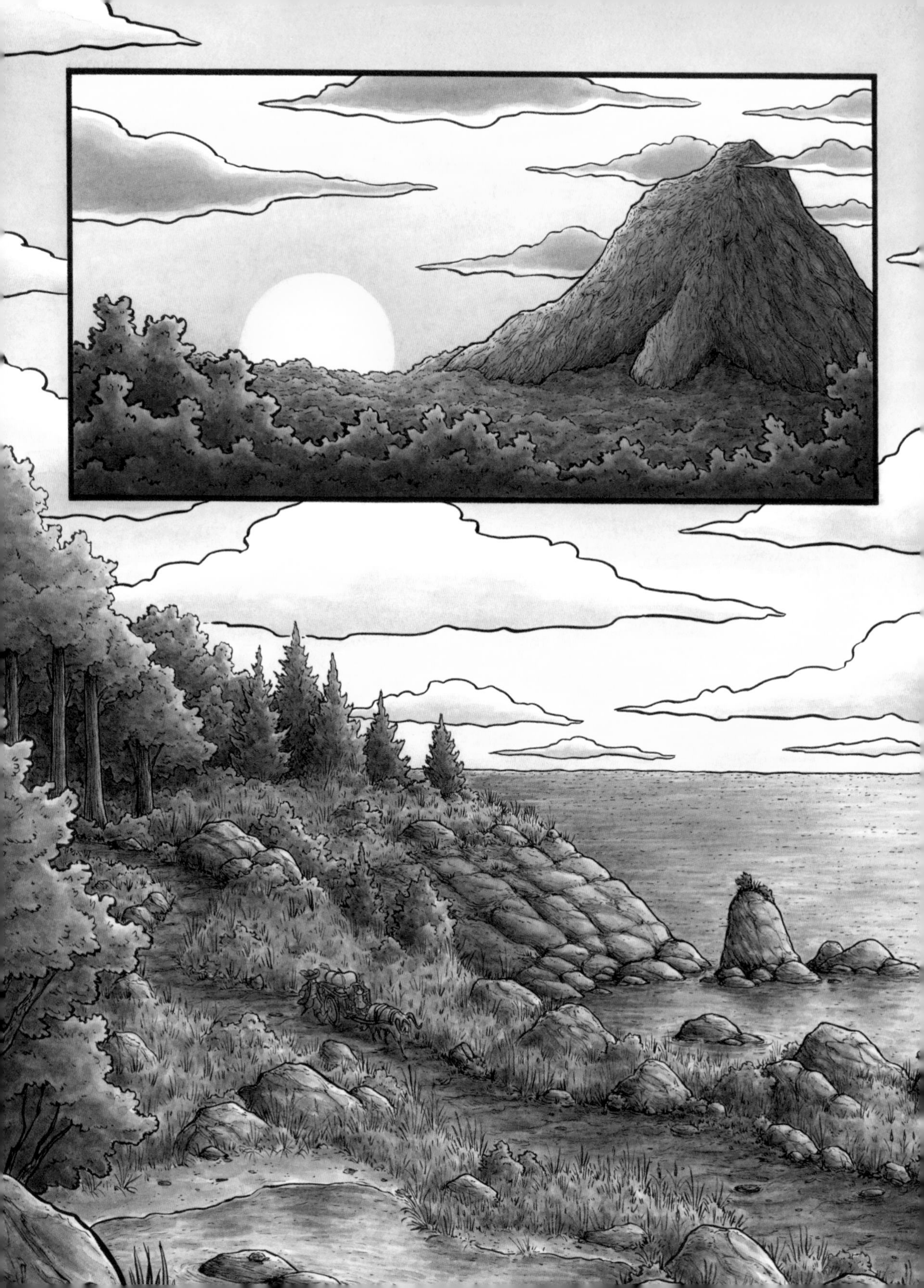

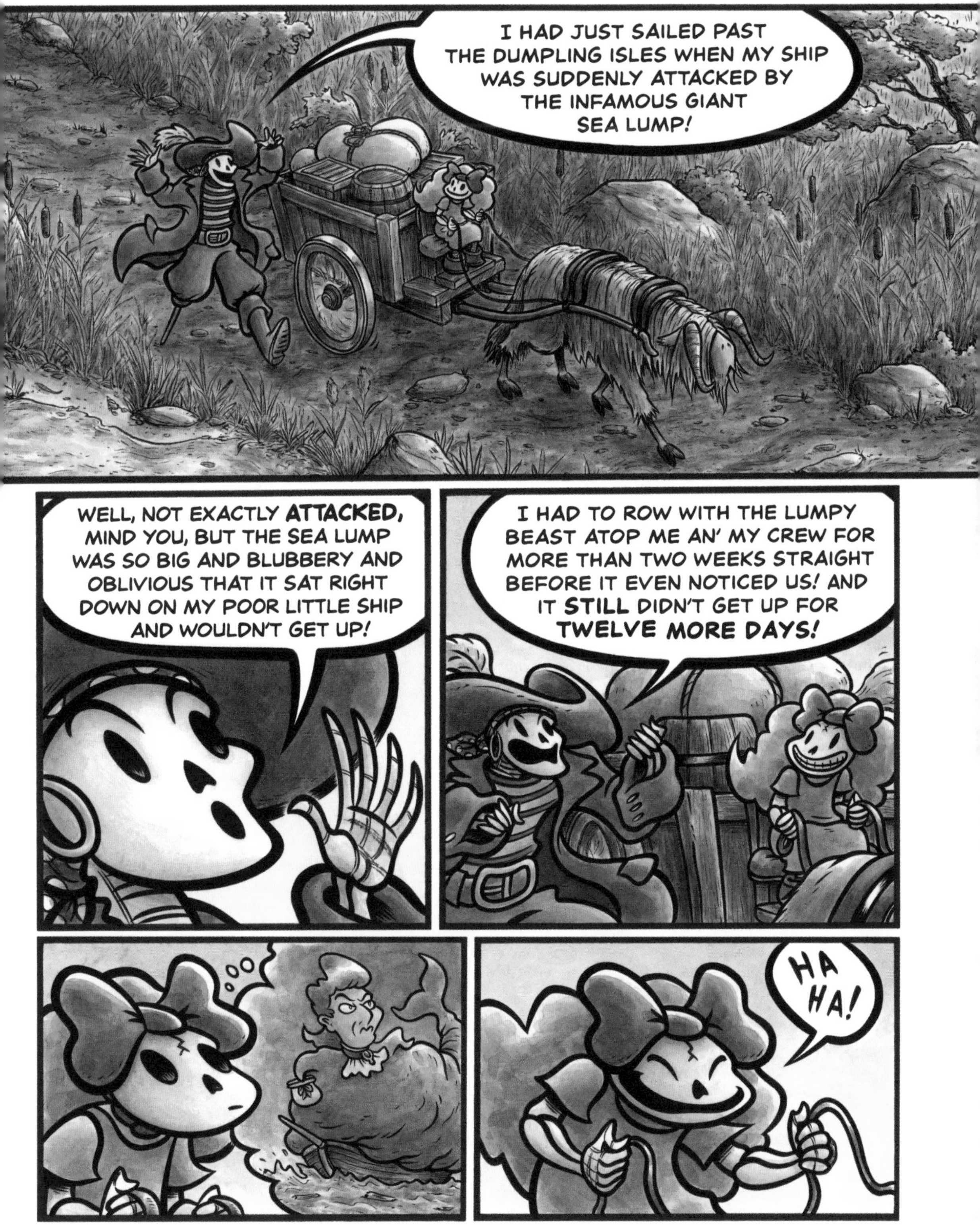
I HAD JUST SAILED PAST THE DUMPLING ISLES WHEN MY SHIP WAS SUDDENLY ATTACKED BY THE INFAMOUS GIANT SEA LUMP!
WELL, NOT EXACTLY ATTACKED, MIND YOU, BUT THE SEA LUMP WAS SO BIG AND BLUBBERY AND OBLIVIOUS THAT IT SAT RIGHT DOWN ON MY POOR LITTLE SHIP AND WOULDN'T GET UP!
I HAD TO ROW WITH THE LUMPY BEAST ATOP ME AN' MY CREW FOR MORE THAN TWO WEEKS STRAIGHT BEFORE IT EVEN NOTICED US! AND IT STILL DIDN'T GET UP FOR TWELVE MORE DAYS!
HA HA!

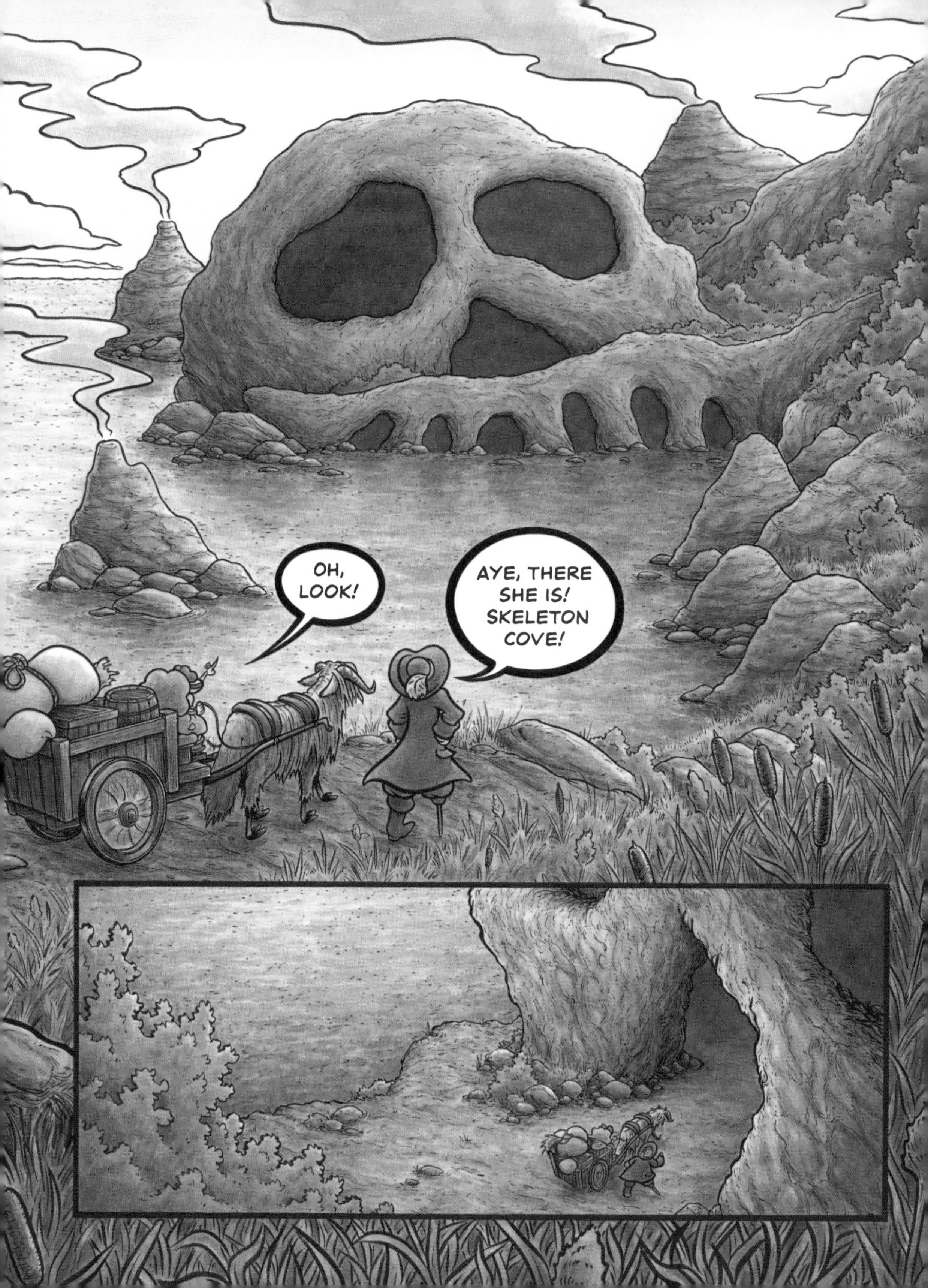
OH, LOOK!
AYE, THERE SHE IS! SKELETON COVE!

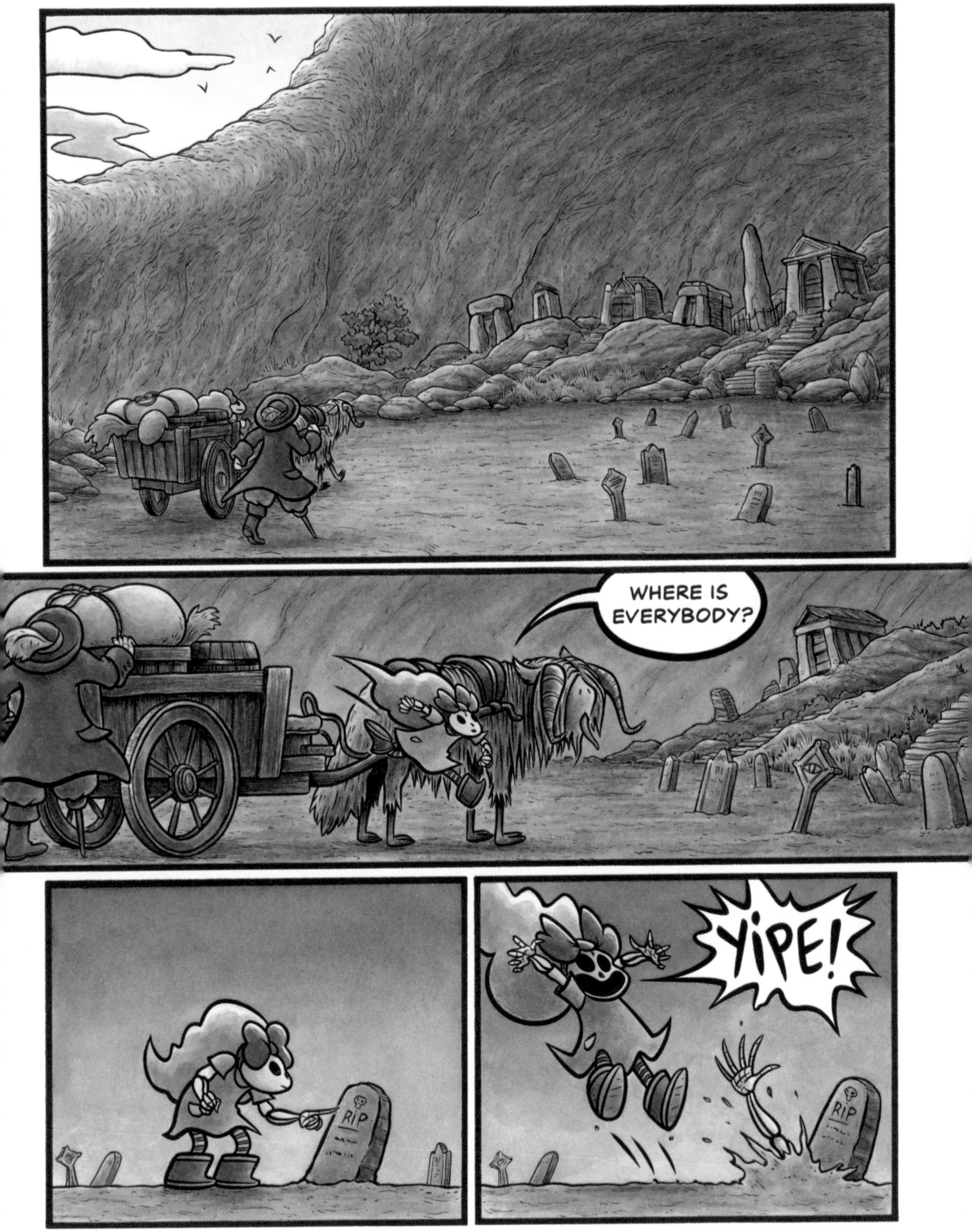
WHERE IS EVERYBODY?
RIP
YIPE!
RIP

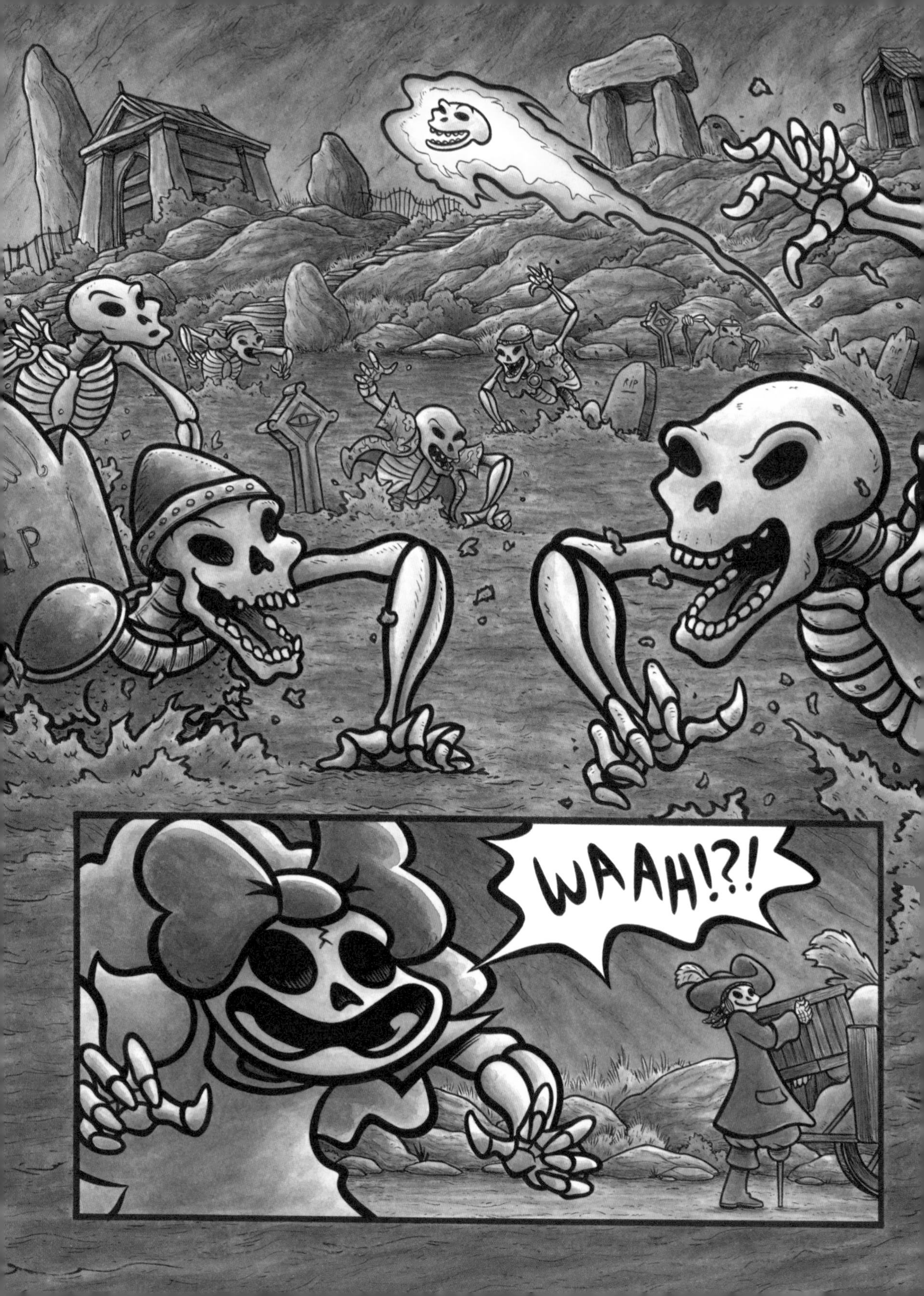
RIP
RIP
WAAH!?!

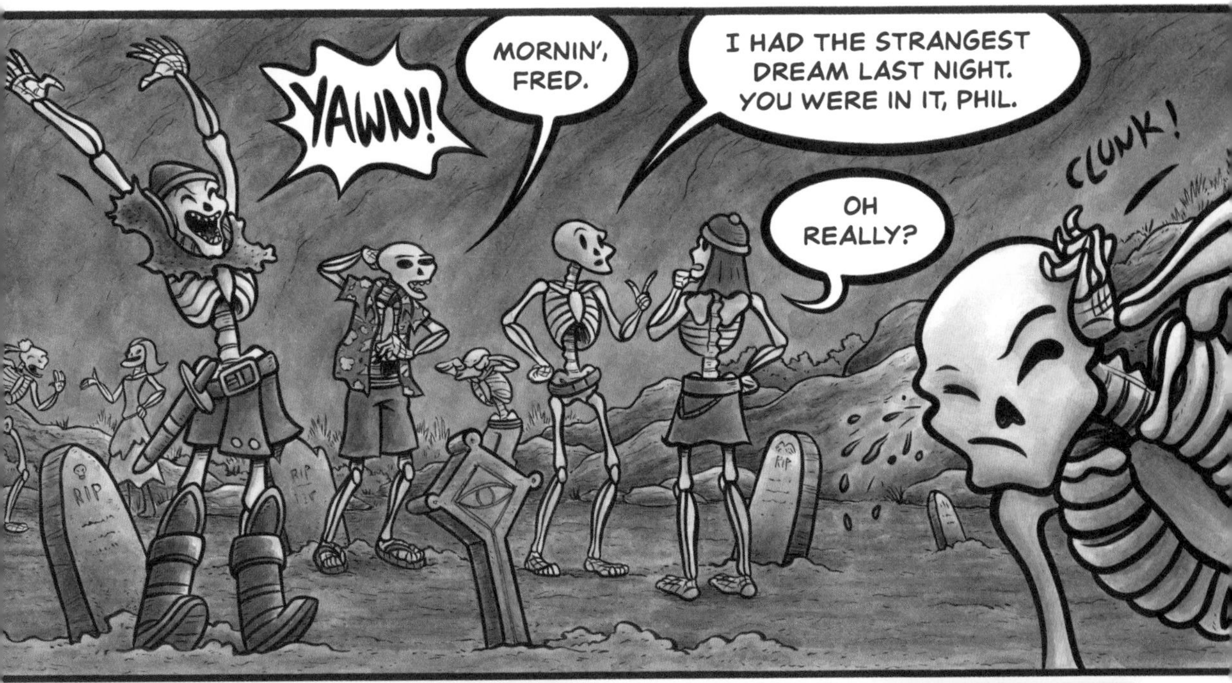
YAWN!
MORNIN', FRED.
I HAD THE STRANGEST DREAM LAST NIGHT. YOU WERE IN IT, PHIL.
OH REALLY?
CLUNK!

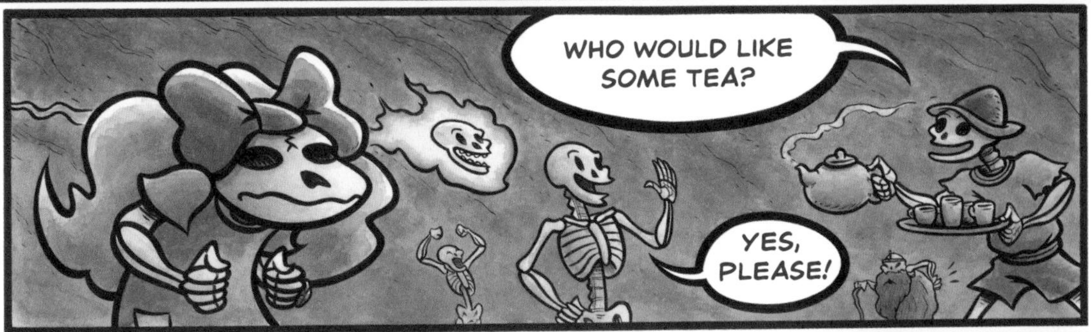
WHO WOULD LIKE SOME TEA?
YES, PLEASE!

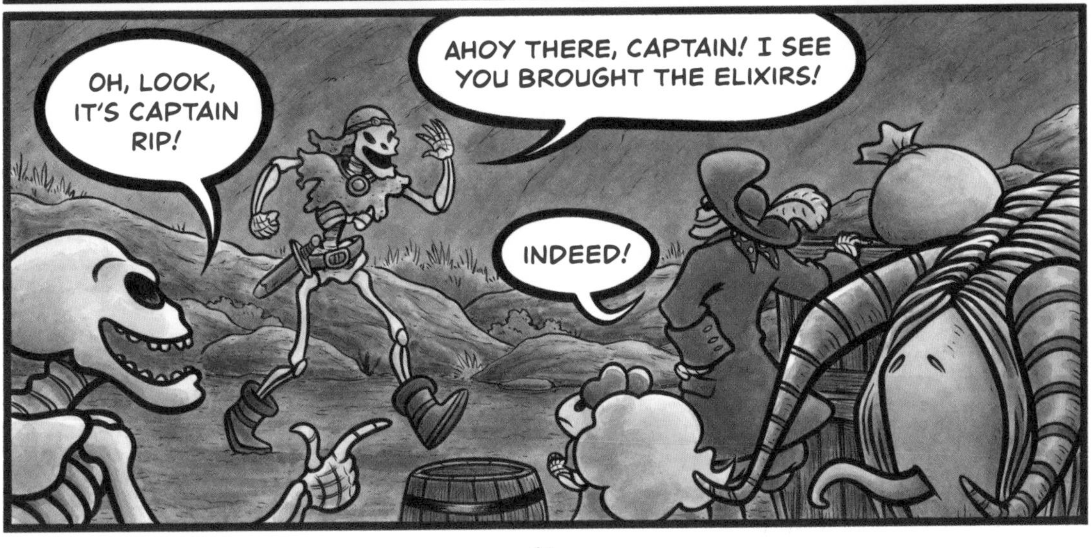
OH, LOOK, IT'S CAPTAIN RIP!
AHOY THERE, CAPTAIN! I SEE YOU BROUGHT THE ELIXIRS!
INDEED!

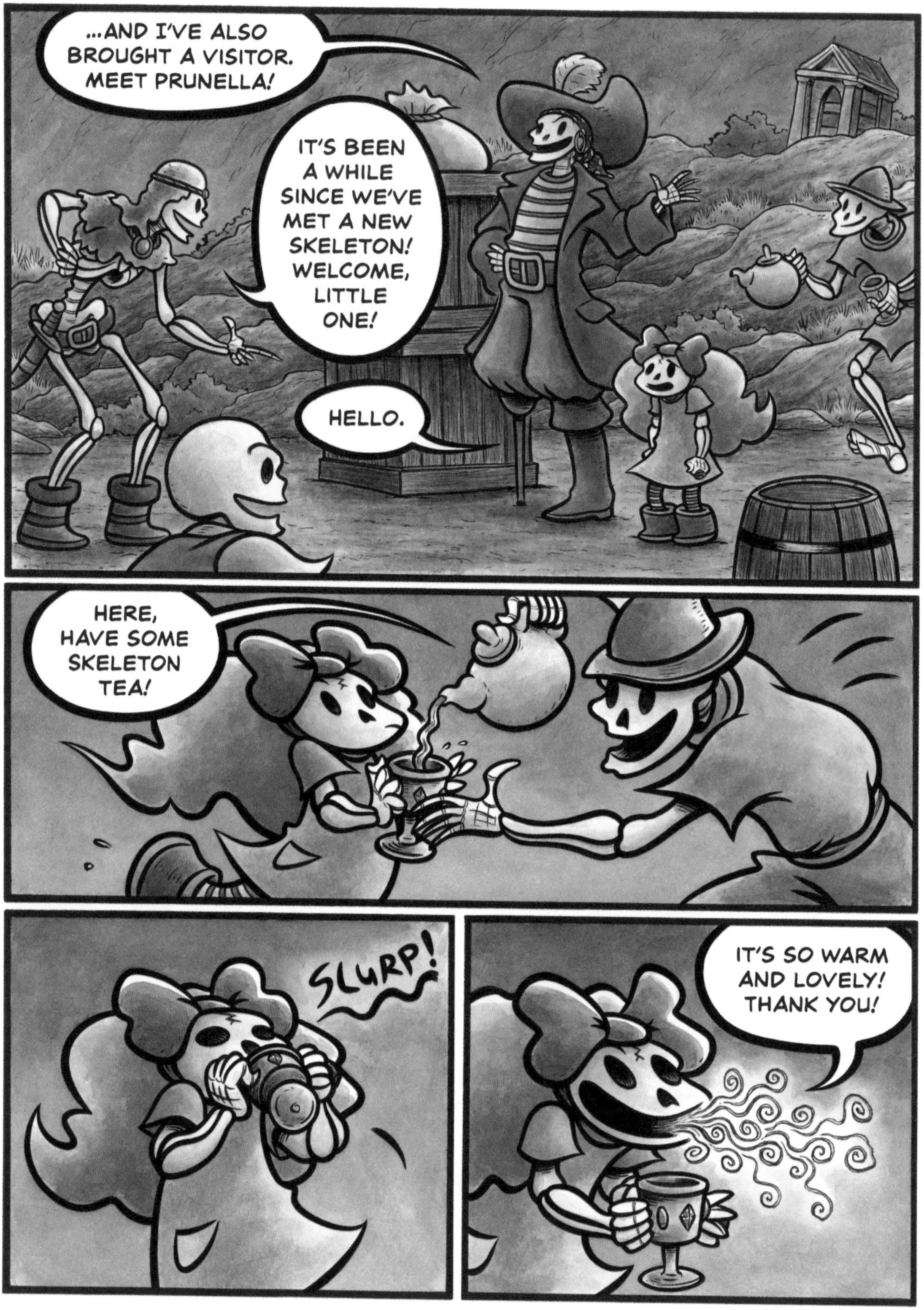
...AND I'VE ALSO BROUGHT A VISITOR. MEET PRUNELLA!
IT'S BEEN A WHILE SINCE WE'VE MET A NEW SKELETON! WELCOME, LITTLE ONE!
HELLO.
HERE, HAVE SOME SKELETON TEA!
SLURP!
IT'S SO WARM AND LOVELY! THANK YOU!

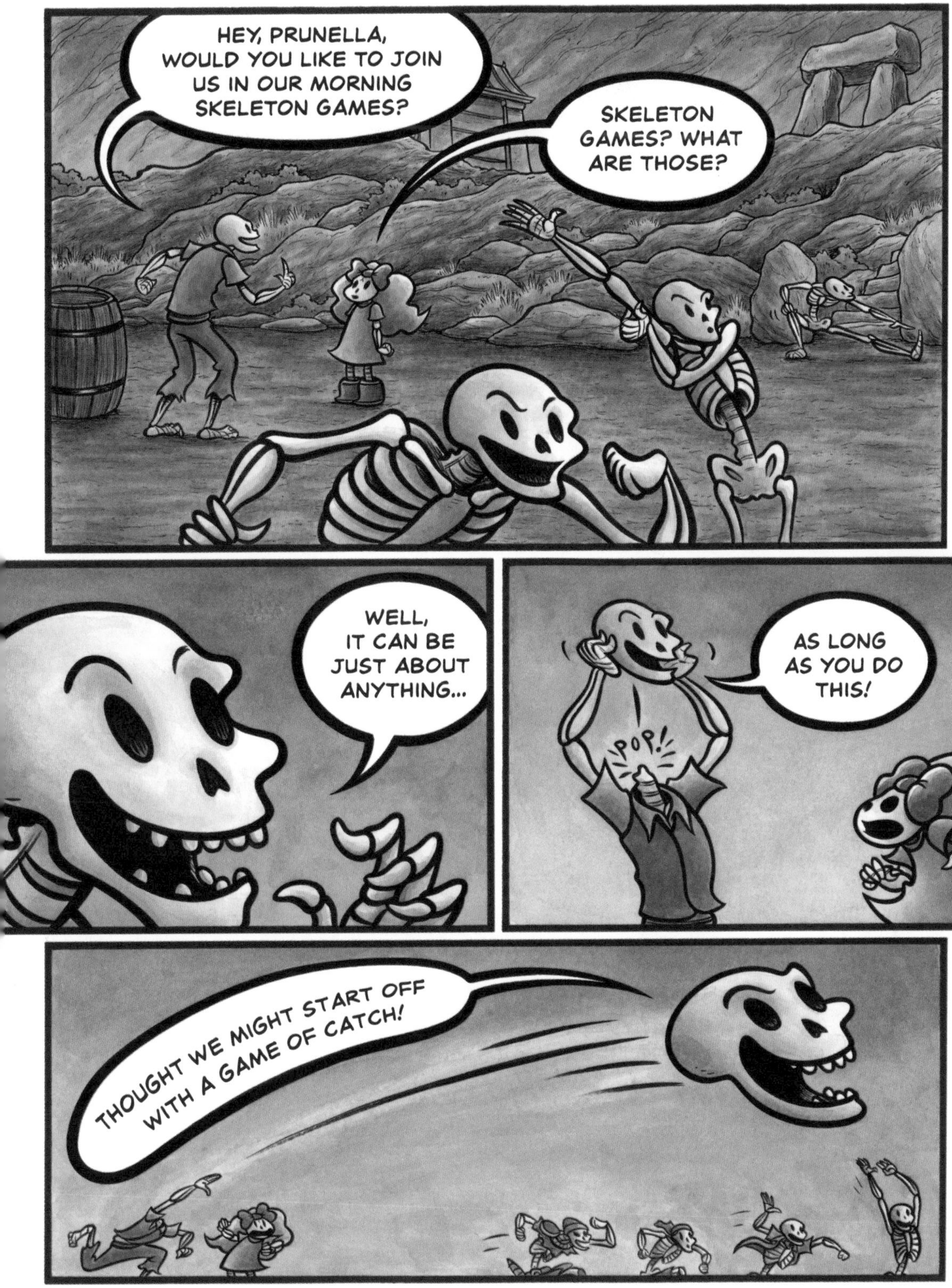
HEY, PRUNELLA, WOULD YOU LIKE TO JOIN US IN OUR MORNING SKELETON GAMES?
SKELETON GAMES? WHAT ARE THOSE?
WELL, IT CAN BE JUST ABOUT ANYTHING...
AS LONG AS YOU DO THIS!
POP!
THOUGHT WE MIGHT START OFF WITH A GAME OF CATCH!

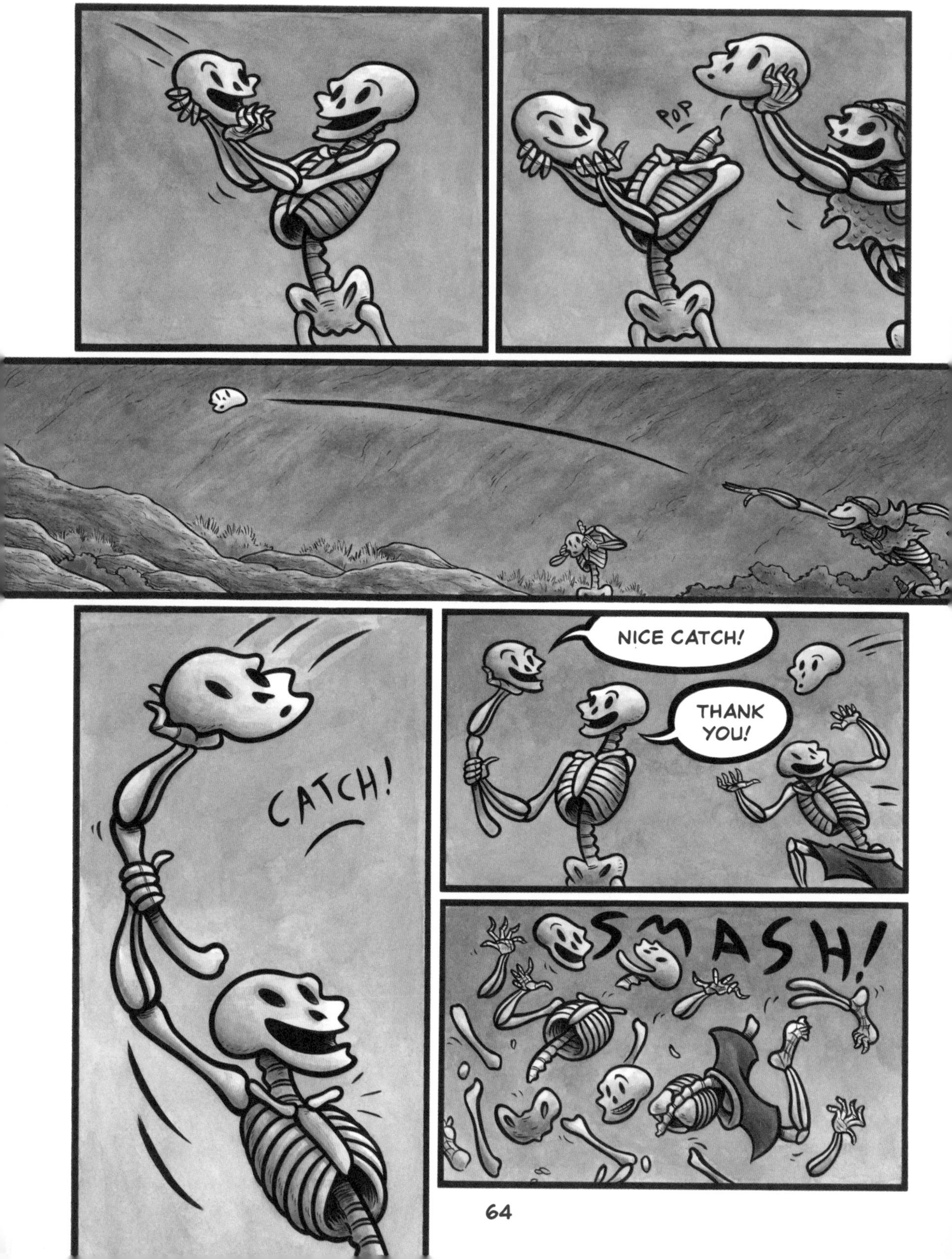
POP
CATCH!
NICE CATCH!
THANK YOU!
SMASH!

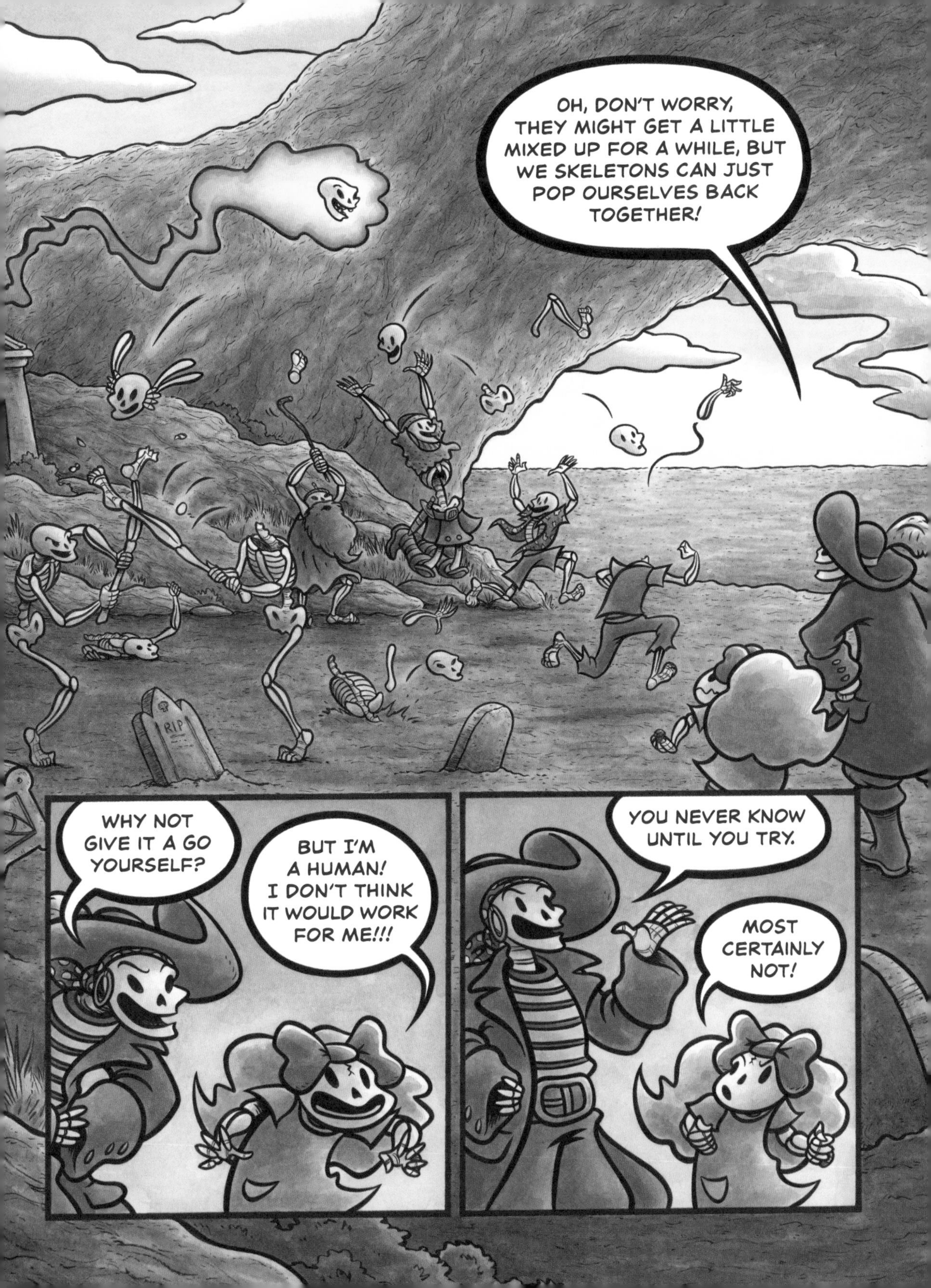
OH, DON'T WORRY, THEY MIGHT GET A LITTLE MIXED UP FOR A WHILE, BUT WE SKELETONS CAN JUST POP OURSELVES BACK TOGETHER!
RIP
WHY NOT GIVE IT A GO YOURSELF?
BUT I'M A HUMAN! I DON'T THINK IT WOULD WORK FOR ME!!!
YOU NEVER KNOW UNTIL YOU TRY.
MOST CERTAINLY NOT!

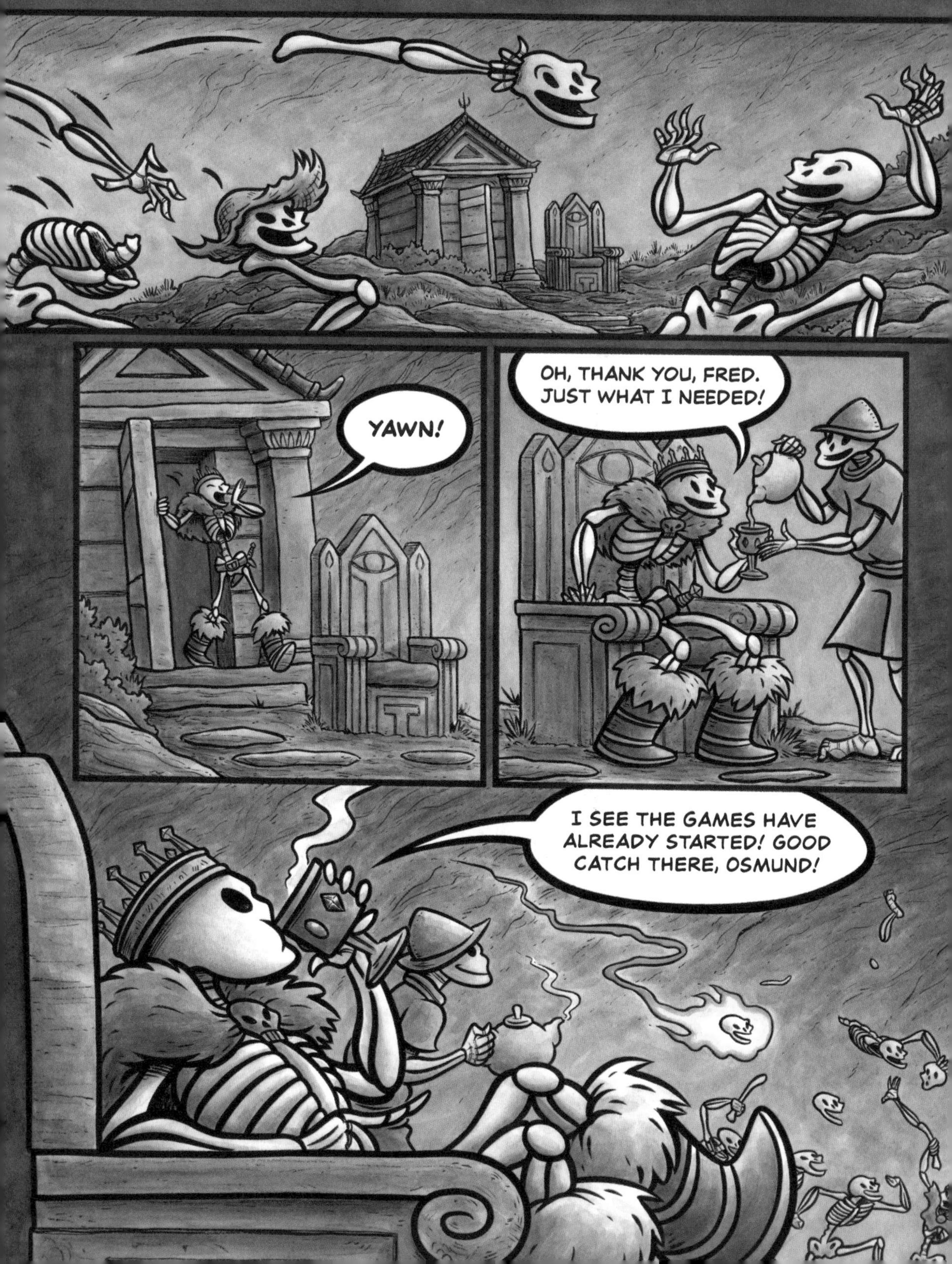
YAWN!
OH, THANK YOU, FRED. JUST WHAT I NEEDED!
I SEE THE GAMES HAVE ALREADY STARTED! GOOD CATCH THERE, OSMUND!

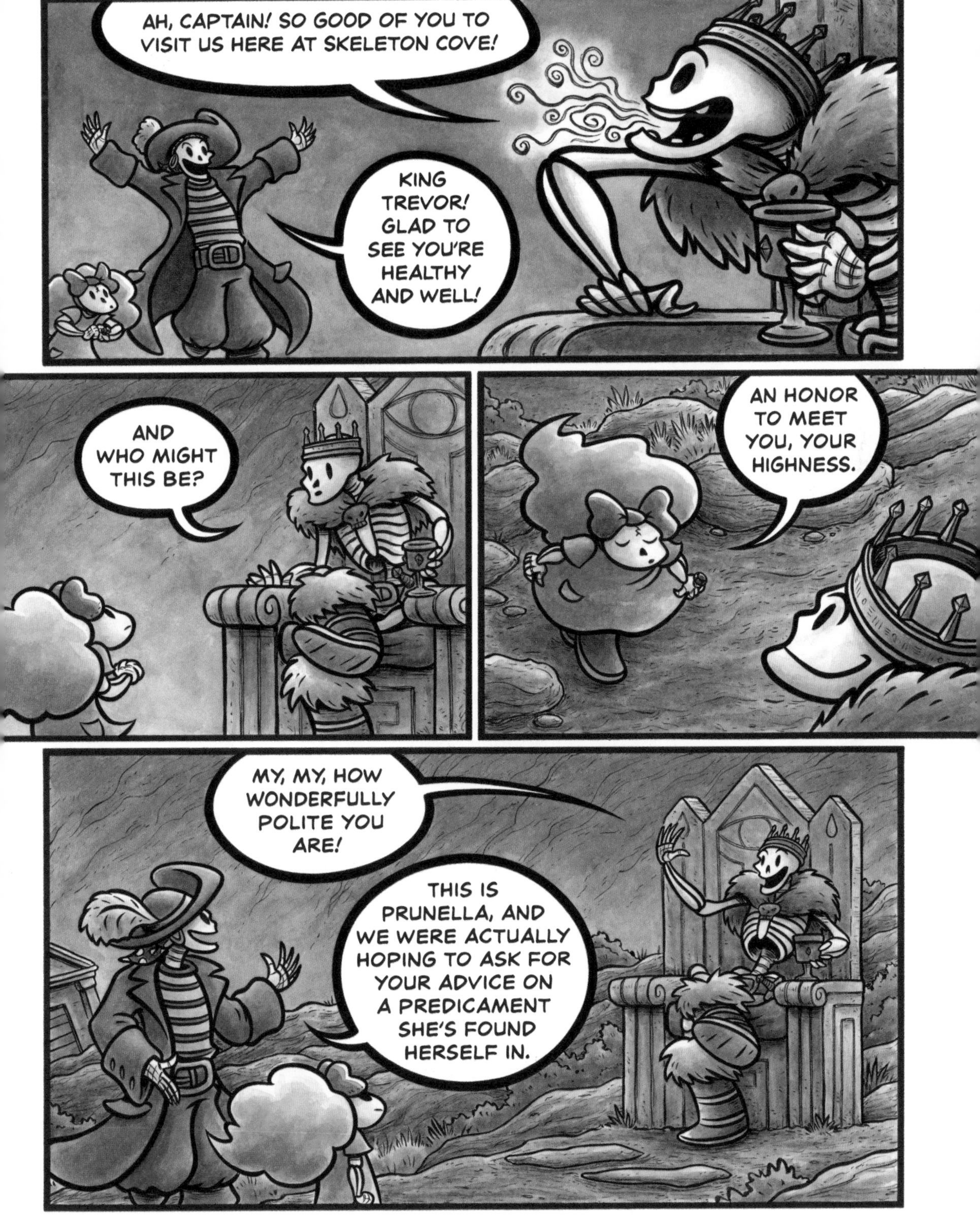
AH, CAPTAIN! SO GOOD OF YOU TO VISIT US HERE AT SKELETON COVE!
KING TREVOR! GLAD TO SEE YOU'RE HEALTHY AND WELL!
AND WHO MIGHT THIS BE?
AN HONOR TO MEET YOU, YOUR HIGHNESS.
MY, MY, HOW WONDERFULLY POLITE YOU ARE!
THIS IS PRUNELLA, AND WE WERE ACTUALLY HOPING TO ASK FOR YOUR ADVICE ON A PREDICAMENT SHE'S FOUND HERSELF IN.

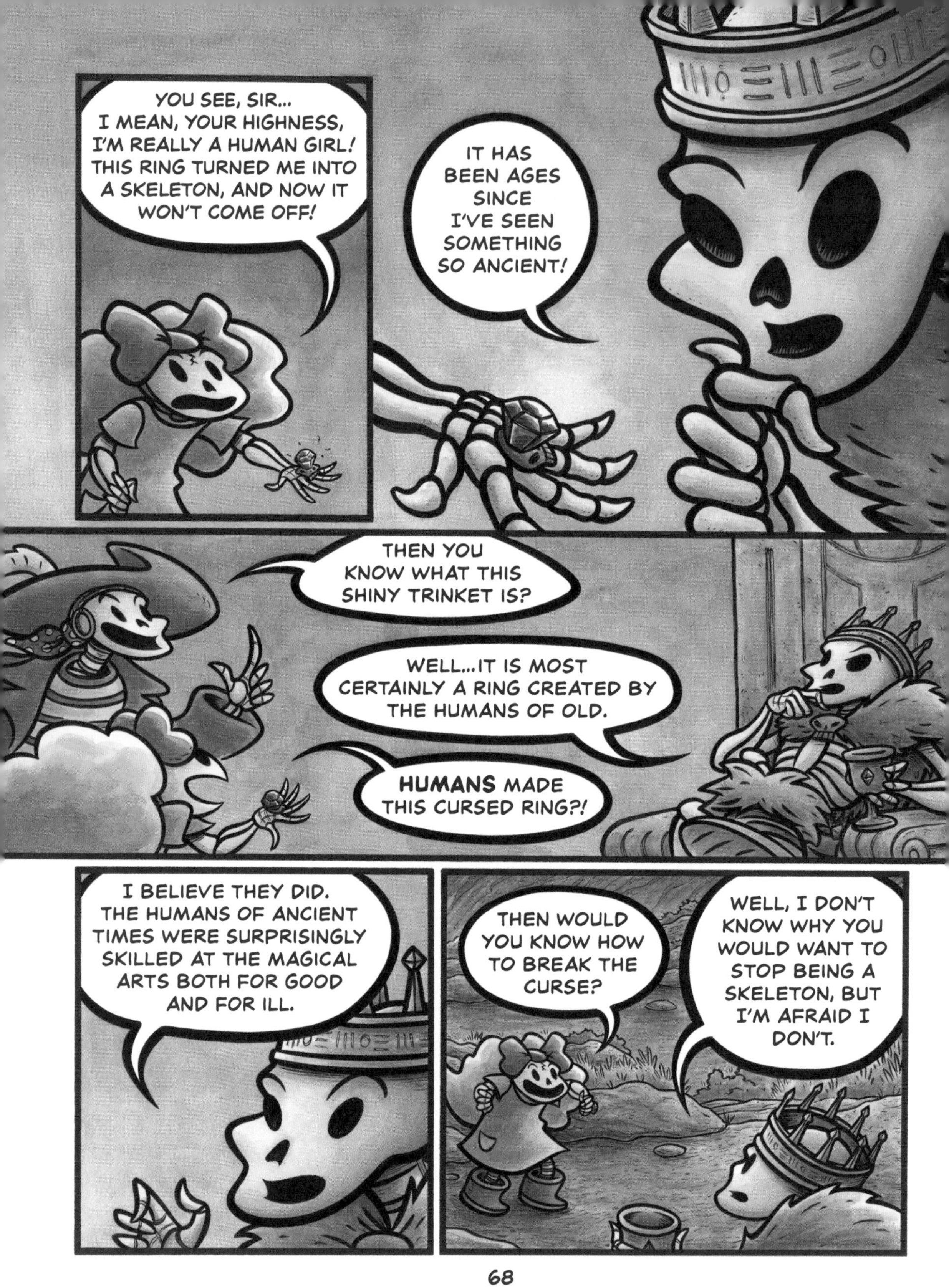
YOU SEE, SIR... I MEAN, YOUR HIGHNESS, I'M REALLY A HUMAN GIRL! THIS RING TURNED ME INTO A SKELETON, AND NOW IT WON'T COME OFF!
IT HAS BEEN AGES SINCE I'VE SEEN SOMETHING SO ANCIENT!
THEN YOU KNOW WHAT THIS SHINY TRINKET IS?
WELL...IT IS MOST CERTAINLY A RING CREATED BY THE HUMANS OF OLD.
HUMANS MADE THIS CURSED RING?!
I BELIEVE THEY DID. THE HUMANS OF ANCIENT TIMES WERE SURPRISINGLY SKILLED AT THE MAGICAL ARTS BOTH FOR GOOD AND FOR ILL.
THEN WOULD YOU KNOW HOW TO BREAK THE CURSE?
WELL, I DON'T KNOW WHY YOU WOULD WANT TO STOP BEING A SKELETON, BUT I'M AFRAID I DON'T.

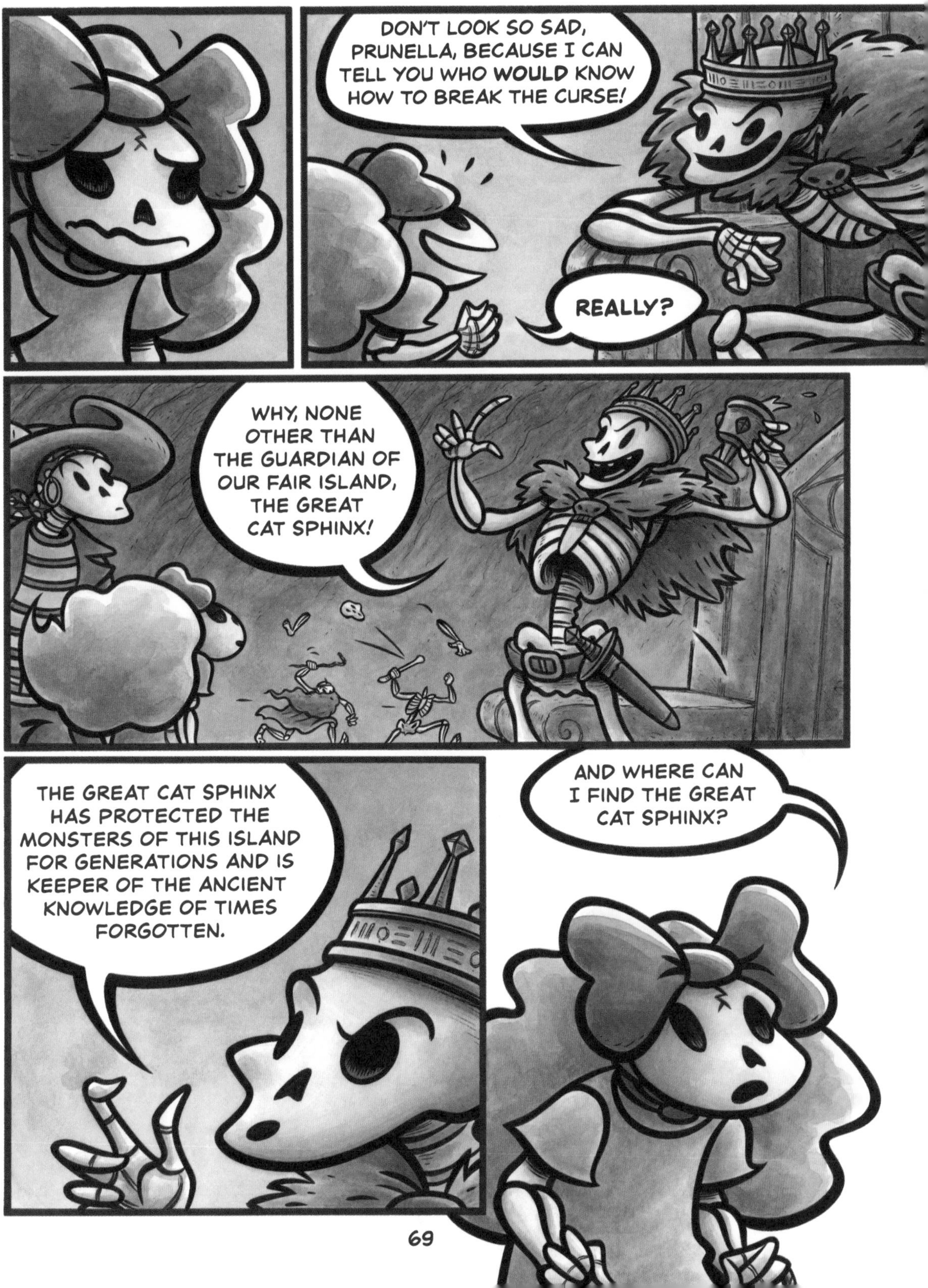
DON'T LOOK SO SAD, PRUNELLA, BECAUSE I CAN TELL YOU WHO **WOULD** KNOW HOW TO BREAK THE CURSE!
REALLY?
WHY, NONE OTHER THAN THE GUARDIAN OF OUR FAIR ISLAND, THE GREAT CAT SPHINX!
THE GREAT CAT SPHINX HAS PROTECTED THE MONSTERS OF THIS ISLAND FOR GENERATIONS AND IS KEEPER OF THE ANCIENT KNOWLEDGE OF TIMES FORGOTTEN.
AND WHERE CAN I FIND THE GREAT CAT SPHINX?

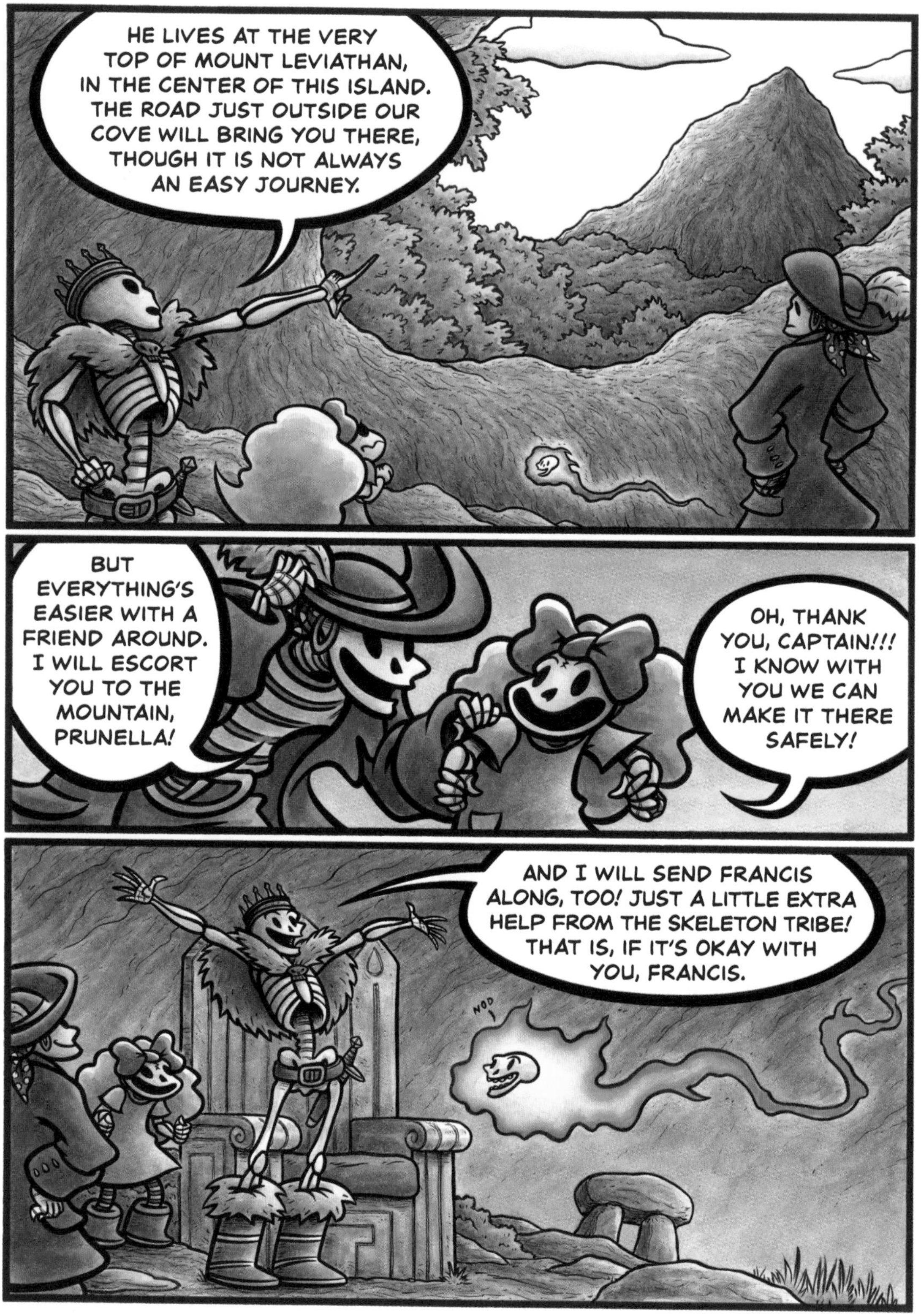
HE LIVES AT THE VERY TOP OF MOUNT LEVIATHAN, IN THE CENTER OF THIS ISLAND. THE ROAD JUST OUTSIDE OUR COVE WILL BRING YOU THERE, THOUGH IT IS NOT ALWAYS AN EASY JOURNEY.
BUT EVERYTHING'S EASIER WITH A FRIEND AROUND. I WILL ESCORT YOU TO THE MOUNTAIN, PRUNELLA!
OH, THANK YOU, CAPTAIN!!! I KNOW WITH YOU WE CAN MAKE IT THERE SAFELY!
AND I WILL SEND FRANCIS ALONG, TOO! JUST A LITTLE EXTRA HELP FROM THE SKELETON TRIBE! THAT IS, IF IT'S OKAY WITH YOU, FRANCIS.
NOD

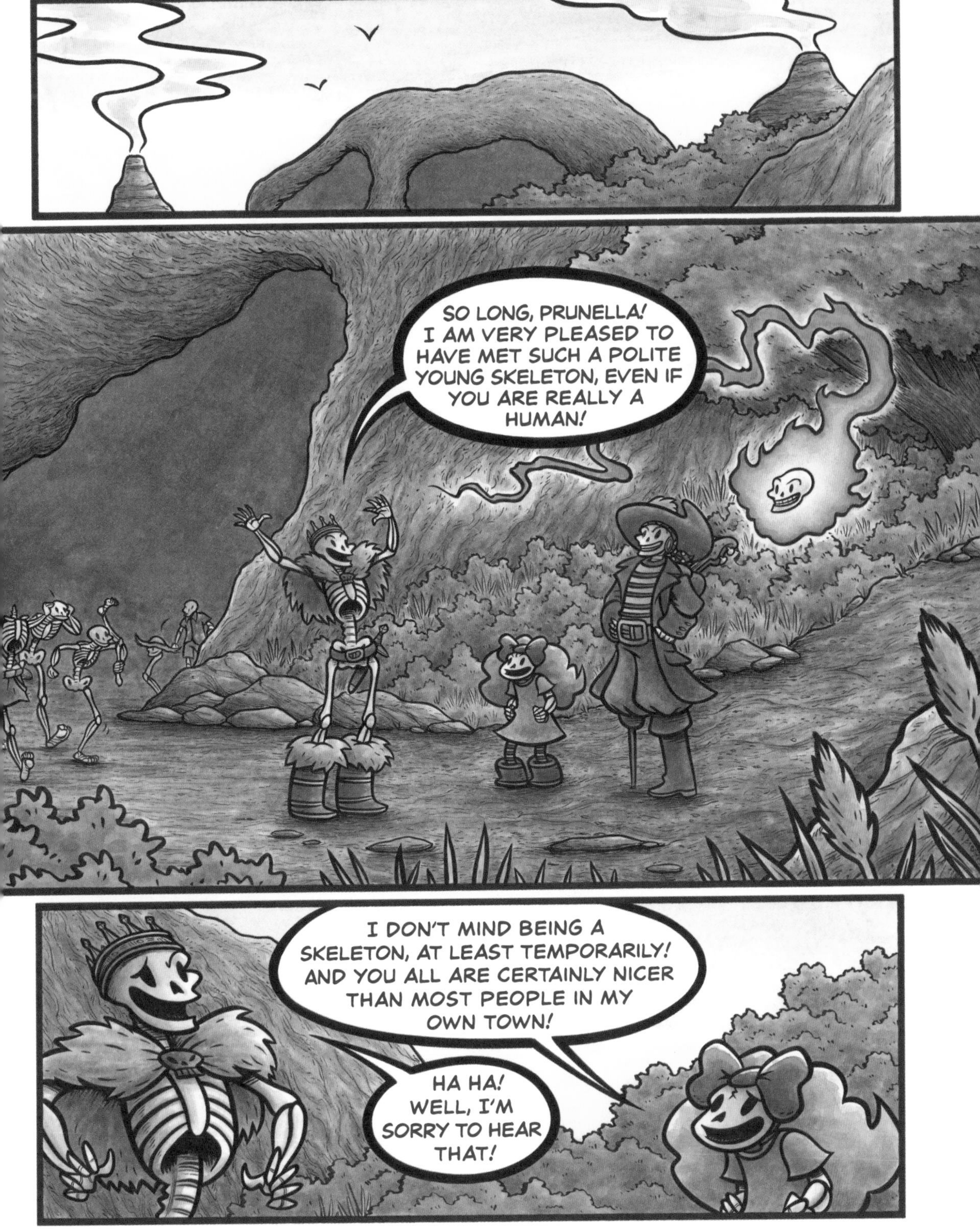
SO LONG, PRUNELLA! I AM VERY PLEASED TO HAVE MET SUCH A POLITE YOUNG SKELETON, EVEN IF YOU ARE REALLY A HUMAN!
I DON'T MIND BEING A SKELETON, AT LEAST TEMPORARILY! AND YOU ALL ARE CERTAINLY NICER THAN MOST PEOPLE IN MY OWN TOWN!
HA HA! WELL, I'M SORRY TO HEAR THAT!

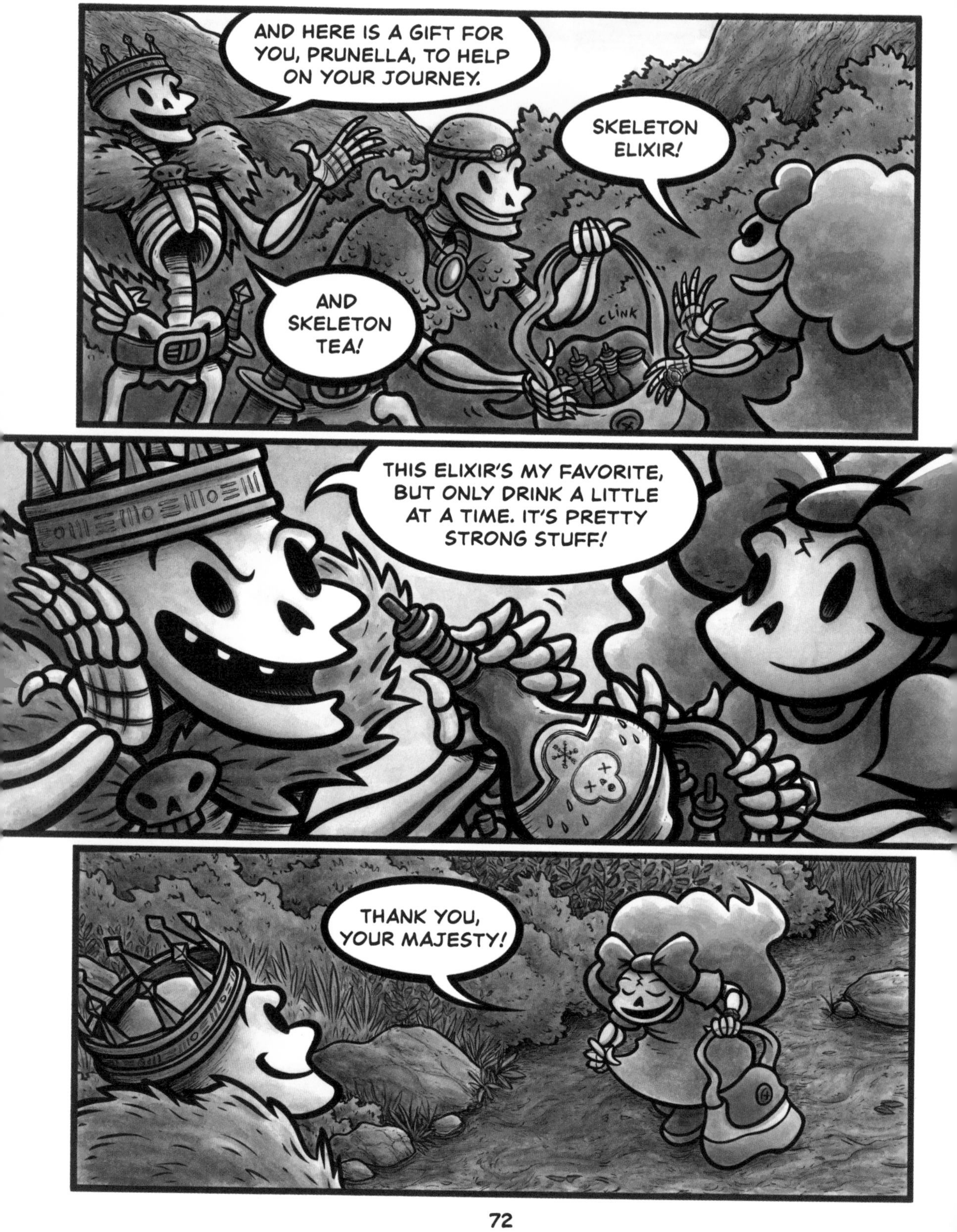
AND HERE IS A GIFT FOR YOU, PRUNELLA, TO HELP ON YOUR JOURNEY.
SKELETON ELIXIR!
AND SKELETON TEA!
CLINK
THIS ELIXIR'S MY FAVORITE, BUT ONLY DRINK A LITTLE AT A TIME. IT'S PRETTY STRONG STUFF!
THANK YOU, YOUR MAJESTY!

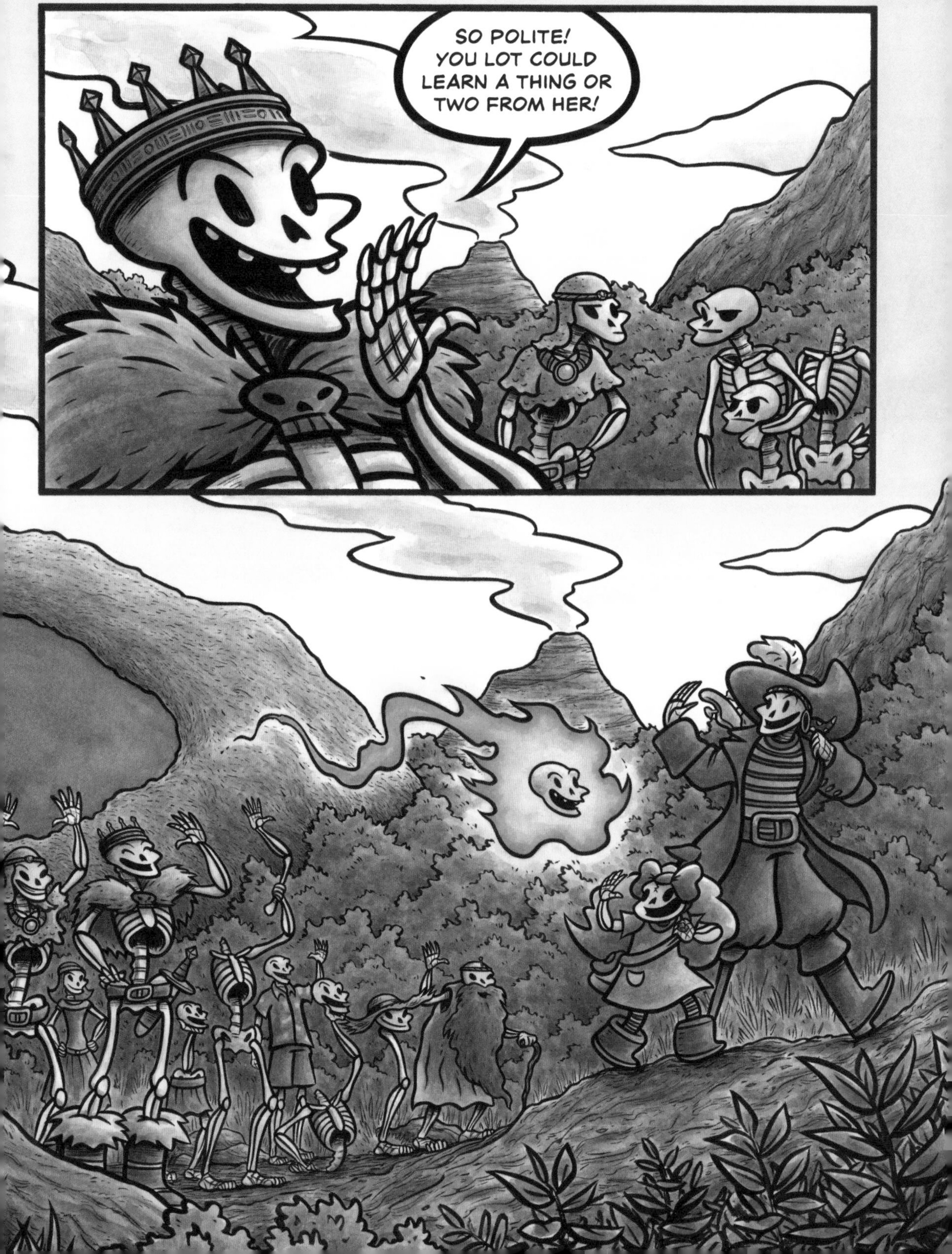
SO POLITE!
YOU LOT COULD
LEARN A THING OR
TWO FROM HER!

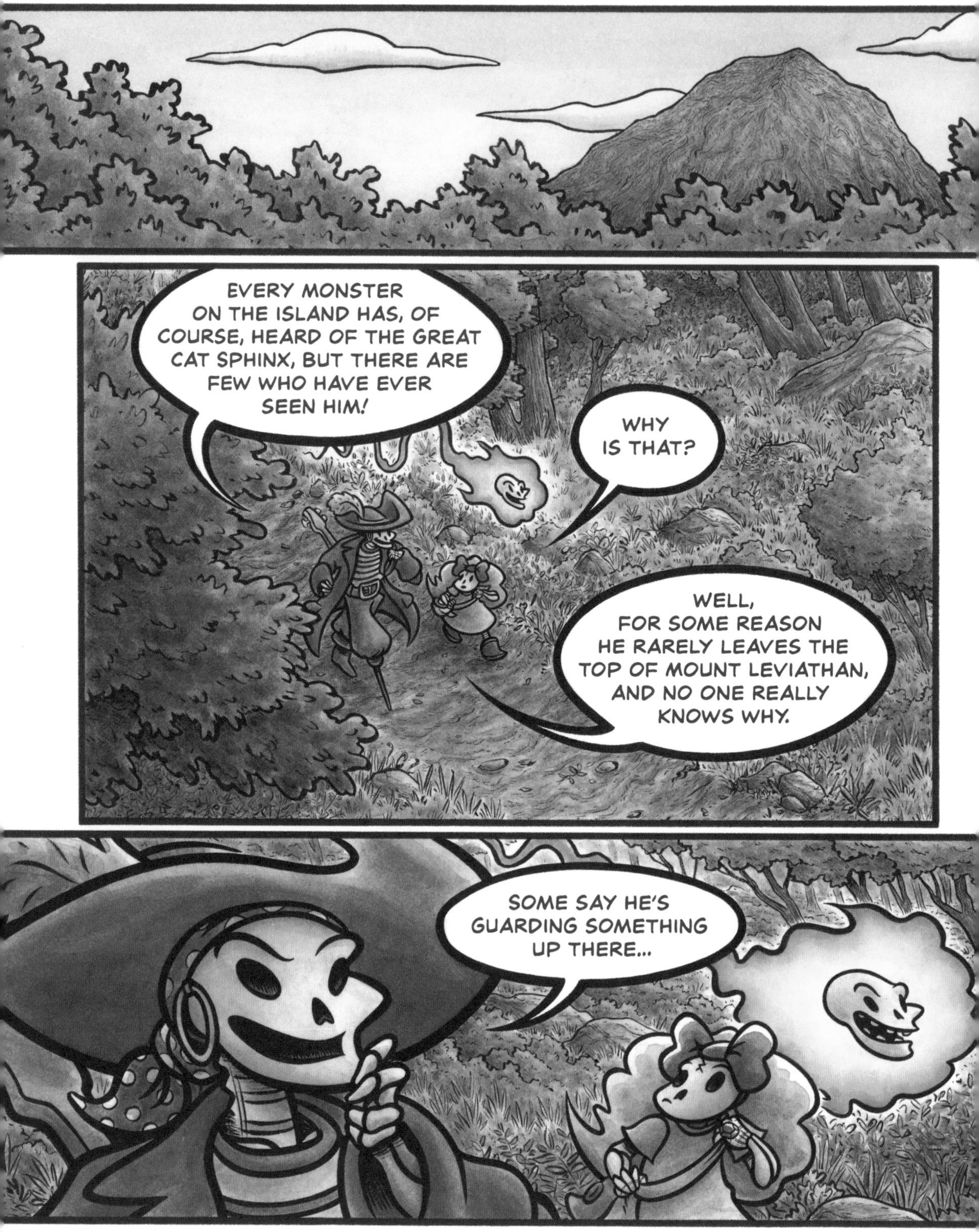
EVERY MONSTER ON THE ISLAND HAS, OF COURSE, HEARD OF THE GREAT CAT SPHINX, BUT THERE ARE FEW WHO HAVE EVER SEEN HIM!
WHY IS THAT?
WELL, FOR SOME REASON HE RARELY LEAVES THE TOP OF MOUNT LEVIATHAN, AND NO ONE REALLY KNOWS WHY.
SOME SAY HE'S GUARDING SOMETHING UP THERE...

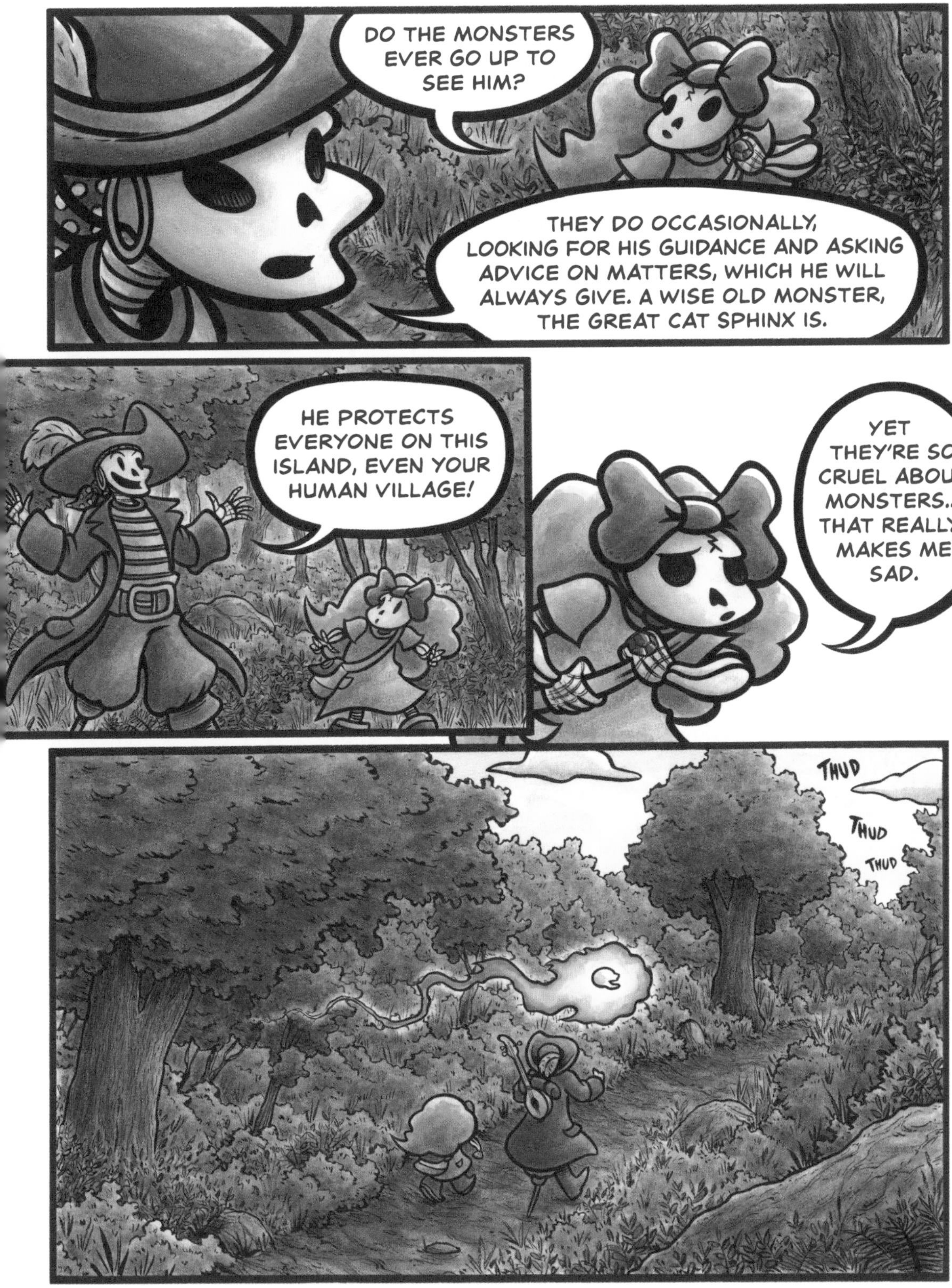
DO THE MONSTERS EVER GO UP TO SEE HIM?
THEY DO OCCASIONALLY, LOOKING FOR HIS GUIDANCE AND ASKING ADVICE ON MATTERS, WHICH HE WILL ALWAYS GIVE. A WISE OLD MONSTER, THE GREAT CAT SPHINX IS.
HE PROTECTS EVERYONE ON THIS ISLAND, EVEN YOUR HUMAN VILLAGE!
YET THEY'RE SO CRUEL ABOUT MONSTERS... THAT REALLY MAKES ME SAD.
THUD
THUD
THUD

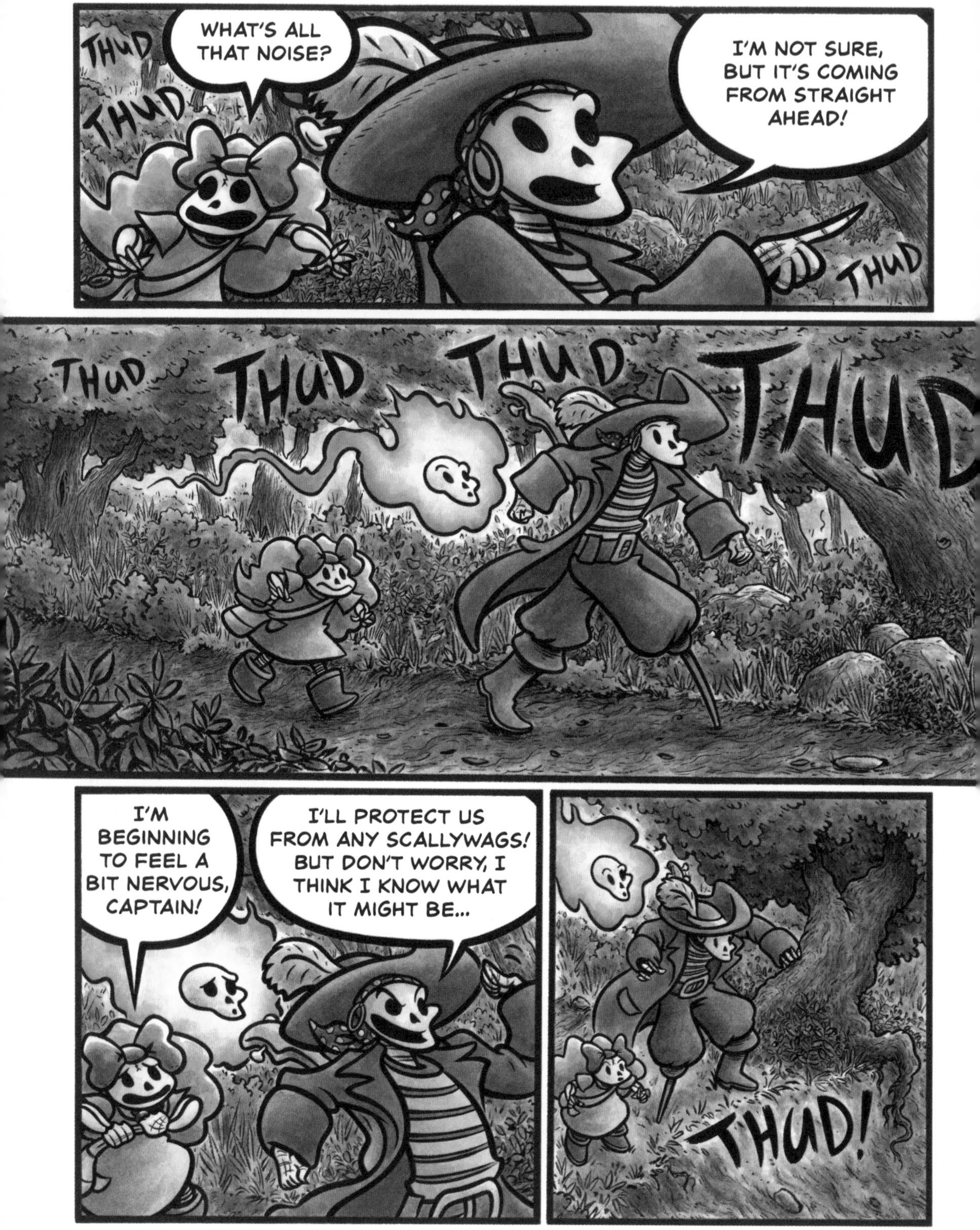
THUD
THUD
WHAT'S ALL THAT NOISE?
I'M NOT SURE, BUT IT'S COMING FROM STRAIGHT AHEAD!
THUD
THUD
THUD
THUD
THUD
I'M BEGINNING TO FEEL A BIT NERVOUS, CAPTAIN!
I'LL PROTECT US FROM ANY SCALLYWAGS! BUT DON'T WORRY, I THINK I KNOW WHAT IT MIGHT BE...
THUD!

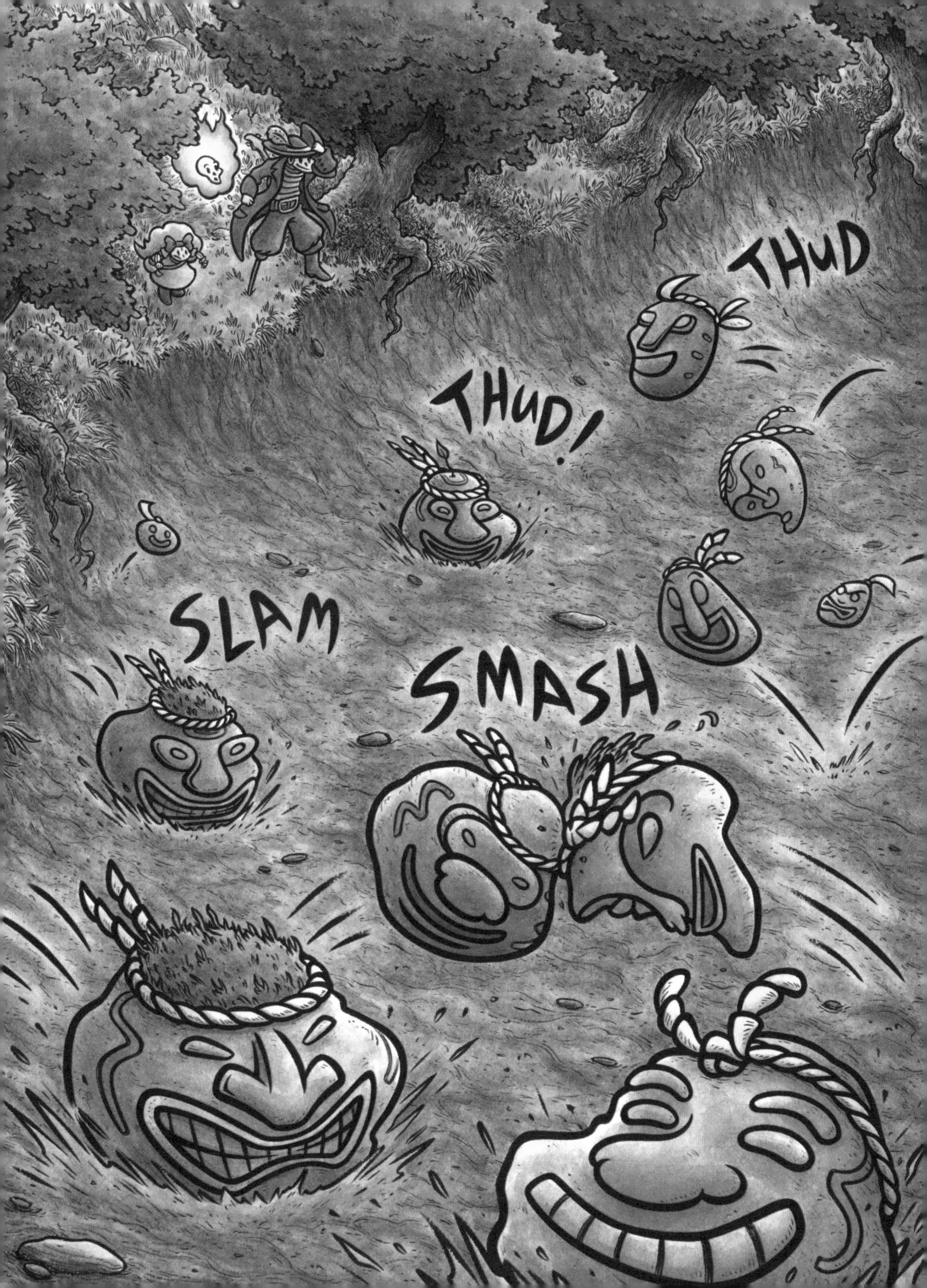

THUD
THUD!
SLAM
SMASH

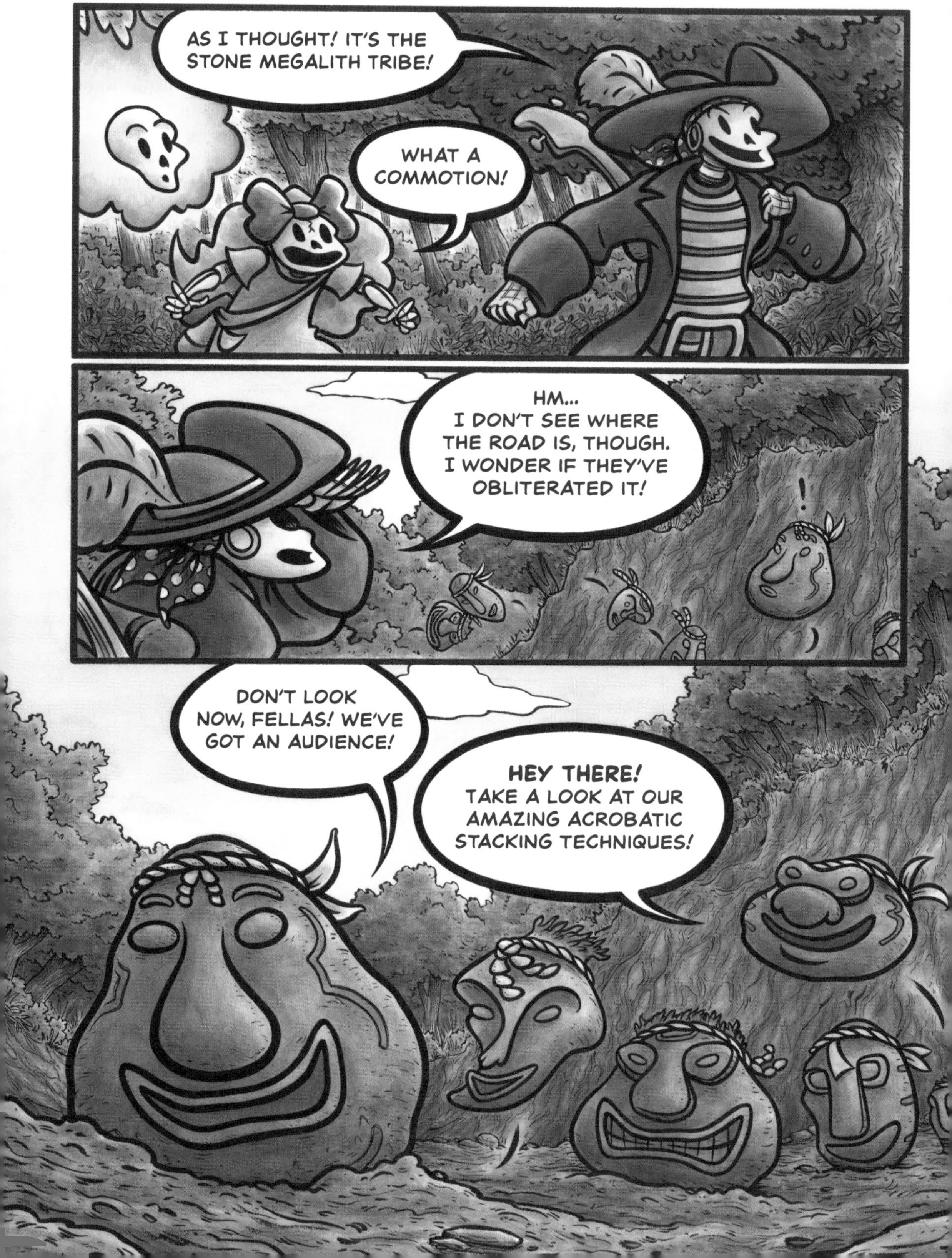
AS I THOUGHT! IT'S THE STONE MEGALITH TRIBE!
WHAT A COMMOTION!
HM... I DON'T SEE WHERE THE ROAD IS, THOUGH. I WONDER IF THEY'VE OBLITERATED IT!
!
DON'T LOOK NOW, FELLAS! WE'VE GOT AN AUDIENCE!
HEY THERE! TAKE A LOOK AT OUR AMAZING ACROBATIC STACKING TECHNIQUES!

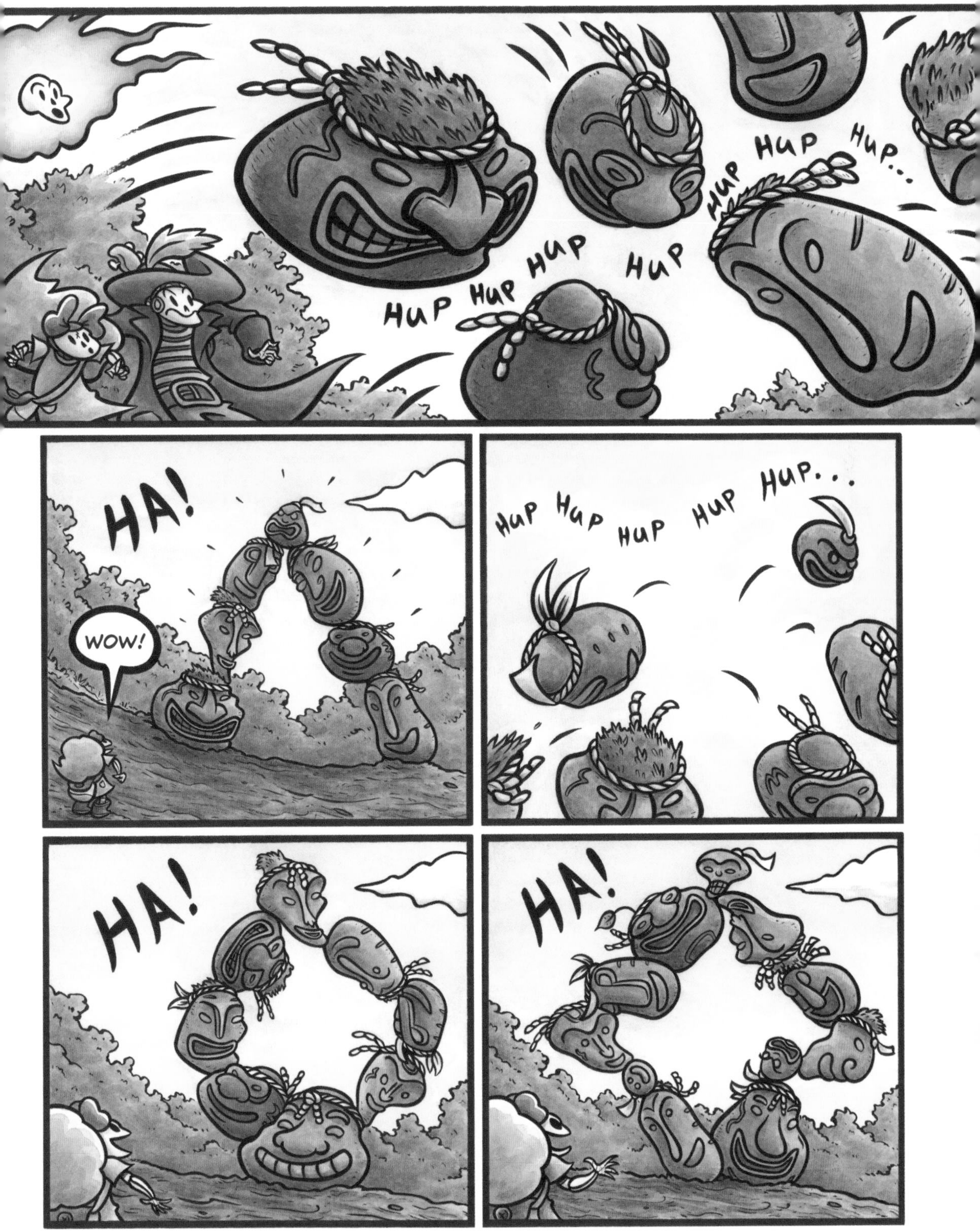
HUP HUP HUP HUP HUP HUP HUP HUP...
HA!
WOW!
HUP HUP HUP HUP HUP...
HA!
HA!

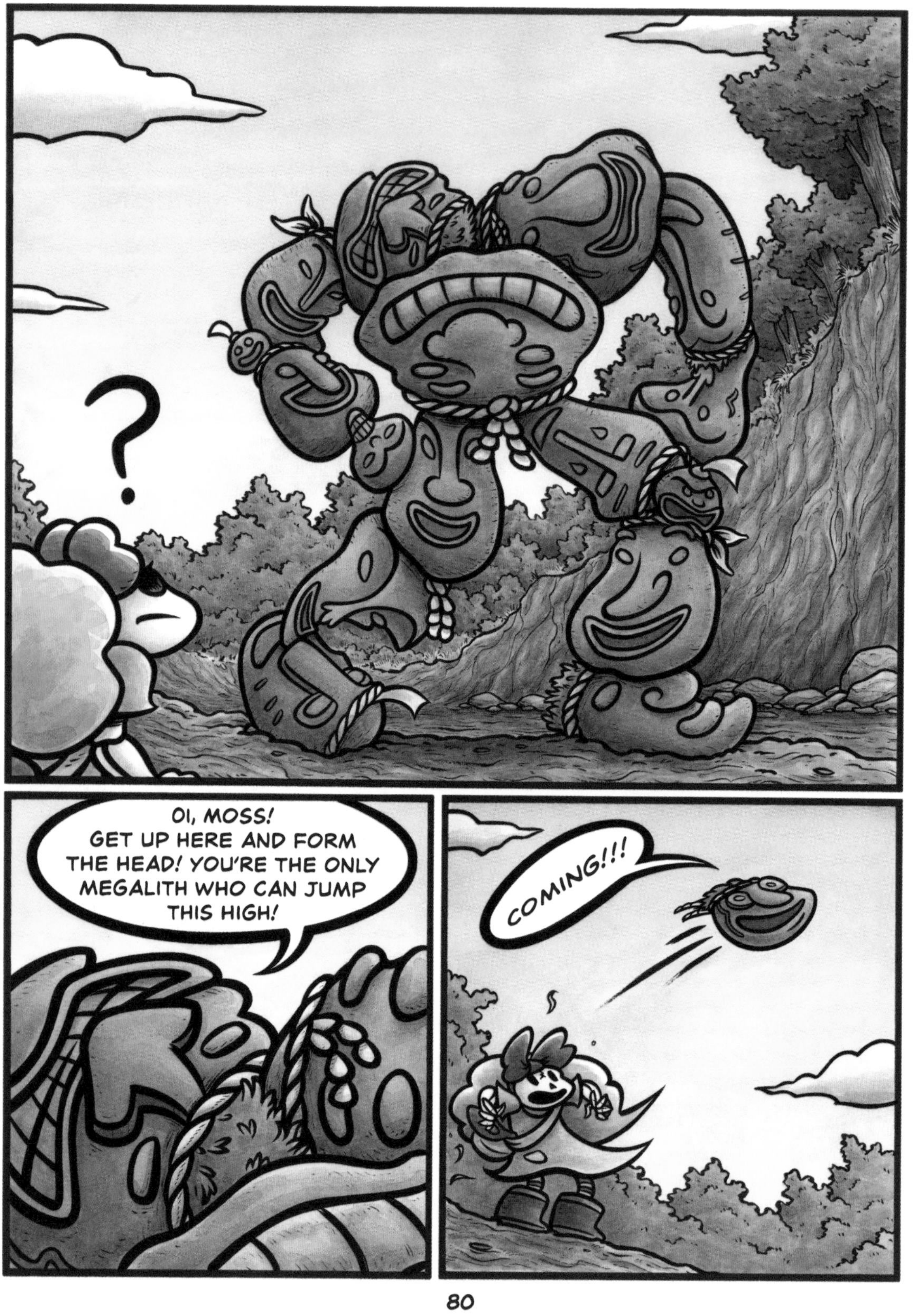
?
OI, MOSS!
GET UP HERE AND FORM
THE HEAD! YOU'RE THE ONLY
MEGALITH WHO CAN JUMP
THIS HIGH!
COMING!!!

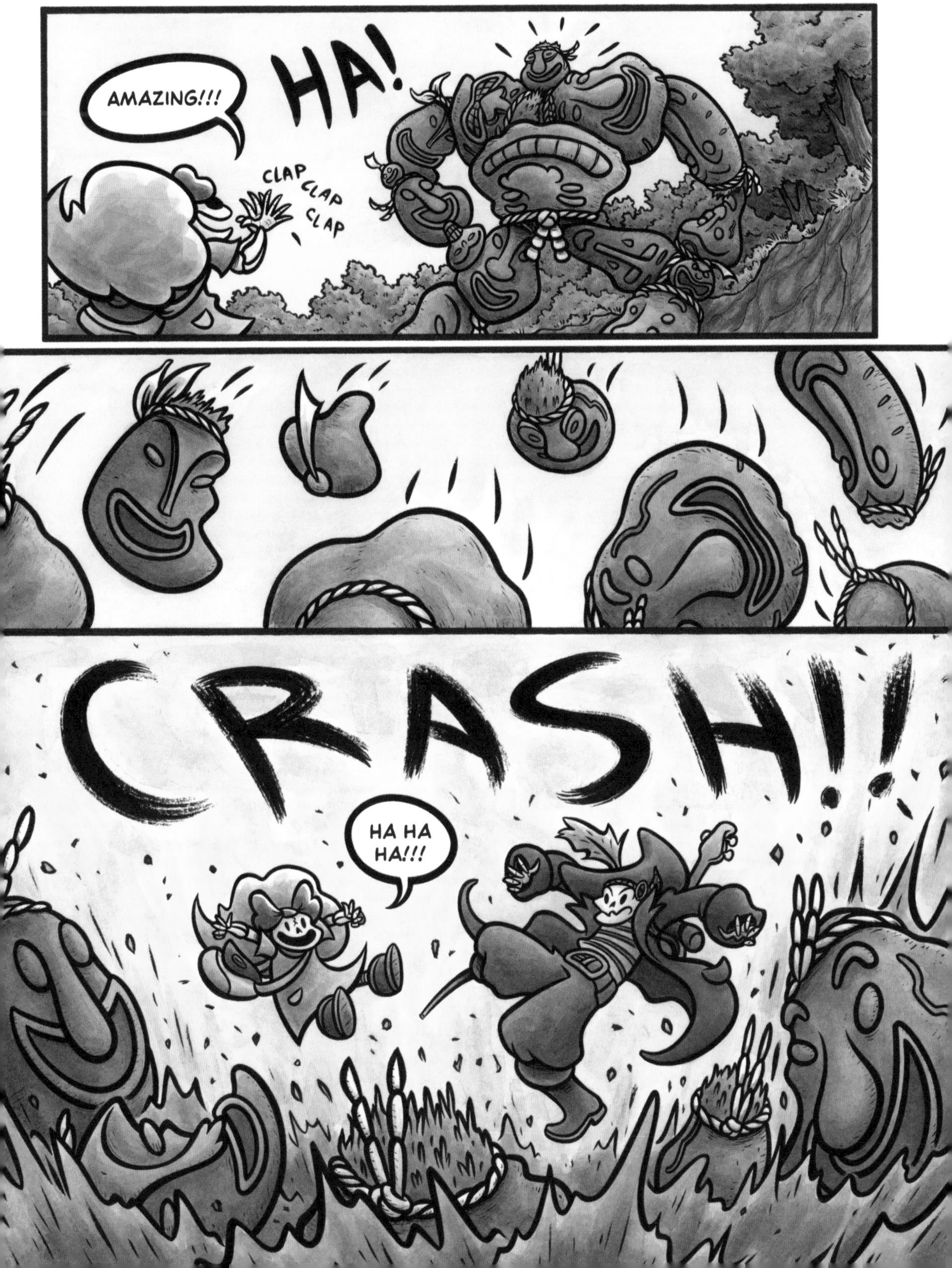
AMAZING!!!
HA!
CLAP CLAP CLAP
CRASH!!
HA HA HA!!!

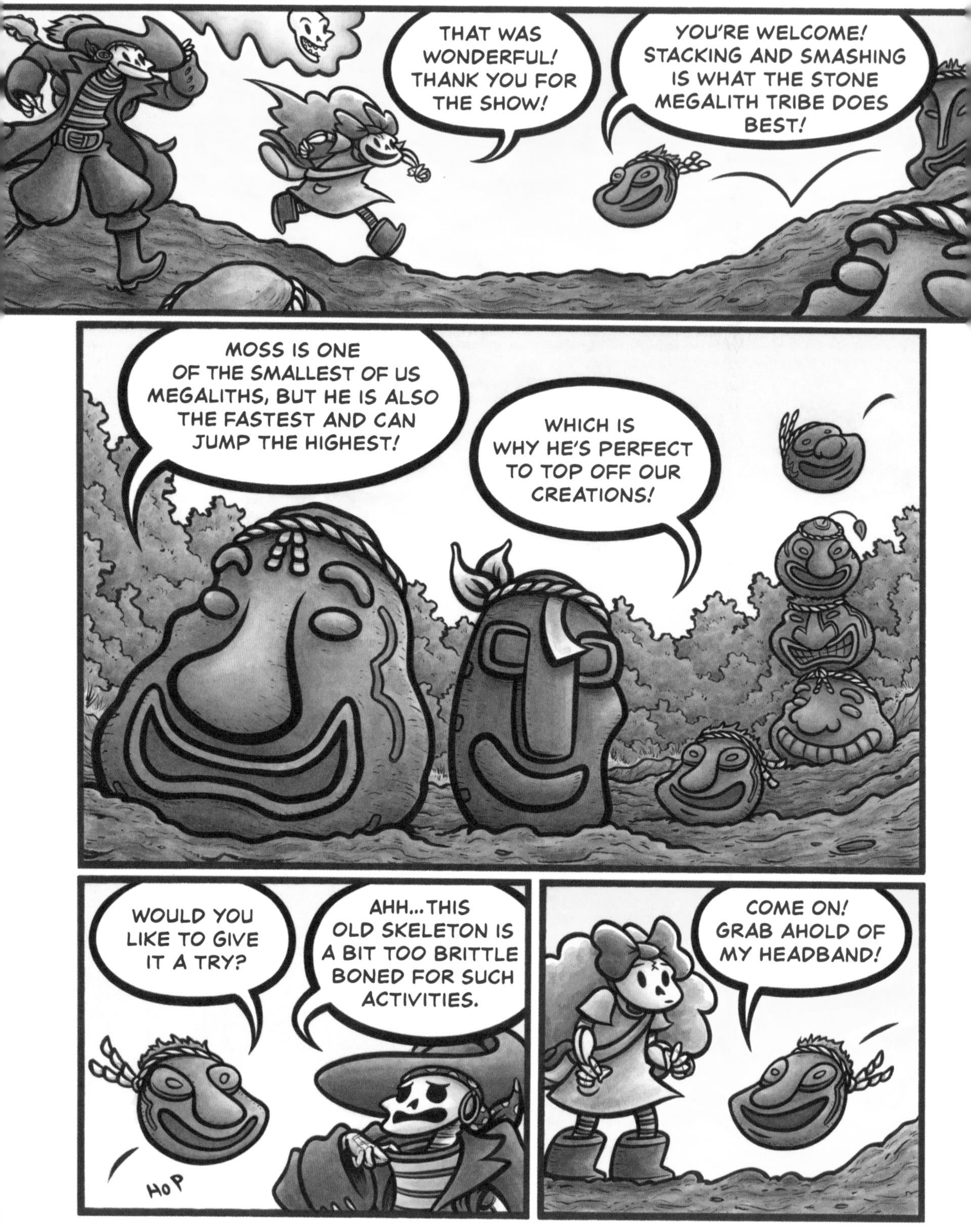
THAT WAS WONDERFUL! THANK YOU FOR THE SHOW!
YOU'RE WELCOME! STACKING AND SMASHING IS WHAT THE STONE MEGALITH TRIBE DOES BEST!
MOSS IS ONE OF THE SMALLEST OF US MEGALITHS, BUT HE IS ALSO THE FASTEST AND CAN JUMP THE HIGHEST!
WHICH IS WHY HE'S PERFECT TO TOP OFF OUR CREATIONS!
WOULD YOU LIKE TO GIVE IT A TRY?
HOP
AHH...THIS OLD SKELETON IS A BIT TOO BRITTLE BONED FOR SUCH ACTIVITIES.
COME ON! GRAB AHOLD OF MY HEADBAND!

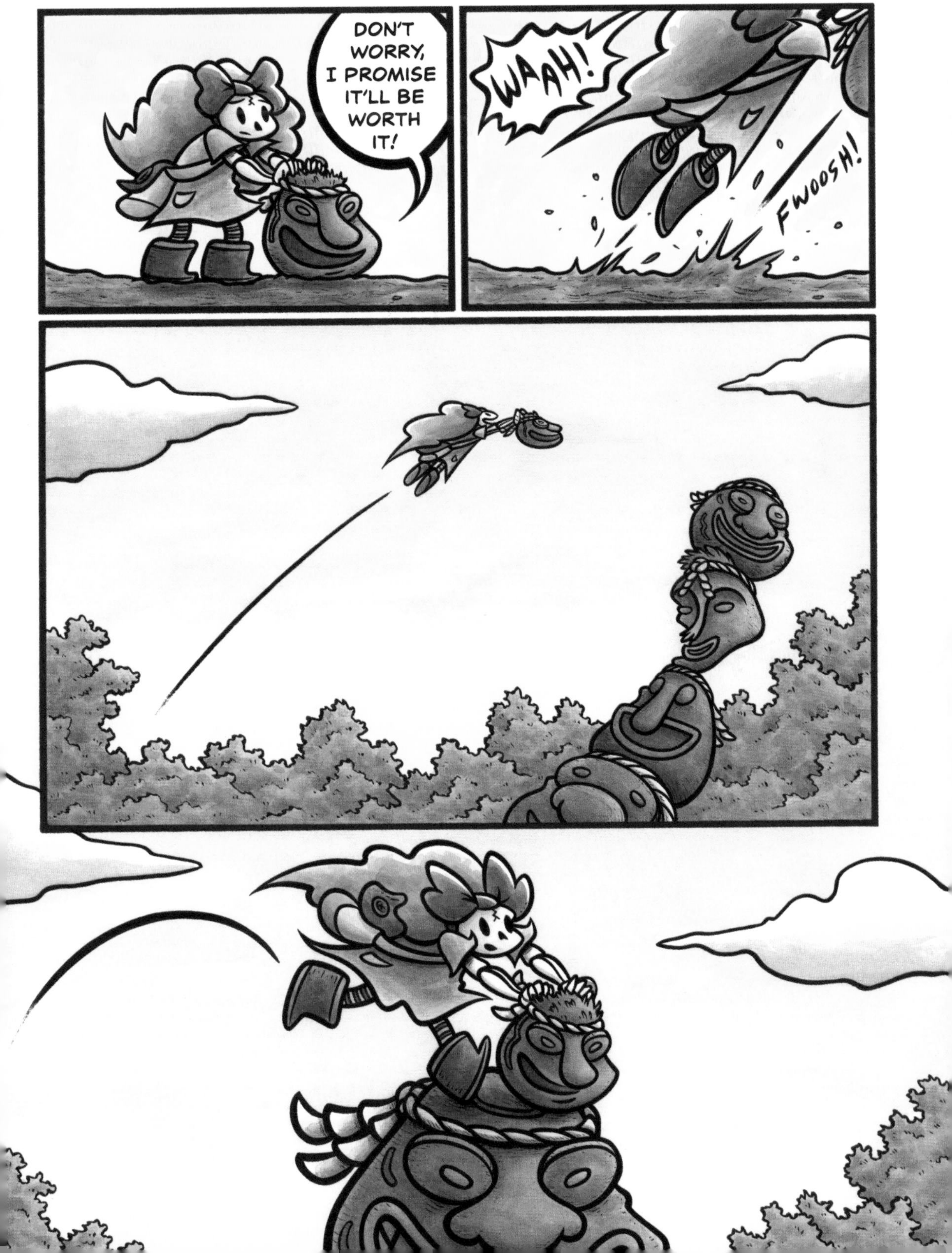
DON'T WORRY, I PROMISE IT'LL BE WORTH IT!
WAAH!
FWOOSH!

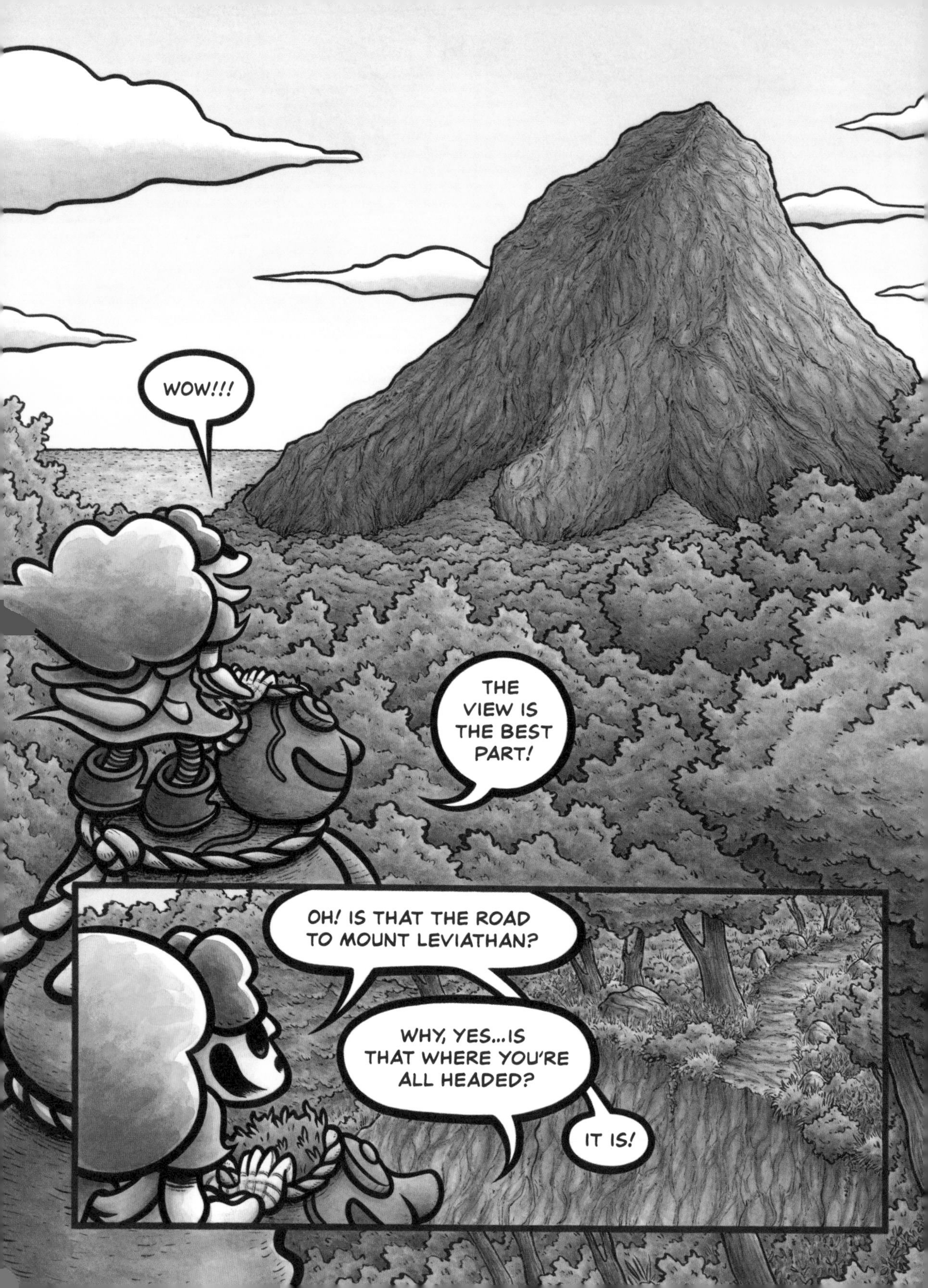
WOW!!!
THE VIEW IS THE BEST PART!
OH! IS THAT THE ROAD TO MOUNT LEVIATHAN?
WHY, YES...IS THAT WHERE YOU'RE ALL HEADED?
IT IS!

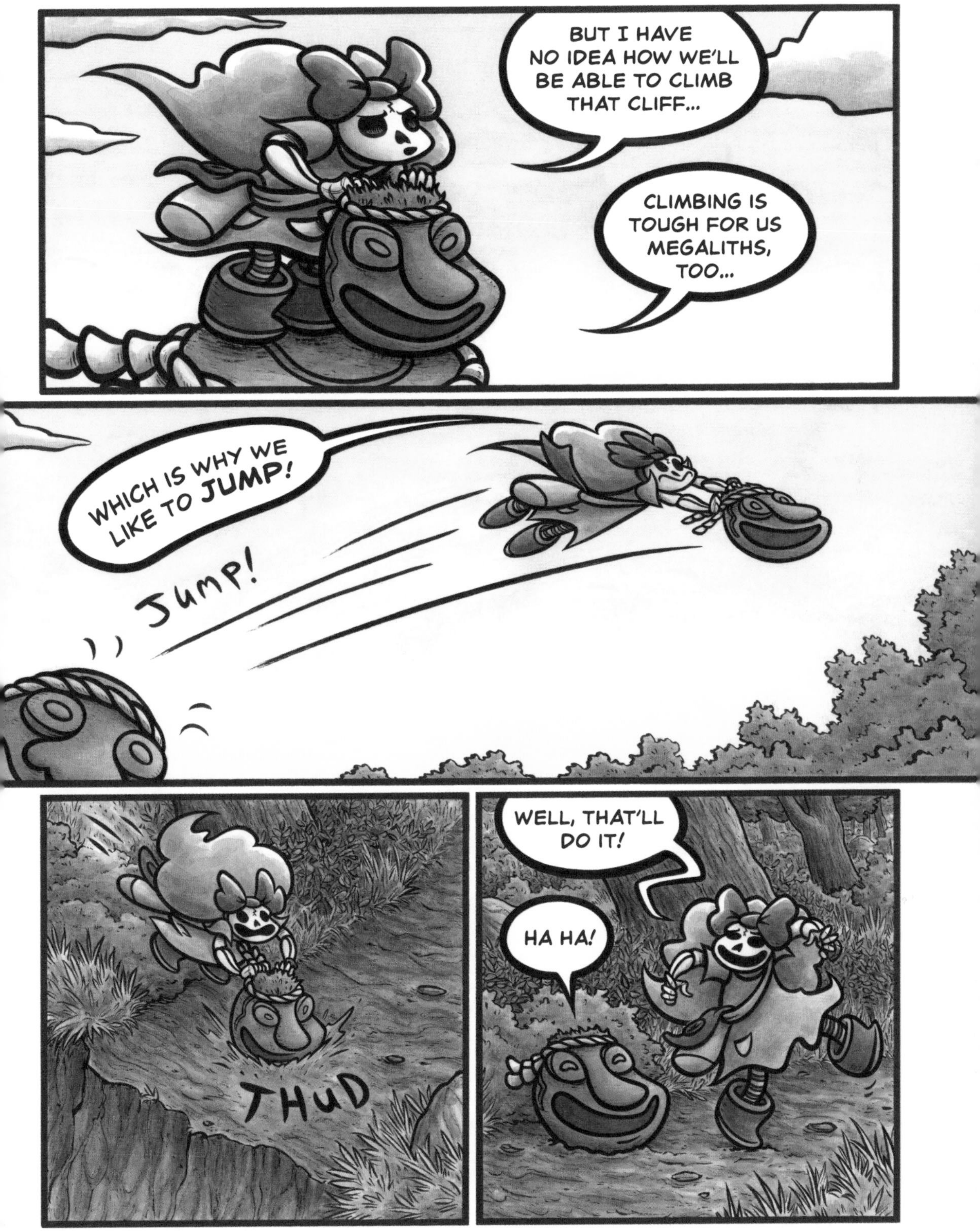
BUT I HAVE NO IDEA HOW WE'LL BE ABLE TO CLIMB THAT CLIFF...
CLIMBING IS TOUGH FOR US MEGALITHS, TOO...
WHICH IS WHY WE LIKE TO JUMP!
JUMP!
THUD
WELL, THAT'LL DO IT!
HA HA!

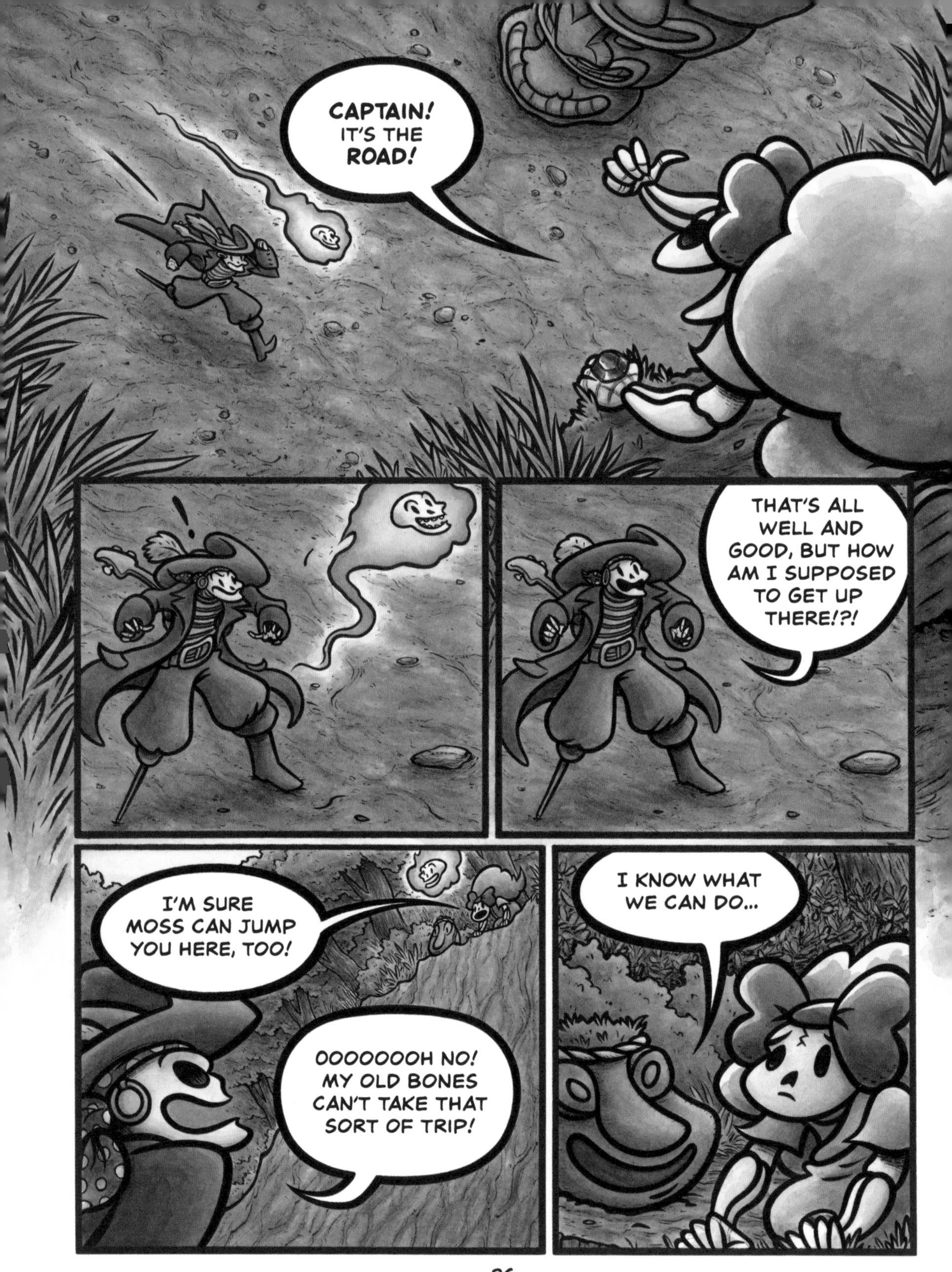

CAPTAIN! IT'S THE ROAD!
THAT'S ALL WELL AND GOOD, BUT HOW AM I SUPPOSED TO GET UP THERE!?!
I'M SURE MOSS CAN JUMP YOU HERE, TOO!
OOOOOOOH NO! MY OLD BONES CAN'T TAKE THAT SORT OF TRIP!
I KNOW WHAT WE CAN DO...

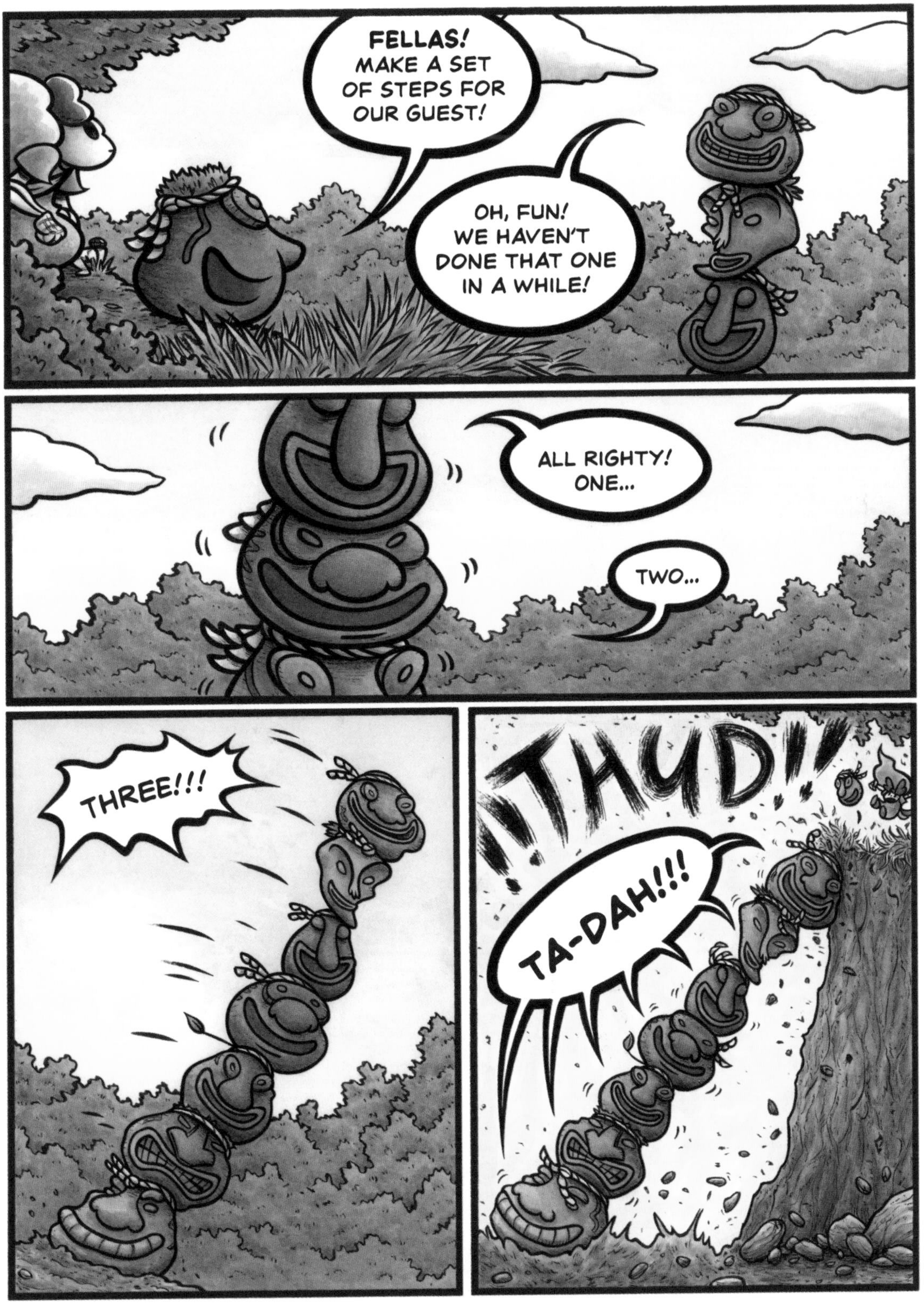
FELLAS! MAKE A SET OF STEPS FOR OUR GUEST!
OH, FUN! WE HAVEN'T DONE THAT ONE IN A WHILE!
ALL RIGHTY! ONE...
TWO...
THREE!!!
THUD!!
TA-DAH!!!

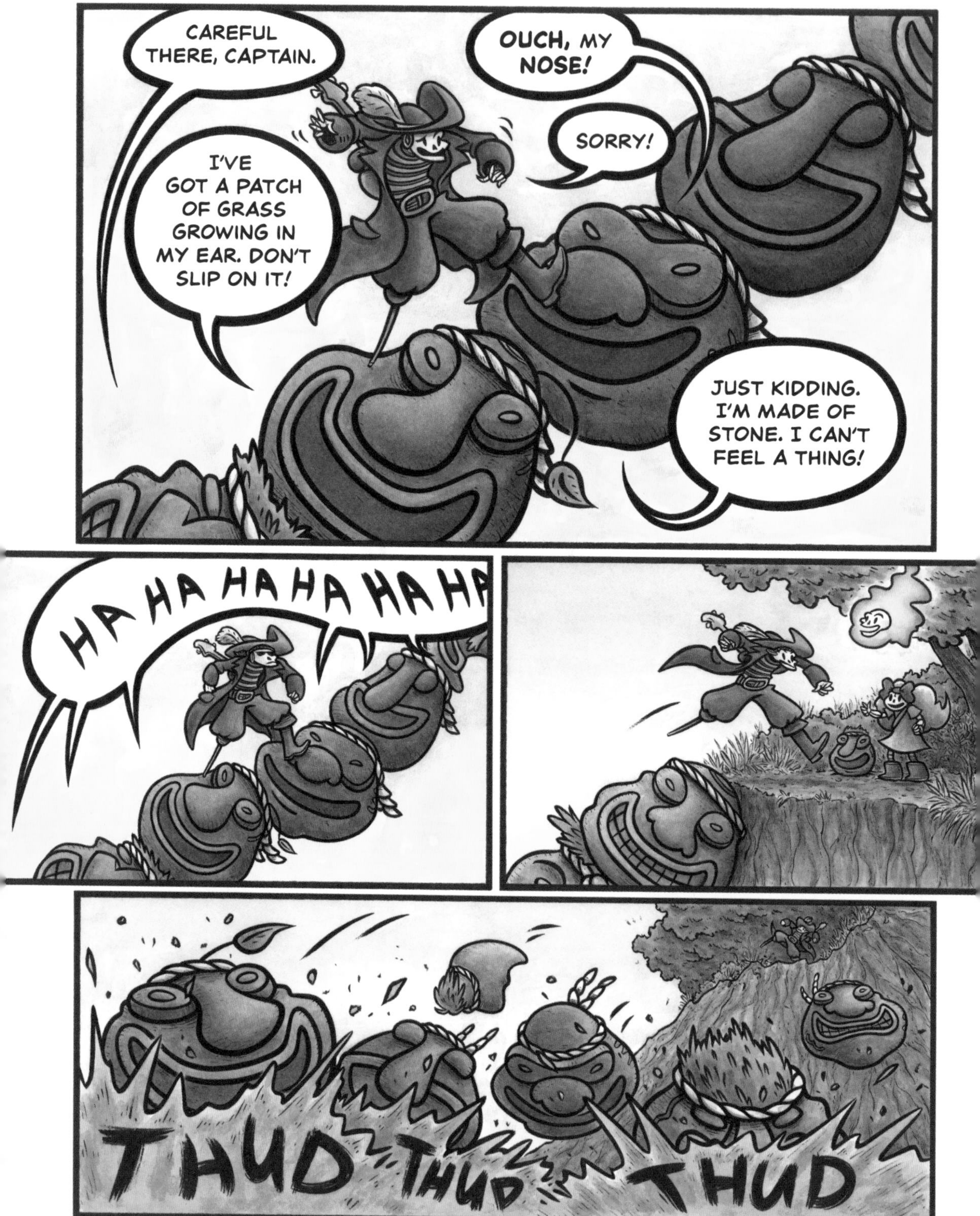
CAREFUL THERE, CAPTAIN.
OUCH, MY NOSE!
SORRY!
I'VE GOT A PATCH OF GRASS GROWING IN MY EAR. DON'T SLIP ON IT!
JUST KIDDING. I'M MADE OF STONE. I CAN'T FEEL A THING!
HA HA HA HA HA HA HA
THUD THUD THUD

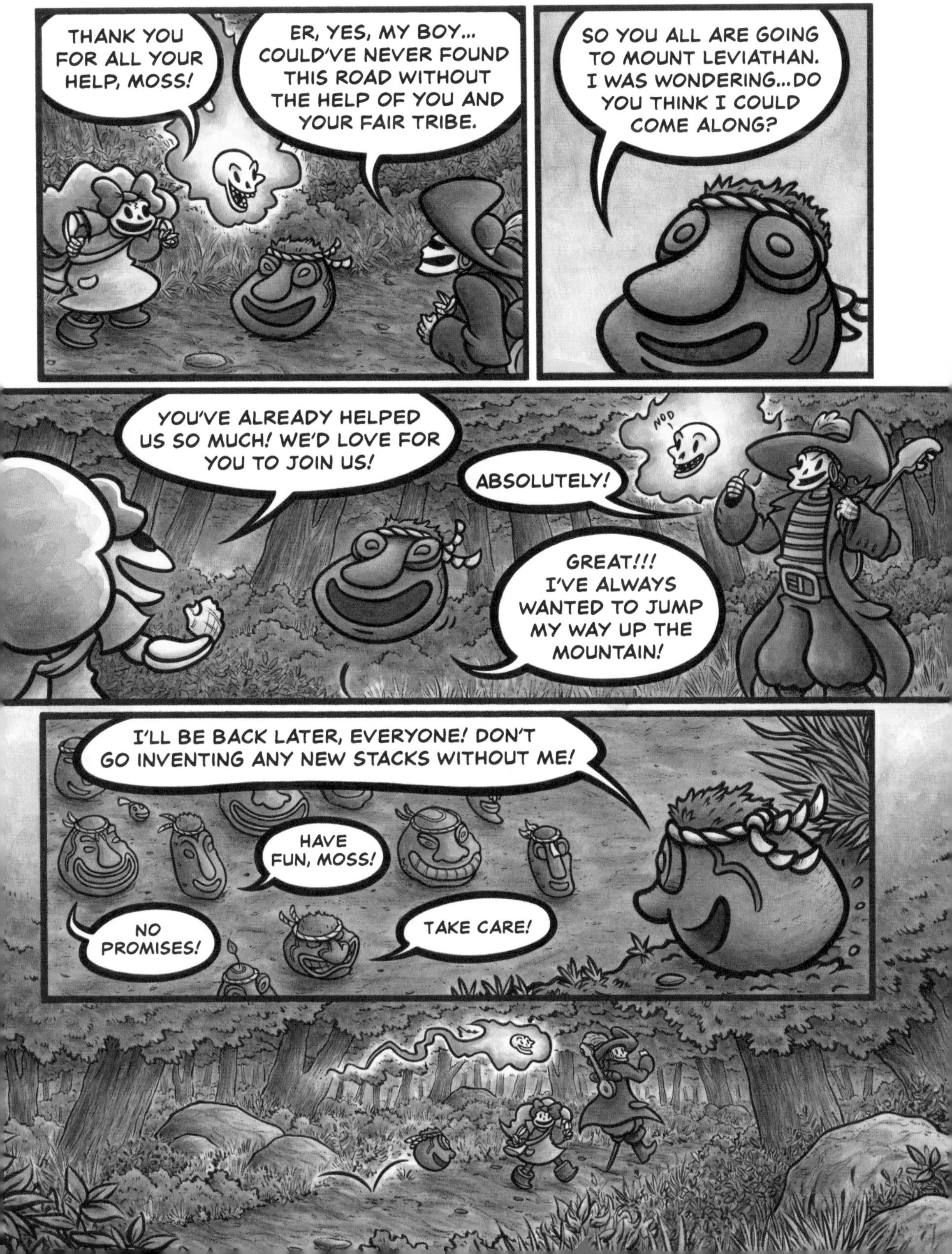
THANK YOU FOR ALL YOUR HELP, MOSS!
ER, YES, MY BOY... COULD'VE NEVER FOUND THIS ROAD WITHOUT THE HELP OF YOU AND YOUR FAIR TRIBE.
SO YOU ALL ARE GOING TO MOUNT LEVIATHAN. I WAS WONDERING...DO YOU THINK I COULD COME ALONG?
YOU'VE ALREADY HELPED US SO MUCH! WE'D LOVE FOR YOU TO JOIN US!
NOD
ABSOLUTELY!
GREAT!!! I'VE ALWAYS WANTED TO JUMP MY WAY UP THE MOUNTAIN!
I'LL BE BACK LATER, EVERYONE! DON'T GO INVENTING ANY NEW STACKS WITHOUT ME!
HAVE FUN, MOSS!
NO PROMISES!
TAKE CARE!

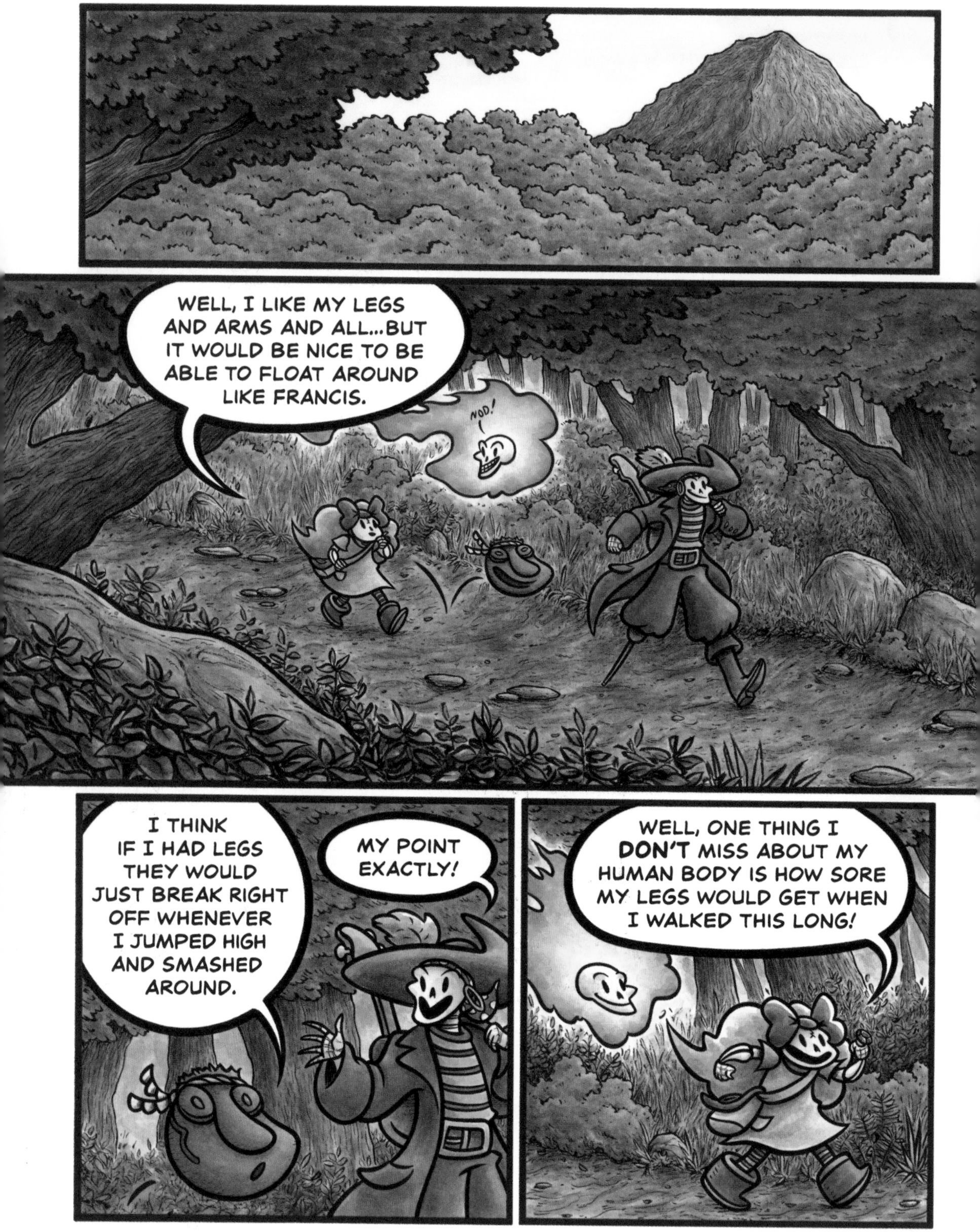
WELL, I LIKE MY LEGS AND ARMS AND ALL...BUT IT WOULD BE NICE TO BE ABLE TO FLOAT AROUND LIKE FRANCIS.
NOD!
I THINK IF I HAD LEGS THEY WOULD JUST BREAK RIGHT OFF WHENEVER I JUMPED HIGH AND SMASHED AROUND.
MY POINT EXACTLY!
WELL, ONE THING I **DON'T** MISS ABOUT MY HUMAN BODY IS HOW SORE MY LEGS WOULD GET WHEN I WALKED THIS LONG!

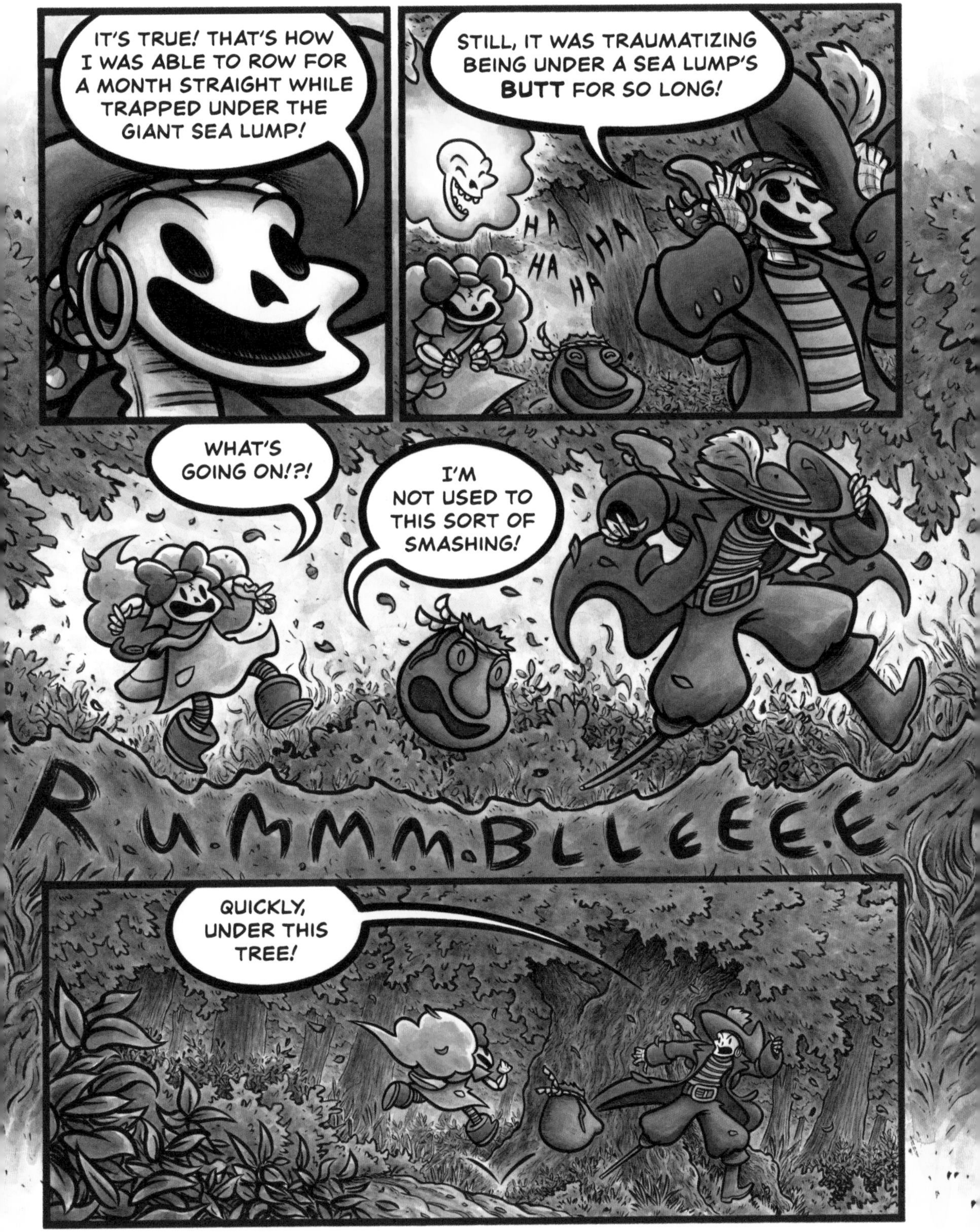
IT'S TRUE! THAT'S HOW I WAS ABLE TO ROW FOR A MONTH STRAIGHT WHILE TRAPPED UNDER THE GIANT SEA LUMP!
STILL, IT WAS TRAUMATIZING BEING UNDER A SEA LUMP'S **BUTT** FOR SO LONG!
HA HA HA HA
WHAT'S GOING ON!?!
I'M NOT USED TO THIS SORT OF SMASHING!
RUMMMBLLEEEE
QUICKLY, UNDER THIS TREE!

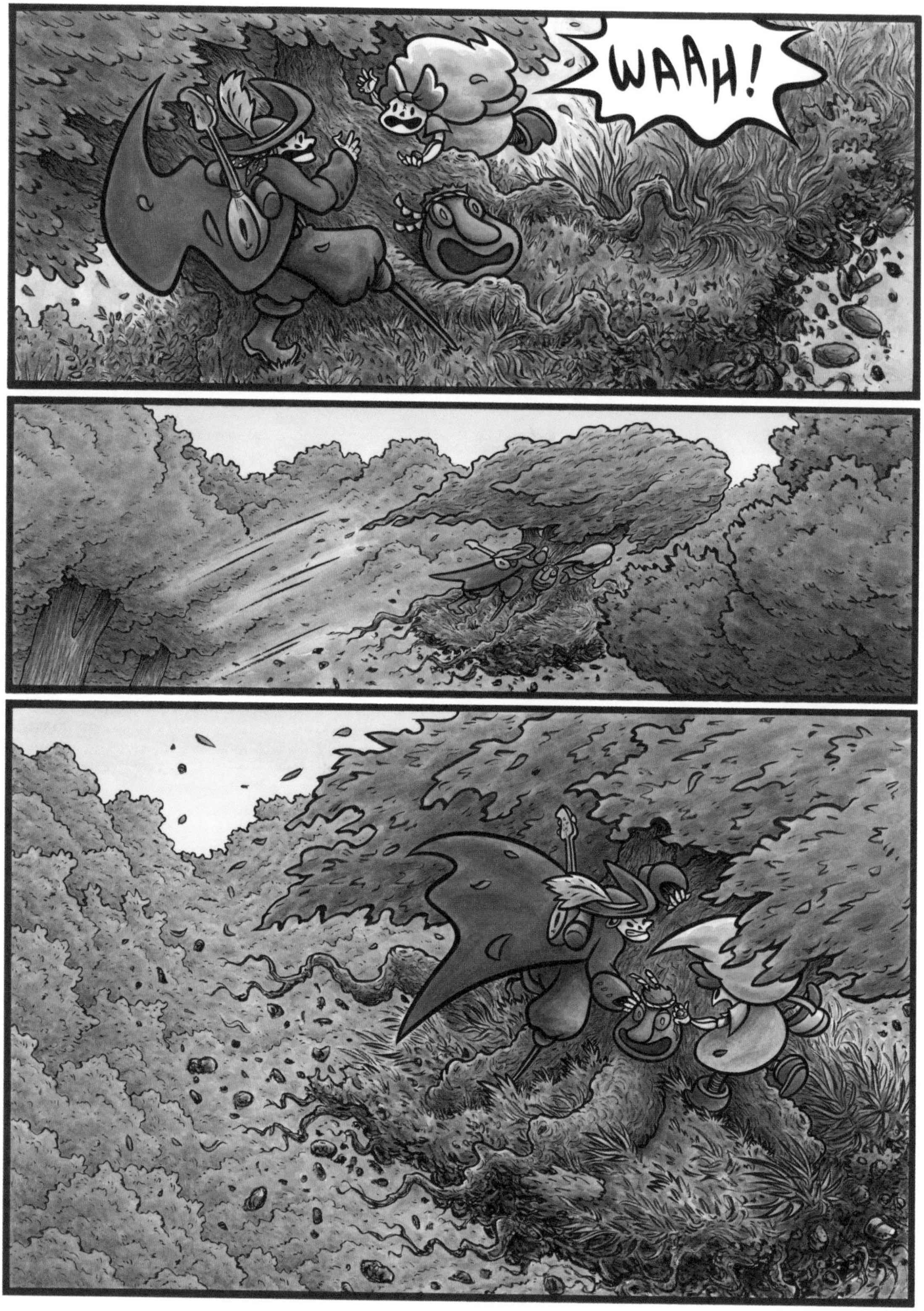
WAAH!

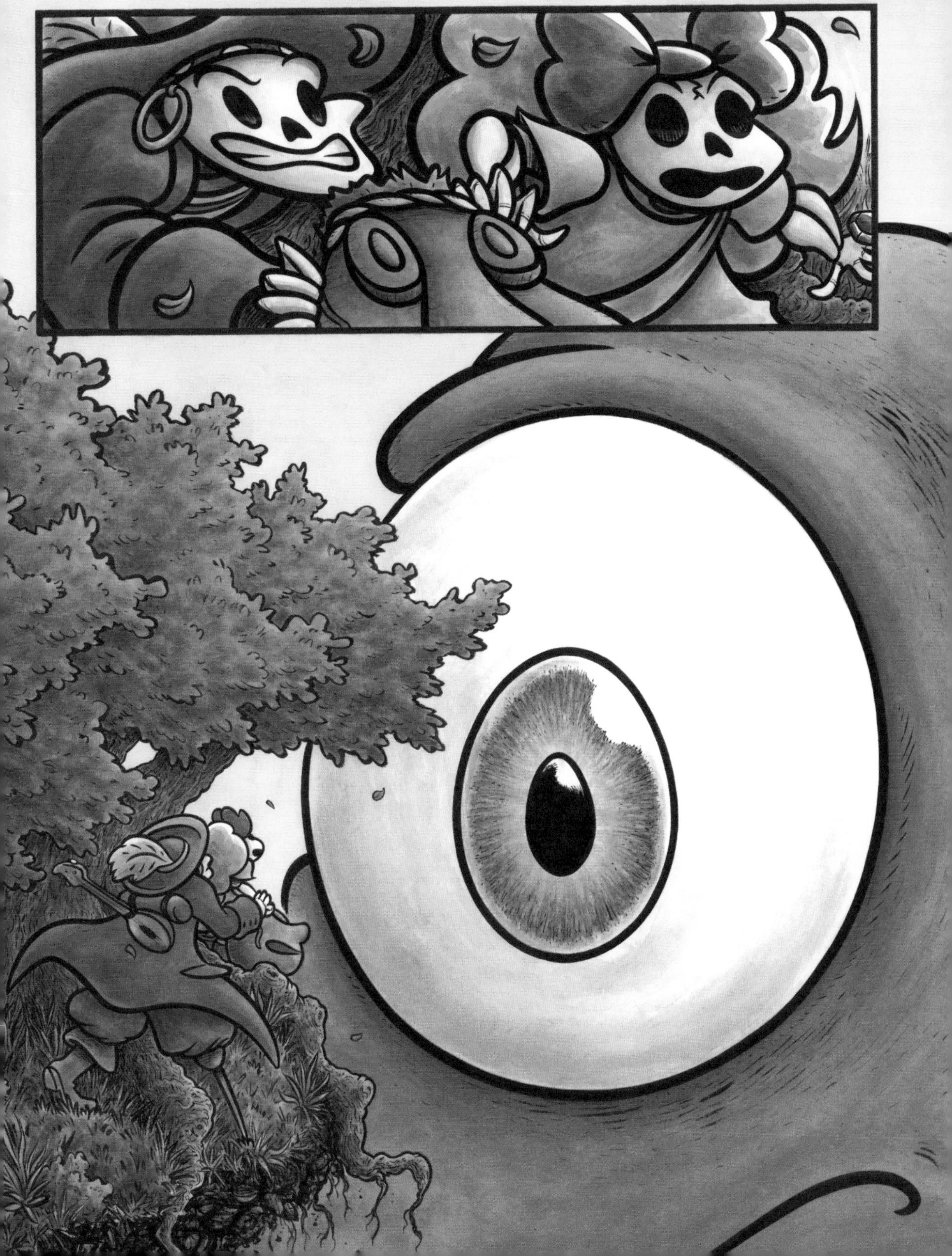

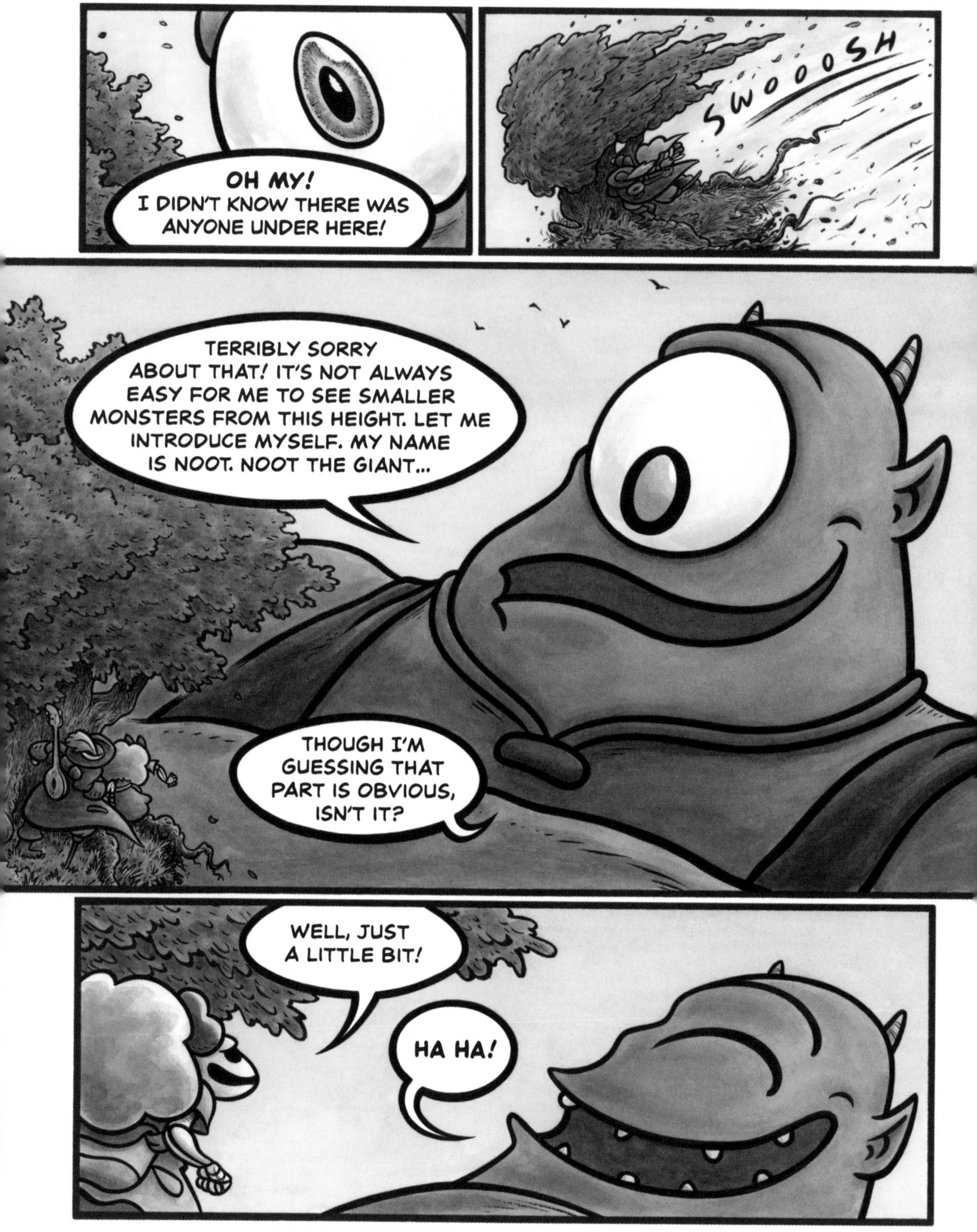
OH MY! I DIDN'T KNOW THERE WAS ANYONE UNDER HERE!
SWOOOSH
TERRIBLY SORRY ABOUT THAT! IT'S NOT ALWAYS EASY FOR ME TO SEE SMALLER MONSTERS FROM THIS HEIGHT. LET ME INTRODUCE MYSELF. MY NAME IS NOOT. NOOT THE GIANT...
THOUGH I'M GUESSING THAT PART IS OBVIOUS, ISN'T IT?
WELL, JUST A LITTLE BIT!
HA HA!

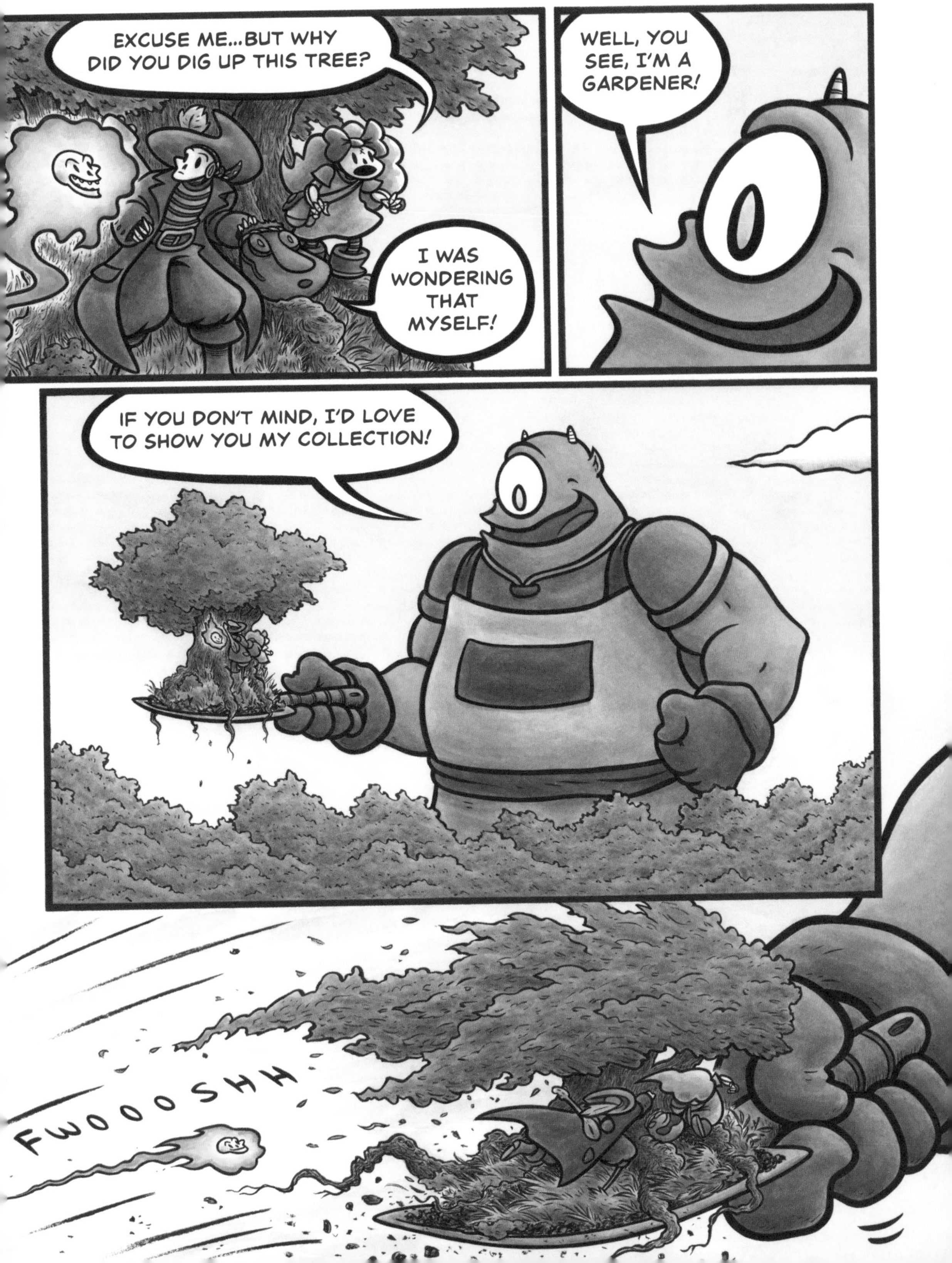
EXCUSE ME...BUT WHY DID YOU DIG UP THIS TREE?
I WAS WONDERING THAT MYSELF!
WELL, YOU SEE, I'M A GARDENER!
IF YOU DON'T MIND, I'D LOVE TO SHOW YOU MY COLLECTION!
FWOOOOSHH

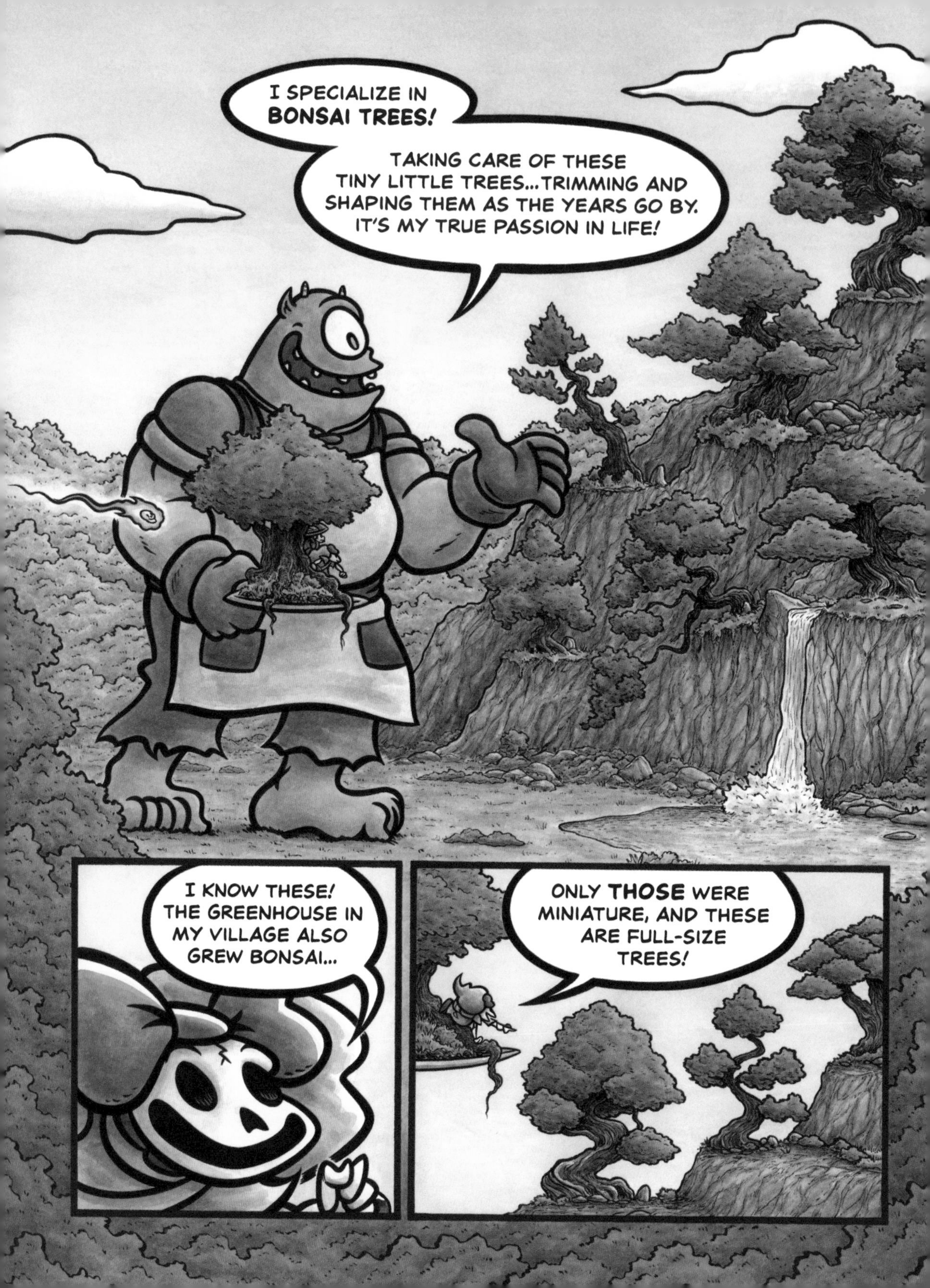
I SPECIALIZE IN BONSAI TREES!
TAKING CARE OF THESE TINY LITTLE TREES...TRIMMING AND SHAPING THEM AS THE YEARS GO BY. IT'S MY TRUE PASSION IN LIFE!
I KNOW THESE! THE GREENHOUSE IN MY VILLAGE ALSO GREW BONSAI...
ONLY THOSE WERE MINIATURE, AND THESE ARE FULL-SIZE TREES!

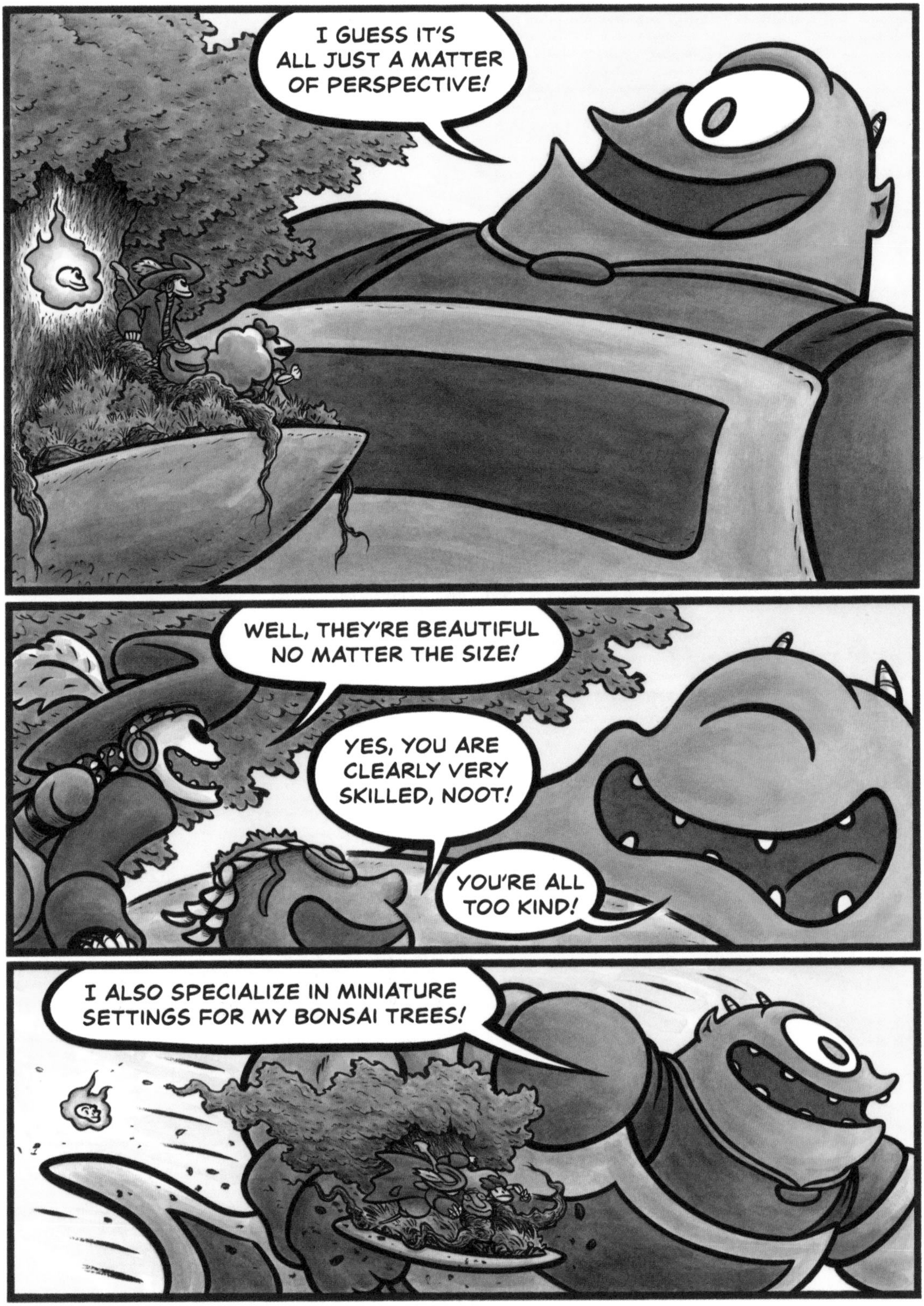
I GUESS IT'S ALL JUST A MATTER OF PERSPECTIVE!
WELL, THEY'RE BEAUTIFUL NO MATTER THE SIZE!
YES, YOU ARE CLEARLY VERY SKILLED, NOOT!
YOU'RE ALL TOO KIND!
I ALSO SPECIALIZE IN MINIATURE SETTINGS FOR MY BONSAI TREES!

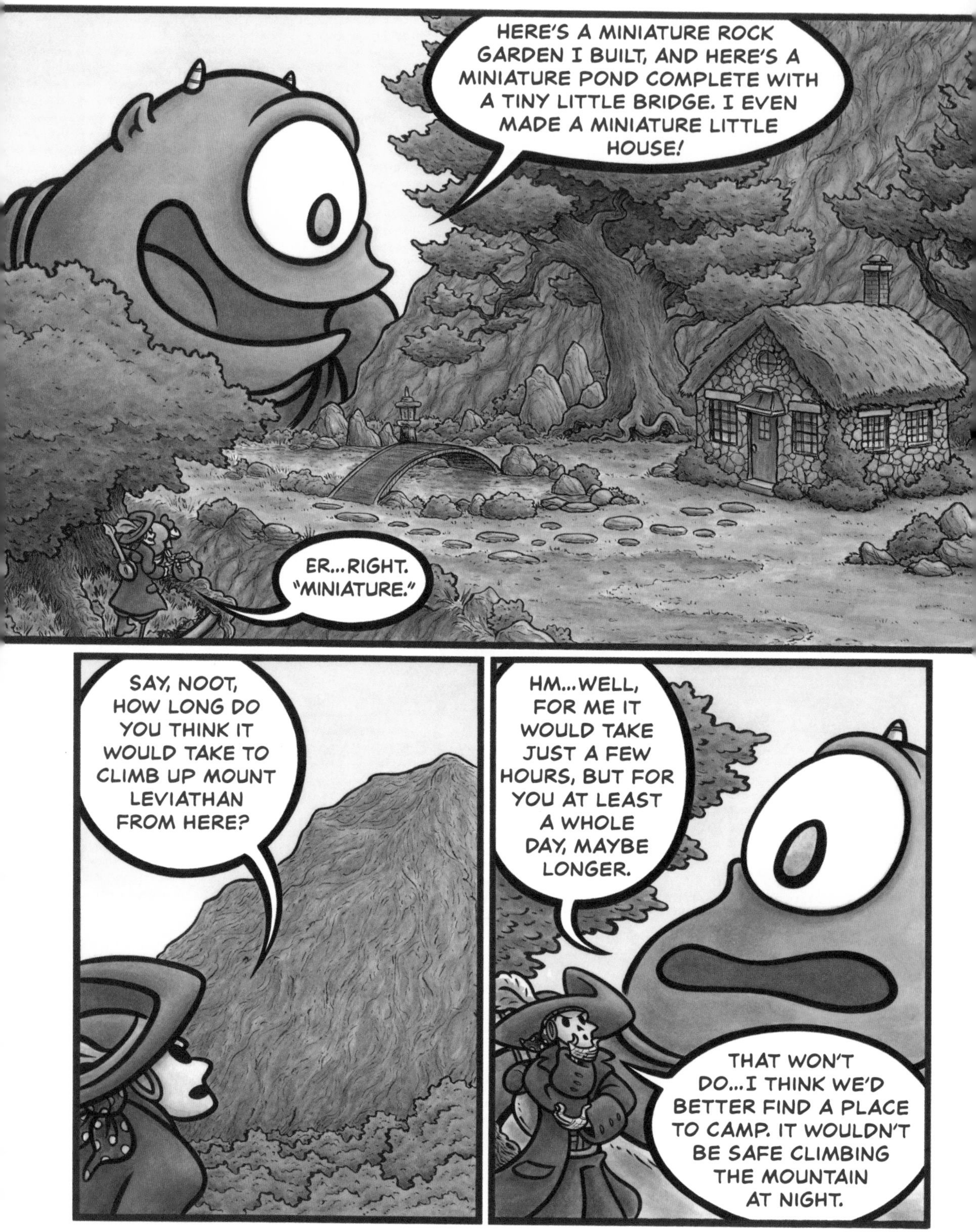
HERE'S A MINIATURE ROCK GARDEN I BUILT, AND HERE'S A MINIATURE POND COMPLETE WITH A TINY LITTLE BRIDGE. I EVEN MADE A MINIATURE LITTLE HOUSE!
ER...RIGHT. "MINIATURE."
SAY, NOOT, HOW LONG DO YOU THINK IT WOULD TAKE TO CLIMB UP MOUNT LEVIATHAN FROM HERE?
HM...WELL, FOR ME IT WOULD TAKE JUST A FEW HOURS, BUT FOR YOU AT LEAST A WHOLE DAY, MAYBE LONGER.
THAT WON'T DO...I THINK WE'D BETTER FIND A PLACE TO CAMP. IT WOULDN'T BE SAFE CLIMBING THE MOUNTAIN AT NIGHT.

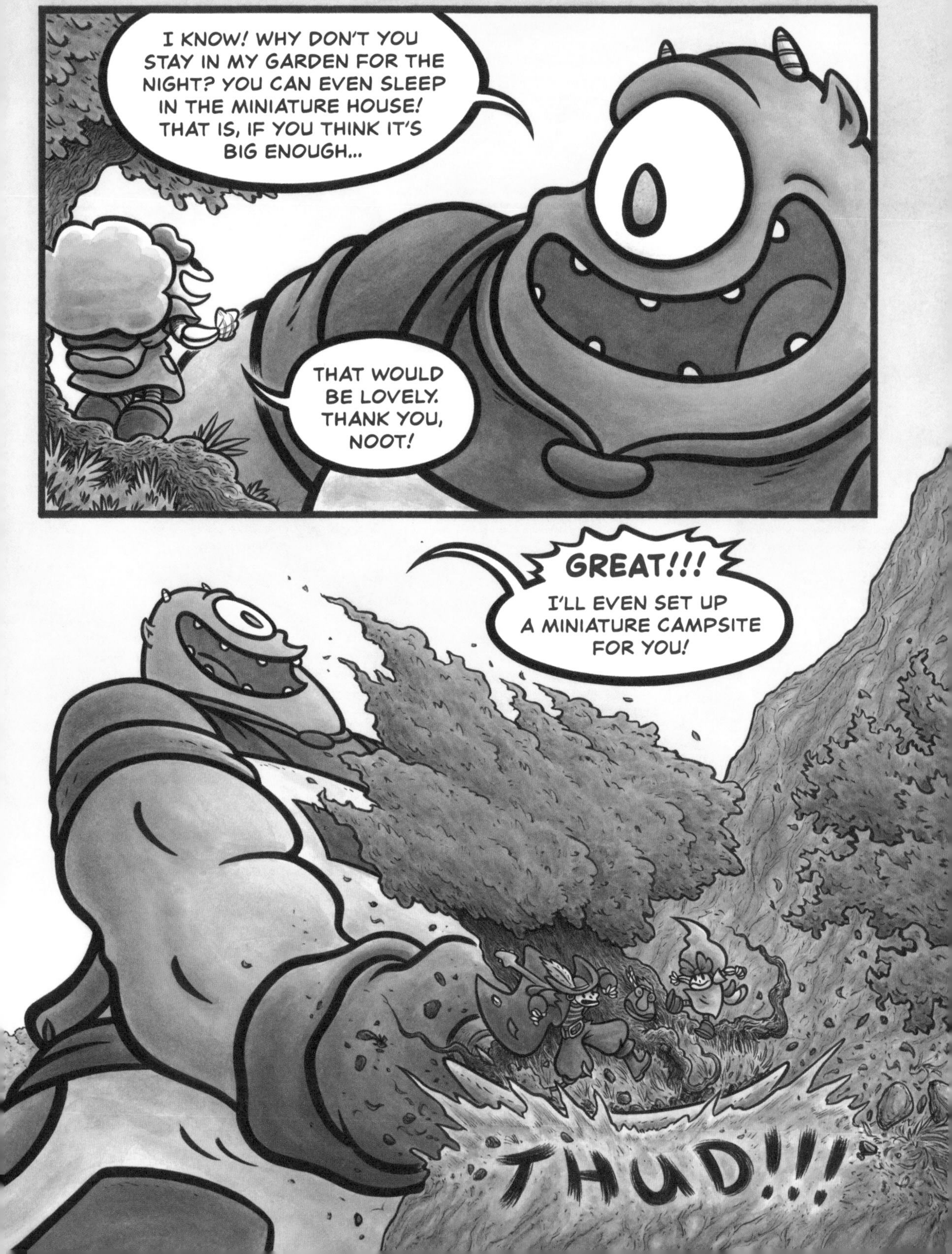
I KNOW! WHY DON'T YOU STAY IN MY GARDEN FOR THE NIGHT? YOU CAN EVEN SLEEP IN THE MINIATURE HOUSE! THAT IS, IF YOU THINK IT'S BIG ENOUGH...
THAT WOULD BE LOVELY. THANK YOU, NOOT!
GREAT!!! I'LL EVEN SET UP A MINIATURE CAMPSITE FOR YOU!
THUD!!!

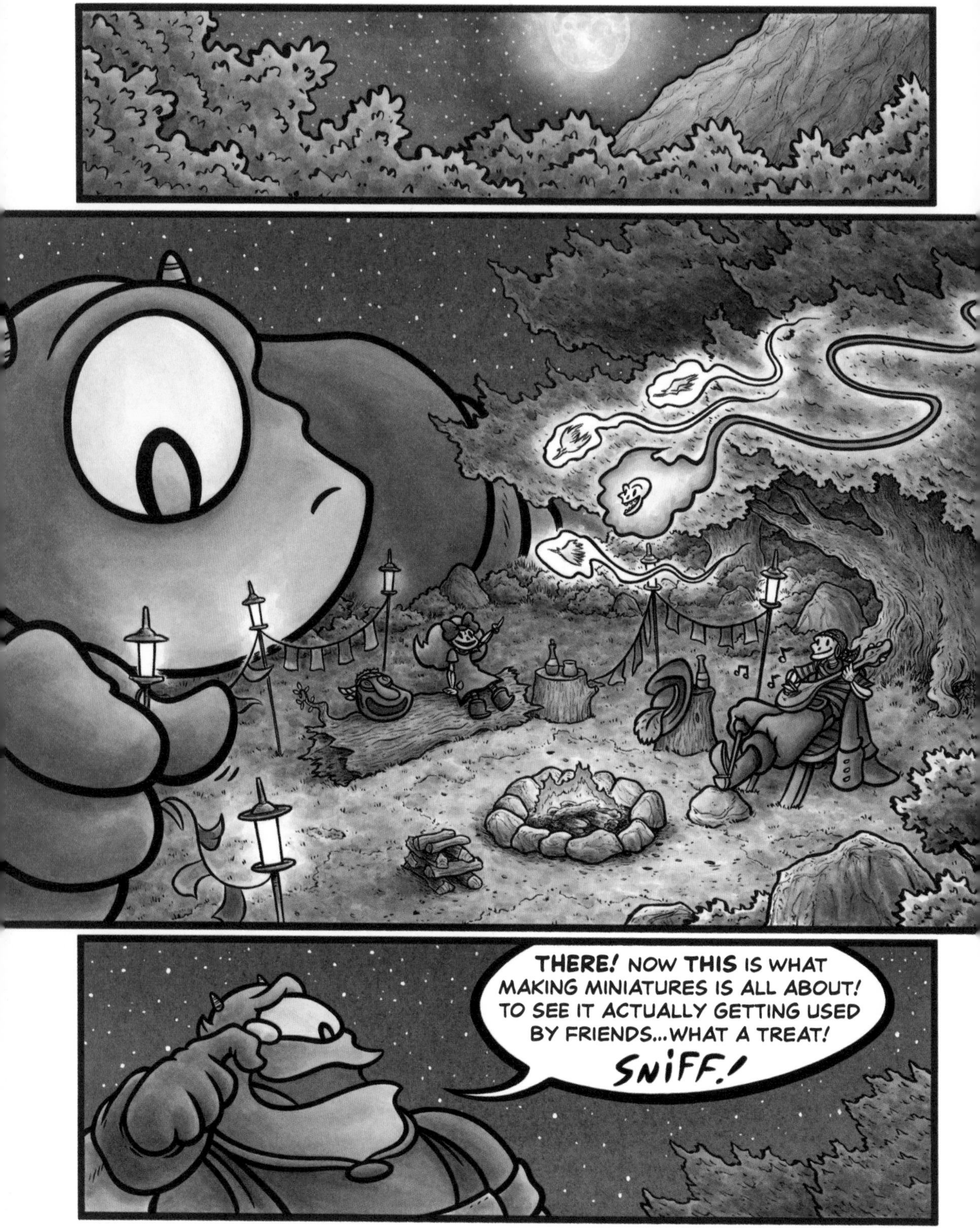
THERE! NOW THIS IS WHAT MAKING MINIATURES IS ALL ABOUT! TO SEE IT ACTUALLY GETTING USED BY FRIENDS...WHAT A TREAT!
SNIFF!

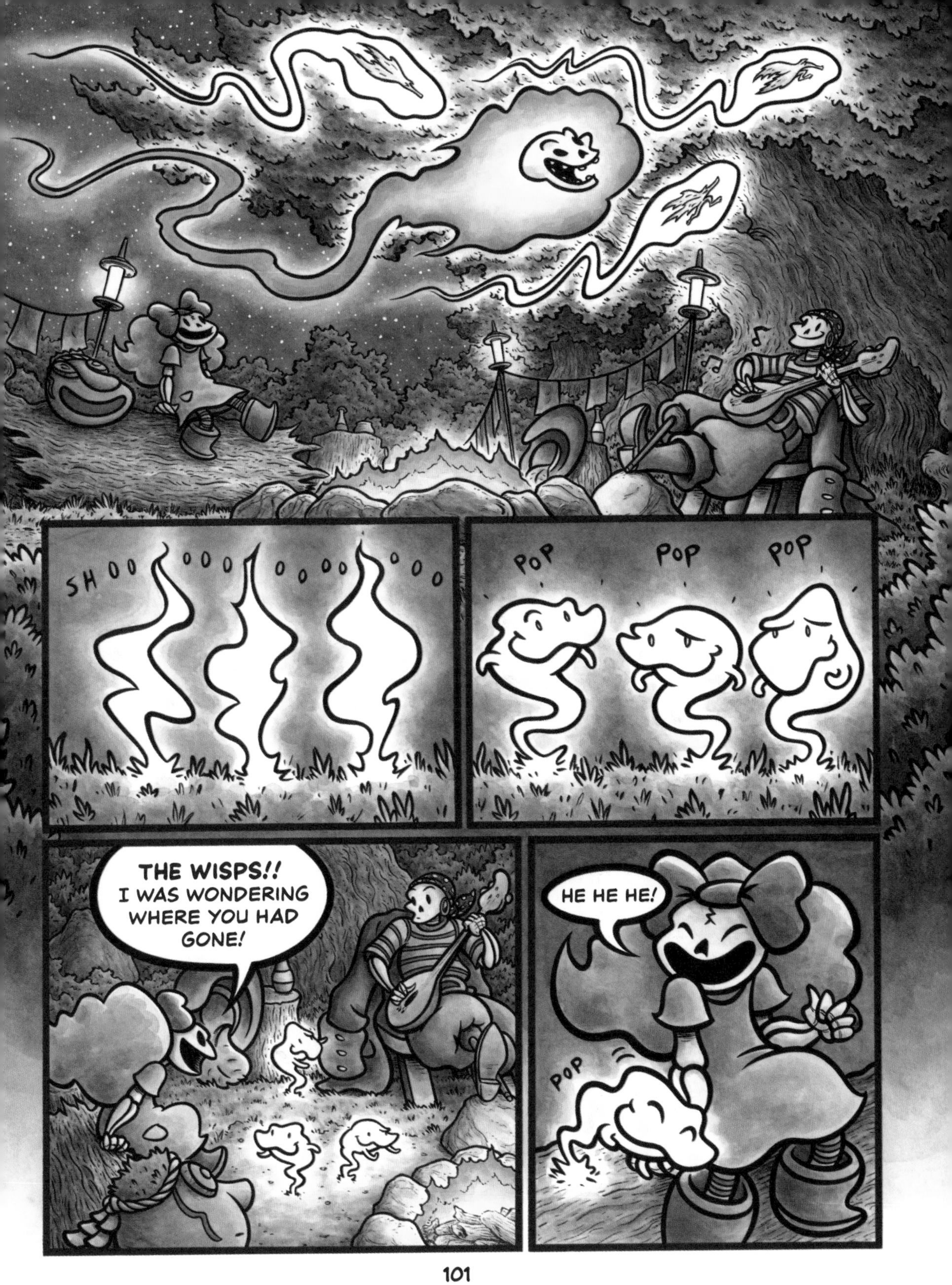

SHOOOOOOOOOOOOO
POP
POP
POP
THE WISPS!! I WAS WONDERING WHERE YOU HAD GONE!
HE HE HE!
POP

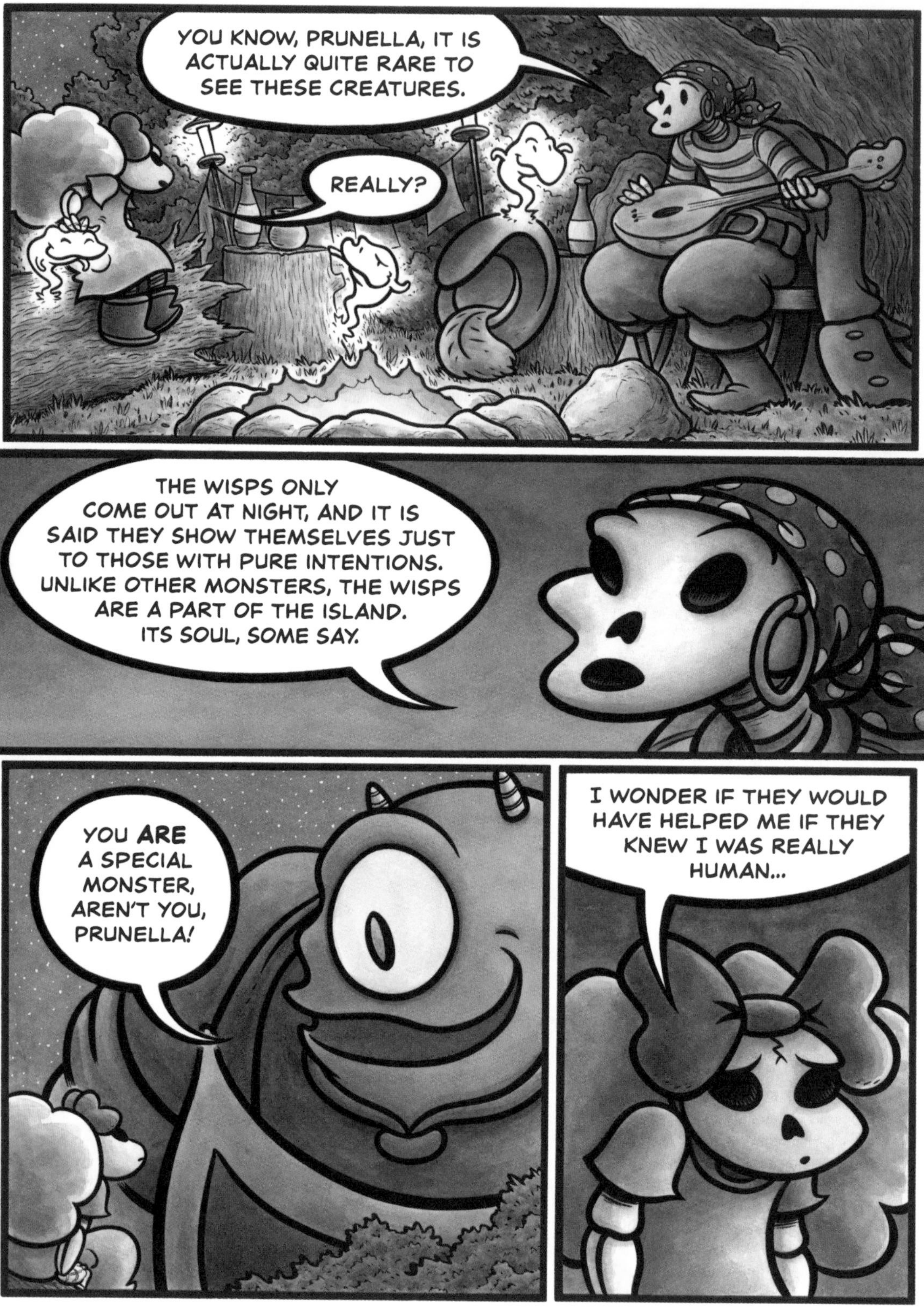
YOU KNOW, PRUNELLA, IT IS ACTUALLY QUITE RARE TO SEE THESE CREATURES.
REALLY?
THE WISPS ONLY COME OUT AT NIGHT, AND IT IS SAID THEY SHOW THEMSELVES JUST TO THOSE WITH PURE INTENTIONS. UNLIKE OTHER MONSTERS, THE WISPS ARE A PART OF THE ISLAND. ITS SOUL, SOME SAY.
YOU **ARE** A SPECIAL MONSTER, AREN'T YOU, PRUNELLA!
I WONDER IF THEY WOULD HAVE HELPED ME IF THEY KNEW I WAS REALLY HUMAN...

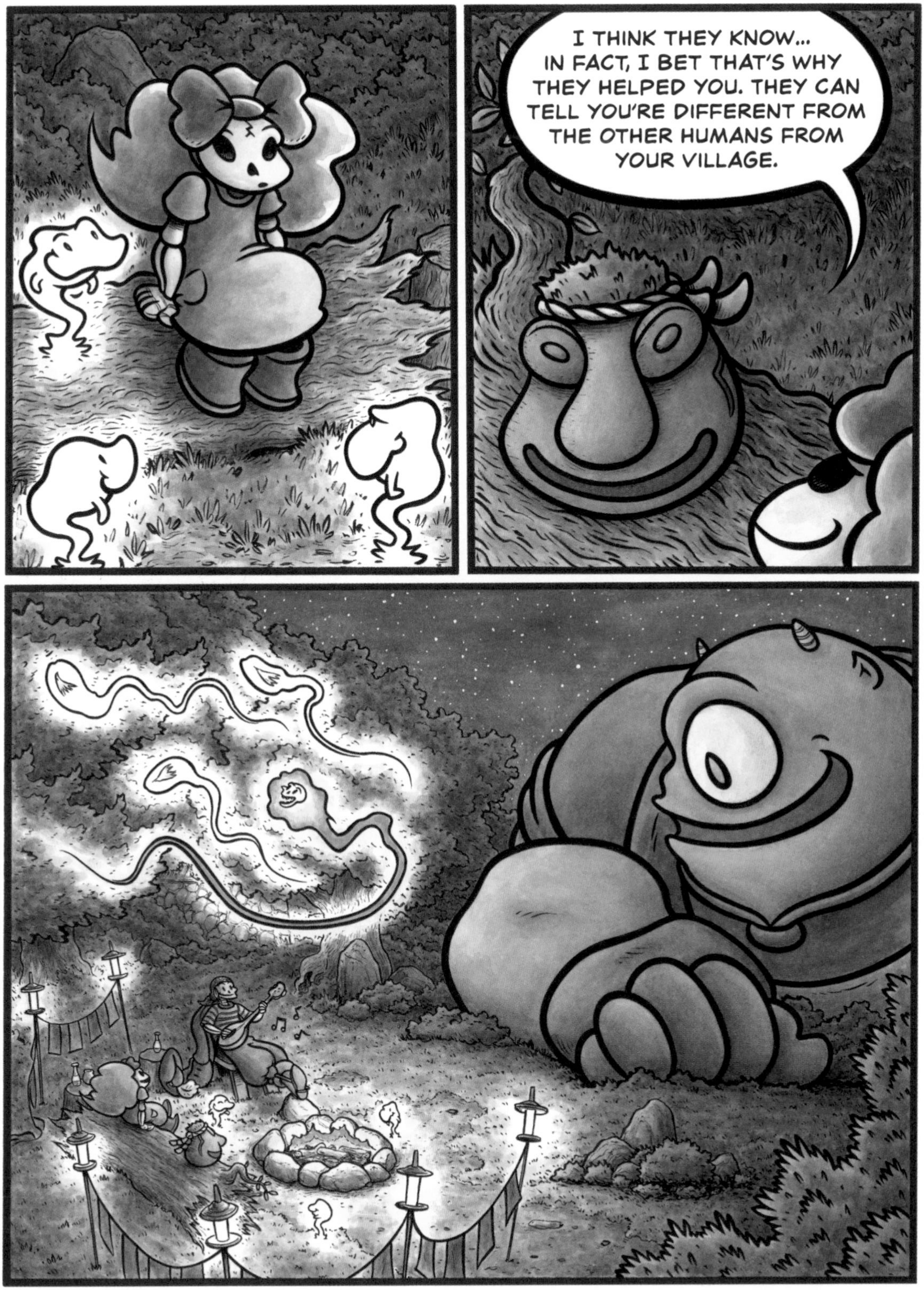
I THINK THEY KNOW... IN FACT, I BET THAT'S WHY THEY HELPED YOU. THEY CAN TELL YOU'RE DIFFERENT FROM THE OTHER HUMANS FROM YOUR VILLAGE.

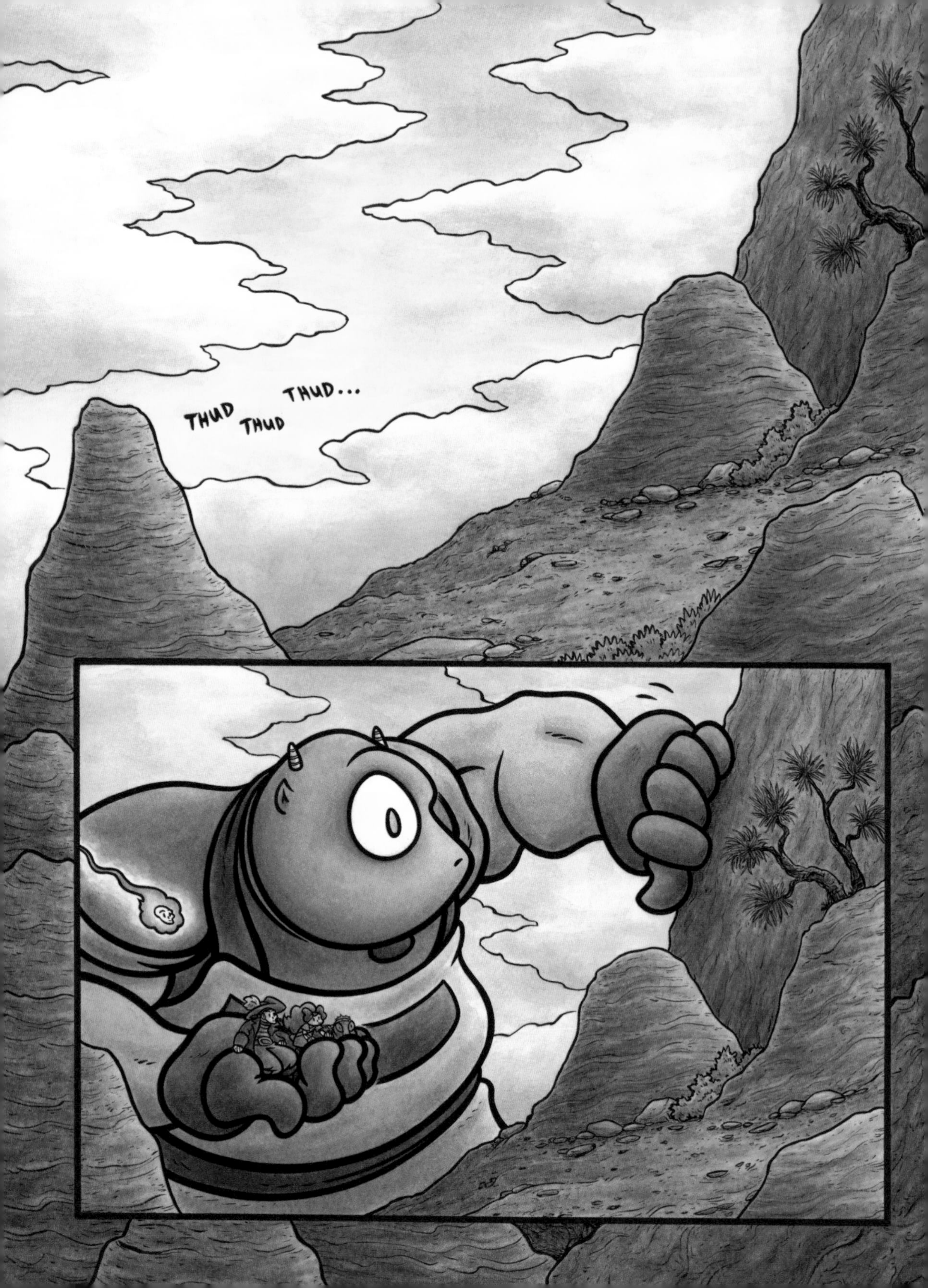
THUD
THUD
THUD...

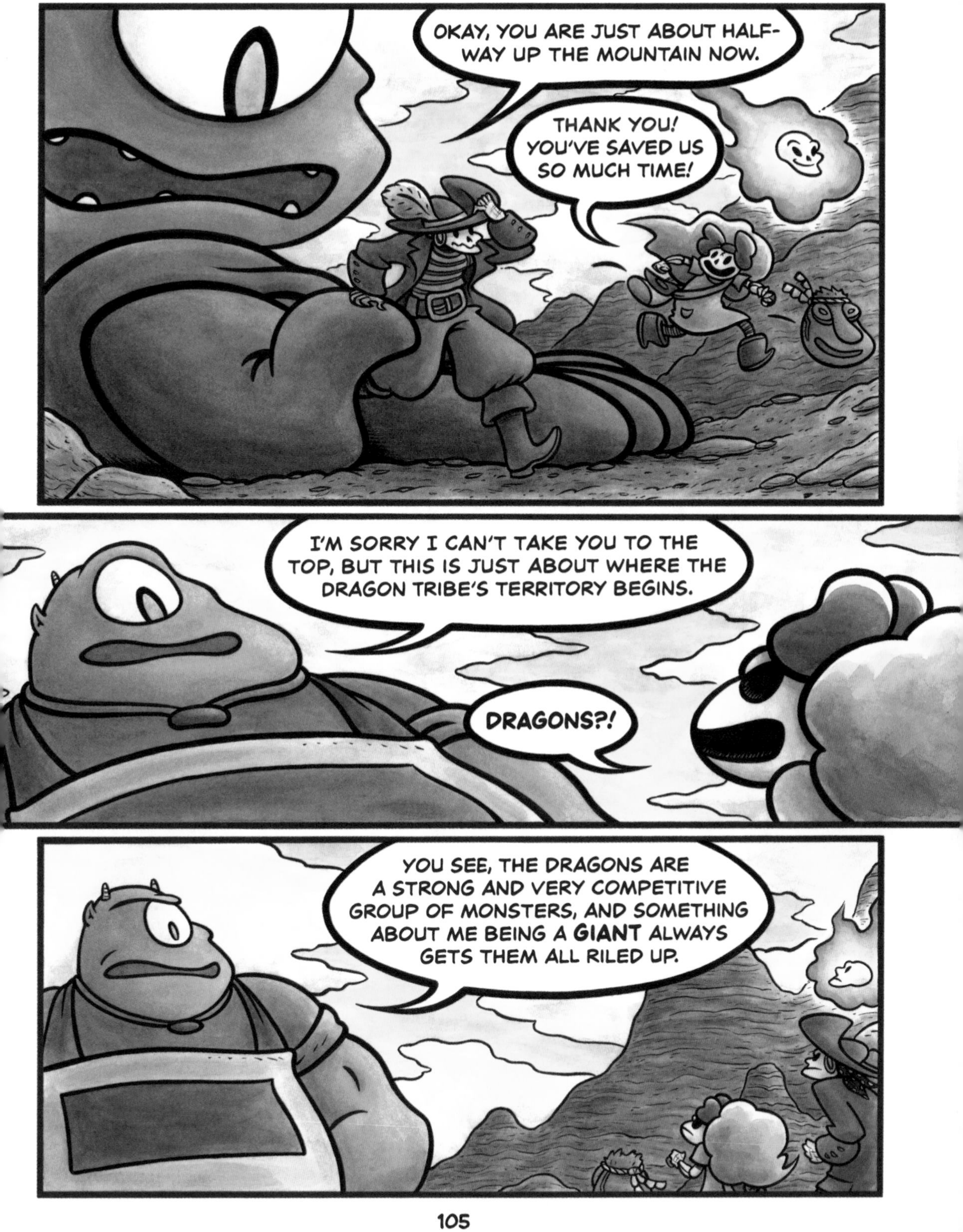
OKAY, YOU ARE JUST ABOUT HALF-WAY UP THE MOUNTAIN NOW.
THANK YOU! YOU'VE SAVED US SO MUCH TIME!
I'M SORRY I CAN'T TAKE YOU TO THE TOP, BUT THIS IS JUST ABOUT WHERE THE DRAGON TRIBE'S TERRITORY BEGINS.
DRAGONS?!
YOU SEE, THE DRAGONS ARE A STRONG AND VERY COMPETITIVE GROUP OF MONSTERS, AND SOMETHING ABOUT ME BEING A GIANT ALWAYS GETS THEM ALL RILED UP.

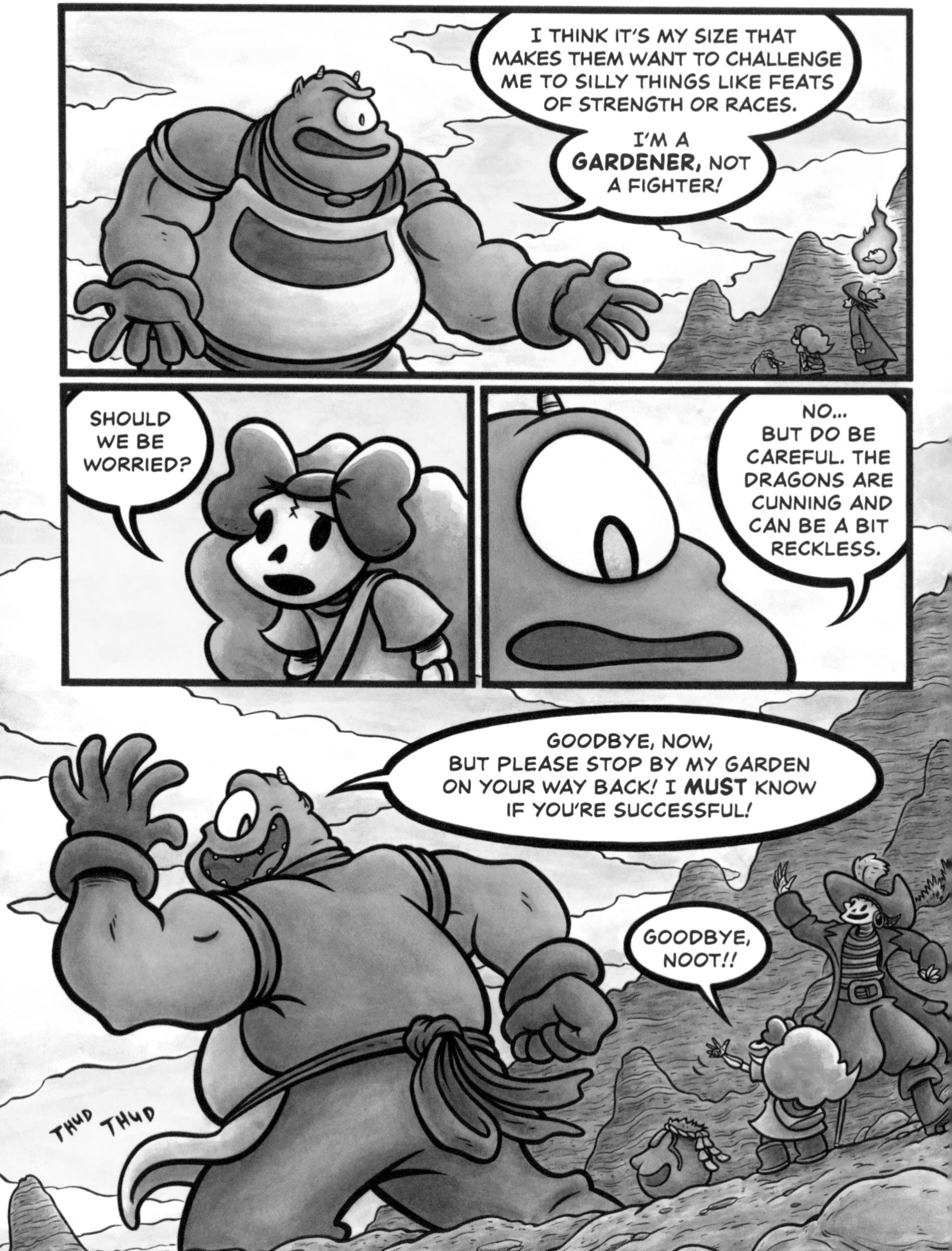
I THINK IT'S MY SIZE THAT MAKES THEM WANT TO CHALLENGE ME TO SILLY THINGS LIKE FEATS OF STRENGTH OR RACES.
I'M A GARDENER, NOT A FIGHTER!
SHOULD WE BE WORRIED?
NO... BUT DO BE CAREFUL. THE DRAGONS ARE CUNNING AND CAN BE A BIT RECKLESS.
GOODBYE, NOW, BUT PLEASE STOP BY MY GARDEN ON YOUR WAY BACK! I MUST KNOW IF YOU'RE SUCCESSFUL!
GOODBYE, NOOT!!
THUD THUD

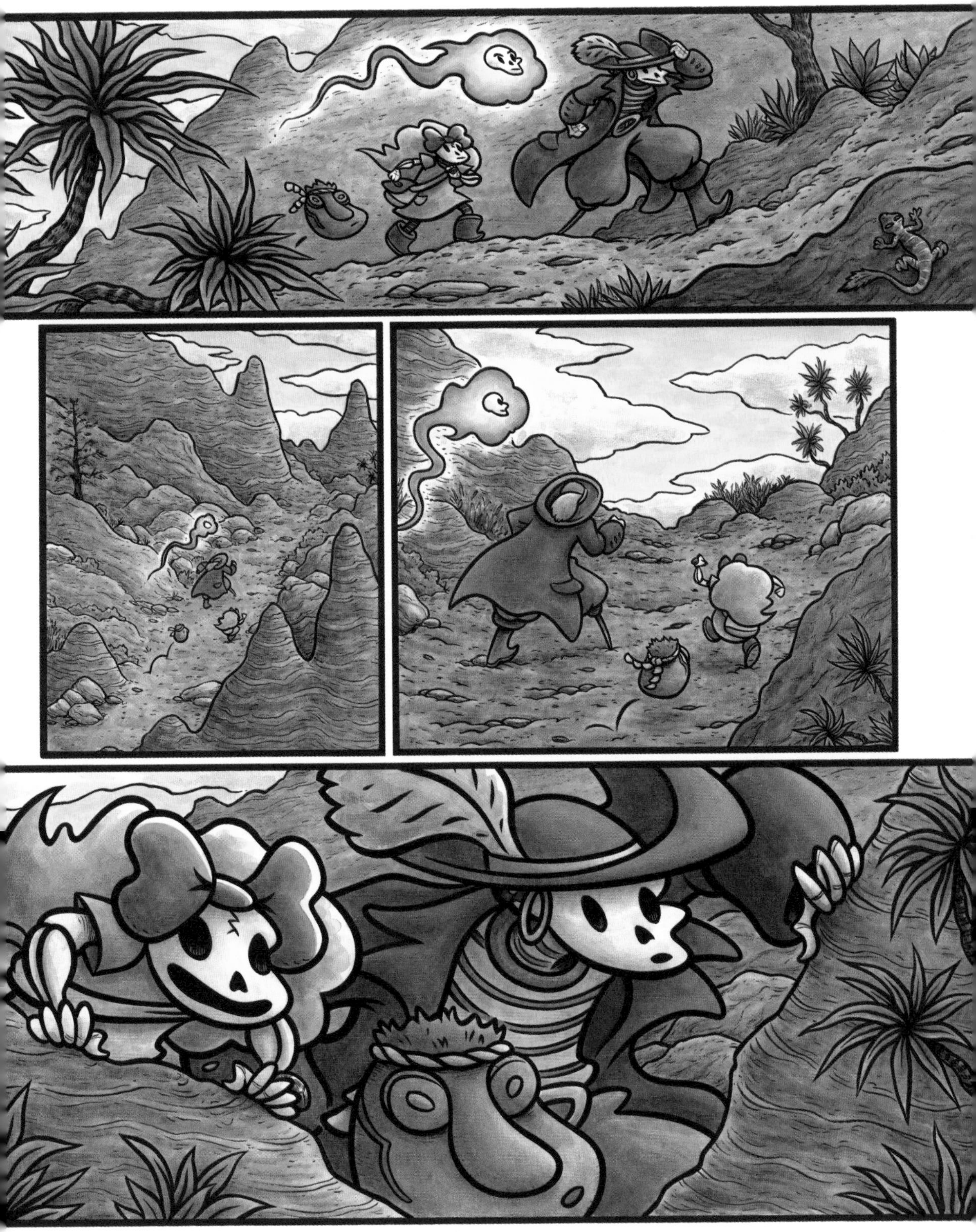

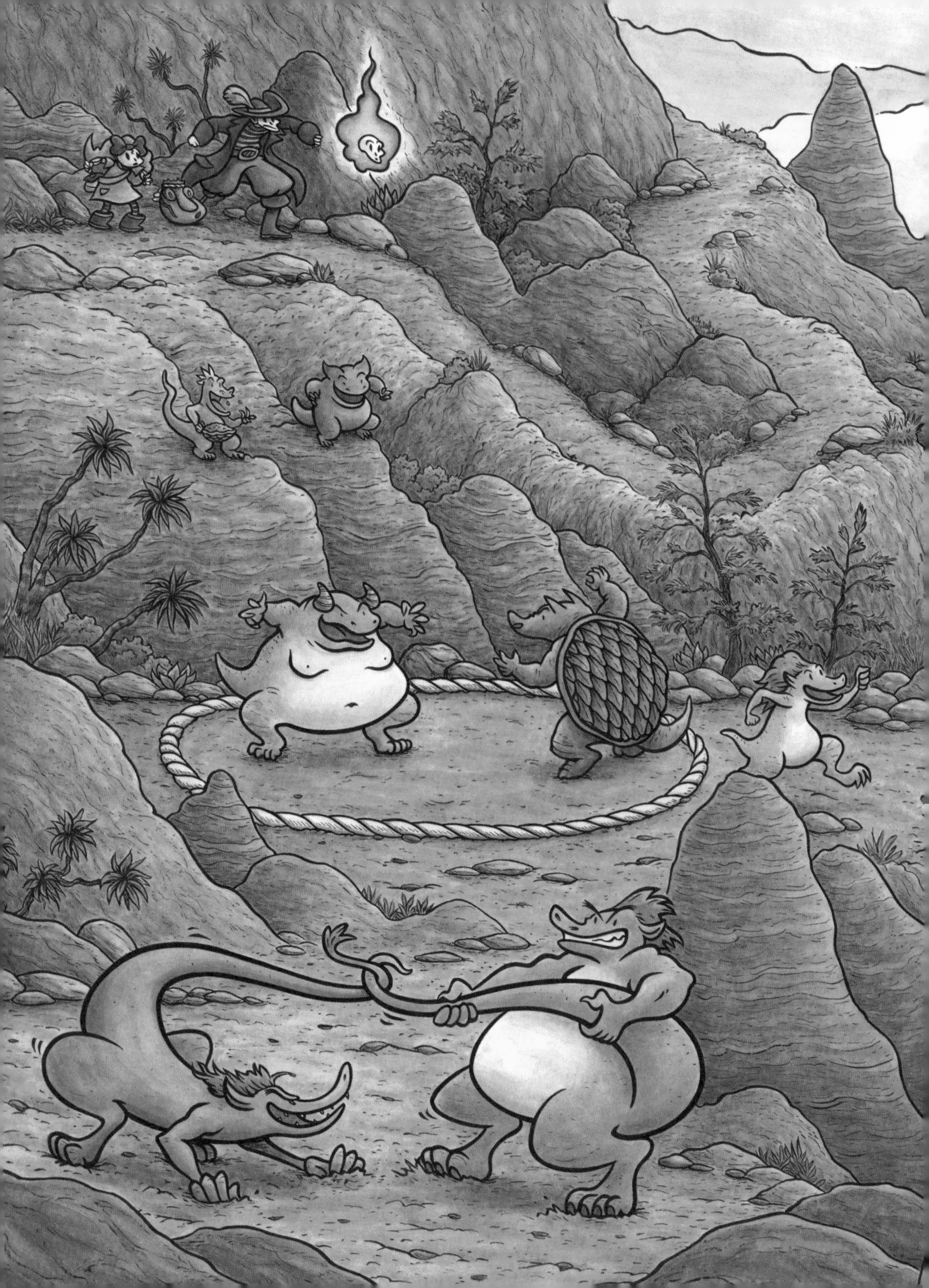

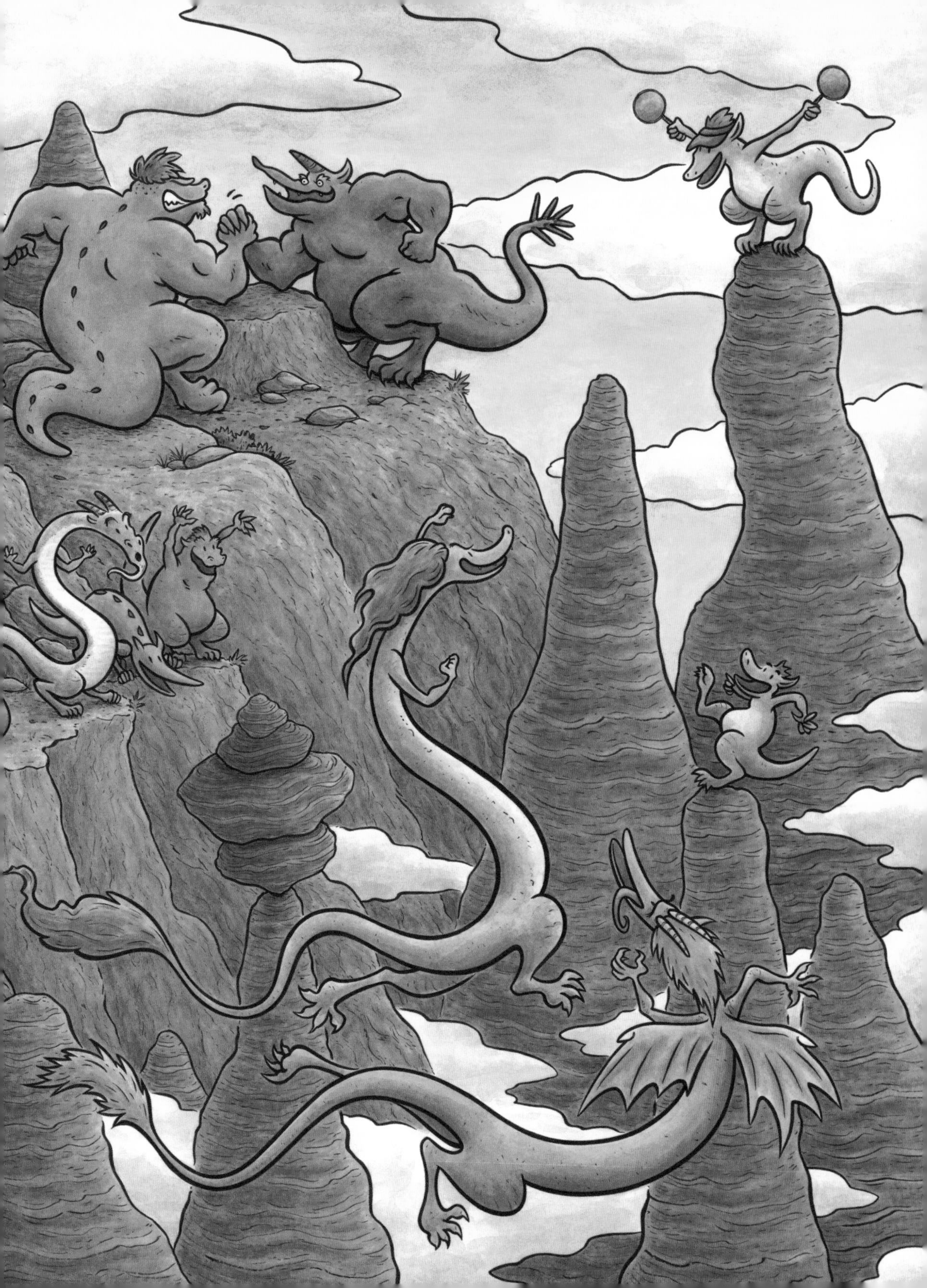

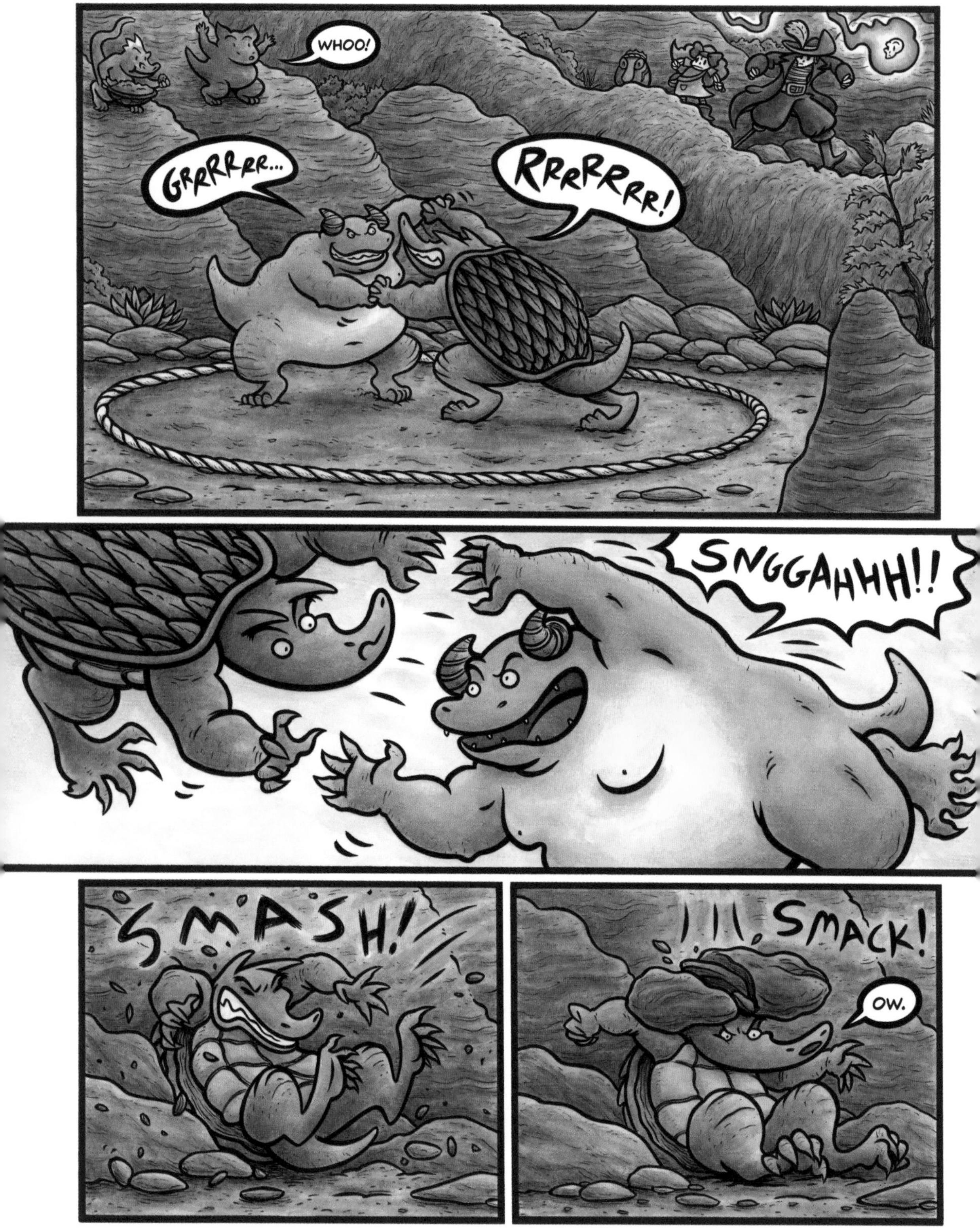
WHOO!
GRRRRRR...
RRRRRRRR!
SNGGAHHH!!
SMASH!
SMACK!
OW.

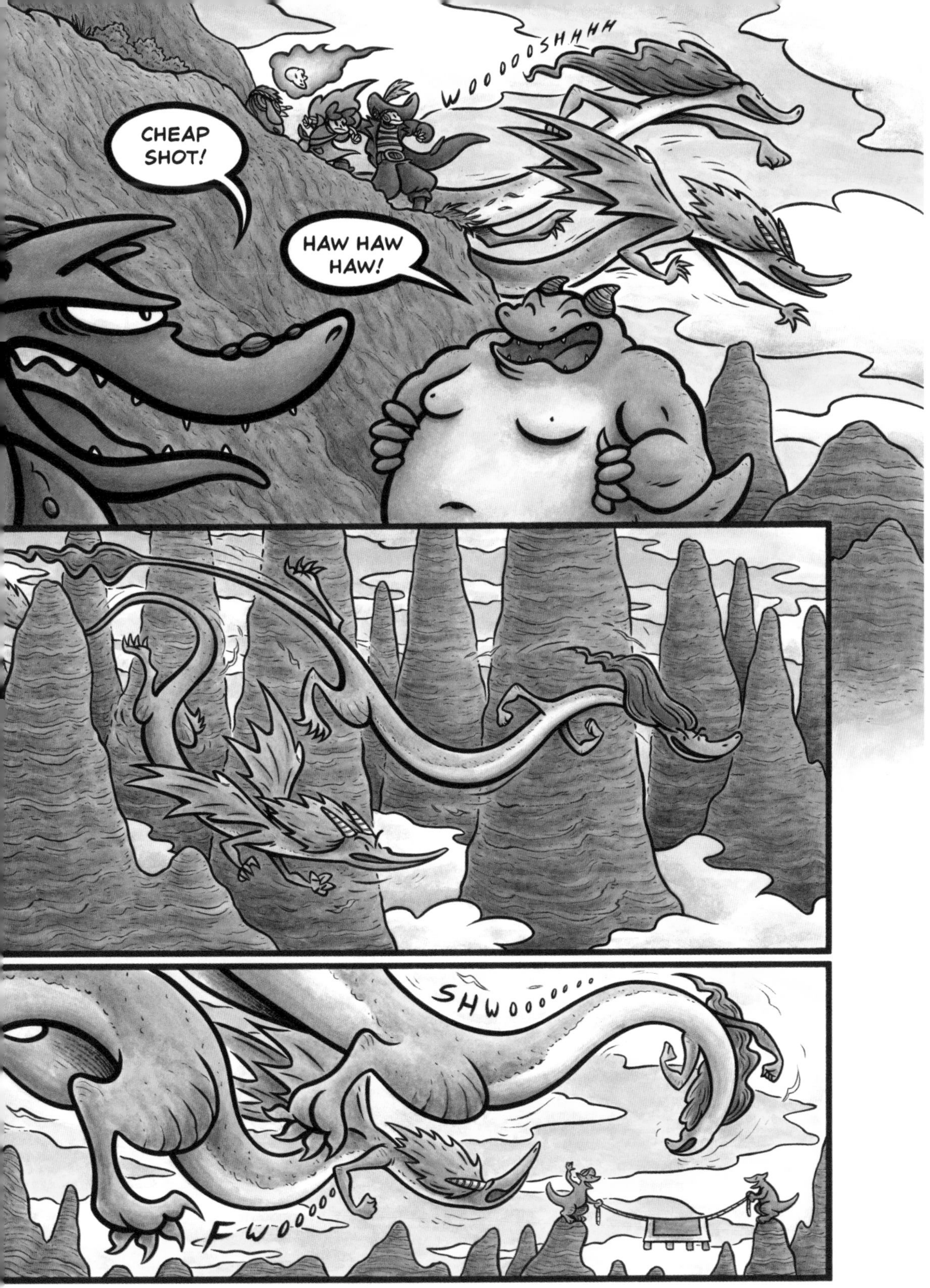

WOOOOOSHHHH
CHEAP SHOT!
HAW HAW HAW!
SHWOOOOOOO
FWOOOOO

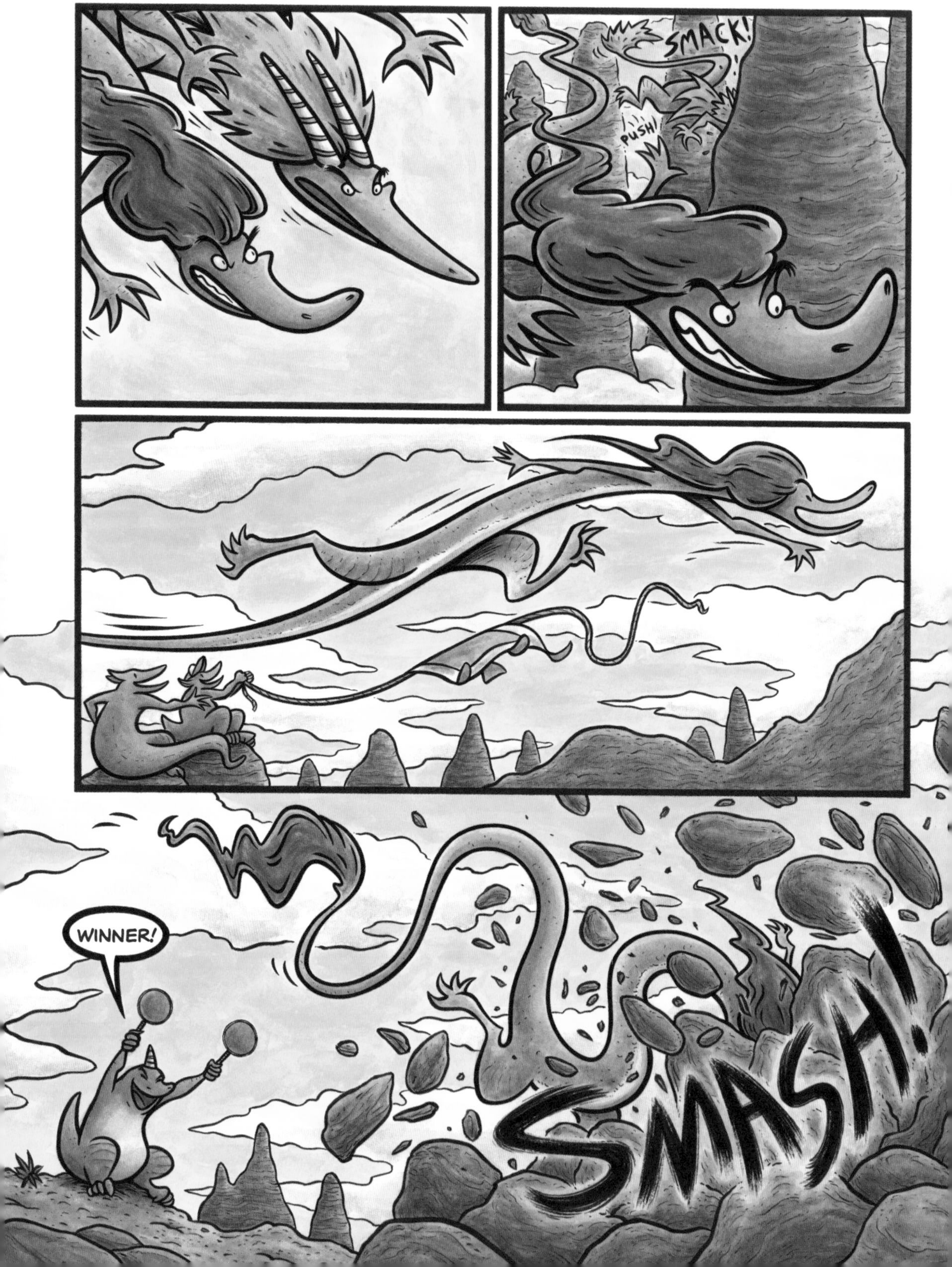
SMACK!
PUSH!
WINNER!
SMASH!

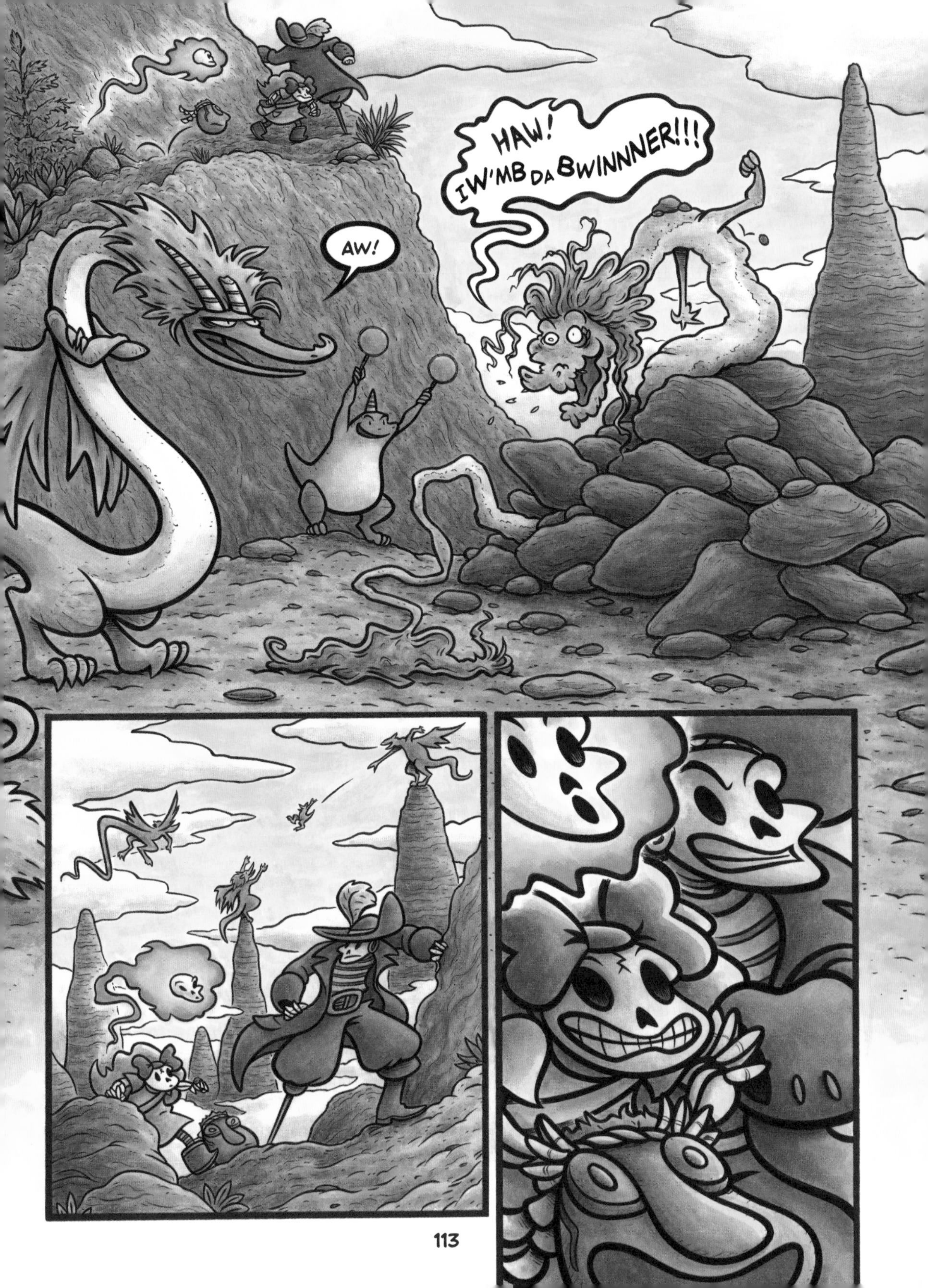
AW!
HAW!
IW'MB DA BWINNNER!!!

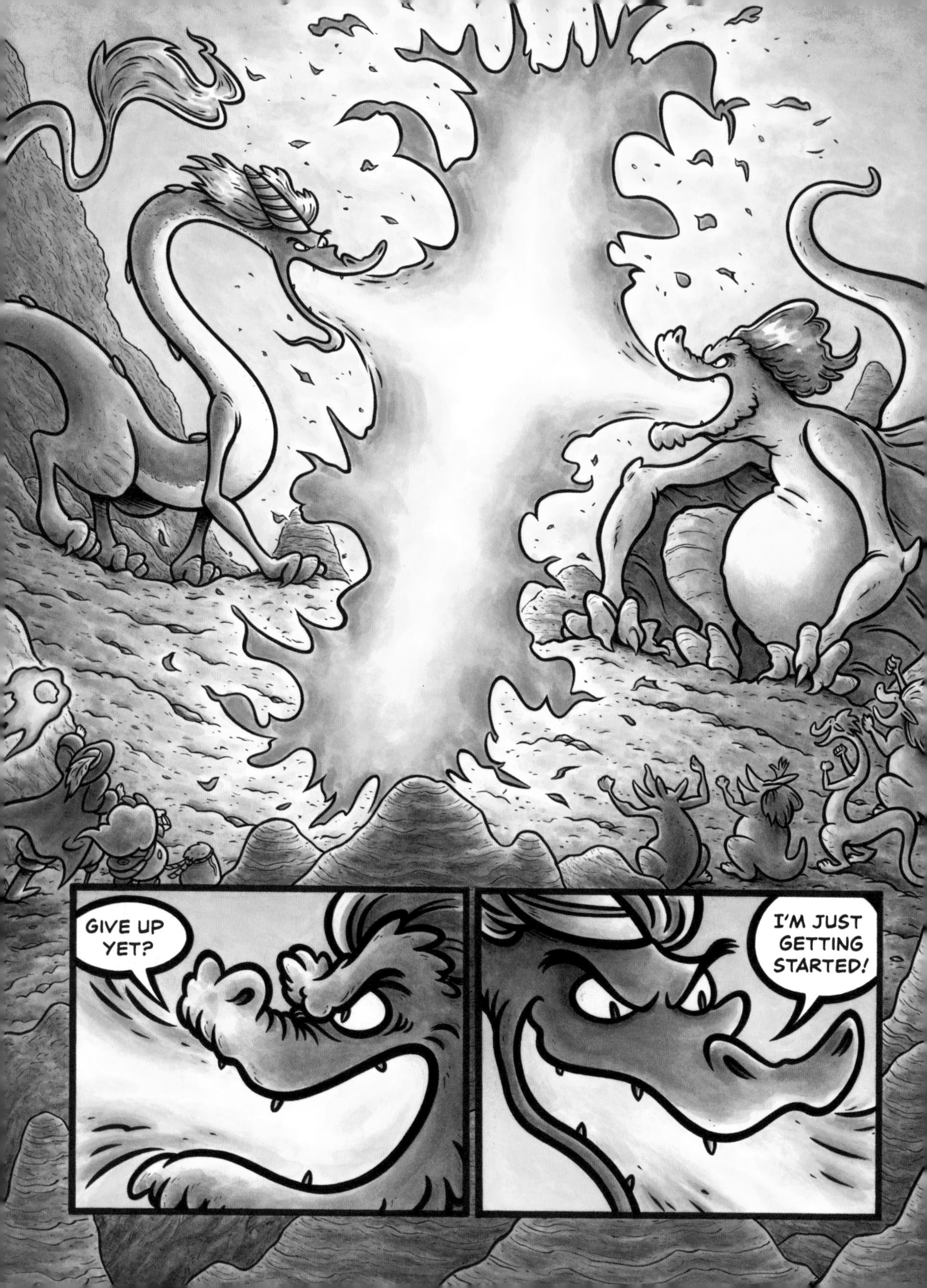
GIVE UP YET?
I'M JUST GETTING STARTED!

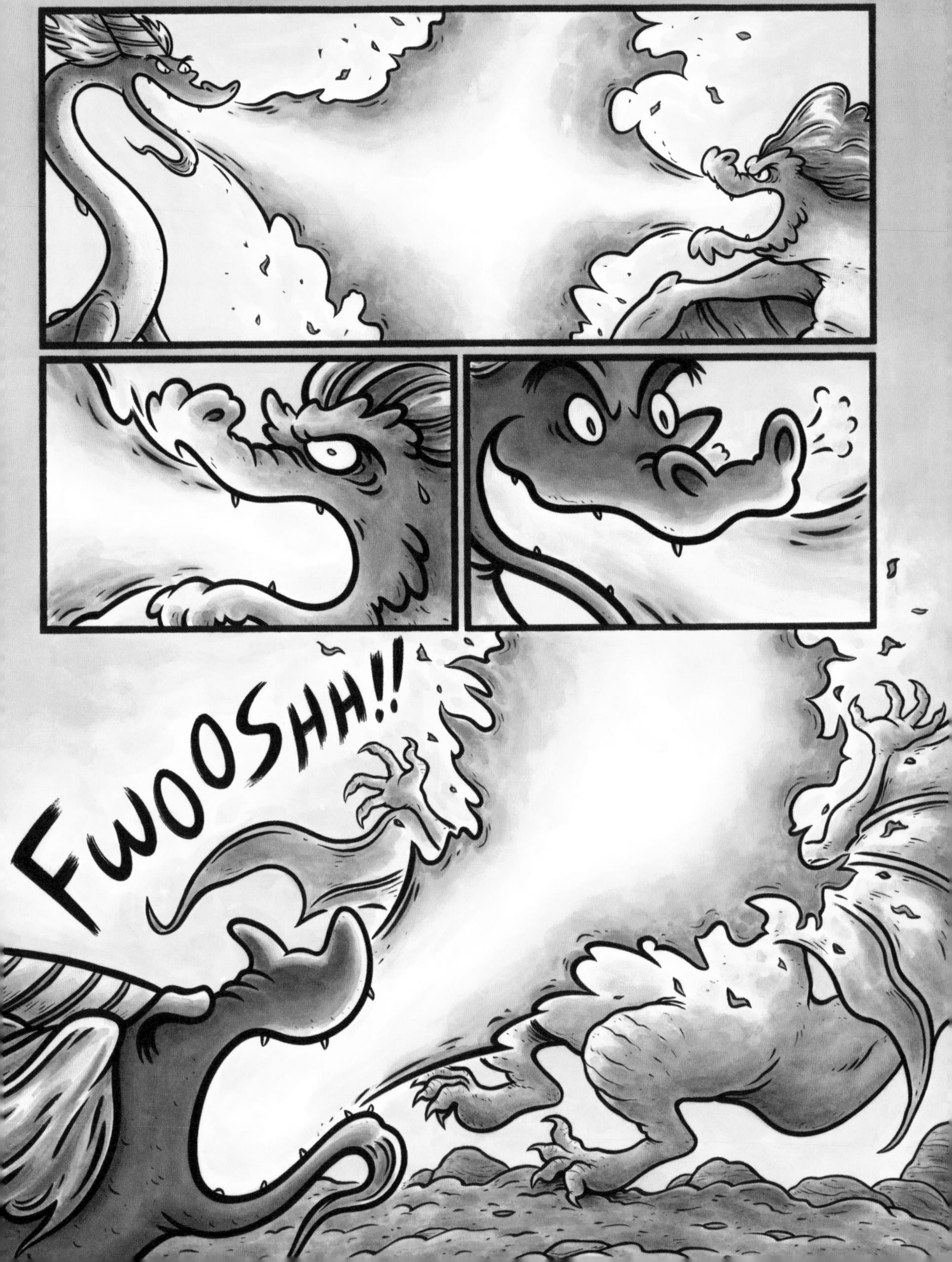
FWOOSHH!!

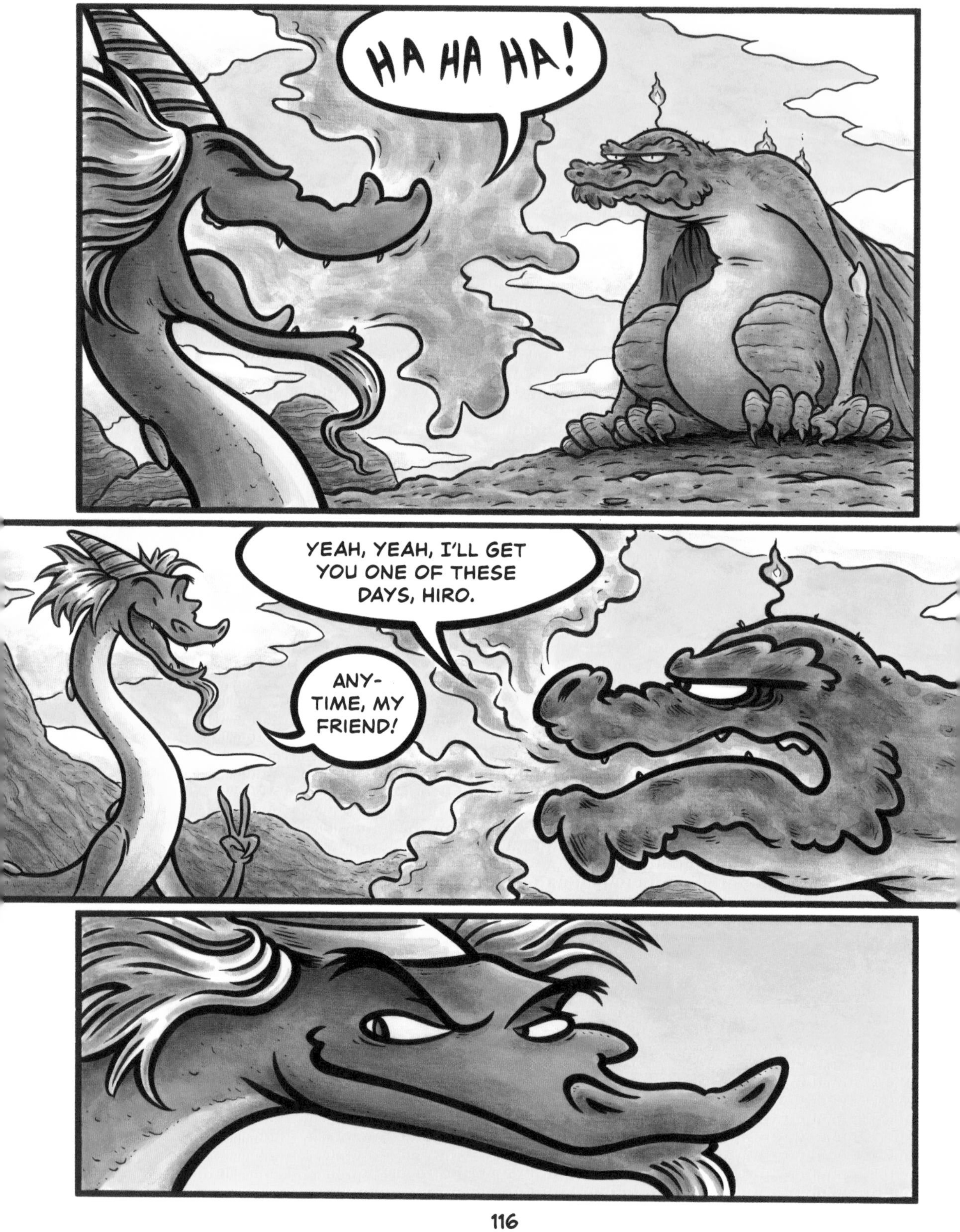
HA HA HA!
YEAH, YEAH, I'LL GET YOU ONE OF THESE DAYS, HIRO.
ANY-TIME, MY FRIEND!

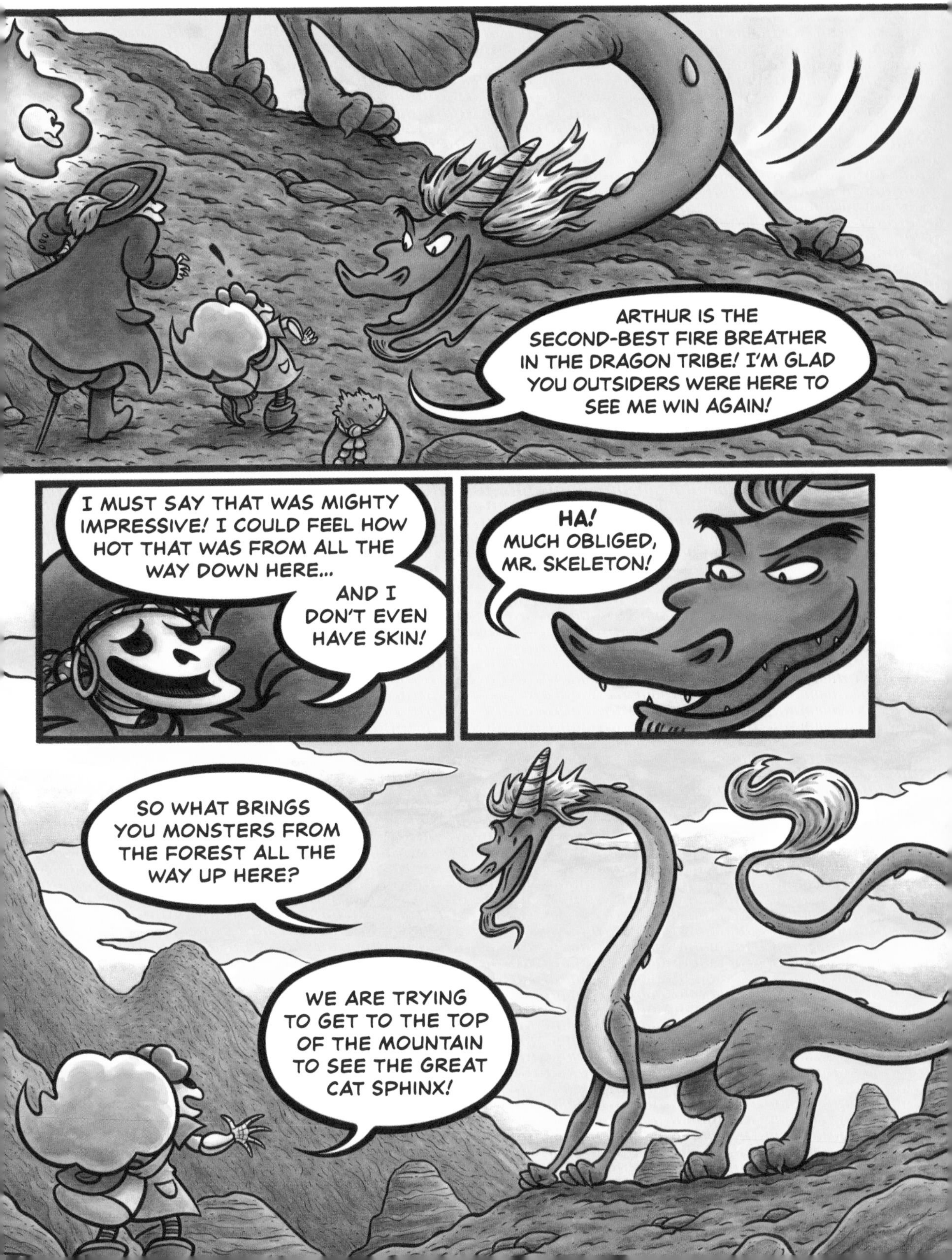
ARTHUR IS THE SECOND-BEST FIRE BREATHER IN THE DRAGON TRIBE! I'M GLAD YOU OUTSIDERS WERE HERE TO SEE ME WIN AGAIN!
I MUST SAY THAT WAS MIGHTY IMPRESSIVE! I COULD FEEL HOW HOT THAT WAS FROM ALL THE WAY DOWN HERE...
AND I DON'T EVEN HAVE SKIN!
HA! MUCH OBLIGED, MR. SKELETON!
SO WHAT BRINGS YOU MONSTERS FROM THE FOREST ALL THE WAY UP HERE?
WE ARE TRYING TO GET TO THE TOP OF THE MOUNTAIN TO SEE THE GREAT CAT SPHINX!

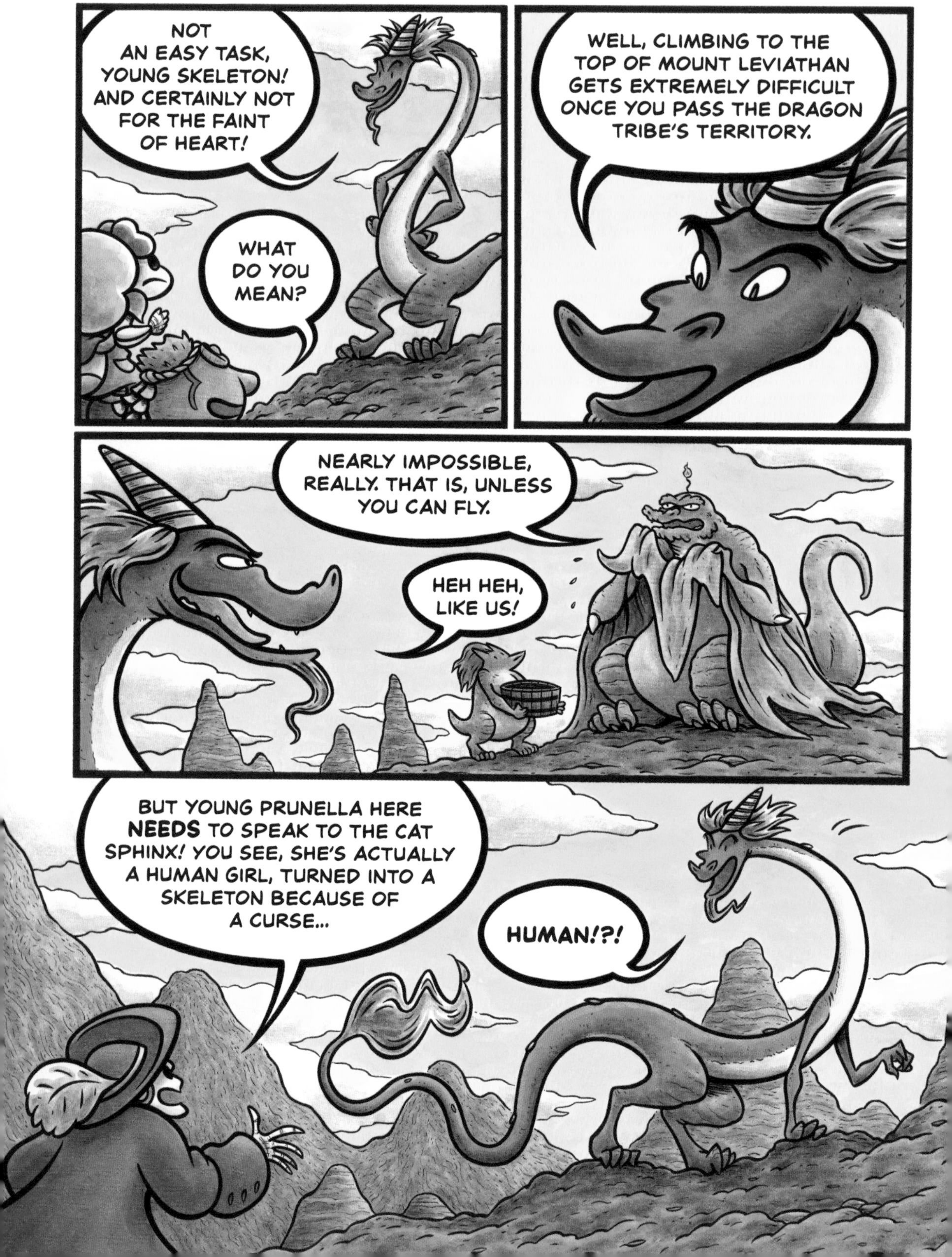
NOT AN EASY TASK, YOUNG SKELETON! AND CERTAINLY NOT FOR THE FAINT OF HEART!
WHAT DO YOU MEAN?
WELL, CLIMBING TO THE TOP OF MOUNT LEVIATHAN GETS EXTREMELY DIFFICULT ONCE YOU PASS THE DRAGON TRIBE'S TERRITORY.
NEARLY IMPOSSIBLE, REALLY. THAT IS, UNLESS YOU CAN FLY.
HEH HEH, LIKE US!
BUT YOUNG PRUNELLA HERE **NEEDS** TO SPEAK TO THE CAT SPHINX! YOU SEE, SHE'S ACTUALLY A HUMAN GIRL, TURNED INTO A SKELETON BECAUSE OF A CURSE...
HUMAN!?!

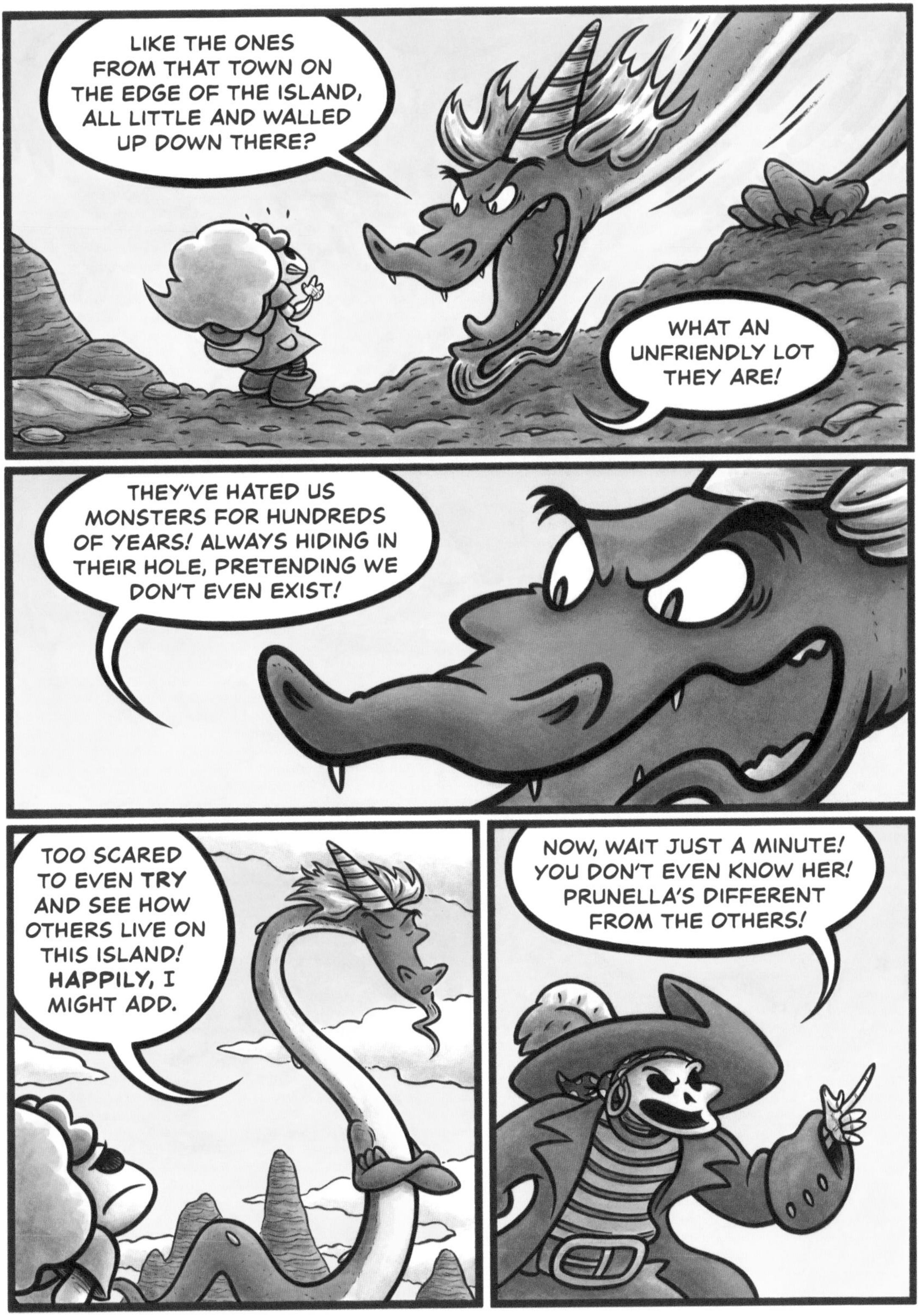

LIKE THE ONES FROM THAT TOWN ON THE EDGE OF THE ISLAND, ALL LITTLE AND WALLED UP DOWN THERE?
WHAT AN UNFRIENDLY LOT THEY ARE!
THEY'VE HATED US MONSTERS FOR HUNDREDS OF YEARS! ALWAYS HIDING IN THEIR HOLE, PRETENDING WE DON'T EVEN EXIST!
TOO SCARED TO EVEN **TRY** AND SEE HOW OTHERS LIVE ON THIS ISLAND! **HAPPILY,** I MIGHT ADD.
NOW, WAIT JUST A MINUTE! YOU DON'T EVEN KNOW HER! PRUNELLA'S DIFFERENT FROM THE OTHERS!

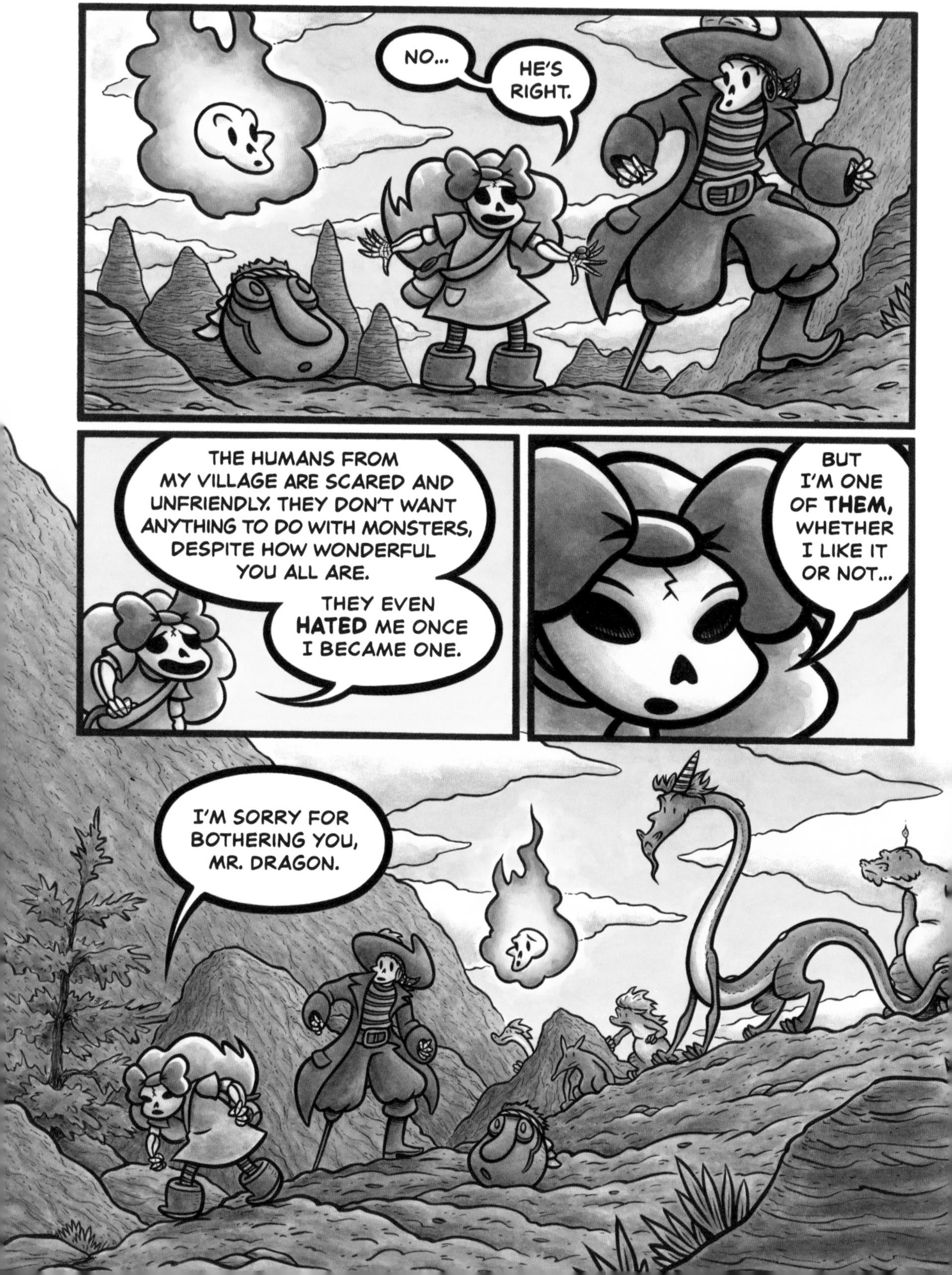
NO...
HE'S RIGHT.
THE HUMANS FROM MY VILLAGE ARE SCARED AND UNFRIENDLY. THEY DON'T WANT ANYTHING TO DO WITH MONSTERS, DESPITE HOW WONDERFUL YOU ALL ARE.
THEY EVEN HATED ME ONCE I BECAME ONE.
BUT I'M ONE OF THEM, WHETHER I LIKE IT OR NOT...
I'M SORRY FOR BOTHERING YOU, MR. DRAGON.

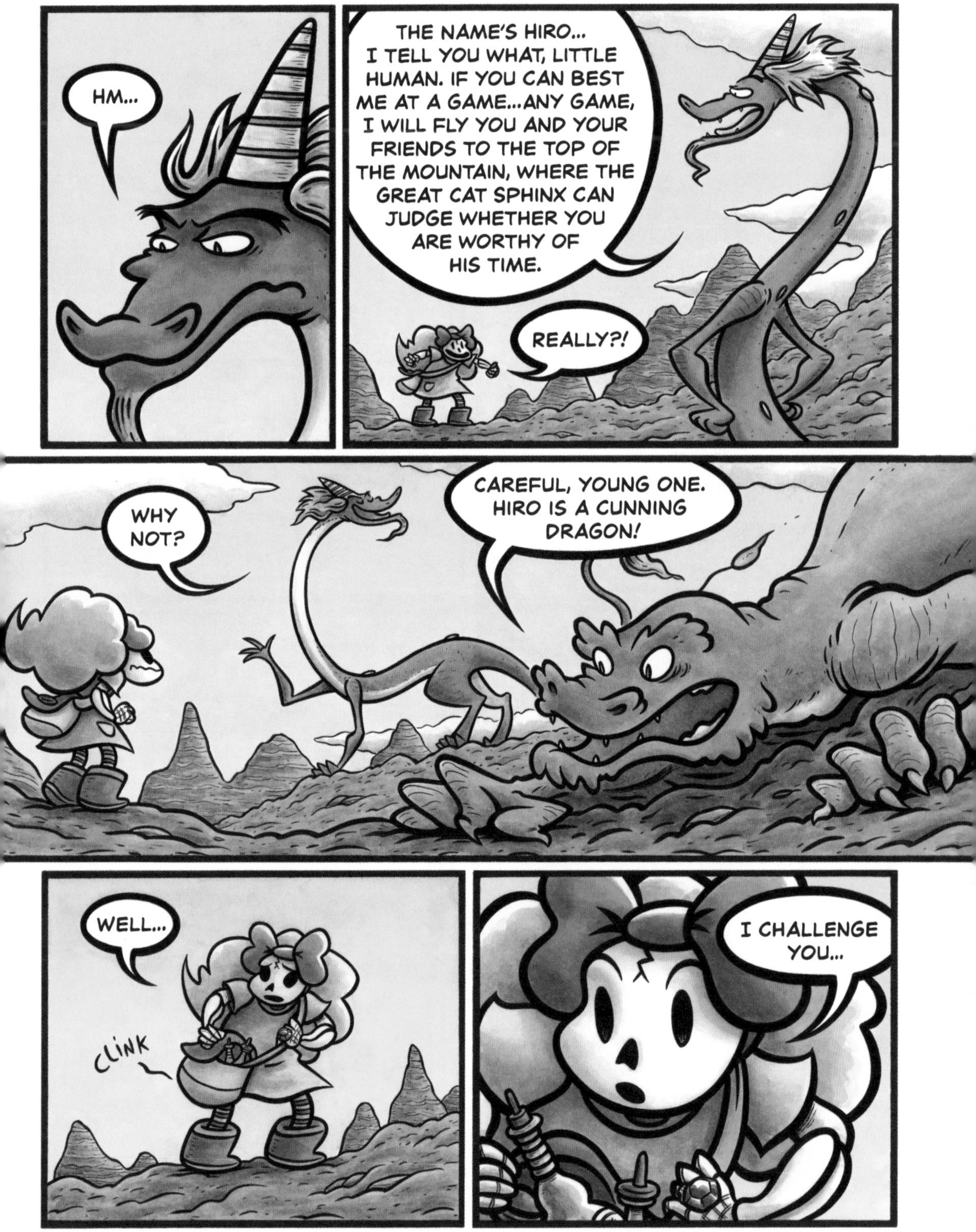
HM...
THE NAME'S HIRO... I TELL YOU WHAT, LITTLE HUMAN. IF YOU CAN BEST ME AT A GAME...ANY GAME, I WILL FLY YOU AND YOUR FRIENDS TO THE TOP OF THE MOUNTAIN, WHERE THE GREAT CAT SPHINX CAN JUDGE WHETHER YOU ARE WORTHY OF HIS TIME.
REALLY?!
WHY NOT?
CAREFUL, YOUNG ONE. HIRO IS A CUNNING DRAGON!
WELL...
CLINK
I CHALLENGE YOU...

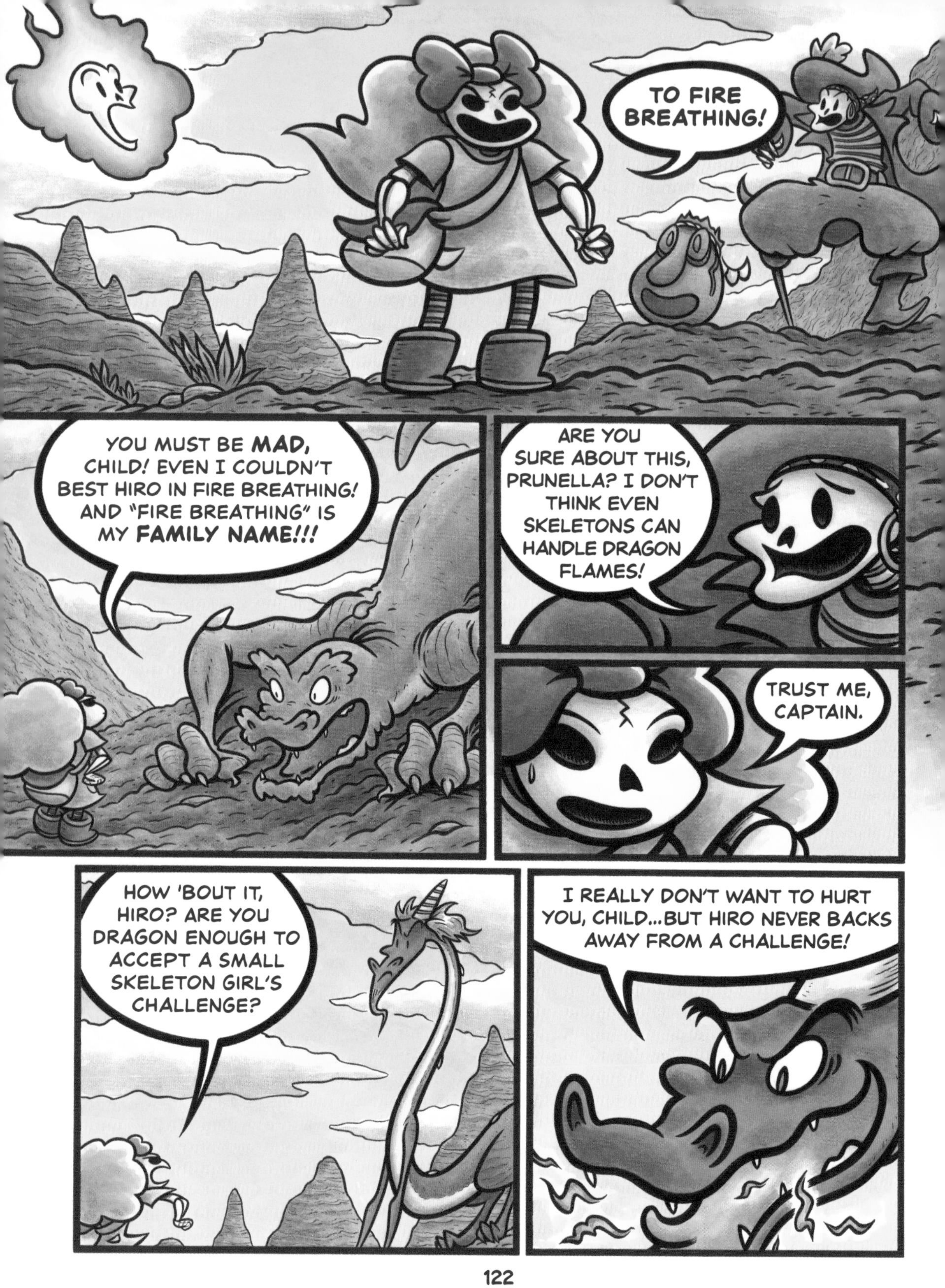
TO FIRE BREATHING!
YOU MUST BE MAD, CHILD! EVEN I COULDN'T BEST HIRO IN FIRE BREATHING! AND "FIRE BREATHING" IS MY FAMILY NAME!!!
ARE YOU SURE ABOUT THIS, PRUNELLA? I DON'T THINK EVEN SKELETONS CAN HANDLE DRAGON FLAMES!
TRUST ME, CAPTAIN.
HOW 'BOUT IT, HIRO? ARE YOU DRAGON ENOUGH TO ACCEPT A SMALL SKELETON GIRL'S CHALLENGE?
I REALLY DON'T WANT TO HURT YOU, CHILD...BUT HIRO NEVER BACKS AWAY FROM A CHALLENGE!

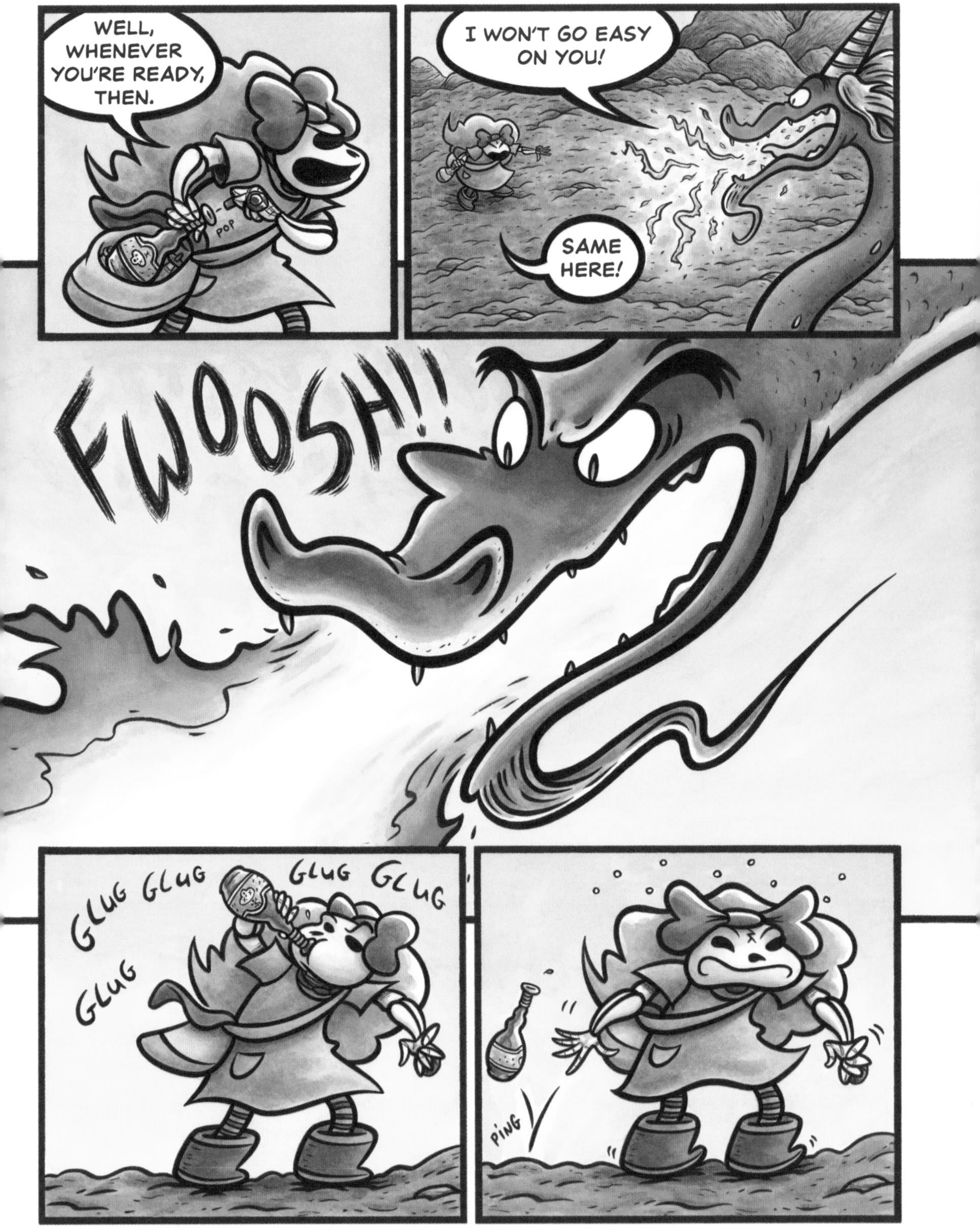

WELL, WHENEVER YOU'RE READY, THEN.
POP
I WON'T GO EASY ON YOU!
SAME HERE!
FWOOSH!!
GLUG GLUG GLUG GLUG
GLUG
PING

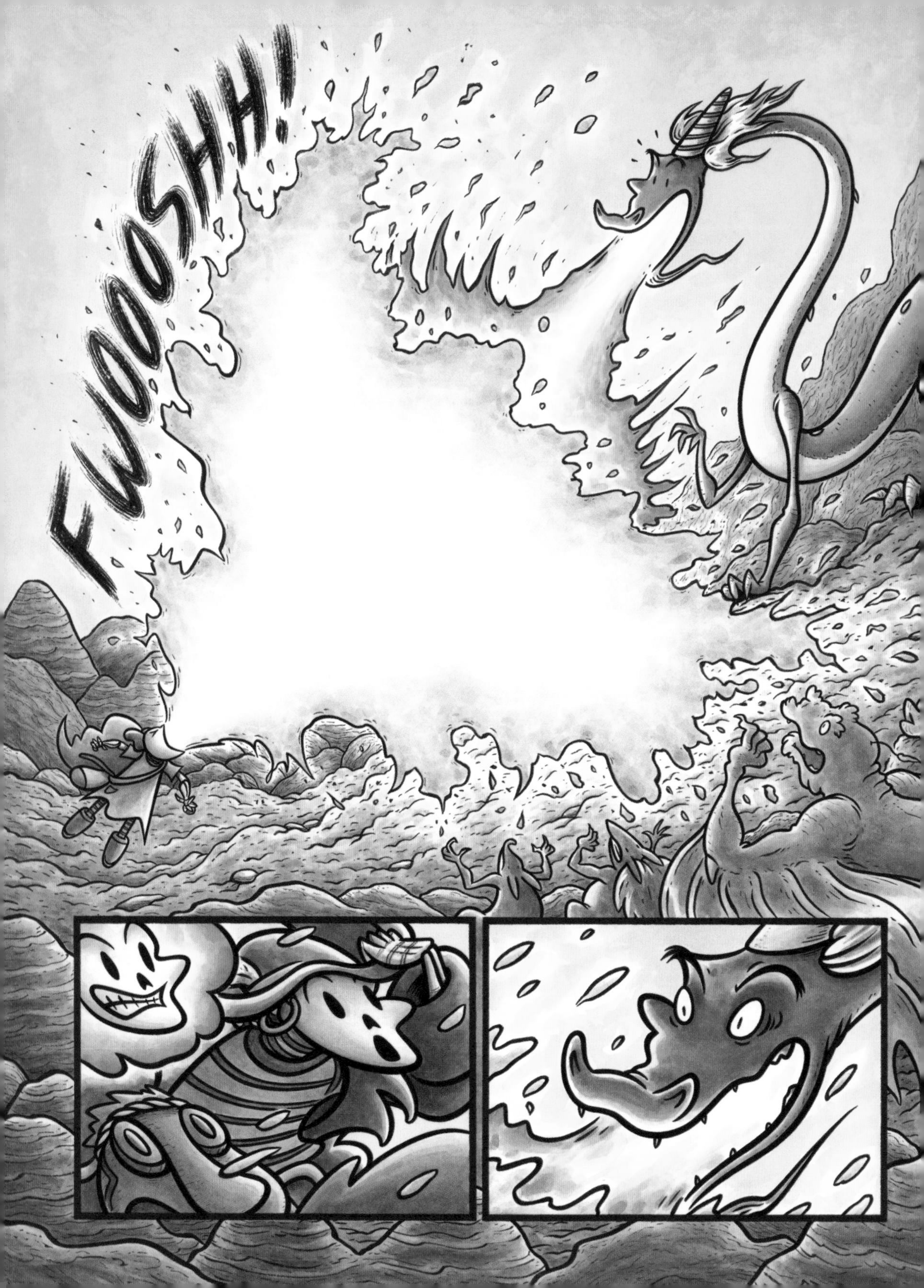
FWOOOSHH!!

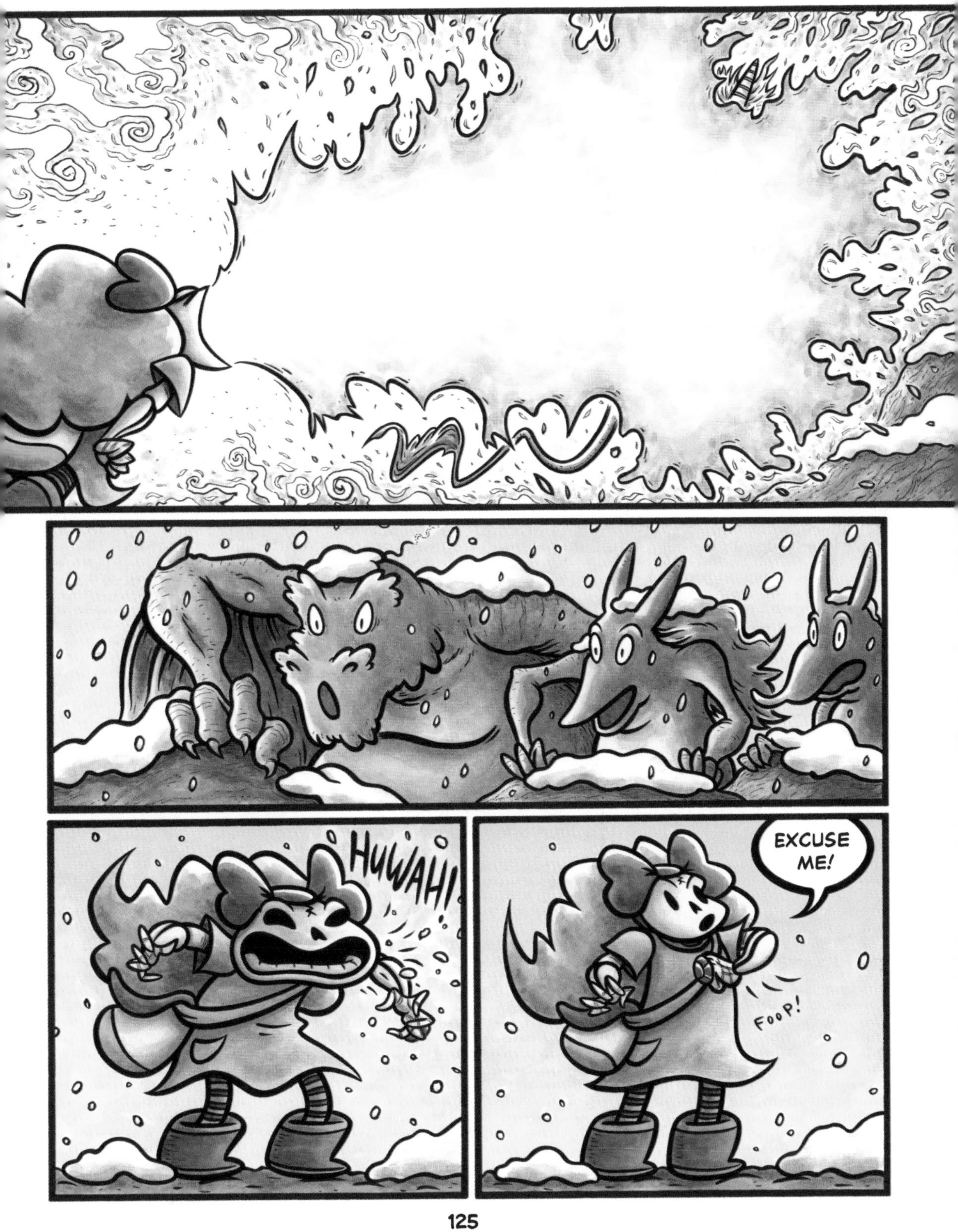
HUWAH!
EXCUSE ME!
FOOP!

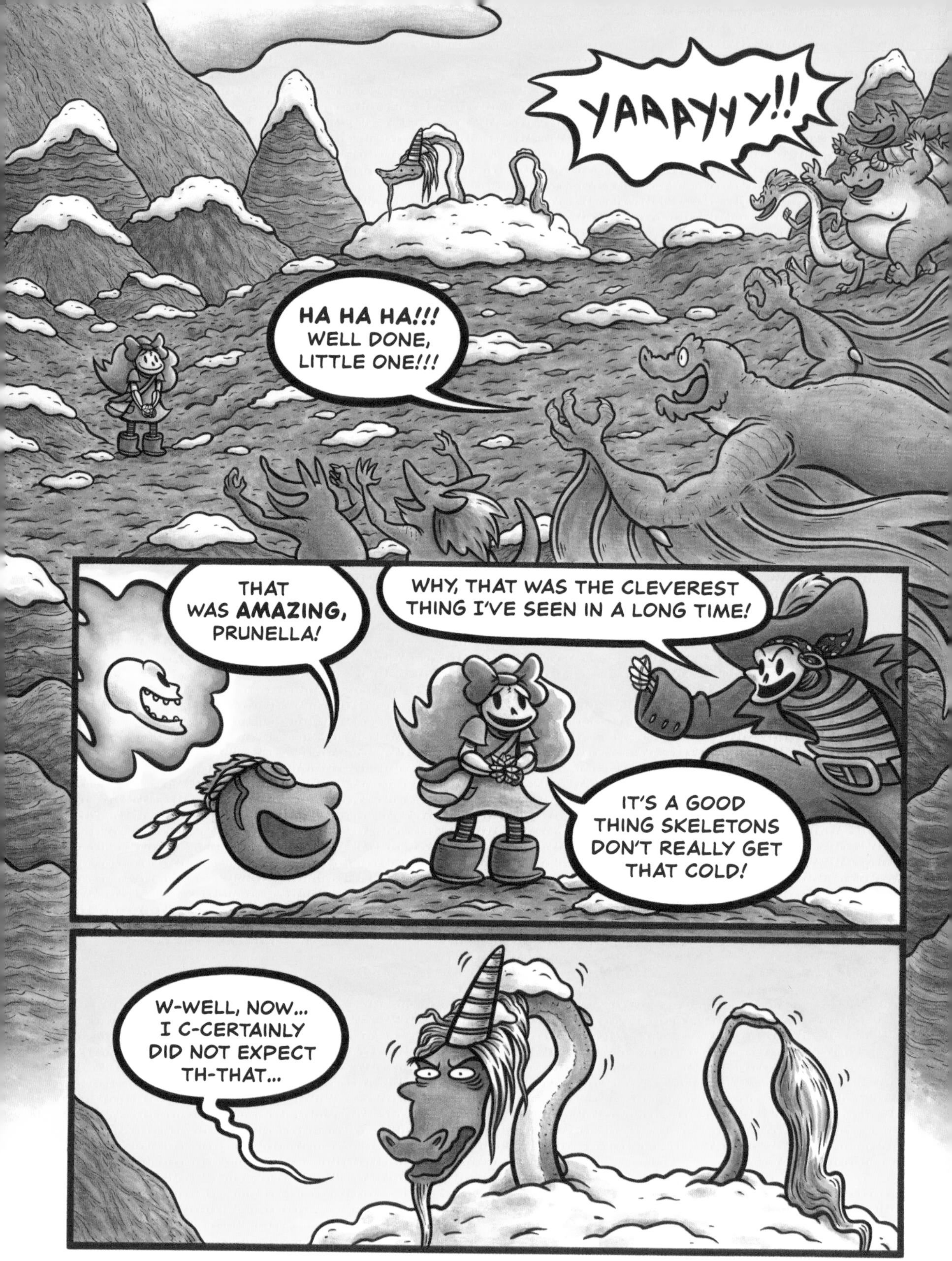
YAAAYYY!!
HA HA HA!!! WELL DONE, LITTLE ONE!!!
THAT WAS AMAZING, PRUNELLA!
WHY, THAT WAS THE CLEVEREST THING I'VE SEEN IN A LONG TIME!
IT'S A GOOD THING SKELETONS DON'T REALLY GET THAT COLD!
W-WELL, NOW... I C-CERTAINLY DID NOT EXPECT TH-THAT...

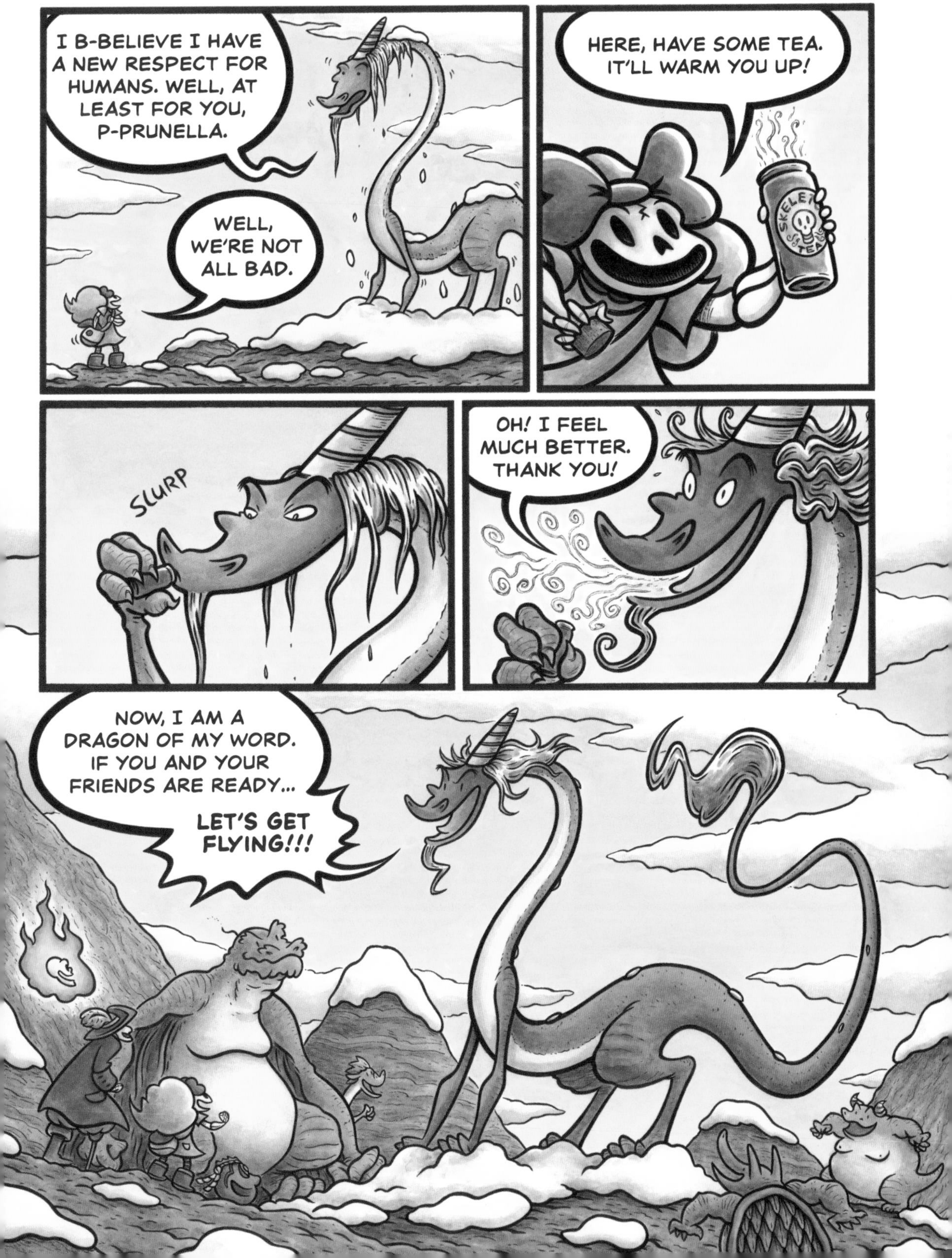
I B-BELIEVE I HAVE A NEW RESPECT FOR HUMANS. WELL, AT LEAST FOR YOU, P-PRUNELLA.
WELL, WE'RE NOT ALL BAD.
HERE, HAVE SOME TEA. IT'LL WARM YOU UP!
SKELETEA
SLURP
OH! I FEEL MUCH BETTER. THANK YOU!
NOW, I AM A DRAGON OF MY WORD. IF YOU AND YOUR FRIENDS ARE READY...
LET'S GET FLYING!!!

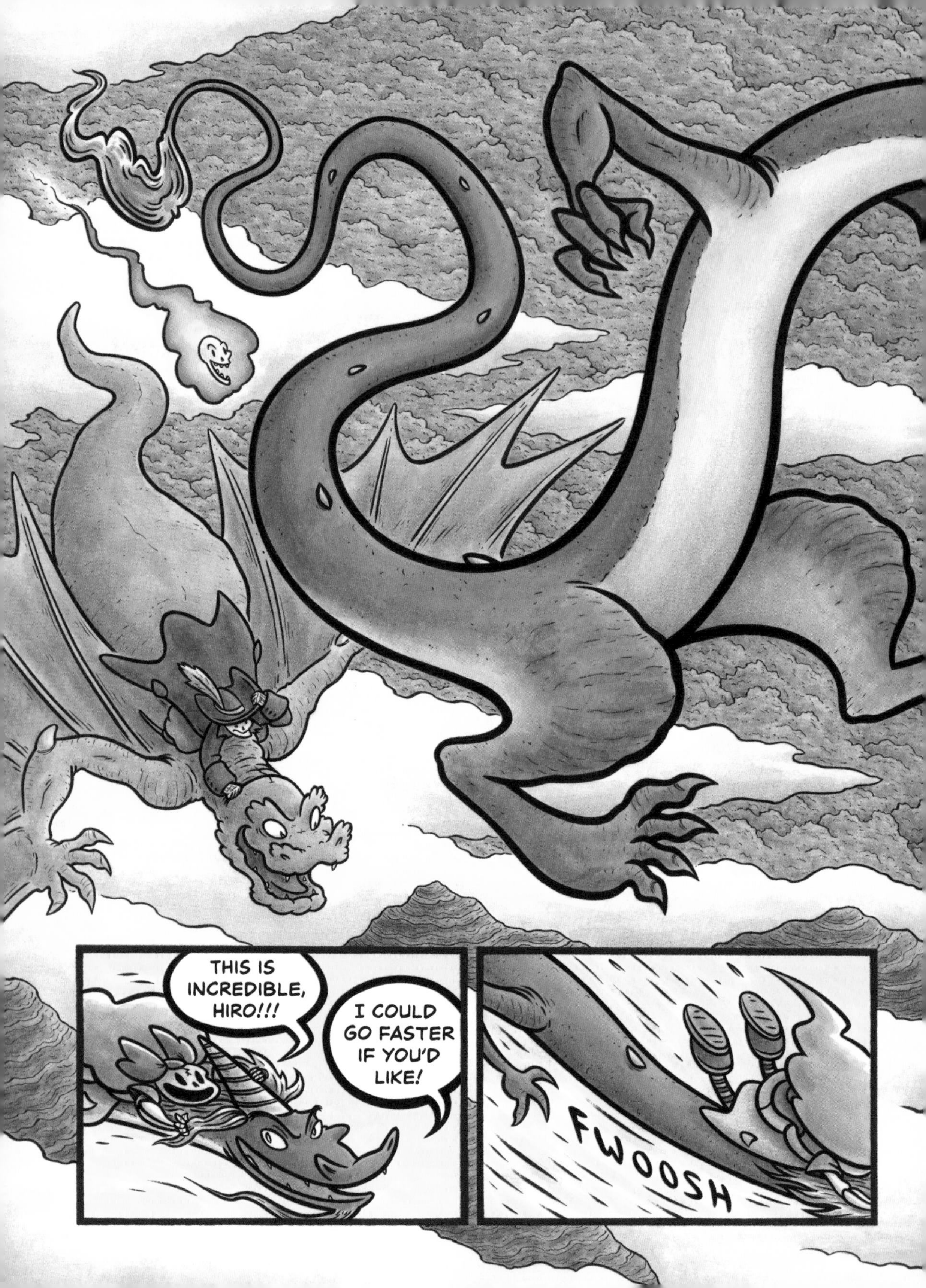
THIS IS INCREDIBLE, HIRO!!!
I COULD GO FASTER IF YOU'D LIKE!
FWOOSH

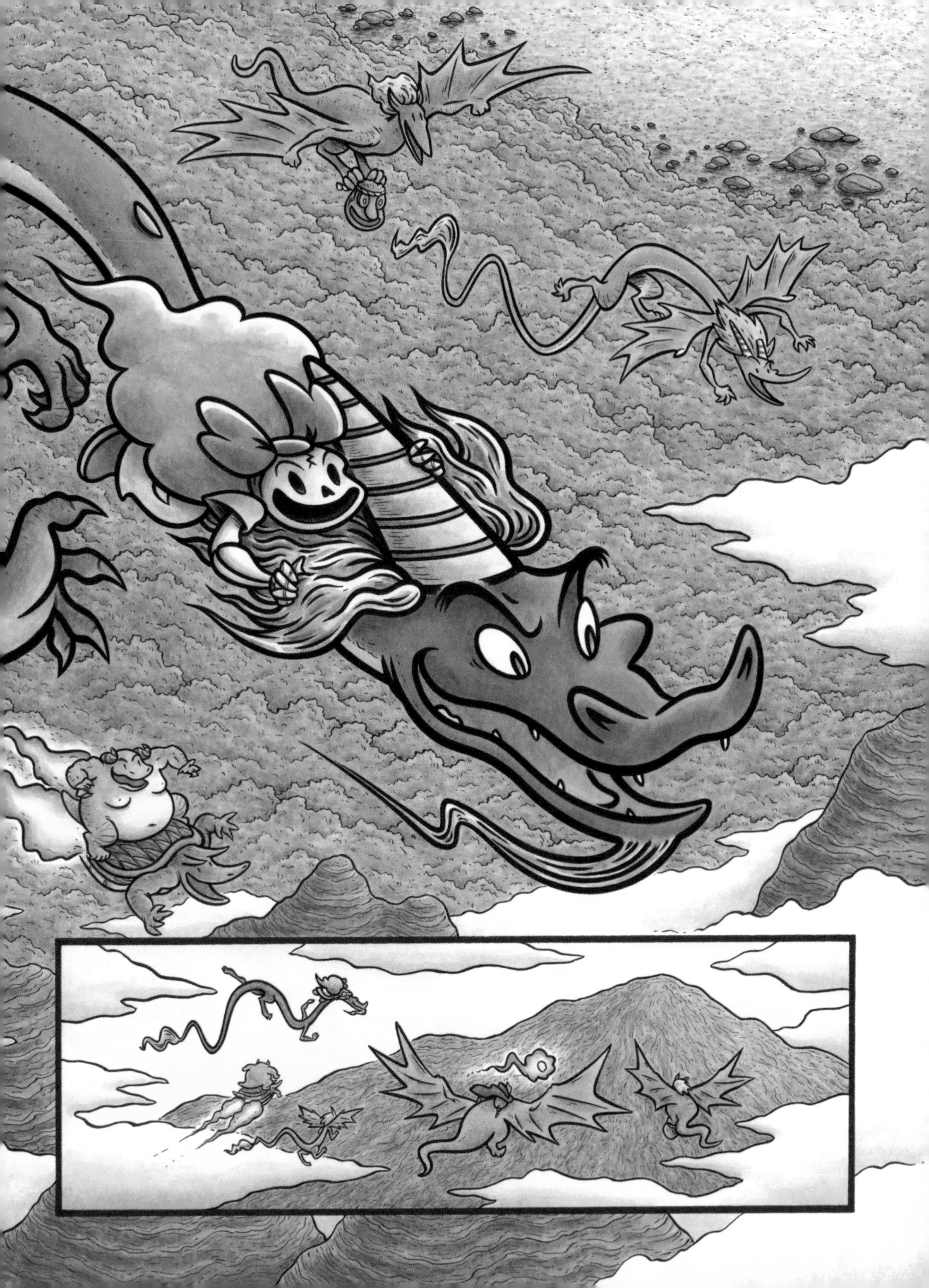

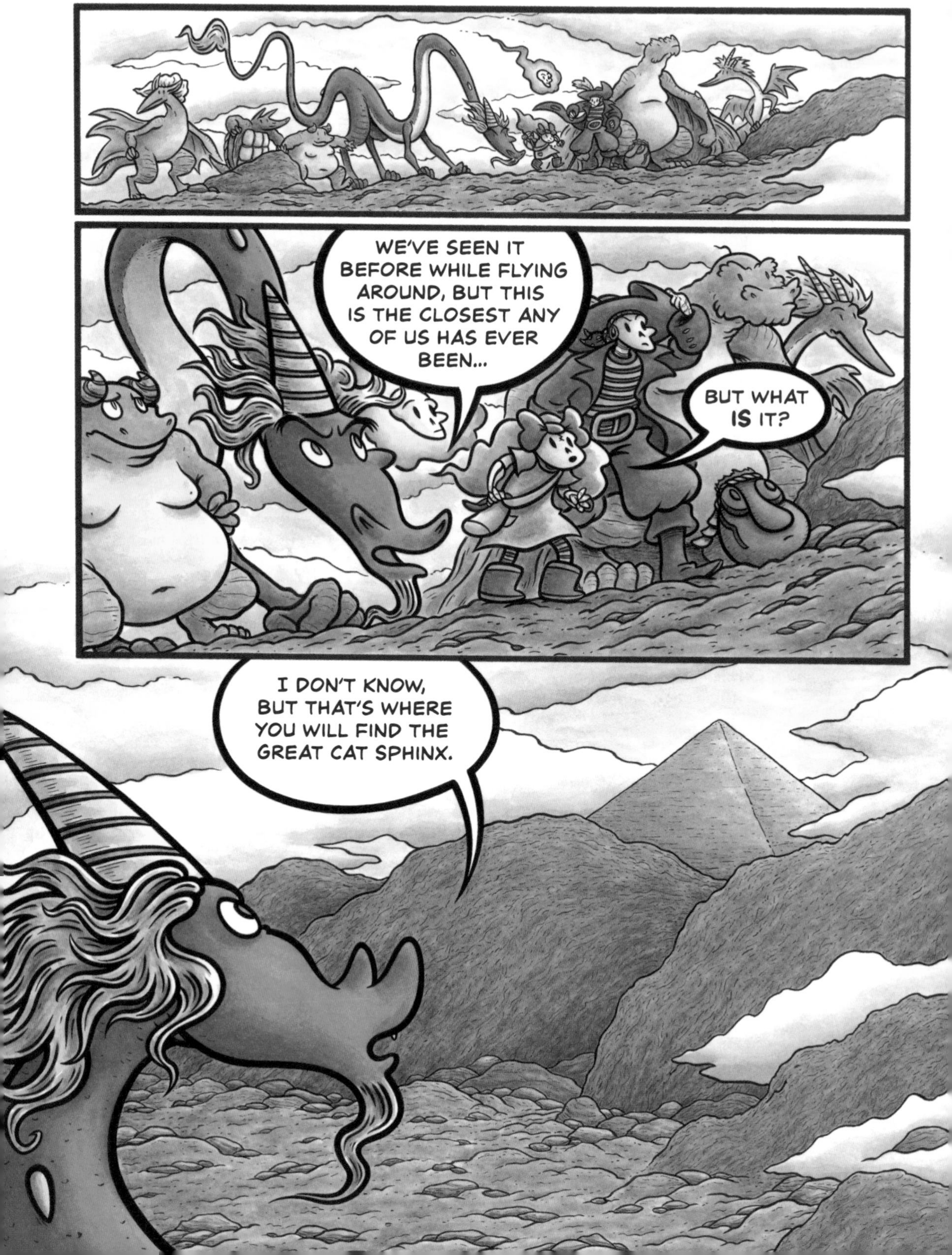
WE'VE SEEN IT BEFORE WHILE FLYING AROUND, BUT THIS IS THE CLOSEST ANY OF US HAS EVER BEEN...
BUT WHAT **IS** IT?
I DON'T KNOW, BUT THAT'S WHERE YOU WILL FIND THE GREAT CAT SPHINX.

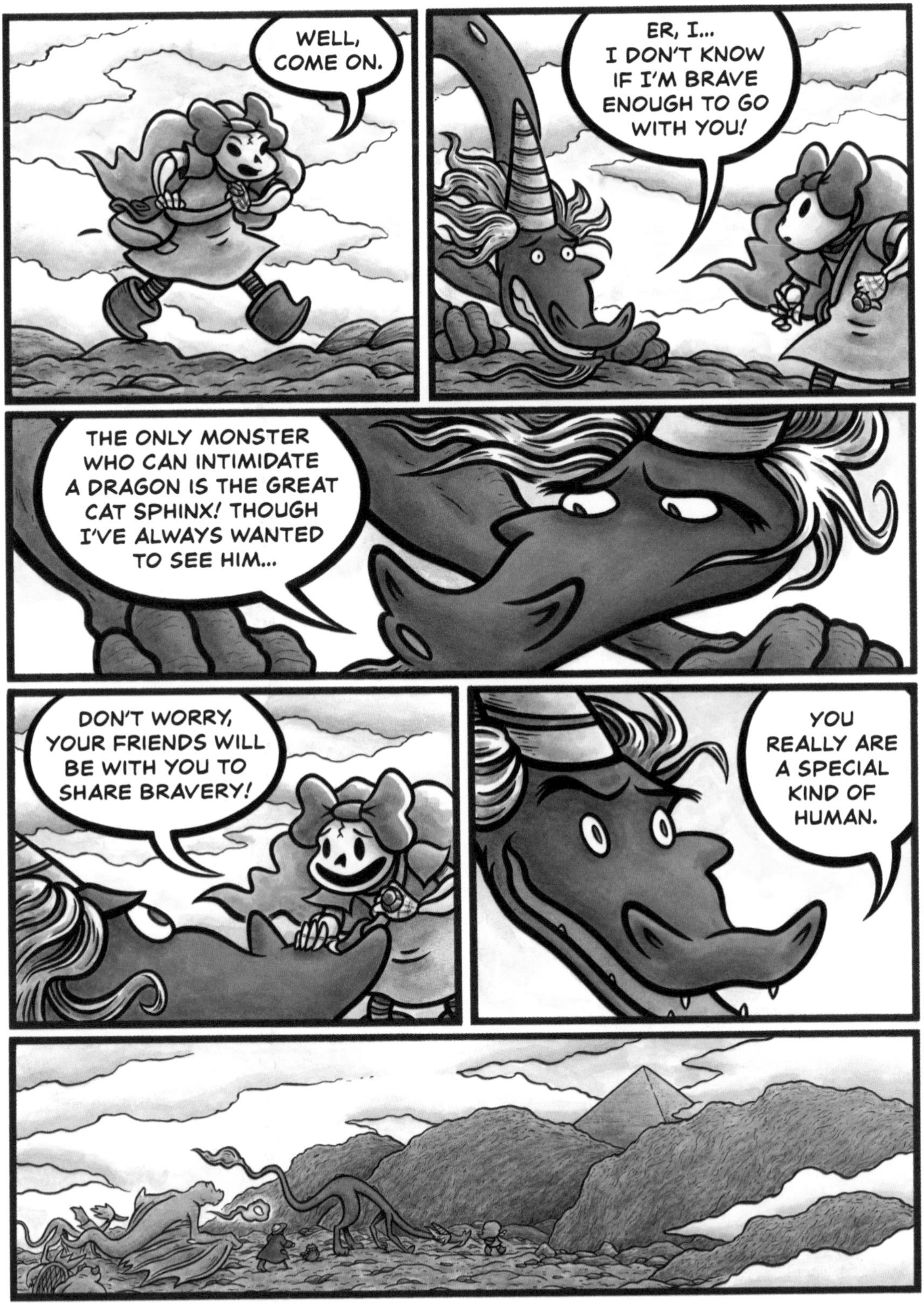
WELL, COME ON.
ER, I... I DON'T KNOW IF I'M BRAVE ENOUGH TO GO WITH YOU!
THE ONLY MONSTER WHO CAN INTIMIDATE A DRAGON IS THE GREAT CAT SPHINX! THOUGH I'VE ALWAYS WANTED TO SEE HIM...
DON'T WORRY, YOUR FRIENDS WILL BE WITH YOU TO SHARE BRAVERY!
YOU REALLY ARE A SPECIAL KIND OF HUMAN.

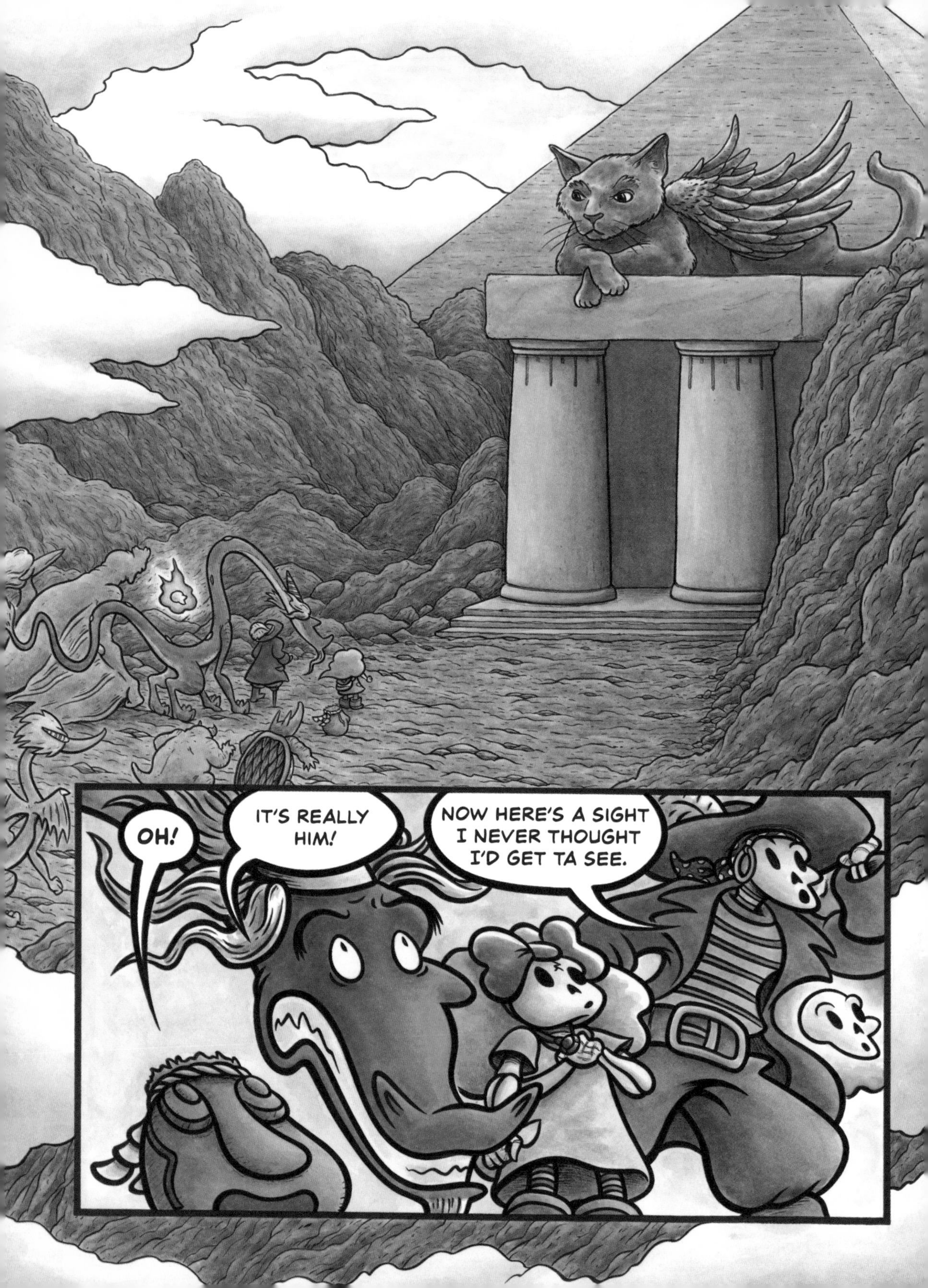
OH!
IT'S REALLY HIM!
NOW HERE'S A SIGHT I NEVER THOUGHT I'D GET TA SEE.

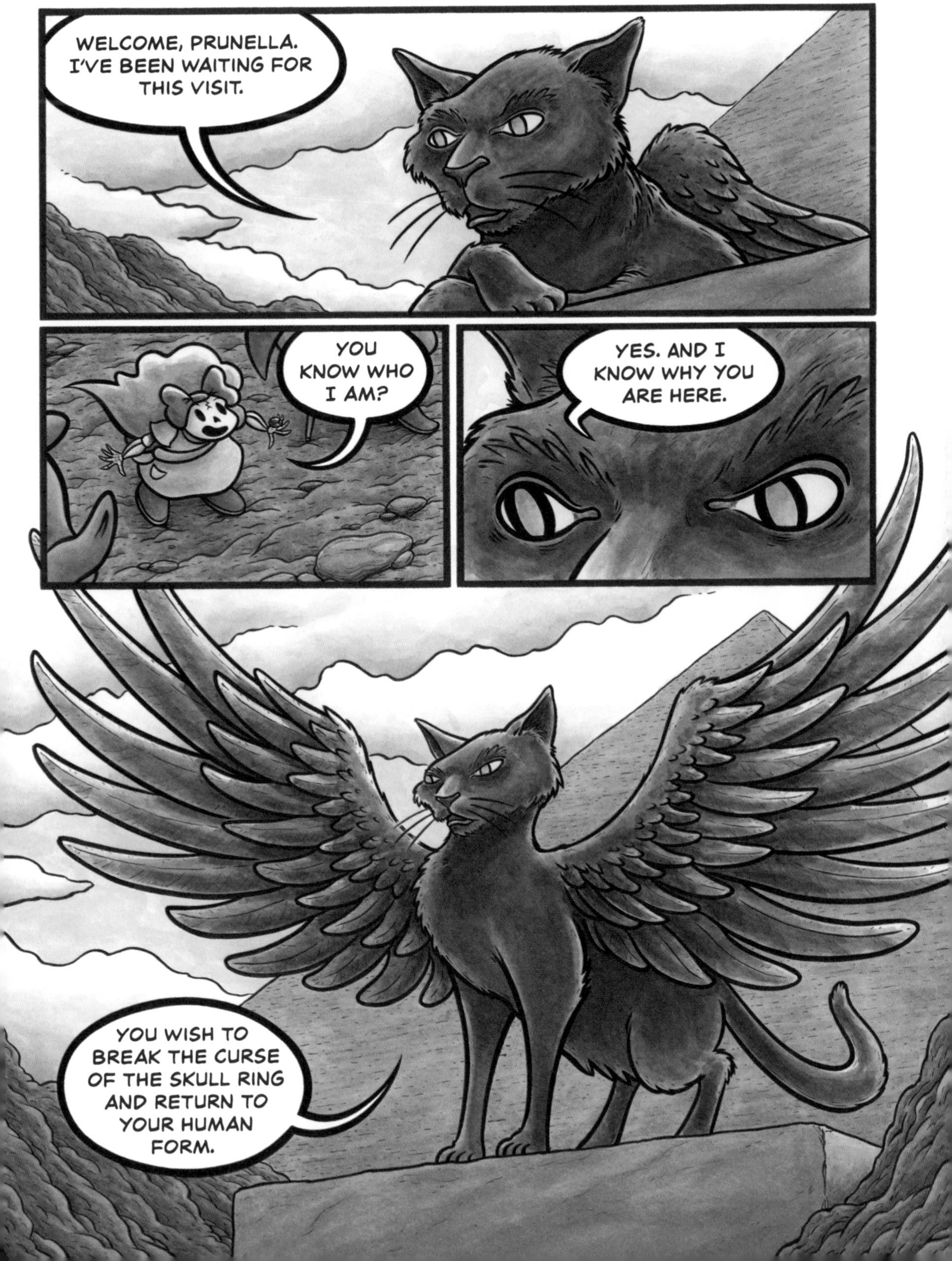
WELCOME, PRUNELLA. I'VE BEEN WAITING FOR THIS VISIT.
YOU KNOW WHO I AM?
YES. AND I KNOW WHY YOU ARE HERE.
YOU WISH TO BREAK THE CURSE OF THE SKULL RING AND RETURN TO YOUR HUMAN FORM.

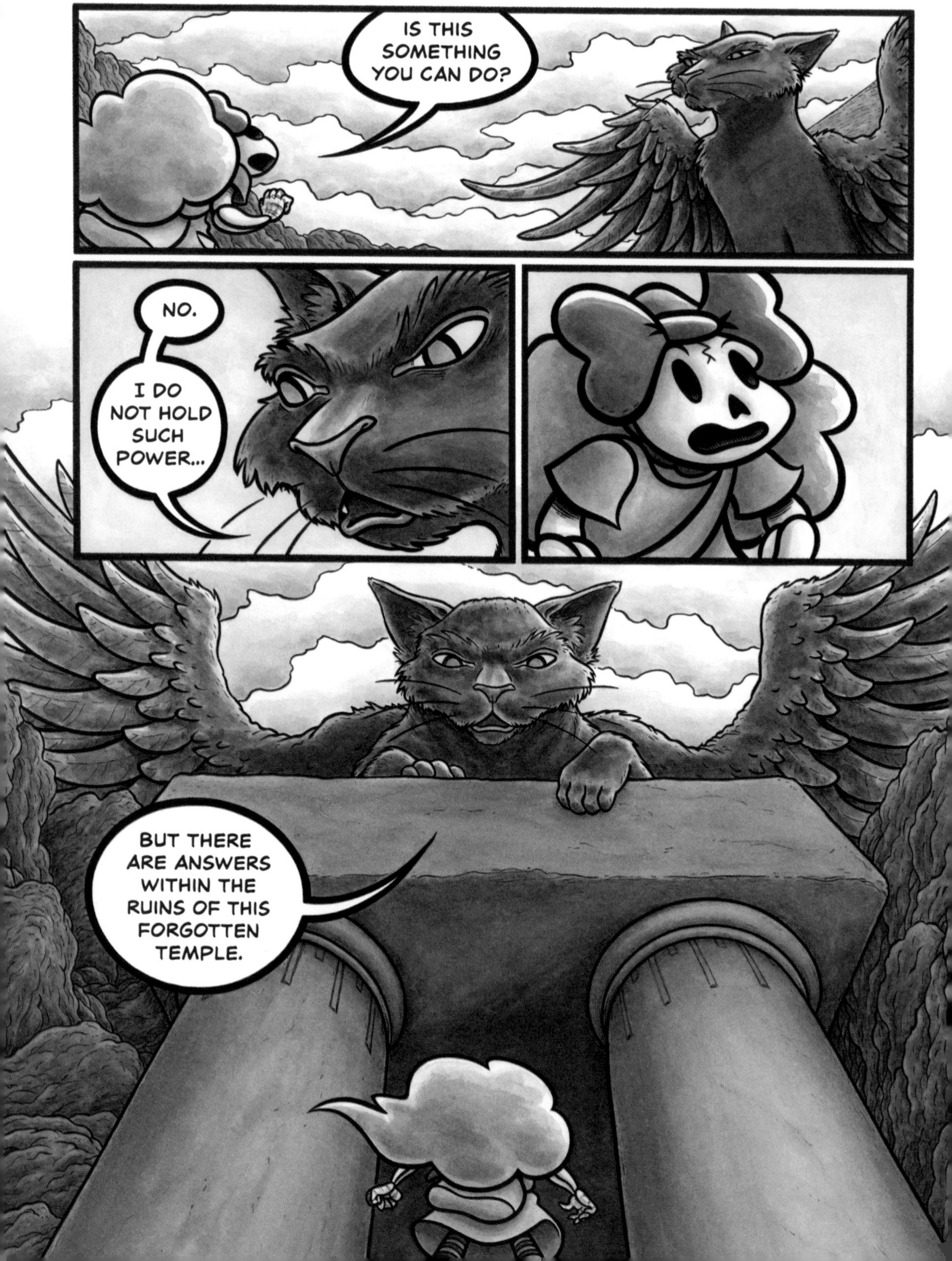
IS THIS SOMETHING YOU CAN DO?
NO.
I DO NOT HOLD SUCH POWER...
BUT THERE ARE ANSWERS WITHIN THE RUINS OF THIS FORGOTTEN TEMPLE.

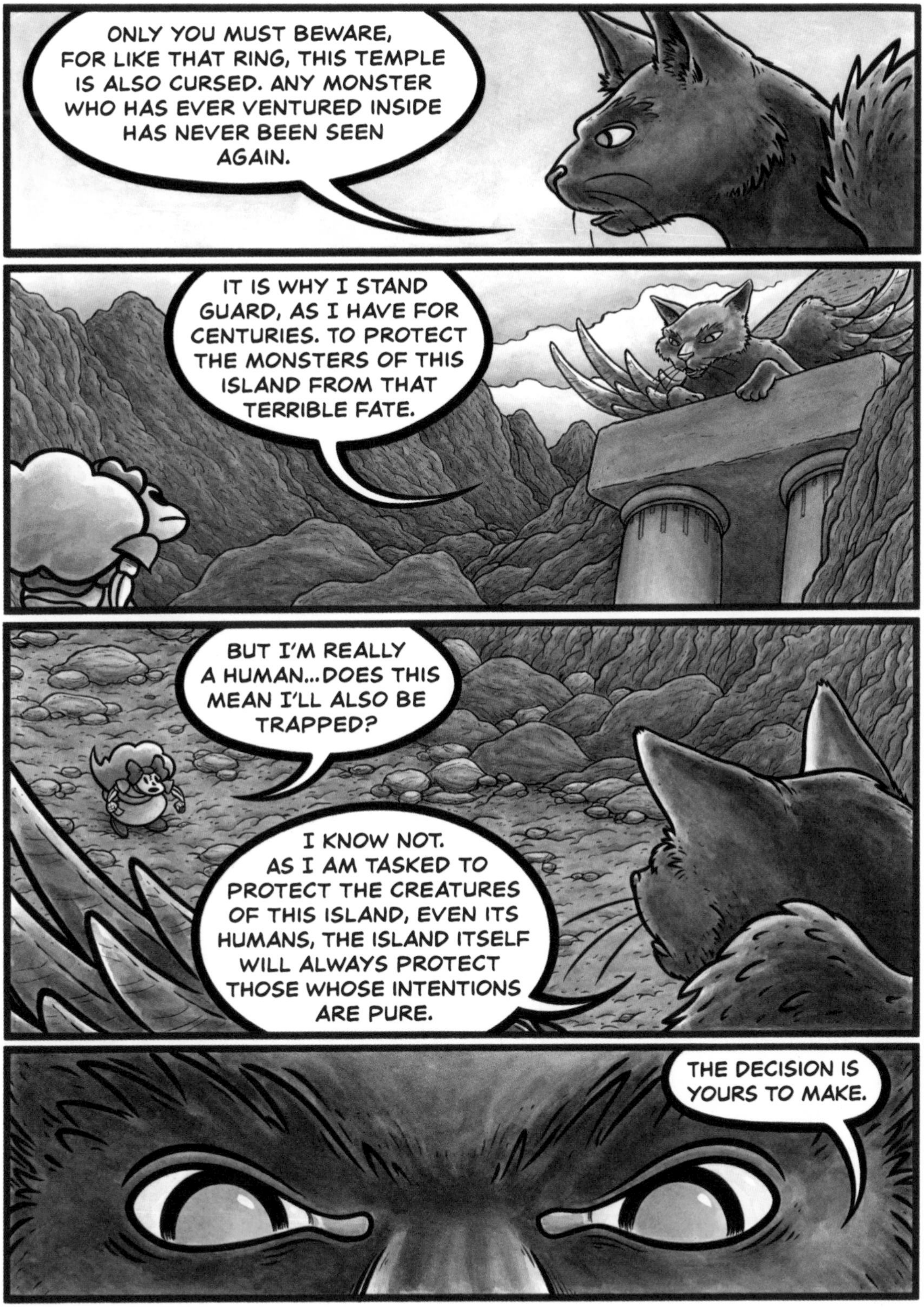
ONLY YOU MUST BEWARE, FOR LIKE THAT RING, THIS TEMPLE IS ALSO CURSED. ANY MONSTER WHO HAS EVER VENTURED INSIDE HAS NEVER BEEN SEEN AGAIN.
IT IS WHY I STAND GUARD, AS I HAVE FOR CENTURIES. TO PROTECT THE MONSTERS OF THIS ISLAND FROM THAT TERRIBLE FATE.
BUT I'M REALLY A HUMAN...DOES THIS MEAN I'LL ALSO BE TRAPPED?
I KNOW NOT. AS I AM TASKED TO PROTECT THE CREATURES OF THIS ISLAND, EVEN ITS HUMANS, THE ISLAND ITSELF WILL ALWAYS PROTECT THOSE WHOSE INTENTIONS ARE PURE.
THE DECISION IS YOURS TO MAKE.

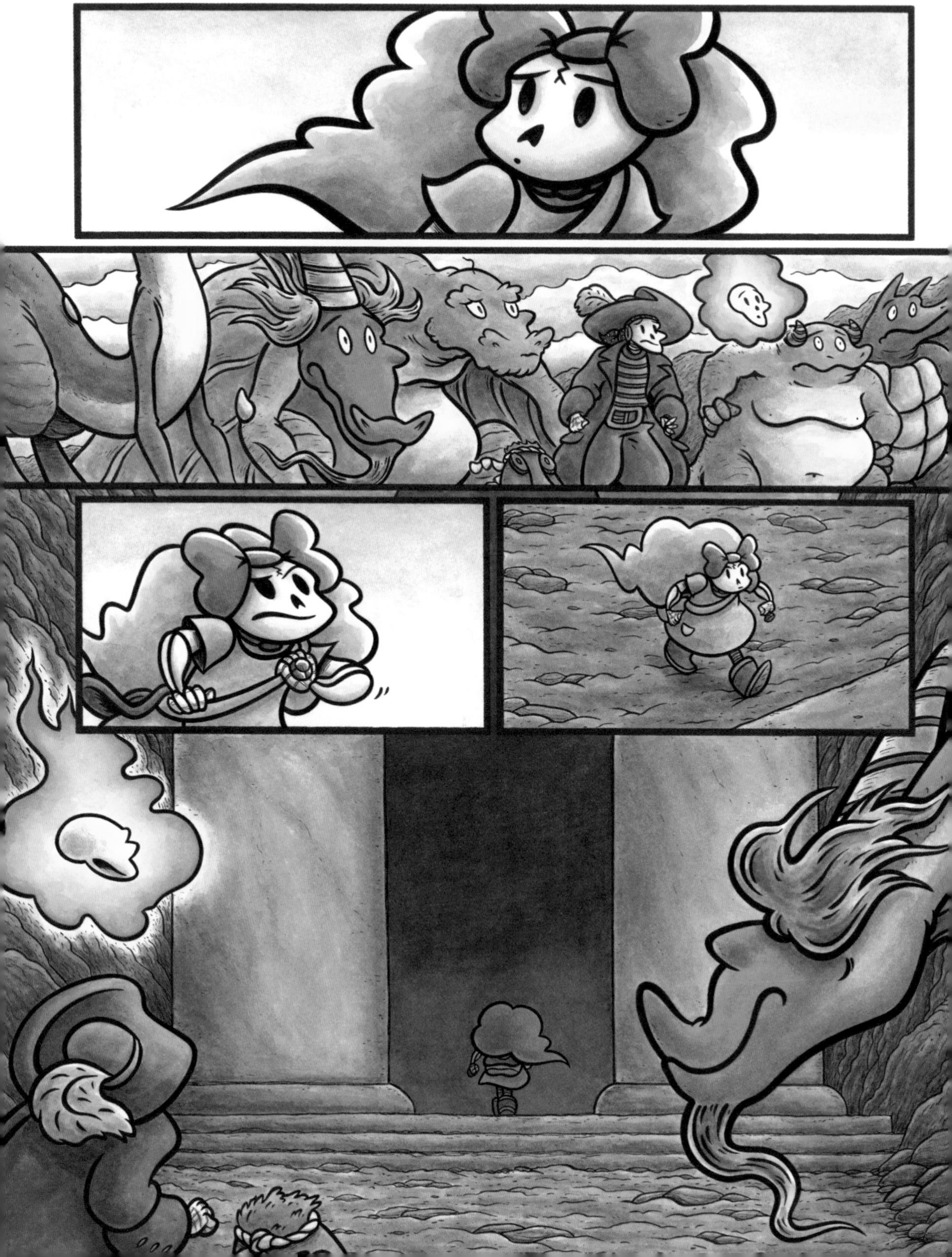

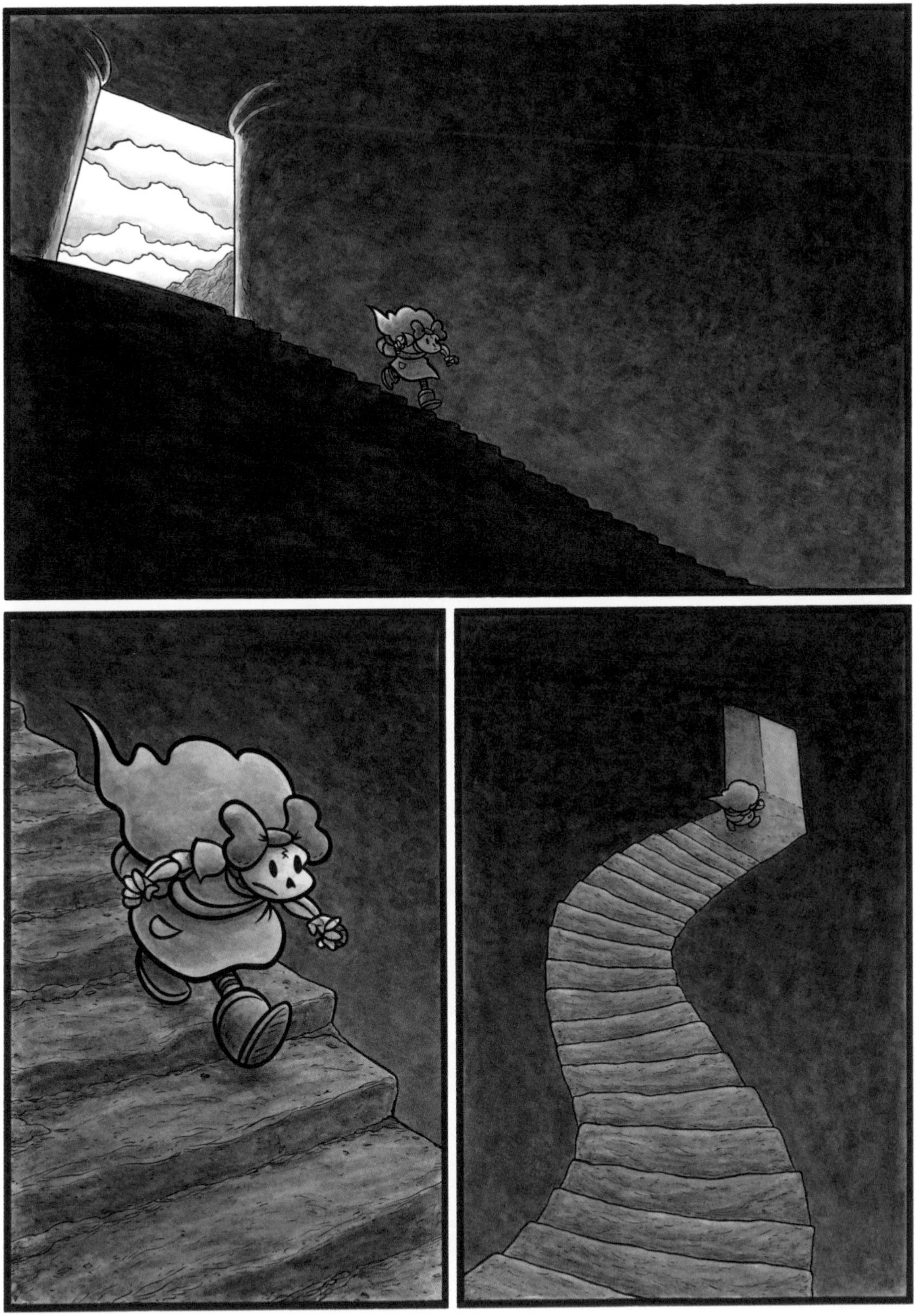

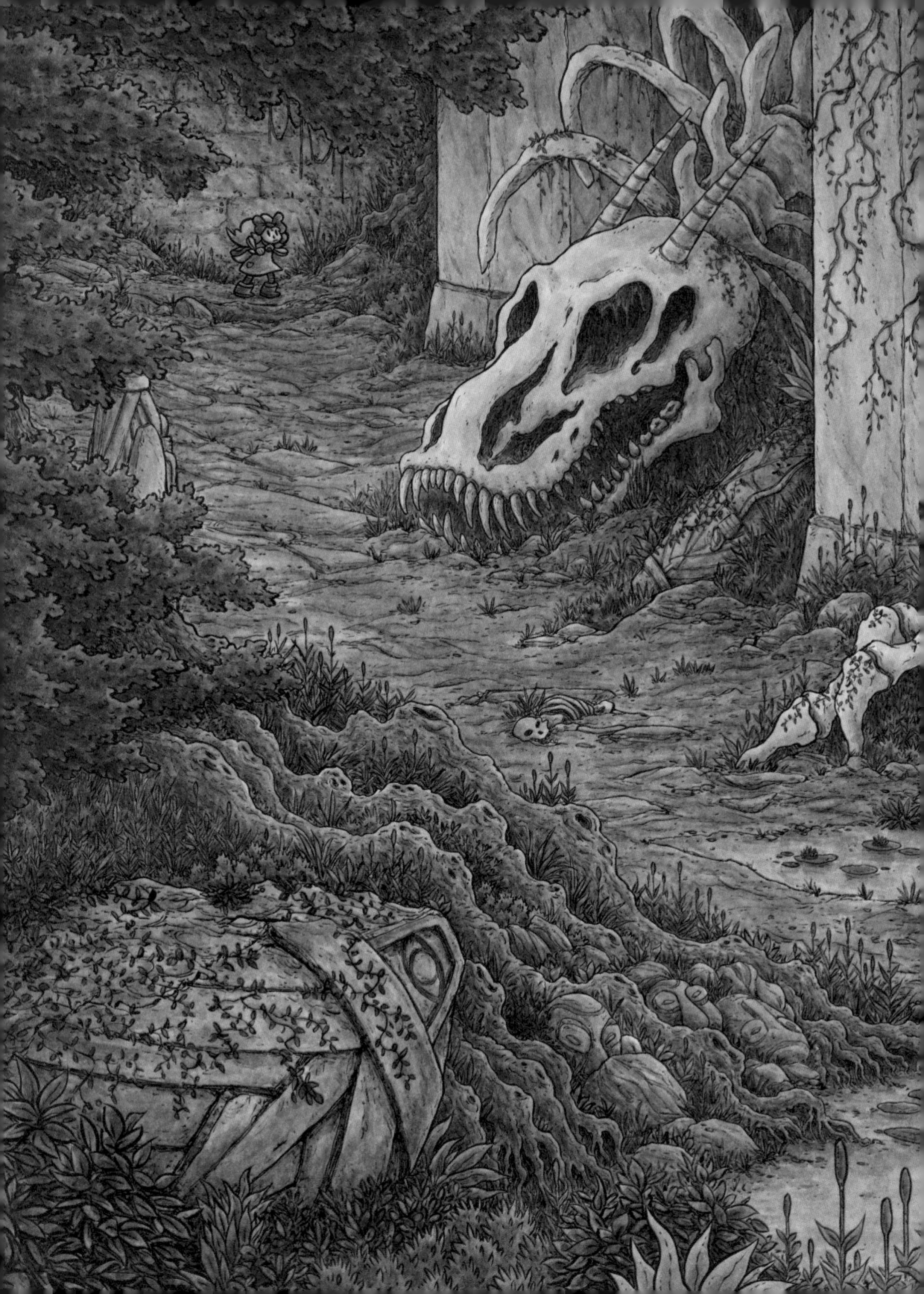

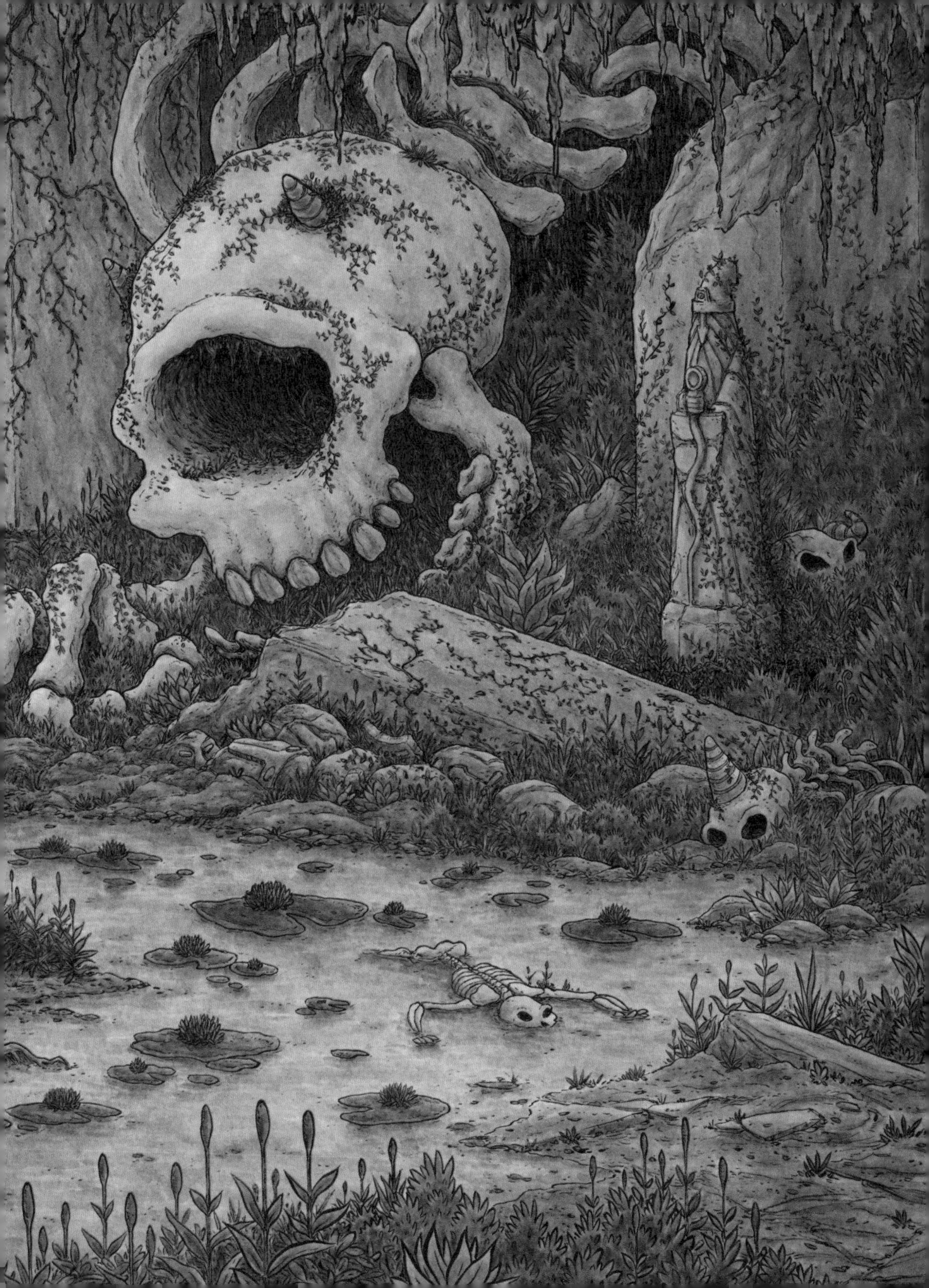

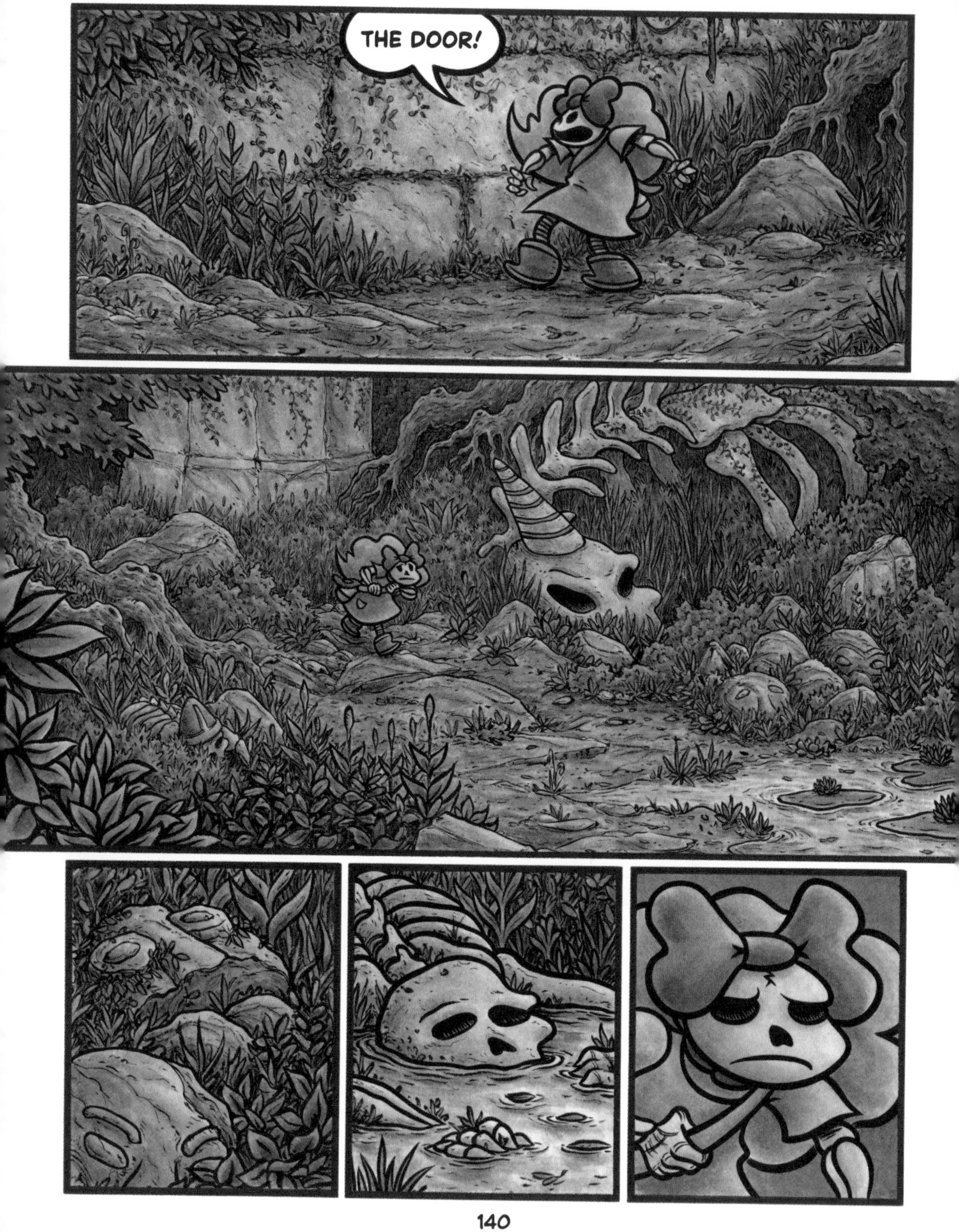
THE DOOR!

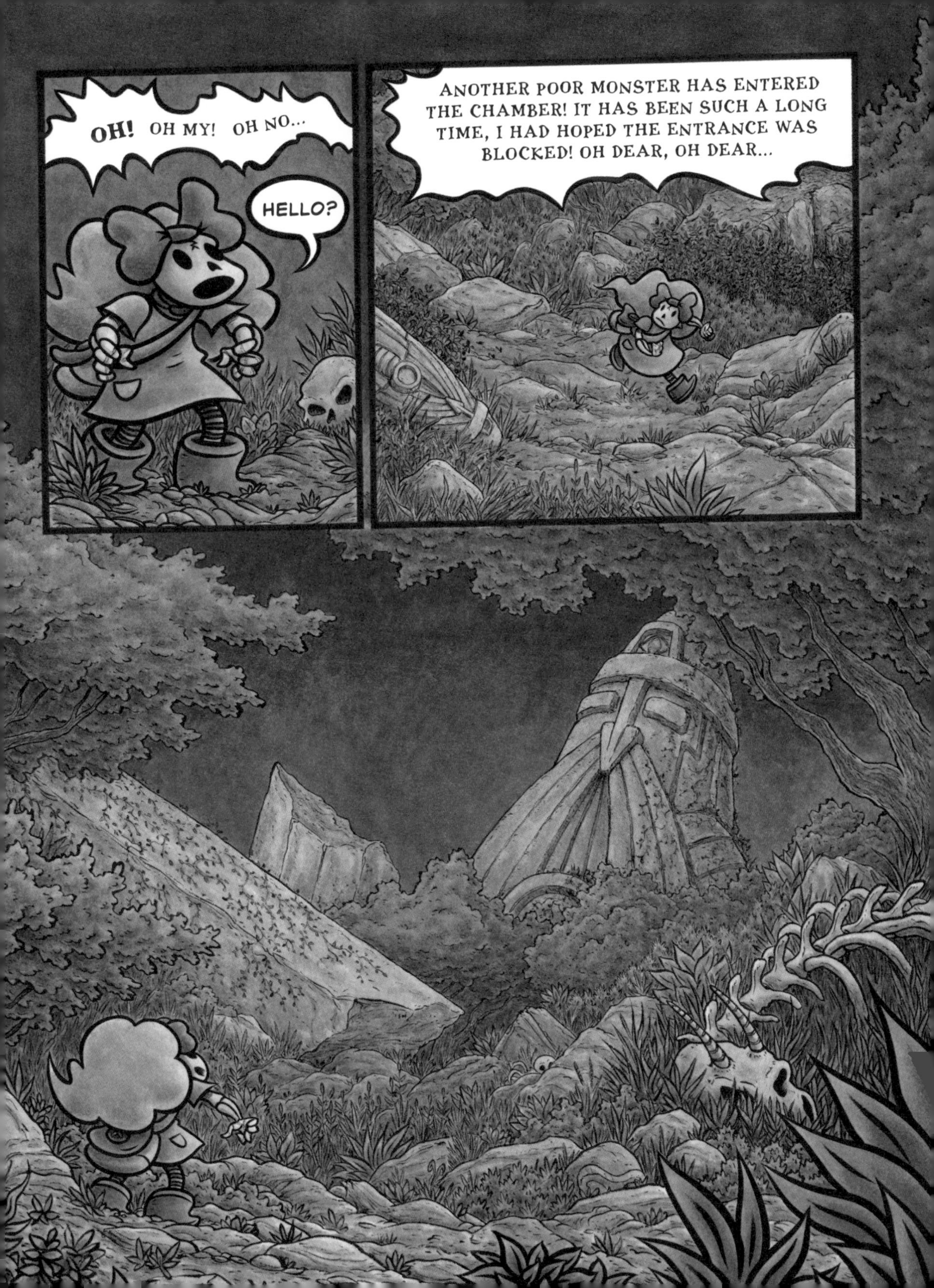
OH! OH MY! OH NO...
HELLO?
ANOTHER POOR MONSTER HAS ENTERED THE CHAMBER! IT HAS BEEN SUCH A LONG TIME, I HAD HOPED THE ENTRANCE WAS BLOCKED! OH DEAR, OH DEAR...

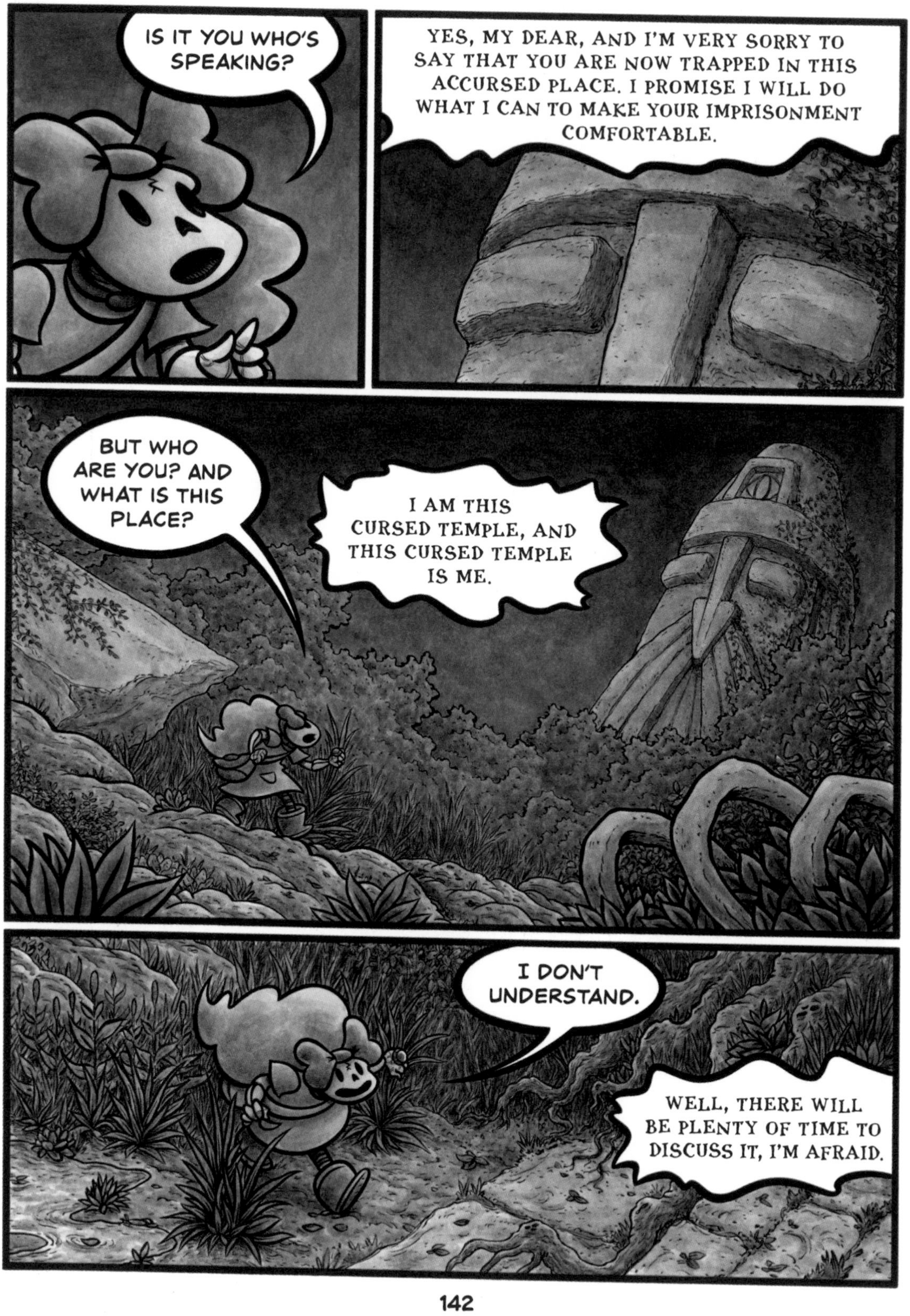
IS IT YOU WHO'S SPEAKING?
YES, MY DEAR, AND I'M VERY SORRY TO SAY THAT YOU ARE NOW TRAPPED IN THIS ACCURSED PLACE. I PROMISE I WILL DO WHAT I CAN TO MAKE YOUR IMPRISONMENT COMFORTABLE.
BUT WHO ARE YOU? AND WHAT IS THIS PLACE?
I AM THIS CURSED TEMPLE, AND THIS CURSED TEMPLE IS ME.
I DON'T UNDERSTAND.
WELL, THERE WILL BE PLENTY OF TIME TO DISCUSS IT, I'M AFRAID.

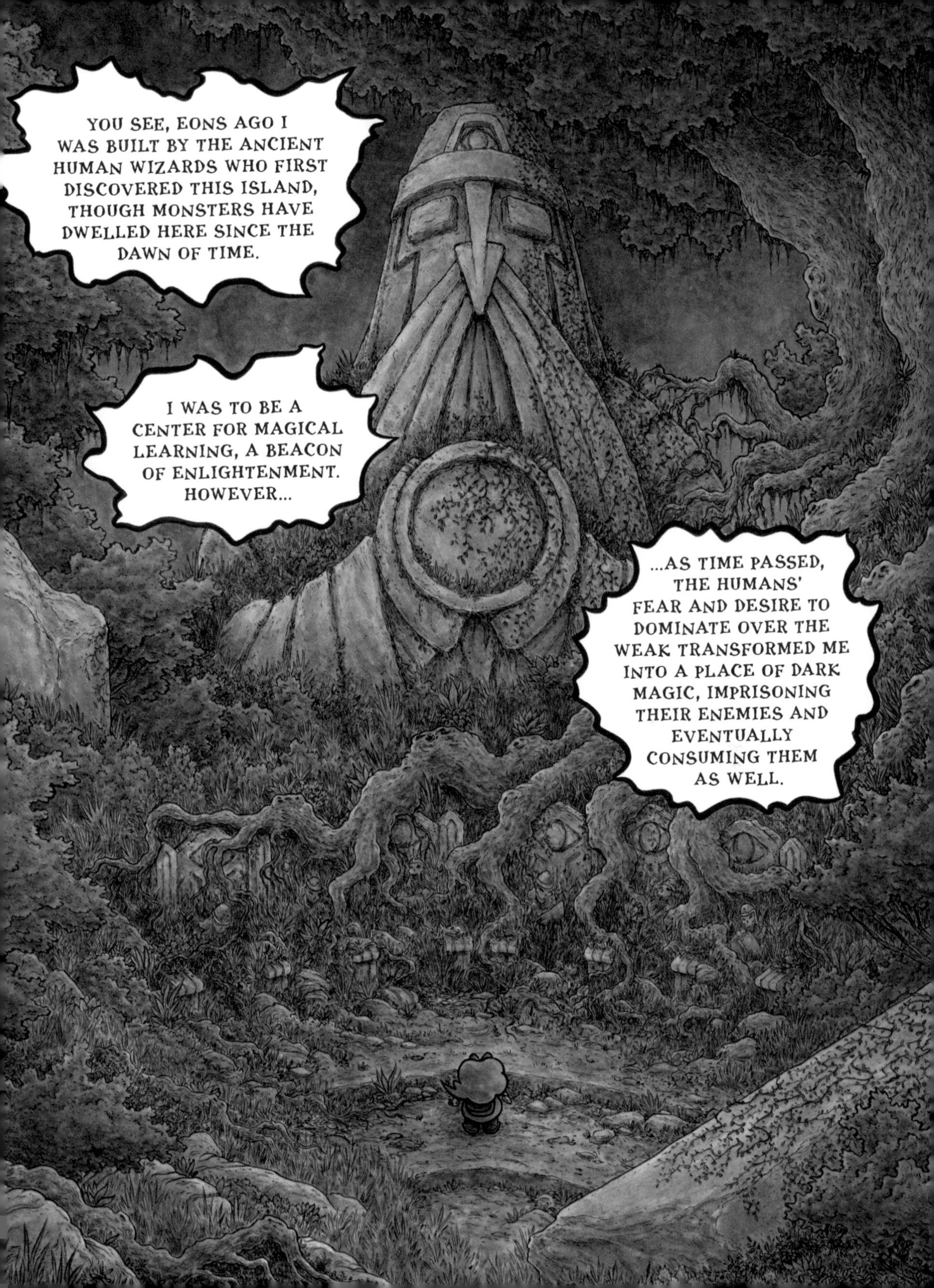
YOU SEE, EONS AGO I WAS BUILT BY THE ANCIENT HUMAN WIZARDS WHO FIRST DISCOVERED THIS ISLAND, THOUGH MONSTERS HAVE DWELLED HERE SINCE THE DAWN OF TIME.
I WAS TO BE A CENTER FOR MAGICAL LEARNING, A BEACON OF ENLIGHTENMENT. HOWEVER...
...AS TIME PASSED, THE HUMANS' FEAR AND DESIRE TO DOMINATE OVER THE WEAK TRANSFORMED ME INTO A PLACE OF DARK MAGIC, IMPRISONING THEIR ENEMIES AND EVENTUALLY CONSUMING THEM AS WELL.

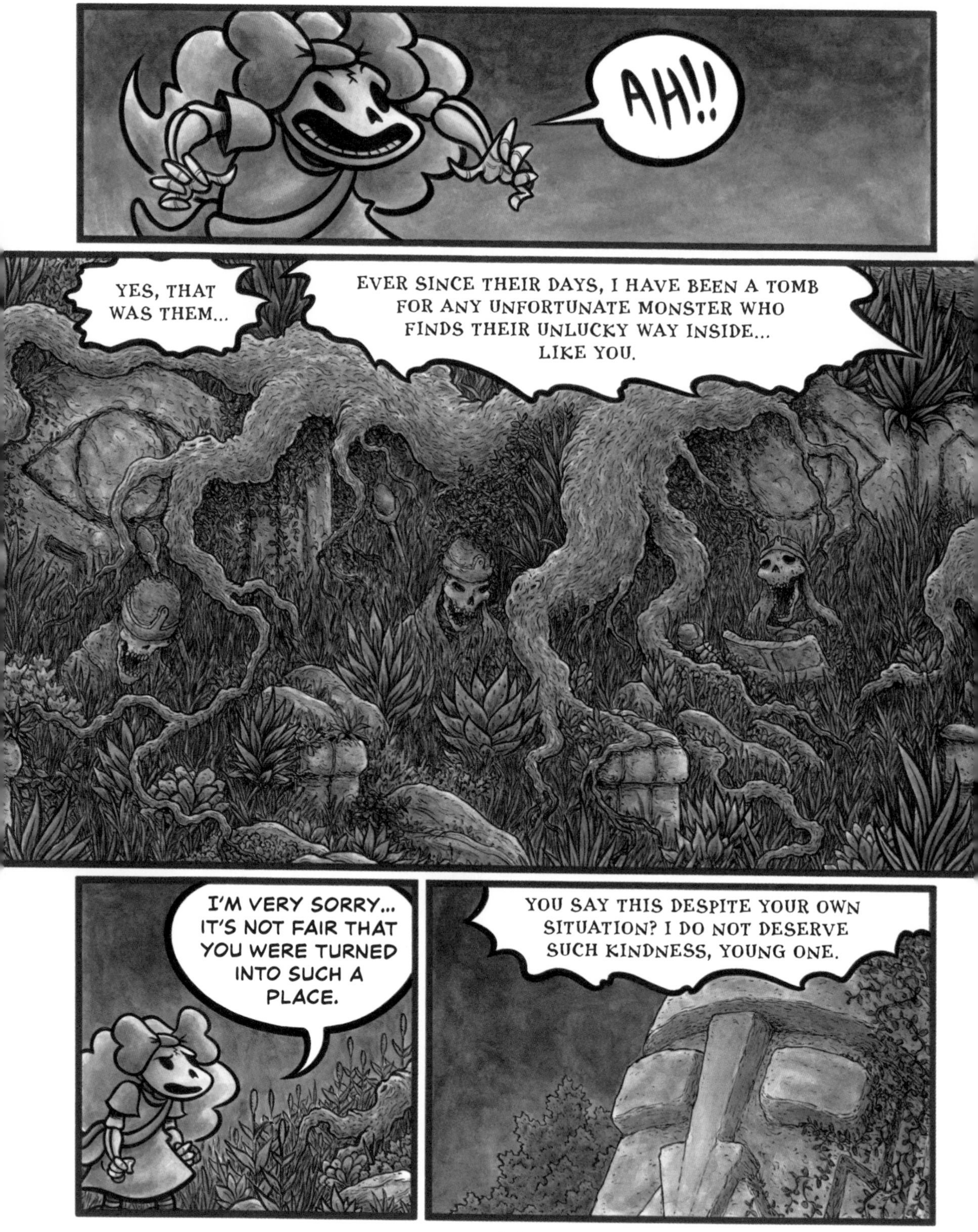
AH!!
YES, THAT WAS THEM...
EVER SINCE THEIR DAYS, I HAVE BEEN A TOMB FOR ANY UNFORTUNATE MONSTER WHO FINDS THEIR UNLUCKY WAY INSIDE... LIKE YOU.
I'M VERY SORRY... IT'S NOT FAIR THAT YOU WERE TURNED INTO SUCH A PLACE.
YOU SAY THIS DESPITE YOUR OWN SITUATION? I DO NOT DESERVE SUCH KINDNESS, YOUNG ONE.

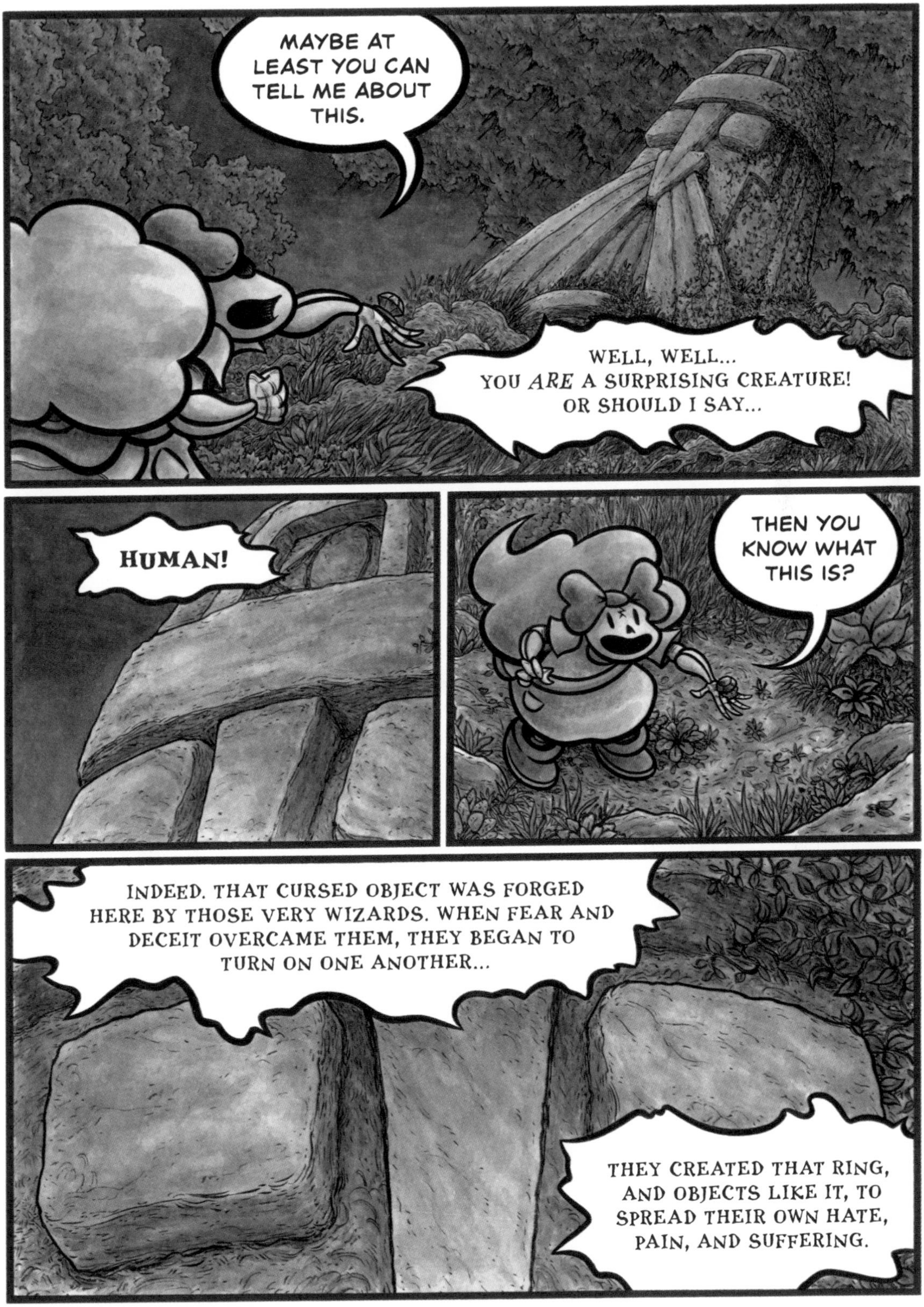
MAYBE AT LEAST YOU CAN TELL ME ABOUT THIS.
WELL, WELL... YOU *ARE* A SURPRISING CREATURE! OR SHOULD I SAY...
HUMAN!
THEN YOU KNOW WHAT THIS IS?
INDEED. THAT CURSED OBJECT WAS FORGED HERE BY THOSE VERY WIZARDS. WHEN FEAR AND DECEIT OVERCAME THEM, THEY BEGAN TO TURN ON ONE ANOTHER...
THEY CREATED THAT RING, AND OBJECTS LIKE IT, TO SPREAD THEIR OWN HATE, PAIN, AND SUFFERING.

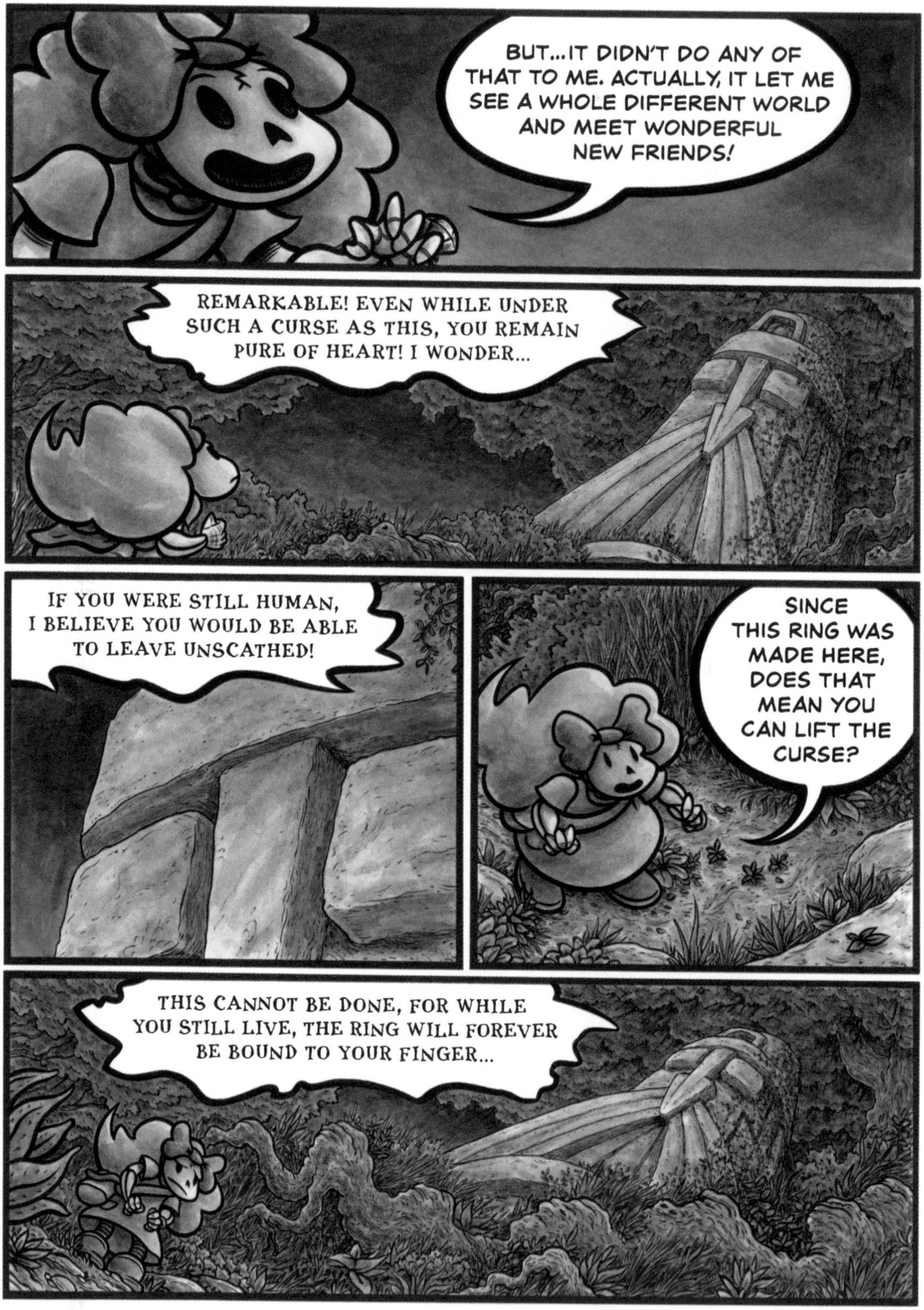

BUT...IT DIDN'T DO ANY OF THAT TO ME. ACTUALLY, IT LET ME SEE A WHOLE DIFFERENT WORLD AND MEET WONDERFUL NEW FRIENDS!
REMARKABLE! EVEN WHILE UNDER SUCH A CURSE AS THIS, YOU REMAIN PURE OF HEART! I WONDER...
IF YOU WERE STILL HUMAN, I BELIEVE YOU WOULD BE ABLE TO LEAVE UNSCATHED!
SINCE THIS RING WAS MADE HERE, DOES THAT MEAN YOU CAN LIFT THE CURSE?
THIS CANNOT BE DONE, FOR WHILE YOU STILL LIVE, THE RING WILL FOREVER BE BOUND TO YOUR FINGER...

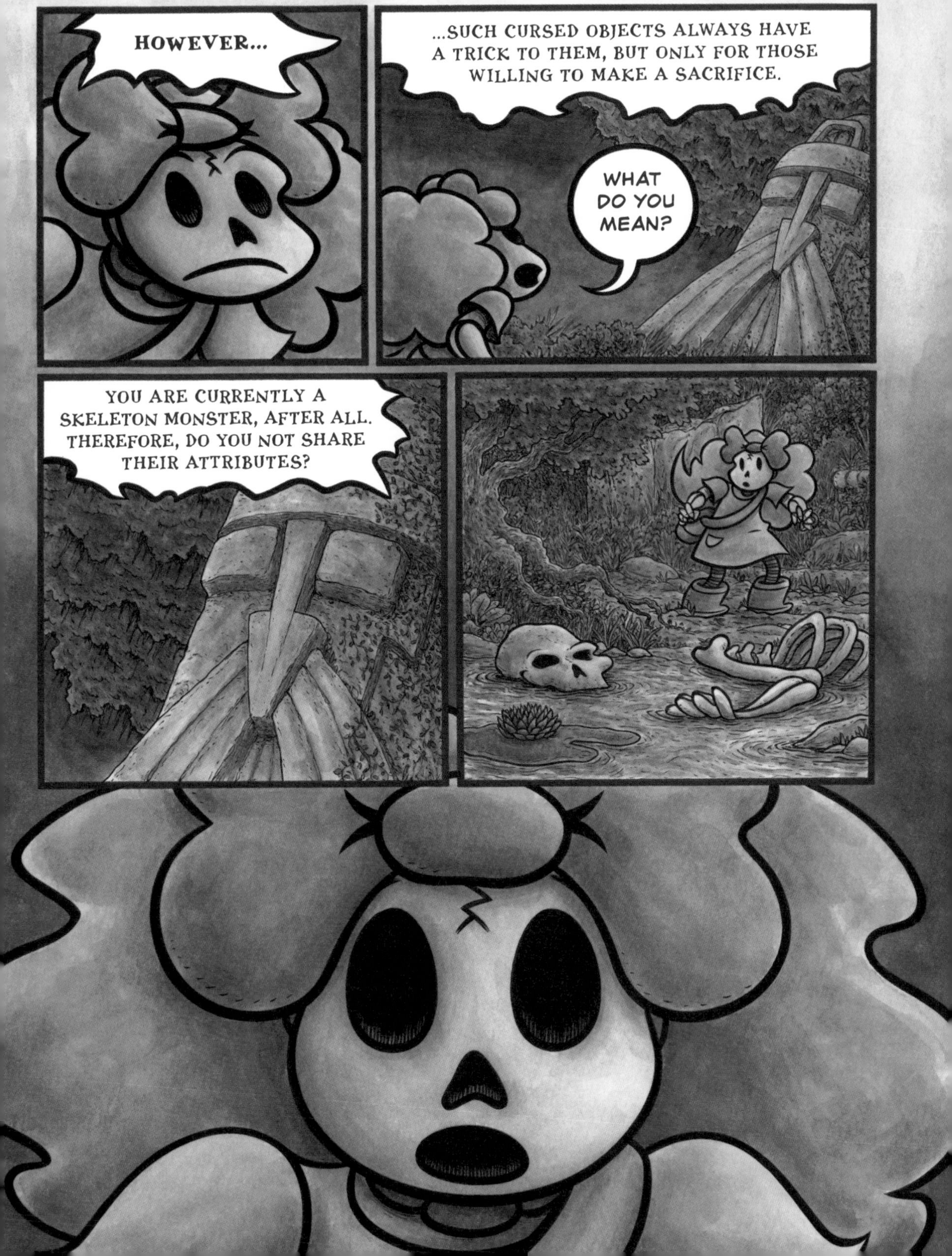
HOWEVER...
...SUCH CURSED OBJECTS ALWAYS HAVE A TRICK TO THEM, BUT ONLY FOR THOSE WILLING TO MAKE A SACRIFICE.
WHAT DO YOU MEAN?
YOU ARE CURRENTLY A SKELETON MONSTER, AFTER ALL. THEREFORE, DO YOU NOT SHARE THEIR ATTRIBUTES?

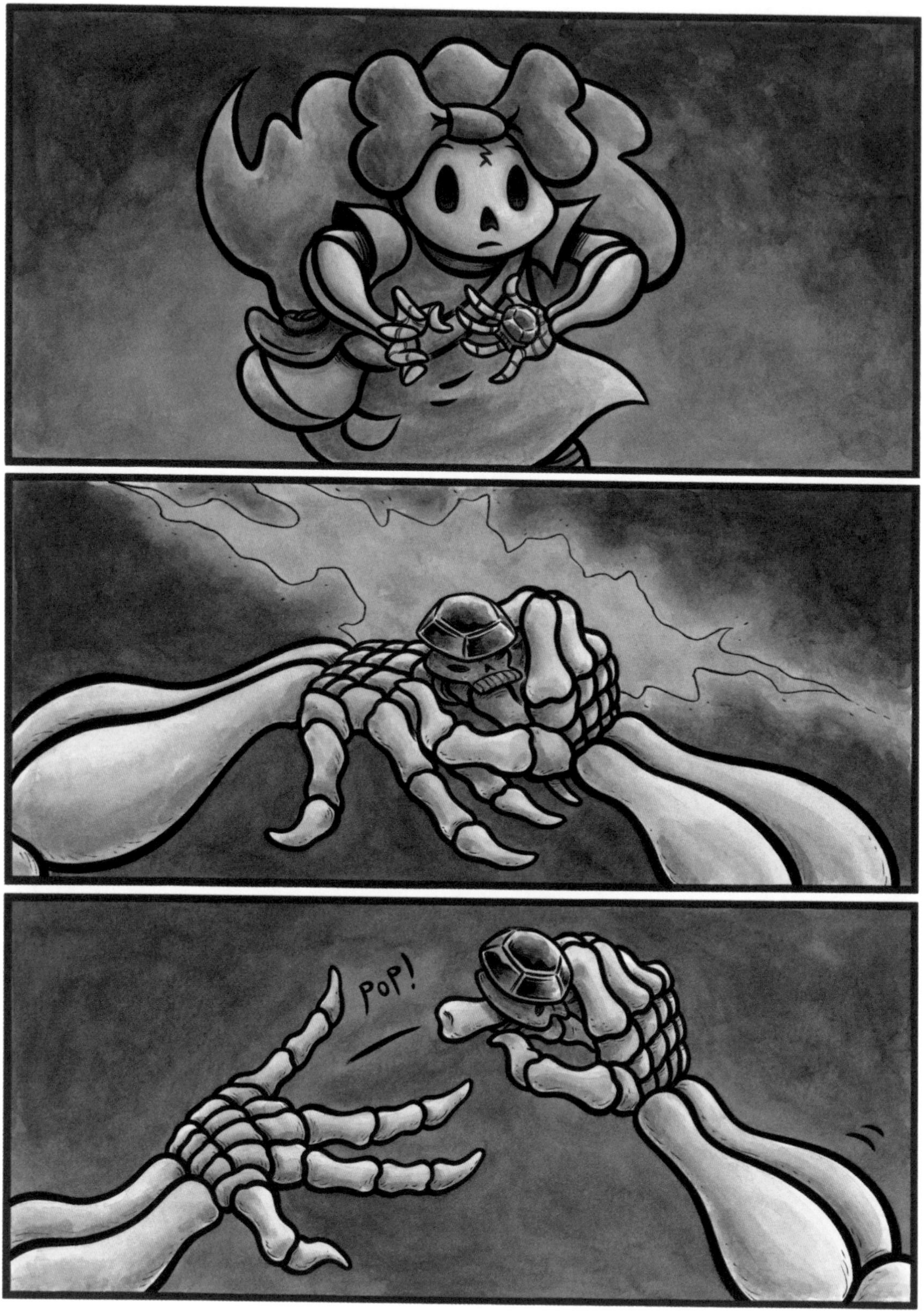
POP!

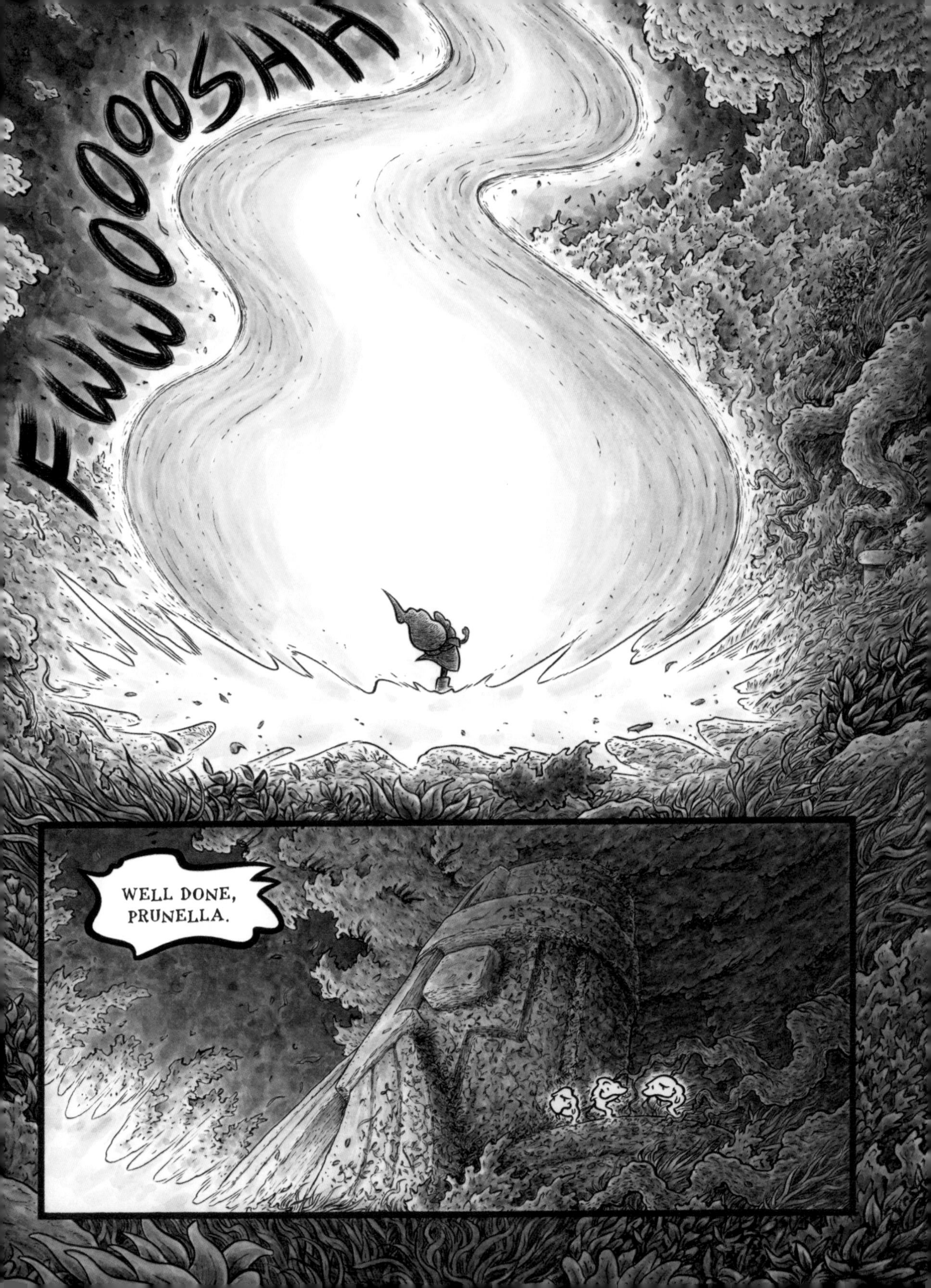
FWOOOOSHH
WELL DONE, PRUNELLA.

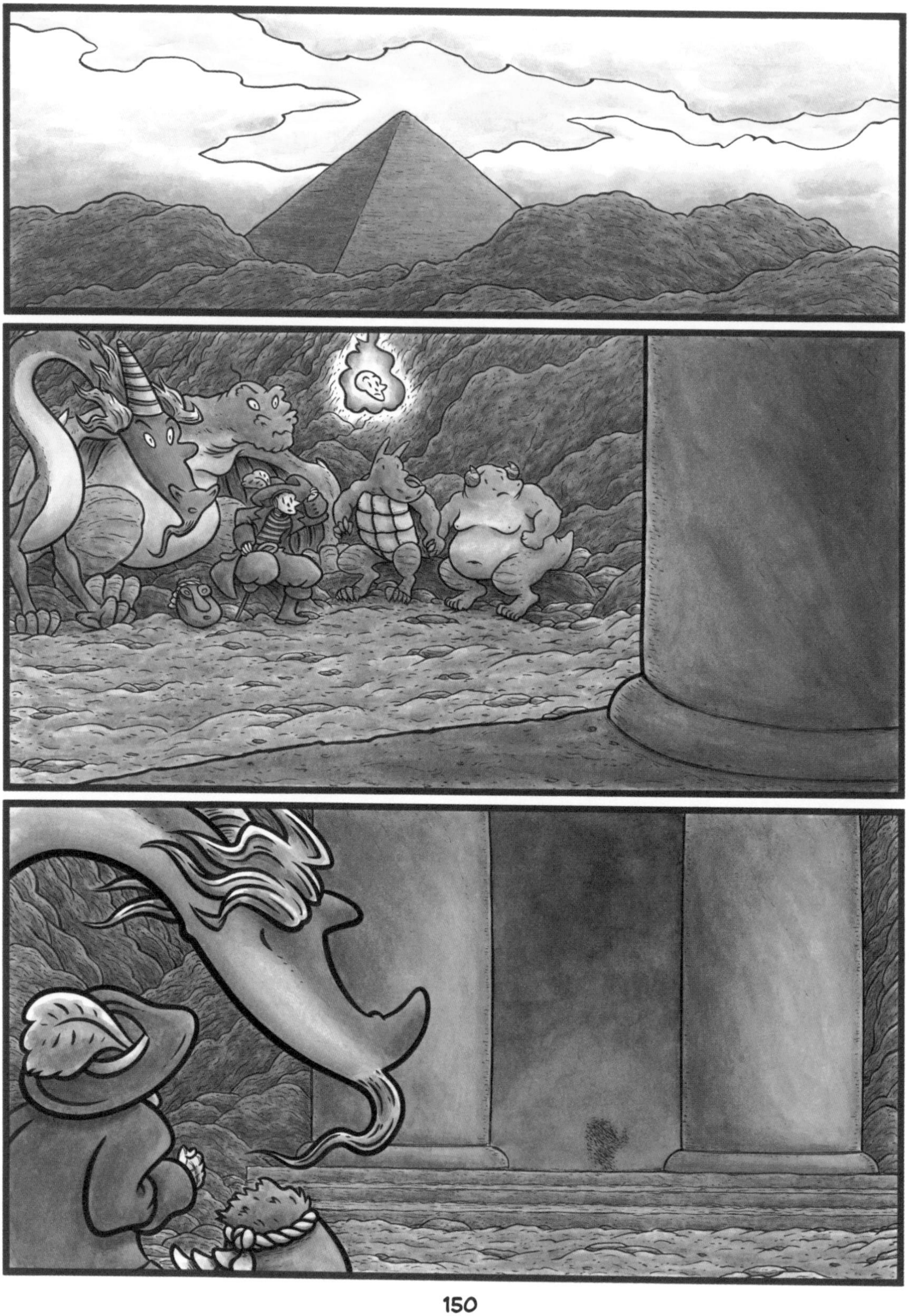

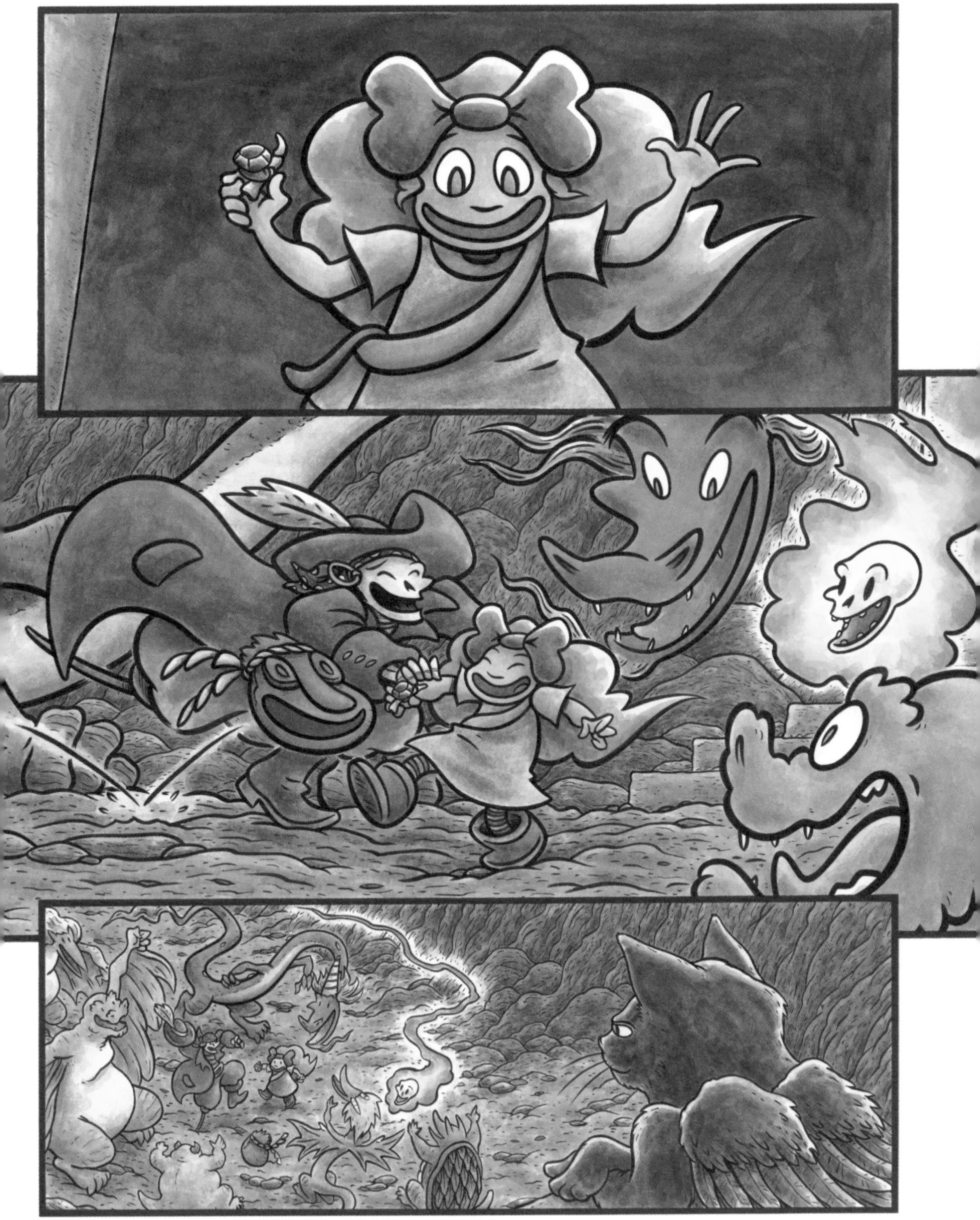

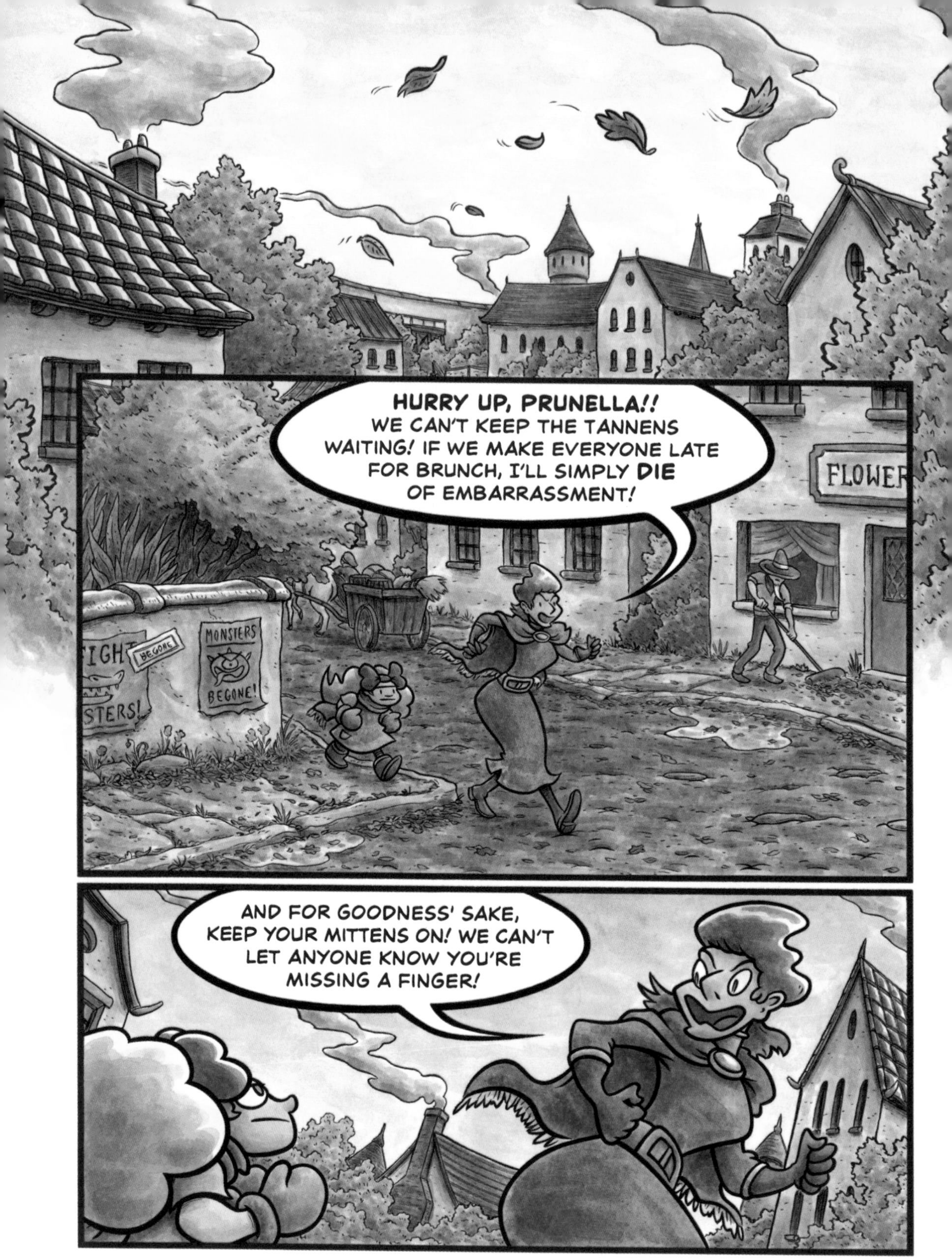
HURRY UP, PRUNELLA!! WE CAN'T KEEP THE TANNENS WAITING! IF WE MAKE EVERYONE LATE FOR BRUNCH, I'LL SIMPLY DIE OF EMBARRASSMENT!
FLOWER
MONSTERS BEGONE!
BEGONE
STERS!
AND FOR GOODNESS' SAKE, KEEP YOUR MITTENS ON! WE CAN'T LET ANYONE KNOW YOU'RE MISSING A FINGER!

I'D NEVER LIVE THAT ONE DOWN!

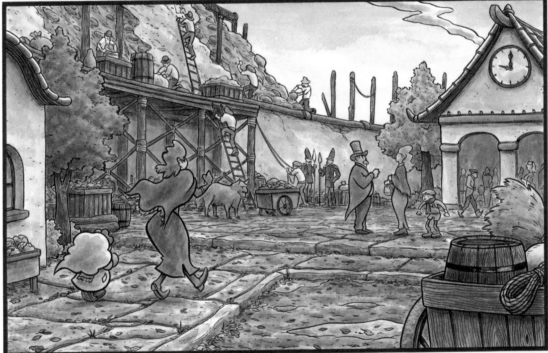

AH, THERE YOU ARE! FRIGHTFULLY CLOSE TO BEING LATE!

IT WAS ALL **THIS ONE'S** FAULT, I ASSURE YOU.

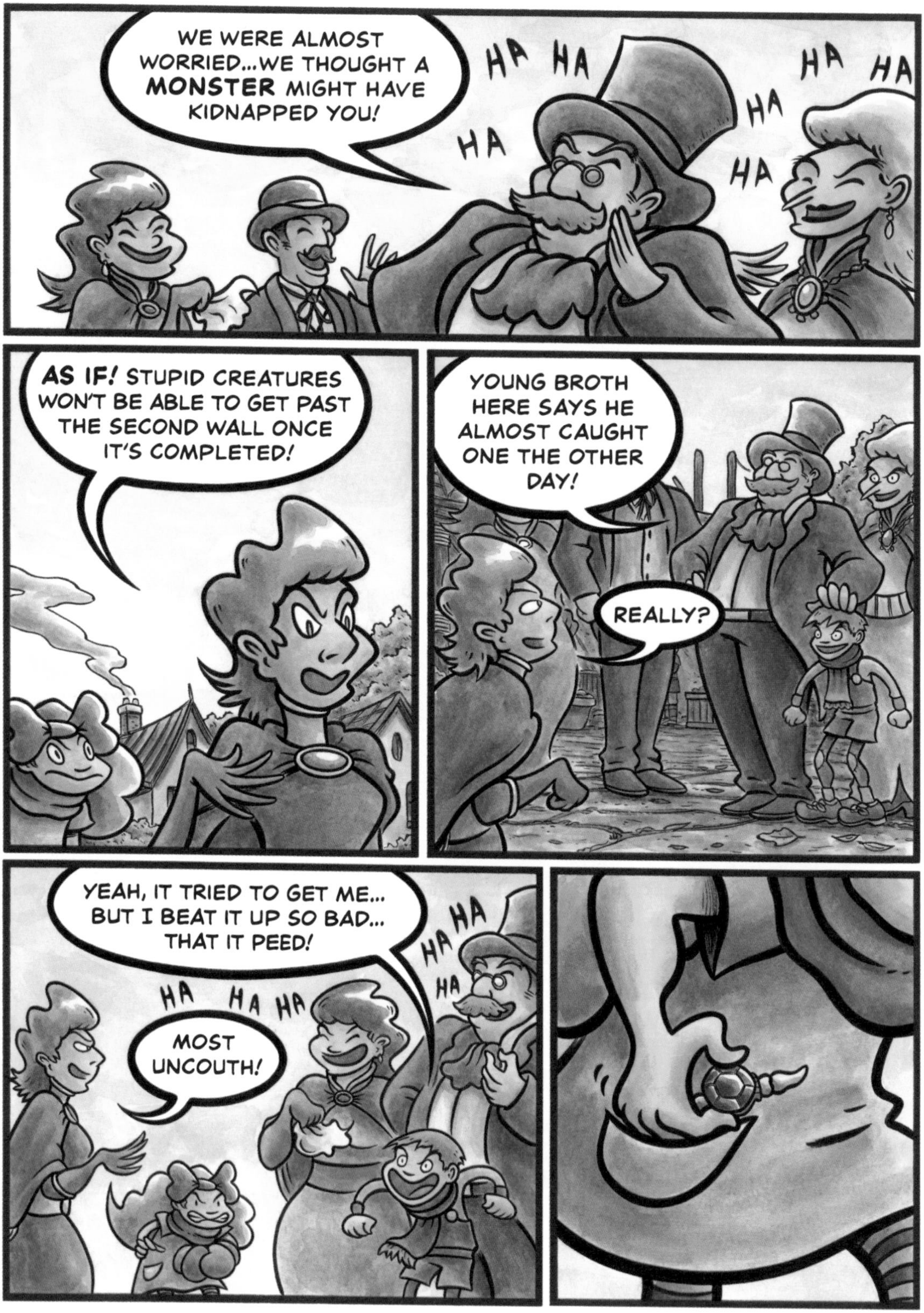

WE WERE ALMOST WORRIED...WE THOUGHT A **MONSTER** MIGHT HAVE KIDNAPPED YOU!
HA HA HA HA HA HA HA
AS IF! STUPID CREATURES WON'T BE ABLE TO GET PAST THE SECOND WALL ONCE IT'S COMPLETED!
YOUNG BROTH HERE SAYS HE ALMOST CAUGHT ONE THE OTHER DAY!
REALLY?
YEAH, IT TRIED TO GET ME... BUT I BEAT IT UP SO BAD... THAT IT PEED!
HA HA HA HA HA HA
MOST UNCOUTH!

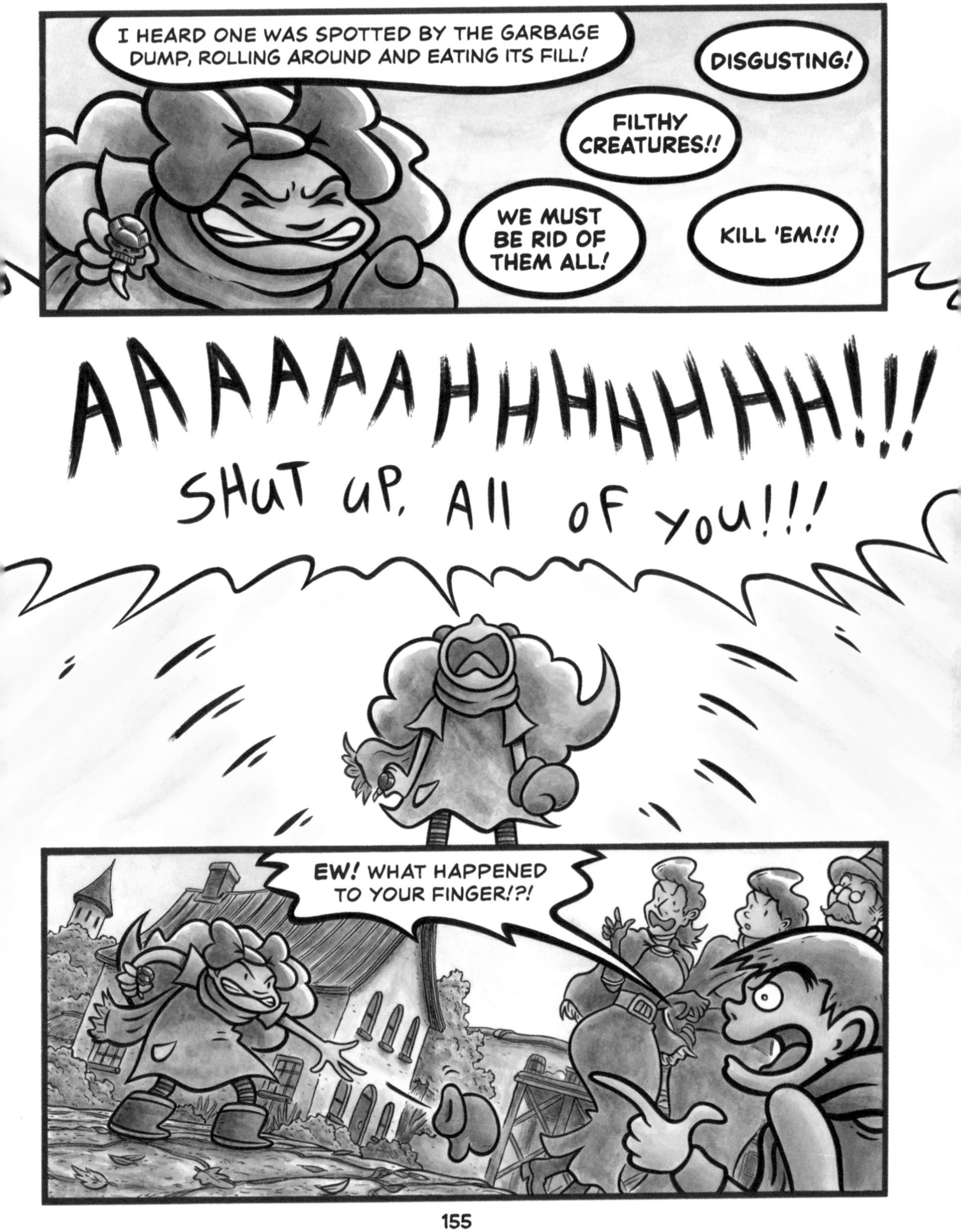
I HEARD ONE WAS SPOTTED BY THE GARBAGE DUMP, ROLLING AROUND AND EATING ITS FILL!
DISGUSTING!
FILTHY CREATURES!!
WE MUST BE RID OF THEM ALL!
KILL 'EM!!!
AAAAAAHHHHHHH!!!
SHUT UP, ALL OF YOU!!!
EW! WHAT HAPPENED TO YOUR FINGER!?!

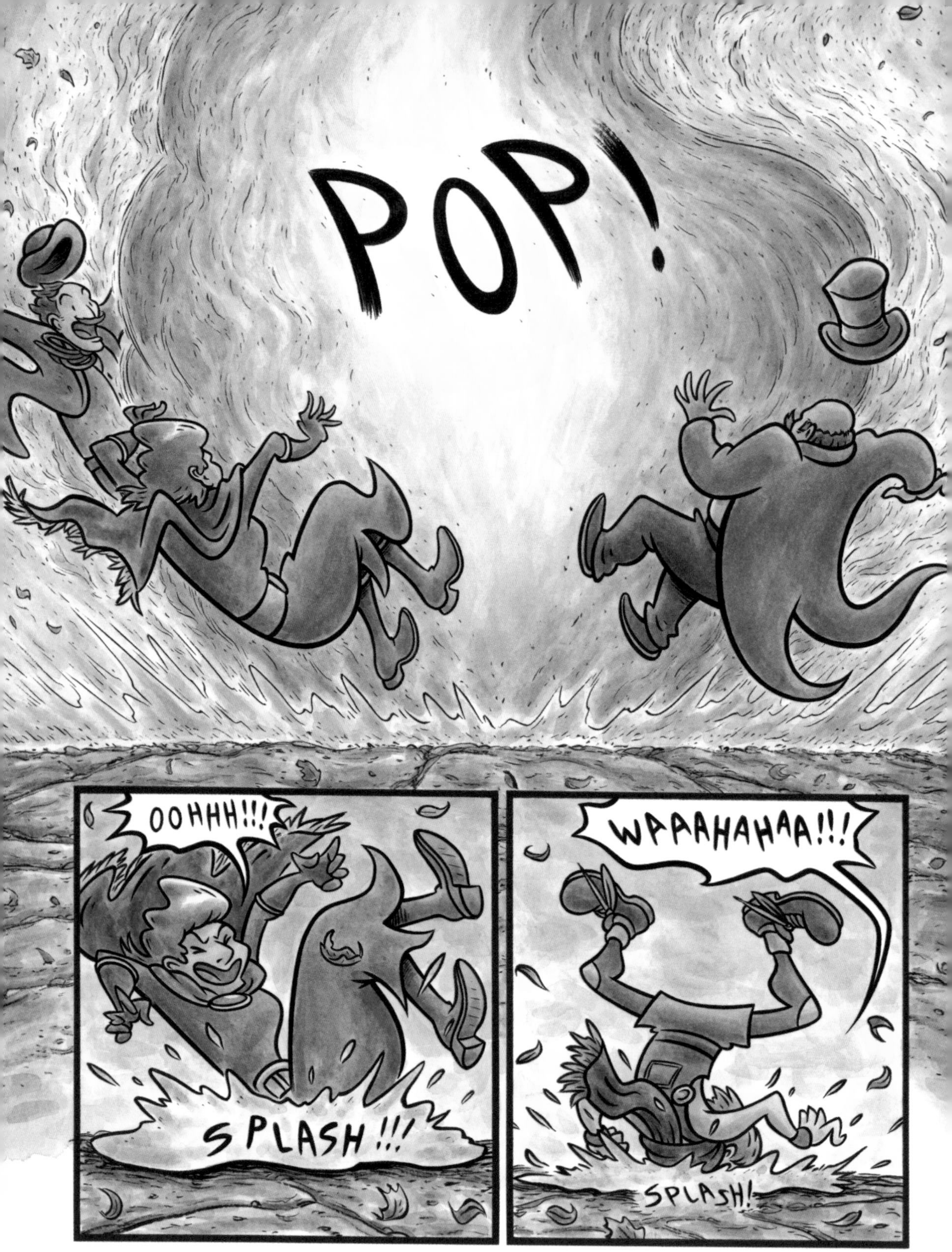
POP!
OOHHH!!!
SPLASH!!!
WAAAHAHAA!!!
SPLASH!

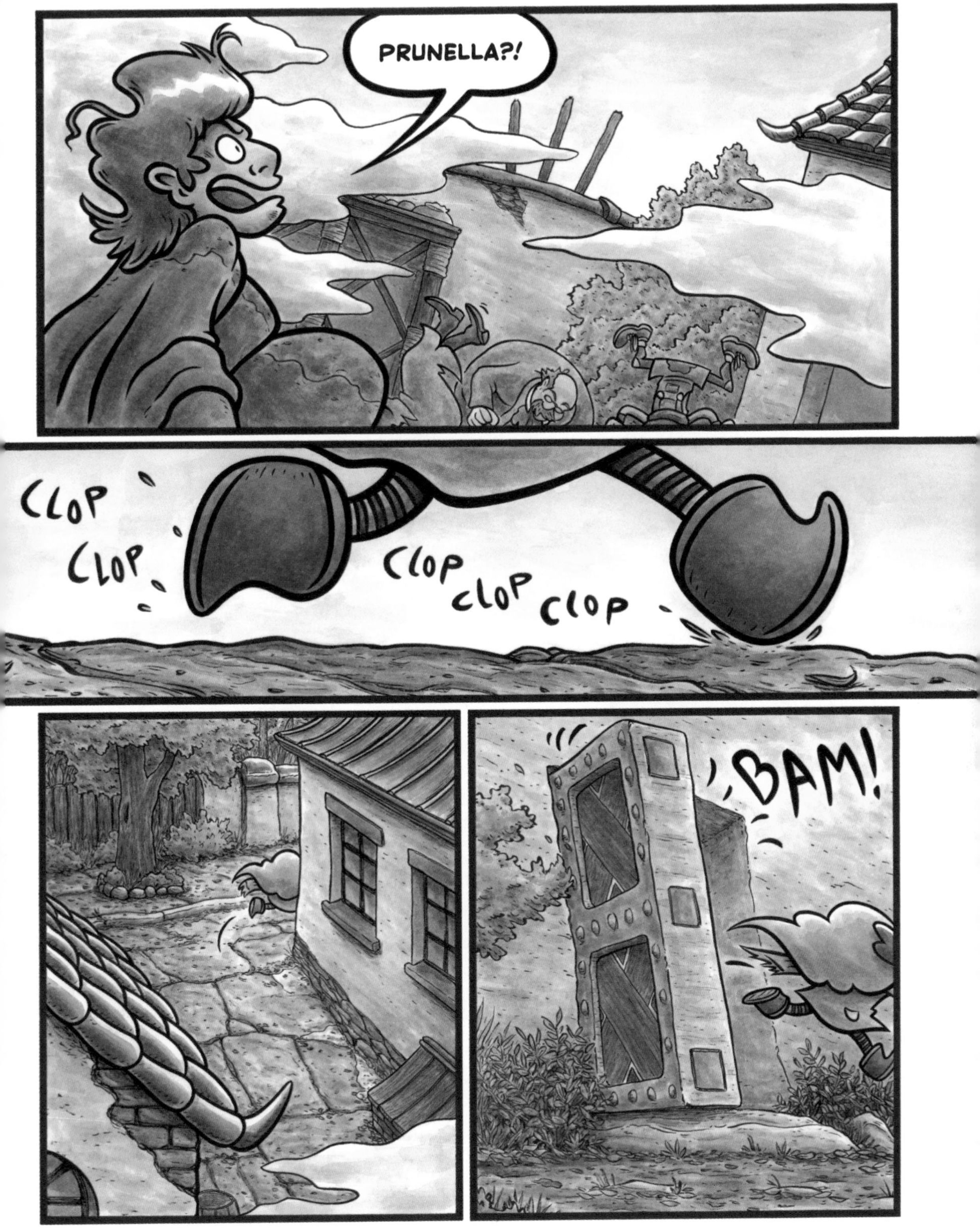
PRUNELLA?!
CLOP
CLOP
CLOP
CLOP
CLOP
BAM!

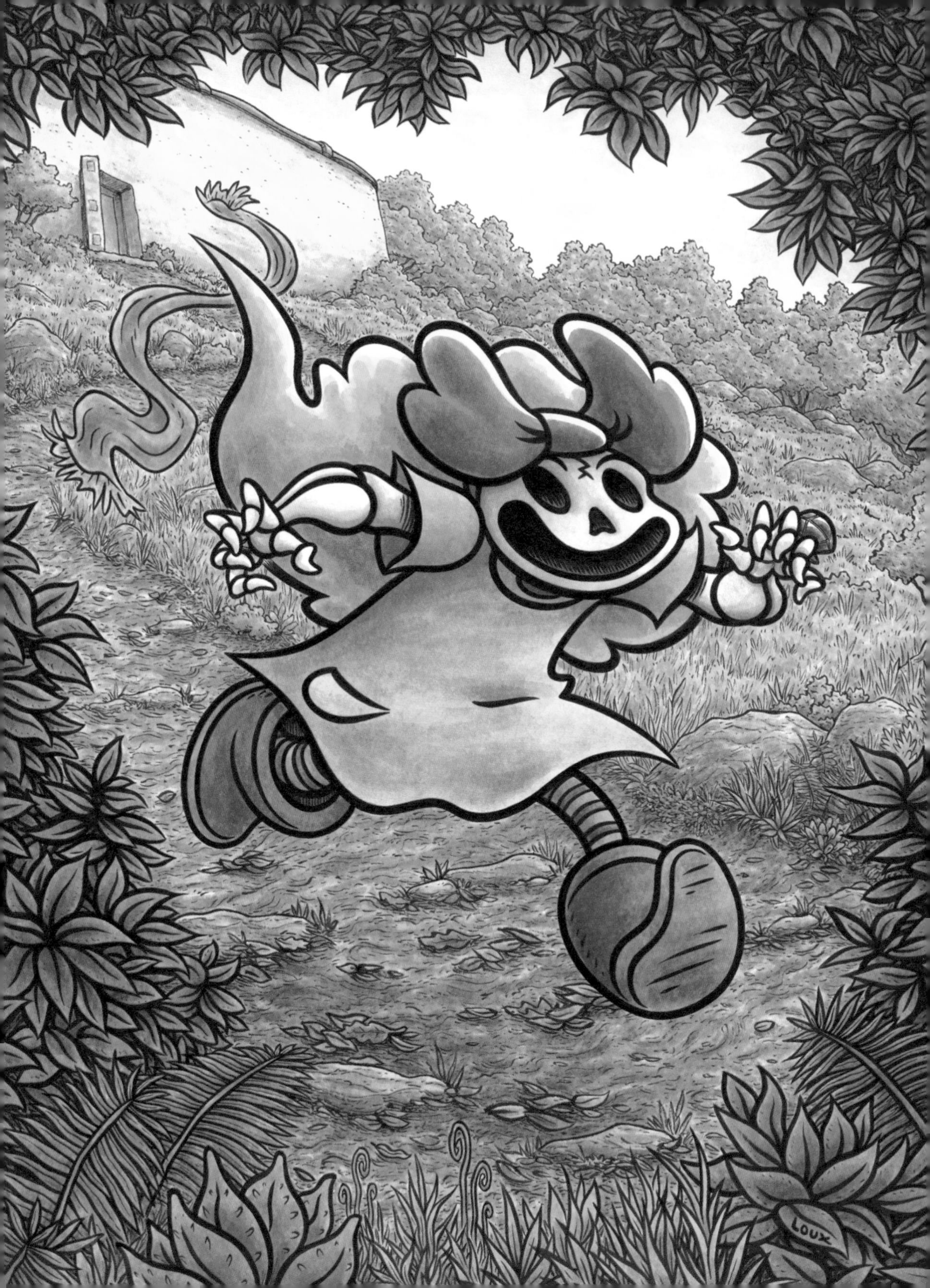
LOUX